LINDA HOWARD

JEOPARDY

HQN™

ISBN-13: 978-0-373-78910-8

Jeopardy

Recycling programs for this product may not exist in your area.

Copyright © 2016 by Harlequin Books S.A.

The publisher acknowledges the copyright holder of the individual works as follows:

A Game of Chance
Copyright © 2000 by Linda Howington

Loving Evangeline
Copyright © 1994 by Linda Howington

www.HQNBooks.com

Printed in U.S.A.

CONTENTS

A GAME OF CHANCE

For the readers

THE BEGINNING

COMING BACK TO WYOMING—coming home—always evoked in Chance Mackenzie such an intense mixture of emotions that he could never decide which was strongest, the pleasure or the acute discomfort. He was, by nature and nurture—not that there had been any nurturing in the first fourteen or so years of his life—a man who was more comfortable alone. If he was alone, then he could operate without having to worry about anyone but himself, and, conversely, there was no one to make him uncomfortable with concern about his own well-being. The type of work he had chosen only reinforced his own inclinations, because covert operations and anti-terrorist activities predicated he be both secretive and wary, trusting no one, letting no one close to him.

And yet… And yet, there was his family. Sprawling, brawling, ferociously overachieving, refusing to let him withdraw, not that he was at all certain he could even if they would allow it. It was always jolting, alarming, to step back into that all-enveloping embrace, to be teased and questioned—*teased,* him, whom some of the most deadly people on earth justifiably feared—hugged and kissed, fussed over and yelled at and…loved, just as if he were like everyone else. He knew he wasn't; the knowledge was always there, in the back of his mind, that he was *not* like them. But he was drawn back, again and again, by something deep inside hungering for the very things that

so alarmed him. Love was scary; he had learned early and
hard how little he could depend on anyone but himself.

The fact that he had survived at all was a testament to
his toughness and intelligence. He didn't know how old
he was, or where he had been born, what he was named
as a child, or if he even had a name—nothing. He had no
memory of a mother, a father, anyone who had taken care
of him. A lot of people simply didn't remember their child-
hoods, but Chance couldn't comfort himself with that possibility, that there had been someone who had loved him
and taken care of him, because he remembered too damn
many other details.

He remembered stealing food when he was so small he
had to stand on tiptoe to reach apples in a bin in a small-
town supermarket. He had been around so many kids now
that, by comparing what he remembered to the sizes they
were at certain ages, he could estimate he had been no
more than three years old at the time, perhaps not even that.

He remembered sleeping in ditches when it was warm,
hiding in barns, stores, sheds, whatever was handy, when
it was cold or raining. He remembered stealing clothes to
wear, sometimes by the simple means of catching a boy
playing alone in a yard, overpowering him and taking the
clothes off his back. Chance had always been much stronger physically than other boys his size, because of the sheer
physical difficulty of staying alive—and he had known
how to fight, for the same reason.

He remembered a dog taking up with him once, a black-
and-white mutt that tagged along and curled up next to
him to sleep, and Chance remembered being grateful for
the warmth. He also remembered that when he reached for
a piece of steak he had stolen from the scraps in back of
a restaurant, the dog bit him and stole the steak. Chance
still had two scars on his left hand from the dog's teeth.

The dog had gotten the meat, and Chance had gone one more day without food. He didn't blame the dog; it had been hungry, too. But Chance ran it off after that, because stealing enough food to keep himself alive was difficult enough, without having to steal for the dog, too. Besides, he had learned that when it came to survival, it was every dog for himself.

He might have been five years old when he learned that particular lesson, but he had learned it well.

Of course, learning how to survive in both rural and urban areas, in all conditions, was what made him so good at his job now, so he supposed his early childhood had its benefits. Even considering that, though, he wouldn't wish his childhood on a dog, not even the damn mutt that had bitten him.

His real life had begun the day Mary Mackenzie found him lying beside a road, deathly ill with a severe case of flu that had turned into pneumonia. He didn't remember much of the next few days—he had been too ill—but he had known he was in a hospital, and he had been wild with fear, because that meant he had fallen into the hands of the system, and he was now, in effect, a prisoner. He was obviously a minor, without identification, and the circumstances would warrant the child welfare services being notified. He had spent his entire life avoiding just such an event, and he had tried to make plans to escape, but his thoughts were vague, hard to get ordered, and his body was too weak to respond to his demands.

But through it all he could remember being soothed by an angel with soft blue-gray eyes and light, silvery brown hair, cool hands and a loving voice. There had also been a big, dark man, a half-breed, who calmly and repeatedly addressed his deepest fear. "We won't let them take you," the big man had said whenever Chance briefly surfaced from his fever-induced stupor.

He didn't trust them, didn't believe the big half-breed's reassurances. Chance had figured out that he himself was part American Indian, but big deal, that didn't mean he could trust these people any more than he could trust that damn thieving, ungrateful mutt. But he was too sick, too weak, to escape or even struggle, and while he was so helpless Mary Mackenzie had somehow hog-tied him with devotion, and he had never managed to break free.

He hated being touched; if someone was close enough to touch him, then they were close enough to attack him. He couldn't fight off the nurses and doctors who poked and prodded and moved him around as if he were nothing more than a mindless piece of meat. He had endured it, gritting his teeth, struggling with both his own panic and the almost overpowering urge to fight, because he knew if he fought them he would be restrained. He had to stay free, so he could run when he recovered enough to move under his own power.

But *she* had been there for what seemed like the entire time, though logically he knew she had to have left the hospital sometimes. When he burned with fever, she washed his face with a cold cloth and fed him slivers of ice. She brushed his hair, stroked his forehead when his head ached so bad he thought his skull would crack; and took over bathing him when she saw how alarmed he became when the nurses did it. Somehow he could bear it better when she bathed him, though even in his illness he had been puzzled by his own reaction.

She touched him constantly, anticipating his needs so that his pillows were fluffed before he was aware of any discomfort, the heat adjusted before he became too hot or too cold, his legs and back massaged when the fever made him ache from head to toe. He was swamped by maternal fussing, enveloped by it. It terrified him, but Mary took advantage of his weakened state and ruthlessly overwhelmed him with her mothering, as if she were determined to pack enough loving care into those few days to make up for a lifetime of nothing.

Sometime during those fever-fogged days, he began to like the feel of her cool hand on his forehead, to listen for that sweet voice even when he couldn't drag his heavy eyelids open, and the sound of it reassured him on some deep, primitive level. Once he dreamed, he didn't know what, but he woke in a panic to find her arms around him, his head pillowed on her narrow shoulder as if he were a baby, her hand gently stroking his hair while she murmured reassuringly to him—and he drifted back to sleep feeling comforted and somehow…safe.

He was always startled, even now, by how small she was. Someone so relentlessly iron-willed should have been seven feet tall and weighed three hundred pounds; at least then it would have made sense that she could bulldoze the hospital staff, even the doctors, into doing what she wanted. She had estimated his age at fourteen, but even then he was over a full head taller than the dainty woman who took over his life, but in this case size didn't matter; he was as helpless against her as was the hospital staff.

There was nothing at all he could do to fight off his growing addiction to Mary Mackenzie's mothering, even though he knew he was developing a weakness, a vulnerability, that terrified him. He had never before cared for anyone or anything, instinctively knowing that to do so would expose his emotional underbelly. But knowledge and wariness couldn't protect him now; by the time he was well enough to leave the hospital, he loved the woman who had decided she was going to be his mother, loved her with all the blind helplessness of a small child.

When he left the hospital it had been with Mary and the big man, Wolf. Because he couldn't bear to leave her just yet, he braced himself to endure her family. Just for a little while, he had promised himself, just until he was stronger.

They had taken him to Mackenzie's Mountain, into their home, their arms, their hearts. A nameless boy had died that day beside the road, and Chance Mackenzie had been born in his place. When Chance had chosen a birthday—at his new sister Maris's insistence—he chose the day Mary found him, rather than the perhaps more logical date that his adoption was final.

He had never had anything, but after that day he had been flooded with...everything. He had always been hungry, but now there was food. He had been starved, too, for learning, and now there were books everywhere, because Mary was a teacher down to her fragile bones, and she had force-fed him knowledge as fast as he could gulp it down. He was accustomed to bedding down wherever and whenever he could, but now he had his own room, his own bed, a routine. He had clothes, new ones, bought specifically for him. No one else had ever worn them, and he hadn't had to steal them.

But most of all, he had always been alone, and abruptly he was surrounded by family. Now he had a mother and a father, *four* brothers, a little sister, a sister-in-law, an infant nephew, and all of them treated him as if he had been there from the beginning. He could still barely tolerate being touched, but the Mackenzie family touched *a lot.* Mary—Mom—was constantly hugging him, tousling his hair, kissing him good-night, fussing over him. Maris, his new sister, pestered the living hell out of him just the way she did her other brothers, then would throw her skinny arms around his waist and fiercely hug him, saying, "I'm so glad you're ours!"

He was always taken aback on those occasions, and would dart a wary glance at Wolf, the big man who was the head of the Mackenzie pack and who was now Chance's dad, too. What did he think, seeing his innocent little daughter hug someone like Chance? Wolf Mackenzie was no innocent; if he didn't know exactly what experiences had molded Chance, he still recognized the dangerous vein in the half-wild boy. Chance always wondered if those knowing eyes could see clear through him, see the blood on his hands, find in his mind the memory of the man he had killed when he was about ten.

Yes, the big half-breed had known very well the type of wild animal he had taken into his family and called son, had known and, like Mary, had loved him, anyway.

His early years had taught Chance how risky life was, taught him not to trust anyone, taught him that love would only make him vulnerable and that vulnerability could cost him his life. He had known all that, and still he hadn't been able to stop himself from loving the Mackenzies. It never stopped scaring him, this weakness in his armor, and yet when he was in the family bosom was the only time he was completely relaxed, because he knew he was safe with them. He couldn't stay away, couldn't distance himself now that he was a man who was more than capable of taking care of himself, because their love for him, and his for them, fed his soul.

He had stopped even trying to limit their access to his heart and instead turned his considerable talents to doing everything he could to make their world, their lives, as safe as possible. They kept making it tougher for him; the Mackenzies constantly assaulted him with expansions: his brothers married, giving him sisters-in-law to love, because his brothers loved them and they were part of the family now. Then there were the babies. When he first came into the family there was only John, Joe and Caroline's first son, newly born. But nephew had followed nephew, and somehow Chance, along with everyone else in the Mackenzie family, found himself rocking infants, changing diapers, holding bottles, letting a dimpled little hand clutch one of his fingers while tottering first steps were made…and each one of those dimpled hands had clutched his heart, too. He had no defense against them. There were twelve nephews now, and one niece against whom he was particularly helpless, much to everyone else's amusement.

Going home was always nerve-racking, and yet he yearned for his family. He was afraid for them, afraid for himself, because he didn't know if he could live now without the warmth the Mackenzies folded about him. His mind told him he would be better off if he gradually severed the ties and isolated himself from both the pleasure and the potential for pain, but his heart always led him home again.

CHAPTER ONE

CHANCE LOVED MOTORCYCLES. The big beast between his legs throbbed with power as he roared along the narrow winding road, the wind in his hair, leaning his body into the curves with the beast so they were one, animal and machine. No other motorcycle in the world sounded like a Harley, with that deep, coughing rumble that vibrated through his entire body. Riding a motorcycle always gave him a hard-on, and his own visceral reaction to the speed and power never failed to amuse him.

Danger was sexy. Every warrior knew it, though it wasn't something people were going to read about in their Sunday newspaper magazines. His brother Josh freely admitted that landing a fighter on a carrier deck had always turned him on. "It falls just short of orgasm," was the way Josh put it. Joe, who could fly any jet built, refrained from commenting but always smiled a slow, knowing smile.

As for both Zane and himself, Chance knew there were times when each had emerged from certain tense situations, usually involving bullets, wanting nothing more than to have a woman beneath him. Chance's sexual need was ferocious at those times; his body was flooded with adrenaline and testosterone, he was *alive,* and he desperately needed a woman's soft body in which he could bury himself and release all the tension. Unfortunately, that need always had to wait: wait until he was in a secure position, maybe even in a different country entirely; wait until there was an available, willing woman at hand; and, most of all, wait until he had settled down enough that he could be relatively civilized in the sack.

But for now, there was only the Harley and himself, the rush of sweet mountain air on his face and the inner mixture of joy and fear of going home. If Mom saw him riding the Harley without a helmet she would tear a strip off his hide, which was why he had the helmet with him, securely fastened behind the seat. He would put it on before sedately riding up the mountain to visit them. Dad wouldn't be fooled, but neither would he say anything, because Wolf Mackenzie knew what it was to fly high and wild.

He crested a ridge, and Zane's house came into view in the broad valley below. The house was large, with five bedrooms and four baths, but not ostentatious; Zane had instinctively built the house so it wouldn't attract undue attention. It didn't look as large as it was, because some of the rooms were underground. He had also built it to be as secure as possible, positioning it so he had an unrestricted view in all directions, but using natural formations of the land to block land access by all but the one road. The doors were steel, with state-of-the-art locks; the windows were shatterproof, and had cost a small fortune. Strategic walls had interior armor, and an emergency generator was installed in the basement. The basement also concealed another means of escape, if escape became necessary. Motion sensors were installed around the house, and as Chance wheeled the motorcycle into the driveway, he knew his arrival had already been signaled.

Zane didn't keep his family locked in a prison, but the security provisions were there if needed. Given their jobs, prudence demanded caution, and Zane had always prepared for emergencies, always had a backup plan.

Chance cut off the motor and sat for a minute, letting

his senses return to normal while he ran a hand through his windswept hair. Then he kicked the stand down and leaned the Harley onto it, and dismounted much the way he would a horse. Taking a thin file from the storage compartment, he went up on the wide, shady porch.

It was a warm summer day, mid-August, and the sky was a cloudless clear blue. Horses grazed contentedly in the pasture, though a few of the more curious had come to the fence to watch with huge, liquid dark eyes as the noisy machine roared into the driveway. Bees buzzed around Barrie's flowers, and birds sang continuously in the trees. Wyoming. Home. It wasn't far away, Mackenzie's Mountain, with the sprawling house on the mountaintop where he had been given…life and everything else in this world that was important to him.

"The door's open." Zane's low, calm voice issued from the intercom beside the door. "I'm in the office."

Chance opened the door and went inside, his booted feet silent as he walked down the hall to Zane's office. With small clicks, the door locks automatically engaged behind him. The house was quiet, meaning Barrie and the kids weren't at home; if Nick was anywhere in the house she would have run squealing to him, hurling herself into his arms, chattering nonstop in her mangled English while holding his face clasped between both her little hands, making certain his attention didn't wander from her—as if he would dare look away. Nick was like a tiny package of unstable explosives; it was best to keep a weather eye on her.

The door to Zane's office was unexpectedly closed. Chance paused a moment, then opened it without knocking.

Zane was behind the desk, computer on, windows open to the warm, fresh air. He gave his brother one of his rare, warm smiles. "Watch where you step," he advised. "Munchkins on deck."

Automatically Chance looked down, checking out the floor, but he didn't see either of the twins. "Where?"

Zane leaned back in his chair a little, looking around for his offspring. Spotting them, he said, "Under the desk. When they heard me let you in, they hid."

Chance raised his eyebrows. To his knowledge, the ten-month-old twins weren't in the habit of hiding from anyone or anything. He looked more carefully and saw four plump, dimpled baby hands peeping from under the cover of Zane's desk. "They aren't very good at it," he observed. "I can see their hands."

"Give them a break, they're new at this stuff. They've only started doing it this week. They're playing Attack."

"Attack?" Fighting the urge to laugh, Chance said, "What am I supposed to do?"

"Just stand there. They'll burst from cover as fast as they can crawl and grab you by the ankles."

"Any biting involved?"

"Not yet."

"Okay. What are they going to do with me once they have me captured?"

"They haven't gotten to that part yet. For now, they just pull themselves up and stand there giggling." Zane scratched his jaw, considering. "Maybe they'll sit on your feet to hold you down, but for the most part they like standing too much to settle for sitting."

The attack erupted. Even with Zane's warning, Chance was a little surprised. They were remarkably quiet, for babies. He had to admire their precision; they launched themselves from under the desk at a rapid crawl, plump little legs pumping, and with identical triumphant crows attached themselves to his ankles. Dimpled hands clutched his jeans. The one on the left plopped down on his foot for a second, then thought better of the tactic and twisted around to begin hauling himself to an upright position. Baby arms wrapped around his knees, and the two little conquerors squealed with delight, their bubbling chuckles eliciting laughter from both men.

"Cool," Chance said admiringly. "Predator babies." He tossed the file onto Zane's desk and leaned down to scoop the little warriors into his arms, settling each diapered bottom on a muscular forearm. Cameron and Zack grinned at him, six tiny white baby teeth shining in each identical dimpled face, and immediately they began patting his face with their fat little hands, pulling his ears, delving into his shirt pockets. It was like being attacked by two squirming, remarkably heavy marshmallows.

"Good God," he said in astonishment. "They weigh a ton." He hadn't expected them to have grown so much in the two months since he had seen them.

"They're almost as big as Nick. She still outweighs them, but I swear they feel heavier." The twins were sturdy and strongly built, the little boys already showing the size of the Mackenzie males, while Nick was as dainty as her grandmother Mary.

"Where are Barrie and Nick?" Chance asked, missing his pretty sister-in-law and exuberant, cheerfully diabolic niece.

"We had a shoe crisis. Don't ask."

"How do you have a shoe crisis?" Chance asked, unable to resist. He sat down in a big, comfortable chair across from Zane's desk, setting the babies more comfortably in his lap. They lost interest in pulling his ears and began babbling to each other, reaching out, entwining their arms and legs as if they sought the closeness they had known while forming in the womb. Chance unconsciously stroked them, enjoying the softness of their skin, the feel of squirming babies in his arms. All the Mackenzie babies grew up accustomed to being constantly, lovingly touched by the entire extended family.

Zane laced his hands behind his head, his big, powerful body relaxed. "First you have a three-year-old who loves her shiny, black, patent leather Sunday shoes. Then you make the severe tactical error of letting her watch *The Wizard of Oz*." His stern mouth twitched, and his pale eyes glittered with amusement.

Chance's agile mind immediately made the connection, and his acquaintance with the three-year-old in question allowed him to make a logical assumption: Nick had decided she had to have a pair of red shoes. "What did she use to try to dye them?"

Zane sighed. "Lipstick, what else?" Each and every young Mackenzie had had an incident with lipstick. It was a family tradition, one John had started when, at the age of two, he had used his mother's favorite lipstick to recolor the impressive rows of fruit salad on Joe's dress uniform. Caroline had been impressively outraged, because the shade had been discontinued and finding a new tube had been much more difficult than replacing the small colored bars that represented medals Joe had earned and services he had performed.

"You couldn't just wipe it off?" The twins had discovered his belt buckle and zipper, and Chance moved the busy little hands that were trying to undress him. They began squirming to get down, and he leaned over to set them on the floor.

"Close the door," Zane instructed, "or they'll escape."

Leaning back, Chance stretched out a long arm and closed the door, just in time. The two diaper-clad escape artists had almost reached it. Deprived of freedom, they plopped down on their padded bottoms and considered the situation, then launched themselves in crawling patrol of the perimeters of the room.

"I *could* have wiped it off," Zane continued, his tone bland, "if I had known about it. Unfortunately, Nick cleaned the shoes herself. She put them in the dishwasher."

Chance threw back his head with a shout of laughter.

"Barrie bought her a new pair of shoes yesterday. Well, you know how Nick's always been so definite about what she wants to wear. She took one look at the shoes, said they were ugly, *even though they were just like the ones she ruined,* and refused to even try them on."

"To be accurate," Chance corrected, "what she said was that they were 'ugwy.'"

Zane conceded the point. "She's getting better with her *L*s, though. She practices, saying the really important words, like lollipop, over and over to herself."

"Can she say 'Chance' yet, instead of 'Dance'?" Chance asked, because Nick stubbornly refused to even acknowledge she couldn't say his name. She insisted everyone else was saying it wrong.

Zane's expression was totally deadpan. "Not a chance."

Chance groaned at the pun, wishing he hadn't asked. "I gather Barrie has taken my little darling shopping, so she can pick out her own shoes."

"Exactly." Zane glanced over to check on his roaming offspring. As if they had been waiting for his parental notice, first Cam and then Zack plopped down on their butts and gave brief warning cries, all the while watching their father expectantly.

"Feeding time," Zane said, swiveling his chair around so he could fetch two bottles from a small cooler behind the desk. He handed one to Chance. "Grab a kid."

"You're prepared, as always," Chance commented as he

went over to the twins and leaned down to lift one in his arms. Holding the baby up, he peered briefly at the scowling little face to make sure he had the one he thought he had. It was Zack, all right. Chance couldn't say exactly how he knew which twin was which, how anyone in the family knew, because the babies were so identical their pediatrician had suggested putting ID anklets on them. But they each had such definite personalities, which were reflected in their expressions, that no one in the family ever confused one twin for the other.

"I have to be prepared. Barrie weaned them last month, and they don't take kindly to having to wait for dinner."

Zack's round blue eyes were fiercely focused on the bottle in Chance's hand. "Why did she wean them so early?" Chance asked as he resumed his seat and settled the baby in the crook of his left arm. "She nursed Nick until he was a year old."

"You'll see," Zane said dryly, settling Cam on his lap.

As soon as Chance brought the bottle within reach of Zack's fat little hands the baby made a grab for it, guiding it to his rapacious, open mouth. He clamped down ferociously on the nipple. Evidently deciding to let his uncle hold the bottle, he nevertheless made certain the situation was stabilized by clutching Chance's wrist with both hands, and wrapping both chubby legs around Chance's forearm. Then he began to growl as he sucked, pausing only to swallow.

An identical growling noise came from Zane's lap. Chance looked over to see his brother's arm captured in the same manner as the two little savages held on to their meals.

Milk bubbled around Zack's rosebud mouth, and Chance blinked as six tiny white teeth gnawed on the plastic nipple.

"Hell, no wonder she weaned you!"

Zack didn't pause in his gnawing, sucking and growling, but he did flick an absurdly arrogant glance at his uncle before returning his full attention to filling his little belly.

Zane was laughing softly, and he lifted Cam enough that he could nuzzle one of the chubby legs so determinedly wrapped around his arm. Cam paused to scowl at the interruption, then changed his mind and instead favored his father with a dimpled, milky smile. The next second the smile was gone and he attacked the bottle again.

Zack's fuzzy black hair was as soft as silk against Chance's arm. Babies were a pure tactile pleasure, he thought, though he hadn't been of that opinion the first time he'd held one. The baby in question had been John, screaming his head off from the misery of teething.

Chance hadn't been with the Mackenzies long, only a few months, and he had still been extremely wary of all these people. He had managed—barely—to control his instinct to attack whenever someone touched him, but he still jumped like a startled wild animal. Joe and Caroline came to visit, and from the expressions on their faces when they entered the house, it had been a very long trip. Even Joe, normally so controlled and unflappable, was frustrated by his futile efforts to calm his son, and Caroline had been completely frazzled by a situation she couldn't handle with her usual impeccable logic. Her blond hair had been mussed, and her green eyes expressed an amazing mixture of concern and outrage.

As she had walked by Chance, she suddenly wheeled and deposited the screaming baby in his arms. Startled, alarmed, he tried to jerk back, but before he knew it he was in sole possession of the wiggling, howling little human. "Here," she said with relief and utmost confidence. "You get him calmed down."

Chance had panicked. It was a wonder he hadn't dropped the baby. He'd never held one before, and he didn't know what to do with it. Another part of him was astounded that Caroline would entrust her adored child to *him,* the mongrel stray Mary—Mom—had brought home with her. Why couldn't these people see what he was? Why couldn't they figure out he had lived wild in a kill-or-be-killed world, and that they would be safer if they kept their distance from him?

Instead, no one seemed to think it unusual or alarming that he was holding the baby, even though in his panic he held John almost at arm's length, clutched between his two strong young hands.

But blessed quiet fell in the house. John was startled out of his screaming. He stared interestedly at this new person and kicked his legs. Automatically Chance changed his grip on the baby, settling him in the cradle of one arm as he had seen the others do. The kid was drooling. A tiny bib was fastened around his neck, and Chance used it to wipe away most of the slobber. John saw this opportunity and grabbed Chance by the thumb, immediately carrying the digit to his mouth and chomping down. Chance had jumped at the force of the hard little gums, with two tiny, sharp teeth already breaking the surface. He grimaced at the pain, but hung in there, letting John use his thumb as a teething ring until Mom rescued him by bringing a cold wet washcloth for the baby to chew.

Chance had expected then to be relieved of baby duty, because Mom usually couldn't wait to get her hands on her grandson. But that day everyone had seemed content to leave John in his hands, even the kid himself, and after a while Chance calmed down enough to start walking around and pointing out things of interest to his little pal, all of which John obediently studied while gnawing on the relief-giving washcloth.

That had been his indoctrination to the ways of babies, and from that day on he had been a sucker for the parade of nephews his virile brothers and fertile sisters-in-law had produced on a regular basis. He seemed to be getting even worse, because with Zane's three he was total mush.

"By the way, Maris is pregnant."

Chance's head jerked up, and a wide grin lit his tanned face. His baby sister had been married nine whole months and had been fretting because she hadn't immediately gotten pregnant.

"When is it due?" He always ruthlessly arranged things so he could be home when a new Mackenzie arrived. Technically, this one would be a MacNeil, but that was a minor point.

"March. She says she'll be crazy before then, because Mac won't let her out of his sight."

Chance chuckled. Other than her father and brothers, Mac was the only man Maris had ever met whom she couldn't intimidate, which was one of the reasons she loved him so much. If Mac had decided he was going to ride herd on Maris during her pregnancy, she had little hope of escaping on one of those long, hard rides she so loved.

Zane nodded toward the file on his desk. "You going to tell me about it?"

Chance knew Zane was asking about more than the contents of the file. He was asking why it hadn't been transmitted by computer, instead of Chance personally bringing a hard copy. Zane knew his brother's schedule; he was the only person, other than Chance himself, who did, so he knew Chance was currently supposed to be in France. He was also asking why he hadn't been notified of Chance's change in itinerary, why his brother hadn't made a simple phone call to let him know he was coming.

"I didn't want to risk even a hint of this leaking out."

Zane's eyebrows rose. "We have security problems?"

"Nothing that I know of," Chance said. "It's what I don't know about that worries me. But, like I said, no one else can hear even a whisper of this. It's between us."

"Now you've made me curious." Zane's cool blue eyes gleamed with interest.

"Crispin Hauer has a daughter."

Zane didn't straighten from his relaxed position, but his expression hardened. Crispin Hauer had been number one on their target list for years, but the terrorist was as elusive as he was vicious. They had yet to find any way to get close to him, any vulnerability they could exploit or bait they could use to lure him into a trap. There was a record of a marriage in London some thirty-five years ago, but Hauer's wife, formerly Pamela Vickery, had disappeared, and no trace of her had ever been found. Chance, along with everyone else, had assumed the woman died soon after the marriage, either by Hauer's hand or by his enemies'.

"Who is she?" Zane asked. "*Where* is she?"

"Her name is Sonia Miller, and she's here, in America."

"I know that name," Zane said, his gaze sharpening.

Chance nodded. "Specifically, she's the courier who was supposedly robbed of her package last week in Chicago."

Zane didn't miss the "supposedly," but then, he never missed anything. "You think it was a setup?"

"I think it's a damn good possibility. I found the link when I checked into her background."

"Hauer would have known she'd be investigated after losing a package, especially one containing aerospace documents. Why take the risk?"

"He might not have thought we would find anything. She was adopted. Hal and Eleanor Miller are listed as her parents, and they're clean as a whistle. I wouldn't have known she was adopted if I hadn't tried to pull up her birth certificate on the computer. Guess what—Hal and Eleanor never had any children. Little Sonia Miller didn't have a birth certificate. So I did some digging and found the adoption file—"

Zane's eyebrows rose. Open adoptions had caused so many problems that the trend had veered sharply back to closed files, which, coupled with electronic privacy laws and safeguards, had made it damn difficult to even locate those closed files, much less get into them. "Did you leave any fingerprints?"

"Nothing that will lead back to us. I went through a couple of relays, then hacked into the Internal Revenue and accessed the file from their system."

Zane grinned. If anyone did notice the electronic snooping, it likely wouldn't even be mentioned; no one messed with the tax people.

Zack had finished his bottle; his ferocious grip on it slackened, and his head lolled against Chance's arm as he briefly struggled against sleep. Automatically Chance lifted the baby to his shoulder and began patting his back. "Ms. Miller has been employed as a courier for a little over five years. She has an apartment in Chicago, but her neighbors say she's seldom there. I have to think this is a long-term setup, that she's been working with her father from the beginning."

Zane nodded. They had to assume the worst, because it was their job to do so. Only by anticipating the worst could they be prepared to handle it.

"Do you have anything in mind?" he asked, taking the

bottle from Cam's slackened grip and gently lifting the sleeping baby to his own shoulder.

"Getting next to her. Getting her to trust me."

"She's not going to be the trusting sort."

"I have a plan," Chance said, and grinned, because that was usually Zane's line.

Zane grinned in return, then paused as a small security console in the wall dinged a soft alarm. He glanced at the security monitor. "Brace yourself," he advised. "Barrie and Nick are home."

Seconds later the front door opened and a shriek filled the house. "Unca *Dance*! UncaDanceUncaDanceUnca*Dance*!" The chant was punctuated by the sound of tiny feet running and jumping down the hall as Nick's celebration of his visit came closer. Chance leaned back in his chair and opened the office door a bare second before Nick barreled through it, her entire little body quivering with joy and eagerness.

She hurled herself at him, and he managed to catch her with his free arm, dragging her onto his lap. She paused to bestow a big-sisterly kiss and a pat on the back of Zack's head—never mind that he was almost as big as she was—then turned all her fierce attention to Chance.

"Are you staying dis time?" she demanded, even as she lifted her face for him to kiss. He did, nuzzling her soft cheek and neck and making her giggle, inhaling the faint sweet scent of baby that still clung to her.

"Just for a few days," he said, to her disappointment. She was old enough now to notice his long and frequent absences, and whenever she saw him she tried to convince him to stay.

She scowled; then, being Nick, she decided to move on to more important matters. Her face brightened. "Den can I wide your moborcycle?"

Alarm flared through him. "No," he said firmly. "You can't ride it, sit on it, lean on it or put any of your toys on it *unless I'm with you.*" With Nick, it was best to close all the loopholes. She seldom disobeyed a direct order, but she was a genius at finding cracks to slip through. Another possibility occurred to him. "You can't put Cam or Zack on it, either." He doubted she could lift either of them, but he wasn't taking any risks.

"Thank you," Barrie said dryly, entering the office in time to catch his addendum. She leaned down to kiss him on the cheek, at the same time lifting Zack from his arms so he could protect himself from Nick's feet. All the Mackenzie males, at one time or another, had fallen victim to a tiny foot in the crotch.

"Mission accomplished?" Zane asked, leaning back in his chair and smiling at his wife with that lazy look in his pale eyes that said he liked what he was seeing.

"Not without some drama and convincing, but, yes, mission accomplished." She pushed a feather lock of red hair out of her eyes. As always, she looked stylish, though she was wearing nothing dressier than beige slacks and a white sleeveless blouse that set off her slim, lightly tanned arms. You could take the girl out of the finishing school, Chance thought admiringly, but you could never take the finishing school out of the girl, and Barrie had gone to the most exclusive one in the world.

Nick was still focused on negotiating riding rights on the motorcycle. She caught his face between her hands and leaned down so her nose practically touched his, insuring his complete attention. He nearly laughed aloud at the fierce intent in her expression. "I wet you wide my twicycle," she said, evidently deciding to cajole instead of demand.

"Somehow I missed that," Zane murmured in amusement, while Barrie laughed softly.

"You *offered* to let me ride your tricycle," Chance corrected. "But I'm too big to ride a tricycle, and you're too little to ride a motorcycle."

"Den when *can* I wide it?" She made her blue eyes wide and winsome.

"When you get your driver's license."

That stymied her. She had no idea what a driver's license was, or how to get it. She stuck a finger in her mouth while she pondered this situation, and Chance tried to divert her interest. "Hey! Aren't those new shoes you're wearing?"

Like magic, her face brightened again. She wriggled around so he could hold one foot up so close to his face she almost kicked him in the nose. "Dey're so *pwetty,*" she crooned in delight.

He caught the little foot in his big hand, admiring the shine of the black patent leather. "Wow, that's so shiny I can see my face in it." He pretended to inspect his teeth, which set her to giggling.

Zane rose to his feet. "We'll put the boys down for their naps while you have her occupied."

Keeping Nick occupied wasn't a problem; she was never at a loss for something to say or do. He curled one silky black strand of her hair around his finger while she chattered about her new shoes, Grampa's new horses and what Daddy had said when he hit his thumb with a hammer. She cheerfully repeated exactly what Daddy had said, making Chance choke.

"But I'm not 'posed to say dat," she said, giving him a solemn look. "Dat's a weally, weally bad word."

"Yeah," he said, his voice strained. "It is."

"I'm not 'posed to say 'damn,' or 'hell,' or 'ass,' or—"

"Then you shouldn't be saying them now." He managed to inject a note of firmness in his tone, though it was a struggle to keep from laughing.

She looked perplexed. "Den how can I tell you what dey are?"

"Does Daddy know what the bad words are?"

The little head nodded emphatically. "He knows dem *all*."

"I'll ask him to tell me, so I'll know which words not to say."

"Otay." She sighed. "But doñ't hit him too hard."

"Hit him?"

"Dat's de only time he says *dat* word, when he hits his dumb wid de hammer. He said so."

Chance managed to turn his laugh into a cough. Zane was an ex-SEAL; his language was as salty as the sea he was so at home in, and Chance had heard "dat word," and worse, many times from his brother. But Mom had also instilled strict courtesy in all her children, so their language was circumspect in front of women and children. Zane must not have known Nick was anywhere near him when he hit his thumb, or no amount of pain could have made him say that in her hearing. Chance only hoped she forgot it before she started kindergarten.

"Aunt Mawis is goin' to have a baby," Nick said, scrambling up to stand in his lap, her feet braced on his thighs. Chance put both hands around her to steady her, though his aid probably wasn't needed; Nick had the balance of an acrobat.

"I know. Your daddy told me."

Nick scowled at not being the first to impart the news. "She's goin' to foal in de spwing," she announced.

He couldn't hold back the laughter this time. He gathered the little darling close to him and stood, whirling her around and making her shriek with laughter as she clung to his neck. He laughed until his eyes were wet. God, he loved this child, who in the three short years of her life had taught them all to be on their toes at all times, because there was no telling what she was going to do or say. It took the entire Mackenzie family to ride herd on her.

Suddenly she heaved a sigh. "When's de spwing? Is it a wong, wong time away?"

"Very long," he said gravely. Seven months was an eternity to a three-year-old.

"Will I be old?"

He put on a sympathetic face and nodded. "You'll be four."

She looked both horrified and resigned. "Four," she said mournfully. "Whodadunkit?"

When he stopped laughing this time, he wiped his eyes and asked, "Who taught you to say *whodathunkit?*"

"John," she said promptly.

"Did he teach you anything else?"

She nodded.

"What? Can you remember it?"

She nodded.

"Will you tell me what they are?"

She rolled her eyes up and studied the ceiling for a moment, then gave him a narrow-eyed look. "Will you wet me wide your moborcycle?"

Damn, she was bargaining! He trembled with fear at the thought of what she would be like when she was sixteen. "No," he said firmly. "If you got hurt, your mommy and daddy would cry, Grampa and Gamma would cry, *I* would cry, Aunt Maris would cry, Mac would cry, Unca Mike would cry—"

She looked impressed at this litany of crying and interrupted before he could name everyone in the family. "I can wide a horse, Unca Dance, so why can't I wide your moborcycle?"

God, she was relentless. Where in the hell were Zane and Barrie? They'd had plenty of time to put the twins down for their naps. If he knew Zane, his brother was taking advantage of having a babysitter for Nick to get in some sexy time with his wife; Zane was always prepared to use a fluid situation to his advantage.

It was another ten minutes before Zane strolled back into the office, his eyes slightly heavy-lidded and his hard face subtly relaxed. Chance scowled at his brother. He'd spent the ten minutes trying to talk Nick into telling him what John had taught her, but she wasn't budging from her initial negotiation. "It's about time," he groused.

"Hey, I hurried," Zane protested mildly.

"Yeah, right."

"As much as possible," he added, smiling. He smoothed his big hand over his daughter's shining black hair. "Have you kept Uncle Chance entertained?"

She nodded. "I told him de weally, weally bad word you said when you hit your dumb."

Zane looked pained, then stern. "How did you tell him when you aren't supposed to say the word?"

She stuck her finger in her mouth and began studying the ceiling again.

"Nick." Zane plucked her from Chance's arms. "Did you say the word?"

Her lower lip stuck out a little, but she nodded, owning up to her transgression.

"Then you can't have a bedtime story tonight. You promised you wouldn't say it."

"I'm sowwy," she said, winding her arms around his neck and laying her head on his shoulder.

Gently he rubbed his hand up and down her back. "I

know you are, sweetheart, but you have to keep your promises." He set her on her feet. "Go find Mommy."

When she was gone, out of curiosity Chance asked, "Why didn't you tell her that she couldn't watch television, instead of taking away the bedtime story?"

"We don't want to make television attractive by using it as a treat or a privilege. Why? Are you taking notes on being a parent?"

Appalled, Chance said, "Not in this lifetime."

"Yeah? Fate has a way of jumping up and biting you on the ass when you least expect it."

"Well, my ass is currently bite-free, and I intend to keep it that way." He nodded at the file on Zane's desk. "We have some planning to do."

CHAPTER TWO

THIS WHOLE ASSIGNMENT was a tribute to Murphy's Law, Sunny Miller thought in disgust as she sat in the Salt Lake City airport, waiting for her flight to be called—if it were called at all, which she was beginning to doubt. This was her fifth airport of the day, and she was still almost a thousand miles from her destination, which was Seattle. She was *supposed* to have been on a direct flight from Atlanta to Seattle, but that flight had been canceled due to mechanical problems and the passengers routed on to other flights, none of which were direct.

From Atlanta she had gone to Cincinnati, from Cincinnati to Chicago, from Chicago to Denver and from Denver to Salt Lake City. At least she was moving west instead of backtracking, and the flight from Salt Lake City, assuming it ever started boarding, was supposed to actually land in Seattle.

The way her day had gone, she expected it to crash instead.

She was tired, she had been fed nothing but peanuts all day, and she was afraid to go get anything to eat in case her flight was called and the plane got loaded and in the air in record time, leaving her behind. When Murphy was in control, anything was possible. She made a mental note to find this Murphy guy and punch him in the nose.

Her normal good humor restored by the whimsy, she

resettled herself in the plastic seat and took out the paperback book she had been reading. She was tired, she was hungry, but she wasn't going to let the stress get to her. If there was one thing she was good at, it was making the best of a situation. Some trips were smooth as silk, and some were a pain in the rear; so long as the good and the bad were balanced, she could cope.

Out of ingrained habit, she kept the strap of her soft leather briefcase looped around her neck, held across her body so it couldn't easily be jerked out of her grasp. Some couriers might handcuff the briefcase or satchel to their wrists, but her company was of the opinion that handcuffs drew unwanted attention; it was better to blend in with the horde of business travelers than to stand out. Handcuffs practically shouted "Important stuff inside!"

After what had happened in Chicago the month before, Sunny was doubly wary and also kept one hand on the briefcase. She had no idea what was in it, but that didn't matter; her job was to get the contents from point A to point B. When the briefcase had been jerked off her shoulder by a green-haired punk in Chicago last month, she had been both humiliated and furious. She was *always* careful, but evidently not careful enough, and now she had a big blotch on her record.

On a very basic level, she was alarmed that she had been caught off guard. She had been taught from the cradle to be both prepared and cautious, to be alert to what was going on around her; if a green-haired punk could get the best of her, then she was neither as prepared nor alert as she had thought. When one slip could mean the difference between life and death, there was no room for error.

Just remembering the incident made her uneasy. She

returned the book to her carry-on bag, preferring to keep her attention on the people around her.

Her stomach growled. She had food in her carry-on, but that was for emergencies, and this didn't qualify. She watched the gate, where the two airline reps were patiently answering questions from impatient passengers. From the dissatisfied expressions on the passengers' faces as they returned to their seats, the news wasn't good; logically, she should have enough time to find something to eat.

She glanced at her watch: 1:45 p.m., local time. She had to have the contents of the briefcase in Seattle by 9:00 p.m. Pacific time tonight, which should have been a breeze, but the way things were going, she was losing faith the assignment could be completed on time. She hated the idea of calling the office to report another failure, even one that wasn't her fault. If the airline didn't get on the ball soon, though, she would have to do something. The customer needed to know if the packet wasn't going to arrive as scheduled.

If the news on the flight delay hadn't improved by the time she returned from eating, she would see about transferring to another airline, though she had already considered that option and none of the possibilities looked encouraging; she was in flight-connection hell. If she couldn't work out something, she would have to make that phone call.

Taking a firm grip on the briefcase with one hand and her carry-on bag with the other, she set off down the concourse in search of food that didn't come from a vending machine. Arriving passengers were pouring out of a gate to her left, and she moved farther to the right to avoid the crush. The maneuver didn't work; someone jostled her left shoulder, and she instinctively looked around to see who it was.

No one was there. A split-second reaction, honed by years of looking over her shoulder, saved her. She automatically tightened her grip on the briefcase just as she felt a tug on the strap, and the leather fell limply from her shoulder.

Damn it, not again!

She ducked and spun, swinging her heavy carry-on bag at her assailant. She caught a glimpse of feral dark eyes and a mean, unshaven face; then her attention locked on his hands. The knife he had used to slice the briefcase strap was in one hand, and he already had his other hand on the briefcase, trying to jerk it away from her. The carry-on bag hit him on the shoulder, staggering him, but he didn't release his grip.

Sunny didn't even think of screaming, or of being scared; she was too angry for either reaction, and both would have splintered her concentration. Instead, she wound up for another swing, aiming the bag for the hand holding the knife.

Around her she heard raised voices, full of confused alarm as people tried to dodge around the disturbance, and jostled others instead. Few, if any, of them would have any idea what the ruckus was about. Vision was hampered; things were happening too fast. She couldn't rely on anyone coming to help, so she ignored the noise, all her attention centered on the cretin whose dirty hand clutched her briefcase.

Whap! She hit him again, but still he held on to the knife.

"Bitch," he snarled, his knife-hand darting toward her.

She jumped back, and her fingers slipped on the leather. Triumphantly he jerked it away from her. Sunny grabbed for the dangling strap and caught it, but the knife made a silver flash as he sliced downward, separating the strap from the briefcase. The abrupt release of tension sent her staggering back.

The cretin whirled and ran. Catching her balance, Sunny shouted, "Stop him!" and ran in pursuit. Her long skirt had a slit up the left side that let her reach full stride, but the cretin not only had a head start, he had longer legs. Her carry-on bag banged against her legs, further hampering her, but she didn't dare leave it behind. Doggedly she kept running, even though she knew it was useless. Despair knotted her stomach. Her only prayer was that someone in the crowd would play hero and stop him.

Her prayer was abruptly answered.

Up ahead, a tall man standing with his back to the concourse turned and glanced almost negligently in the direction of the ruckus. The cretin was almost abreast of him. Sunny drew breath to yell out another "Stop him," even though she knew the cretin would be past before the man could react. She never got the words out of her mouth.

The tall man took in with one glance what was happening, and in a movement as smooth and graceful as a ballet pirouette, he shifted, pivoted and lashed out with one booted foot. The kick landed squarely on the cretin's right knee, taking his leg out from under him. He cartwheeled once and landed flat on his back, his arms flung over his head. The briefcase skidded across the concourse before bouncing against the wall, then back into the path of a stream of passengers. One man hopped over the briefcase, while others stepped around it.

Sunny immediately swerved in that direction, snatching up the briefcase before any other quick-fingered thief could grab it, but she kept one eye on the action.

In another of those quick, graceful movements, the tall

man bent and flipped the cretin onto his stomach, then wrenched both arms up high behind his back and held them with one big hand.

"Owww!" the cretin howled. "You bastard, you're breaking my arms!"

The name-calling got his arms roughly levered even higher. He howled again, this time wordlessly and at a much higher pitch.

"Watch your language," said his captor.

Sunny skidded to a halt beside him. "Be careful," she said breathlessly. "He had a knife."

"I saw it. It landed over there when he fell." The man didn't look up but jerked his chin to the left. As he spoke he efficiently stripped the cretin's belt from its loop and wound the leather in a simple but effective snare around his captive's wrists. "Pick it up before someone grabs it and disappears. Use two fingers, and touch only the blade."

He seemed to know what he was doing, so Sunny obeyed without question. She took a tissue out of her skirt pocket and gingerly picked up the knife as he had directed, being careful not to smear any fingerprints on the handle.

"What do I do with it?"

"Hold it until Security gets here." He angled his dark head toward the nearest airline employee, a transportation escort who was hovering nervously as if unsure what to do. "Security *has* been called, hasn't it?"

"Yes, sir," said the escort, his eyes round with excitement.

Sunny squatted beside her rescuer. "Thank you," she said. She indicated the briefcase, with the two dangling pieces of its strap. "He cut the strap and grabbed it away from me."

"Any time," he said, turning his head to smile at her and giving her her first good look at him.

Her first look was almost her last. Her stomach fluttered. Her heart leaped. Her lungs seized. *Wow,* she thought, and tried to take a deep breath without being obvious about it.

He was probably the best-looking man she had ever seen, without being pretty in any sense of the word. *Drop-dead handsome* was the phrase that came to mind. Slightly dazed, she took in the details: black hair, a little too long and a little too shaggy, brushing the collar at the back of his battered brown leather jacket; smooth, honey-tanned skin; eyes of such a clear, light brown that they looked golden, framed by thick black lashes. As if that wasn't enough, he had also been blessed with a thin, straight nose, high cheekbones and such clearly delineated, well-shaped lips that she had the wild impulse to simply lean forward and kiss him.

She already knew he was tall, and now she had the time to notice the broad shoulders, flat belly and lean hips. Mother Nature had been in a *really* good mood when he was made. He should have been too perfect and pretty to be real, but there was a toughness in his expression that was purely masculine, and a thin, crescent-shaped scar on his left cheekbone only added to the impression. Looking down, she saw another scar slashing across the back of his right hand, a raised line that was white against his tanned skin.

The scars in no way detracted from his attractiveness; the evidence of rough living only accentuated it, stating unequivocally that this was a *man.*

She was so bemused that it took her several seconds to realize he was watching her with mingled amusement and interest. She felt her cheeks heat in embarrassment at being caught giving him a blatant once-over. Okay, twice-over.

But she didn't have time to waste in admiration, so she

forced her attention back to more pressing concerns. The cretin was grunting and making noises designed to show he was in agony, but she doubted he was in any great pain, despite his bound hands and the way her hero had a knee pressed into the small of his back. She had the briefcase back, but the cretin still presented her with a dilemma: It was her civic duty to stay and press charges against him, but if her flight left any time soon, she might very well miss it while she was answering questions and filling out forms.

"Jerk," she muttered at him. "If I miss my flight…"

"When is it?" asked her hero.

"I don't know. It's been delayed, but they could begin boarding at any time. I'll check at the gate and be right back."

He nodded with approval. "I'll hold your friend here and deal with Security until you get back."

"I'll only be a minute," she said, and walked swiftly back to her gate. The counter was now jammed with angry or upset travelers, their mood far more agitated than when she had left just a few moments before. Swiftly she glanced at the board, where CANCELED had been posted in place of the DELAYED sign.

"Damn," she said, under her breath. "Damn, damn, damn." There went her last hope for getting to Seattle in time to complete her assignment, unless there was another miracle waiting for her. Two miracles in one day was probably too much to ask for, though.

She needed to call in, she thought wearily, but first she could deal with the cretin and airport security. She retraced her steps and found that the little drama was now mobile; the cretin was on his feet, being frog-marched under the control of two airport policemen into an office where they would be out of the view of curious passersby.

Her hero was waiting for her, and when he spotted her, he said something to the security guys, then began walking to meet her.

Her heart gave a little flutter of purely feminine appreciation. My, he was good to look at. His clothes were nothing special: a black T-shirt under the old leather jacket, faded jeans and scuffed boots, but he wore them with a confidence and grace that said he was utterly comfortable. Sunny allowed herself a moment of regret that she would never see him again after this little contretemps was handled, but then she pushed it away. She couldn't take the chance of letting anything develop into a relationship—assuming there was anything there to develop—with him or anyone else. She never even let anything start, because it wouldn't be fair to the guy, and she didn't need the emotional wear and tear, either. Maybe one day she would be able to settle down, date, eventually find someone to love and marry and maybe have kids, but not now. It was too dangerous.

When he reached her, he took her arm with old-fashioned courtesy. "Everything okay with your flight?"

"In a way. It's been canceled," she said ruefully. "I have to be in Seattle tonight, but I don't think I'm going to make it. Every flight I've had today has either been delayed or rerouted, and now there's no other flight that would get me there in time."

"Charter a plane," he said as they walked toward the office where the cretin had been taken.

She chuckled. "I don't know if my boss will spring for that kind of money, but it's an idea. I have to call in, anyway, when we're finished here."

"If it makes any difference to him, I'm available right now. I was supposed to meet a customer on that last flight in from Dallas, but he wasn't on the plane, and he hasn't contacted me, so I'm free."

"You're a charter pilot?" She couldn't believe it. It—*he*—was too good to be true. Maybe she did qualify for two miracles in one day after all.

He looked down at her and smiled, making a tiny dimple dance in his cheek. God, he had a dimple, too! Talk about overkill! He held out his hand. "Chance McCall—pilot, thief-catcher, jack-of-all-trades—at your service, ma'am."

She laughed and shook his hand, noticing that he was careful not to grip her fingers too hard. Considering the strength she could feel in that tough hand, she was grateful for his restraint. Some men weren't as considerate. "Sunny Miller, tardy courier and target of thieves. It's nice to meet you, Mr. McCall."

"Chance," he said easily. "Let's get this little problem taken care of, then you can call your boss and see if he thinks a charter flight is just what the doctor ordered."

He opened the door of the unmarked office for her, and she stepped inside to find the two security officers, a woman dressed in a severe gray suit and the cretin, who had been handcuffed to his chair. The cretin glared at her when she came in, as if all this were her fault instead of his.

"You lyin' bitch—" the cretin began.

Chance McCall reached out and gripped the cretin's shoulder. "Maybe you didn't get the message before," he said in that easy way of his that in no way disguised the iron behind it, "but I don't care for your language. Clean it up." He didn't issue a threat, just an order—and his grip on the cretin's shoulder didn't look gentle.

The cretin flinched and gave him an uneasy look, perhaps remembering how effortlessly this man had manhandled him before. Then he looked at the two airport policemen, as if expecting them to step in. The two men crossed their arms and grinned. Deprived of allies, the cretin opted for silence.

The gray-suited woman looked as if she wanted to protest the rough treatment of her prisoner, but she evidently decided to get on with the business at hand. "I'm Margaret Fayne, director of airport security. I assume you're going to file charges?"

"Yes," Sunny said.

"Good," Ms. Fayne said in approval. "I'll need statements from both of you."

"Any idea how long this will take?" Chance asked. "Ms. Miller and I are pressed for time."

"We'll try to hurry things along," Ms. Fayne assured him.

Whether Ms. Fayne was super-efficient or yet another small miracle took place, the paperwork was completed in what Sunny considered to be record time. Not much more than half an hour passed before the cretin was taken away in handcuffs, all the paperwork was prepared and signed, and Sunny and Chance McCall were free to go, having done their civic duty.

He waited beside her while she called the office and explained the situation. The supervisor, Wayne Beesham, wasn't happy, but bowed to reality.

"What's this pilot's name again?" he asked.

"Chance McCall."

"Hold on, let me check him out."

Sunny waited. Their computers held a vast database of information on both commercial airlines and private charters. There were some unsavory characters in the charter business, dealing more in drugs than in passengers, and a courier company couldn't afford to be careless.

"Where's his home base?"

Sunny repeated the question to Chance.

"Phoenix," he said, and once again she relayed the information.

"Okay, got it. He looks okay. How much is his fee?" Sunny asked.

Mr. Beesham grunted at the reply. "That's a bit high."

"He's here, and he's ready to go."

"What kind of plane is it? I don't want to pay this price for a crop-duster that still won't get you there in time."

Sunny sighed. "Why don't I just put him on the line? It'll save time." She handed the receiver to Chance. "He wants to know about your plane."

Chance took the receiver. "McCall." He listened a moment. "It's a Cessna Skylane. The range is about eight hundred miles at seventy-five percent power, six hours flying time. I'll have to refuel, so I'd rather it be around the midway point, say at Roberts Field in Redmond, Oregon. I can radio ahead and have everything rolling so we won't spend much time on the ground." He glanced at his wristwatch. "With the hour we gain when we cross into the Pacific time zone, she can make it—barely."

He listened for another moment, then handed the receiver back to Sunny. "What's the verdict?" she asked.

"I'm authorizing it. For God's sake, get going."

She hung up and grinned at Chance, her blood pumping at the challenge. "It's a go! How long will it take to get airborne?"

"If you let me carry that bag, and we run...fifteen minutes."

Sunny never let the bag out of her possession. She hated to repay his courtesy with a refusal, but caution was so ingrained in her that she couldn't bring herself to take the risk. "It isn't heavy," she lied, tightening her grip on it. "You lead, I'll follow."

One dark eyebrow went up at her reply, but he didn't argue, just led the way through the busy concourse. The private planes were in a different area of the airport, away from the commercial traffic. After several turns and a flight of stairs, they left the terminal and walked across the concrete, the hot afternoon sun beating down on their heads and making her squint. Chance slipped on a pair of sunglasses, then shrugged out of the jacket and carried it in his left hand.

Sunny allowed herself a moment of appreciation at the way his broad shoulders and muscled back filled out the black T-shirt he wore. She might not indulge, but she could certainly admire. If only things were different—but they weren't, she thought, reining in her thoughts. She had to deal with reality, not wishful thinking.

He stopped beside a single-engine airplane, white with gray-and-red striping. After storing her bag and briefcase and securing them with a net, he helped her into the co-pilot's seat. Sunny buckled herself in and looked around with interest. She'd never been in a private plane before, or flown in anything this small. It was surprisingly comfortable. The seats were gray leather, and behind her was a bench seat with individual backs. Carpet covered the metal floor.

There were two sun visors, just like in a car. Amused, she flipped down the one in front of her and laughed aloud when she saw the small mirror attached to it.

Chance walked around the plane, checking details one last time before climbing into the seat to her left and buckling himself in. He put on a set of headphones and began flipping switches while he talked to the air traffic control tower. The engine coughed, then caught, and the propeller on the nose began to spin, slowly at first, then gaining speed until it was an almost invisible blur.

He pointed to another set of headphones, and Sunny put them on. "It's easier to talk using the headphones," came his voice in her ear, "but be quiet until we get airborne."

"Yes, sir," she said, amused, and he flashed a quick grin at her.

They were airborne within minutes, faster than she had ever experienced on a commercial carrier. Being in the small plane gave her a sense of speed that she had never before felt, and when the wheels left the ground the lift was incredible, as if she had sprouted wings and jumped into the air. The ground quickly fell away below, and the vast, glistening blue lake spread out before her, with the jagged mountains straight ahead.

"Wow," she breathed, and brought one hand up to shield her eyes from the sun.

"There's an extra pair of sunglasses in the glove box," he said, indicating the compartment in front of her. She opened it and dug out a pair of inexpensive but stylish Foster Grants with dark red frames. They were obviously some woman's sunglasses, and abruptly she wondered if he was married. He would have a girlfriend, of course; not only was he very nice to look at, he seemed to be a nice person. It was a combination that was hard to find and impossible to beat.

"Your wife's?" she asked as she put on the glasses and breathed a sigh of relief as the uncomfortable glare disappeared.

"No, a passenger left them in the plane."

Well, that hadn't told her anything. She decided to be blunt, even while she wondered why she was bothering, since she would never see him again after they arrived in Seattle. "Are you married?"

Again she got that quick grin. "Nope." He glanced at her, and though she couldn't see his eyes through the dark glasses, she got the impression his gaze was intense. "Are you?"

"No."

"Good," he said.

CHAPTER THREE

CHANCE WATCHED HER from behind the dark lenses of his sunglasses, gauging her reaction to his verbal opening. The plan was working better than he'd hoped; she was attracted to him and hadn't been trying very hard to hide it. All he had to do was take advantage of that attraction and win her trust, which normally might take some doing, but what he had planned would throw her into a situation that wasn't *normal* in any sense of the word. Her life and safety would depend on him.

To his faint surprise, she faced forward and pretended she hadn't heard him. Wryly, he wondered if he'd misread her and she wasn't attracted to him after all. No, she had been watching him pretty blatantly, and in his experience, a woman didn't stare at a man unless she found him attractive.

What was *really* surprising was how attractive he found *her*. He hadn't expected that, but sexual chemistry was an unruly demon that operated outside logic. He had known she was pretty, with brilliant gray eyes and golden-blond hair that swung smoothly to her shoulders, from the photographs in the file he had assembled on her. He just hadn't realized how damn *fetching* she was.

He slanted another glance at her, this time one of pure male assessment. She was of average height, maybe, though a little more slender than he liked, almost delicate. Almost. The muscles of her bare arms, revealed by a white sleeveless blouse, were well-toned and lightly tanned, as if she worked out. A good agent always stayed in good physical condition, so he had to expect her to be stronger than she looked. Her delicate appearance probably took a lot of people off guard.

She sure as hell had taken Wilkins off guard. Chance had to smother a smile. While Sunny had gone back to her gate to check on the status of her flight, which Chance had arranged to be canceled, Wilkins had told him how she had swung her carry-on bag at him, one-armed, and that the damn thing had to weigh a ton, because it had almost knocked him off his feet.

By now, Wilkins and the other three, "Ms. Fayne" and the two security "policemen," would have vanished from the airport. The real airport security had been briefed to stay out of the way, and everything had worked like a charm, though Wilkins had groused at being taken down so roughly. "First that little witch damn near breaks my arm with that bag, then you try to break my back," he'd growled, while they all laughed at him.

Just what was in that bag, anyway? She had held on to it as if it contained the crown jewels, not letting him carry it even when she was right there with him, and only reluctantly letting him take it to stow in the luggage compartment behind them. He'd been surprised at how heavy it was, too heavy to contain the single change of clothes required by an overnight trip, even with a vast array of makeup and a hairdryer thrown in for good measure. The bag had to weigh a good fifty pounds, maybe more. Well, he would find out soon enough what was in it.

"What were you going to do with that guy if you'd caught him?" he asked in a lazy tone, partly to keep her talking, establishing a link between them, and partly because he was curious. She had been chasing after Wilkins with a fiercely determined expression on her face, so determined that, if Wilkins were still running, she would probably still be chasing him.

"I don't know," she said darkly. "I just knew I couldn't let it happen again."

"Again?" Damn, was she going to tell him about Chicago?

"Last month, a green-haired cretin snatched my briefcase in the airport in Chicago." She slapped the arm of the seat. "That's the first time anything like that has ever happened on one of my jobs, then to have it happen again just a month later—I'd have been fired. Heck, *I* would fire me, if I were the boss."

"You didn't catch the guy in Chicago?"

"No. I was in Baggage Claims, and he just grabbed the briefcase, zipped out the door and was gone."

"What about security? They didn't try to catch him?"

She peered at him over the top of the oversize sunglasses. "You're kidding, right?"

He laughed. "I guess I am."

"Losing another briefcase would have been a catastrophe, at least to me, and it wouldn't have done the company any good, either."

"Do you ever know what's in the briefcases?"

"No, and I don't want to. It doesn't matter. Someone could be sending a pound of salami to their dying uncle Fred, or it could be a billion dollars' worth of diamonds—not that I think anyone would ever ship diamonds by a courier service, but you get the idea."

"What happened when you lost the briefcase in Chicago?"

"My company was out a lot of money—rather, the insurance company was. The customer will probably never use us again, or recommend us."

"What happened to you? Any disciplinary action?" He knew there hadn't been.

"No. In a way, I would have felt better if they had at least fined me."

Damn, she was good, he thought in admiration—either that, or she was telling the truth and hadn't had anything to do with the incident in Chicago last month. It was possible, he supposed, but irrelevant. Whether or not she'd had anything to do with losing that briefcase, he was grateful it had happened, because otherwise she would never have come to his notice, and he wouldn't have this lead on Crispin Hauer.

But he didn't think she was innocent; he thought she was in this up to her pretty neck. She was better than he had expected, an actress worthy of an Oscar—so good he might have believed she didn't know anything about her father, if it wasn't for the mystery bag and her deceptive strength. He was trained to put together seemingly insignificant details and come up with a coherent picture, and experience had made him doubly cynical. Few people were as honest as they wanted you to believe, and the people who put on the best show were often the ones with the most to hide. He should know—he was an expert at hiding the black secrets of his soul.

He wondered briefly what it said about him that he was willing to sleep with her as part of his plan to gain her trust, but maybe it was better not to think about it. Someone had to be willing to work in the muck, to do things from which ordinary people would shrink, just to protect those ordinary people. Sex was...just sex. Part of the job. He could even divorce his emotions to the point that he actually looked forward to the task.

Task? Who was he kidding? He couldn't wait to slide into her. She intrigued him, with her toned, tight body and the twinkle that so often lit her clear gray eyes, as if she was often amused at both herself and the world around her. He was fascinated by her eyes, by the white striations that made her eyes look almost faceted, like the palest of blue diamonds. Most people thought of gray eyes as a pale blue, but when he was close to her, he could see that they were, very definitely, brilliantly gray. But most of all he was intrigued by her expression, which was so open and good-humored she could almost trademark the term "Miss Congeniality." How could she look like that, as sweet as apple pie, when she was working hand in glove with the most-wanted terrorist in his files?

Part of him, the biggest part, despised her for what she was. The animal core of him, however, was excited by the dangerous edge of the game he was playing, by the challenge of getting her into bed with him and convincing her to trust him. When he was inside her, he wouldn't be thinking about the hundreds of innocent people her father had killed, only about the linking of their bodies. He wouldn't let himself think of anything else, lest he give himself away with some nuance of expression that women were so good at reading. No, he would make love to her as if he had found his soul mate, because that was the only way he could be certain of fooling her.

But he was good at that, at making a woman feel as if he desired her more than anything else in the world. He knew just how to make her aware of him, how to push hard without panicking her—which brought him back to the fact that she had totally ignored his first opening. He smiled slightly to himself. Did she really think that would work?

"Will you have dinner with me tonight?"

She actually jumped, as if she had been lost in her thoughts. "What?"

"Dinner. Tonight. After you deliver your package."

"Oh. But—I'm supposed to deliver it at nine. It'll be late, and—"

"And you'll be alone, and I'll be alone, and you have to eat. I promise not to bite. I may lick, but I won't bite."

She surprised him by bursting into laughter.

Of all the reactions he had anticipated, laughter wasn't one of them. Still, her laugh was so free and genuine, her head tilted back against the seat, that he found himself smiling in response.

"'I may lick, but I won't bite.' That was good. I'll have to remember it," she said, chuckling.

After a moment, when she said nothing else, he realized that she was ignoring him again. He shook his head. "Does that work with most men?"

"Does what work?"

"Ignoring them when they ask you out. Do they slink away with their tails tucked between their legs?"

"Not that I've ever noticed." She grinned. "You make me sound like a femme fatale, breaking hearts left and right."

"You probably are. We guys are tough, though. We can be bleeding to death on the inside and we'll put up such a good front that no one ever knows." He smiled at her. "Have dinner with me."

"You're persistent, aren't you?"

"You still haven't answered me."

"All right—no. There, I've answered you."

"Wrong answer. Try again." More gently, he said, "I know you're tired, and with the time difference, nine o'clock is really midnight to you. It's just a meal, Sunny, not an evening of dancing. That can wait until our second date."

She laughed again. "Persistent *and* confident." She

paused, made a wry little face. "The answer is still no. I don't date."

This time he was more than surprised, he was stunned. Of all the things he had expected to come out of her mouth, that particular statement had never crossed his mind. Damn, had he so badly miscalculated? "At all? Or just men?"

"At all." She gestured helplessly. "See, this is why I tried to ignore you, because I didn't want to go into an explanation that you wouldn't accept, anyway. No, I'm not gay, I like men very much, but I don't date. End of explanation."

His relief was so intense, he felt a little dizzy. "If you like men, why don't you date?"

"See?" she demanded on a frustrated rush of air. "You didn't accept it. You immediately started asking questions."

"Damn it, did you think I'd just let it drop? There's something between us, Sunny. I know it, and you know it. Or are you going to ignore that, too?"

"That's exactly what I'm going to do."

He wondered if she realized what she had just admitted. "Were you raped?"

"No!" she half shouted, goaded out of control. "I just… don't…date."

She was well on her way to losing her temper, he thought, amused. He grinned. "You're pretty when you're mad."

She sputtered, then began laughing. "How am I supposed to stay mad when you say things like that?"

"You aren't. That's the whole idea."

"Well, it worked. What it didn't do was change my mind. I'm sorry," she said gently, sobering. "It's just… I have my reasons. Let it drop. Please."

"Okay." He paused. "For now."

She gave an exaggerated groan that had him smiling

again. "Why don't you try to take a nap?" he suggested. "You have to be tired, and we still have a long flight ahead of us."

"That's a good idea. You can't badger me if I'm asleep."

With that wry shot, she leaned her head back against the seat. Chance reached behind her seat and produced a folded blanket. "Here. Use this as a pillow, or you'll get a stiff neck."

"Thanks." She took off the headset and tucked the blanket between her head and shoulder, then shifted around in her seat to get more comfortable.

Chance let silence fall, occasionally glancing at her to see if she really fell asleep. About fifteen minutes later, her breathing deepened and evened out into a slow rhythm. He waited a few minutes longer, then eased the plane into a more westerly direction, straight into the setting sun.

CHAPTER FOUR

"SUNNY." THE VOICE was insistent, a little difficult to hear and accompanied by a hand on her shoulder, shaking her. "Sunny, wake up."

She stirred and opened her eyes, stretching a little to relieve the kinks in her back and shoulders. "Are we there?"

Chance indicated the headset in her lap, and she slipped it on. "We have a problem," he said quietly.

The bottom dropped out of her stomach, and her heartbeat skittered. No other words, she thought, could be quite as terrifying when one was in an airplane. She took a deep breath, trying to control the surge of panic. "What's wrong?" Her voice was surprisingly steady. She looked around, trying to spot the problem in the cluster of dials in the cockpit, though she had no idea what any of them meant. Then she looked out of the window at the rugged landscape below them, painted in stark reds and blacks as the setting sun threw shadows over jagged rock. "Where are we?"

"Southeastern Oregon."

The engine coughed and sputtered. Her heart felt as if it did, too. As soon as she heard the break in the rhythm, she became aware that the steady background whine of the motor had been interrupted several times while she slept. Her subconscious had registered the change in sound but not put it in any context. Now the context was all too clear.

"I think it's the fuel pump," he added, in answer to her first question.

Calm. She had to stay calm. She pulled in a deep breath, though her lungs felt as if they had shrunk in size. "What do we do?"

He smiled grimly. "Find a place to set it down before it falls down."

"I'll take setting over falling any day." She looked out the side window, studying the ground below. Jagged mountain ridges, enormous boulders and sharp-cut arroyos slicing through the earth were all she could see. "Uh-oh."

"Yea. I've been looking for a place to land for the past half hour."

This was not good, not good at all. In the balance of good and bad, this weighed heavily on the bad side.

The engine sputtered again. The whole frame of the aircraft shook. So did her voice, when she said, "Have you radioed a Mayday?"

Again that grim smile. "We're in the middle of a great big empty area, between navigational beacons. I've tried a couple of times to raise someone, but there haven't been any answers."

The scale tipped even more out of balance. "I knew it," she muttered. "The way today has gone, I *knew* I'd crash if I got on another plane."

The grouchiness in her voice made him chuckle, despite the urgency of their situation. He reached over and gently squeezed the back of her neck, startling her with his touch, his big hand warm and hard on her sensitive nape. "We haven't crashed yet, and I'm going to try damn hard to make sure we don't. The landing may be rough, though."

She wasn't used to being touched. She had accustomed herself to doing without the physical contact that it was human nature to crave, to keep people at a certain distance. Chance McCall had touched her more in one afternoon than she had been touched in the past five years. The shock of pleasure almost distracted her from their situation—almost. She looked down at the unforgiving landscape again. "How rough does a landing have to get before it qualifies as a crash?"

"If we walk away from it, then it was a landing." He put his hand back on the controls, and she silently mourned that lost connection.

The vast mountain range spread out around them as far as she could see in any direction. Their chances of walking away from this weren't good. How long would it be before their bodies were found, if ever? Sunny clenched her hands, thinking of Margreta. Her sister, not knowing what had happened, would assume the worst—and dying in an airplane crash was *not* the worst. In her grief, she might well abandon her refuge and do something stupid that would get her killed, too.

She watched Chance's strong hands, so deft and sure on the controls. His clear, classic profile was limned against the pearl and vermillion sky, the sort of sunset one saw only in the western states, and likely the last sunset she would ever see. He would be the last person she ever saw, or touched, and she was suddenly, bitterly angry that she had never been able to live the life most women took for granted, that she hadn't been free to accept his offer of dinner and spend the trip in a glow of anticipation, free to flirt with him and maybe see the glow of desire in his golden-brown eyes.

She had been denied a lot, but most of all she had been denied opportunity, and she would never, never forgive her father for that.

The engine sputtered, caught, sputtered again. This time the reassuring rhythm didn't return. The bottom dropped out of her stomach. God, oh God, they were going to crash. Her nails dug into her palms as she fought to contain her panic. She had never before felt so small and helpless, so fragile, with soft flesh and slender bones that couldn't withstand such battering force. She was going to die, and she had yet to live.

The plane jerked and shuddered, bucking under the stress of spasmodic power. It pitched to the right, throwing Sunny against the door so hard her right arm went numb.

"That's it," Chance said between gritted teeth, his knuckles white as he fought to control the pitching aircraft. He brought the wings level again. "I have to take it down now, while I have a little control. Look for the best place."

Best place? There *was* no best place. They needed somewhere that was relatively flat and relatively clear; the last location she had seen that fit that description had been in Utah.

He raised the right wingtip, tilting the plane so he had a better side view.

"See anything?" Sunny asked, her voice shaking just a little.

"Nothing. Damn."

"Damn is the wrong word. Pilots are supposed to say something else just before they crash." Humor wasn't much of a weapon with which to face death, but it was how she had always gotten herself through the hard times.

Unbelievably, he grinned. "But I haven't crashed yet, sweetheart. Have a little faith. I promise I'll say the right word if I don't find a good-looking spot pretty soon."

"If you don't find a good-looking spot, I'll say it for you," she promised fervently.

They crossed a jagged, boulder-strewn ridge, and a long, narrow black pit yawned beneath them like a doorway to hell. "There!" Chance said, nosing the plane down.

"What? Where?" She sat erect, desperate hope flaring inside her, but all she could see was that black pit.

"The canyon. That's our best bet."

The black pit was a canyon? Weren't canyons supposed to be big? That looked like an arroyo. How on earth would the plane ever fit inside it? And what difference did it make, when this was their only chance? Her heart lodged itself in her throat, and she gripped the edge of the seat as Chance eased the pitching aircraft lower and lower.

The engine stopped.

For a moment all she heard was the awful silence, more deafening than any roar.

Then she became aware of the air rushing past the metal skin of the plane, air that no longer supported them. She heard her own heart beating, fast and heavy, heard the whisper of her breath. She heard everything except what she most wanted to hear, the sweet sound of an airplane engine.

Chance didn't say anything. He concentrated fiercely on keeping the plane level, riding the air currents down, down, aiming for that long, narrow slit in the earth. The plane spiraled like a leaf, coming so close to the jagged mountainside on the left that she could see the pits in the dark red rock.

Sunny bit her lip until blood welled in her mouth, fighting back the terror and panic that threatened to erupt in screams. She couldn't distract him now, no matter what. She wanted to close her eyes, but resolutely kept them open. If she died now, she didn't want to do it in craven fear. She couldn't help the fear, but she didn't have to be craven. She would watch death come at her, watch Chance as he fought to bring them down safely and cheat the grim horseman.

They slipped below the sunshine, into the black shadows, deeper and deeper. It was colder in the shadows, a chill that immediately seeped through the windows into her bones. She couldn't see a thing. Quickly she snatched off the sunglasses and saw that Chance had done the same. His eyes were narrowed, his expression hard and intent as he studied the terrain below.

The ground was rushing at them now, a ground that was pocked and scored with rivulets, and dotted with boulders. It was flat enough, but not a nice, clear landing spot at all. She braced her feet against the floor, her body rigid as if she could force the airplane to stay aloft.

"Hold on." His voice was cool. "I'm going to try to make it to the stream bed. The sand will help slow us down before we hit one of those rocks."

A stream bed? He was evidently much better at reading the ground than she was. She tried to see a ribbon of water, but finally realized the stream was dry; the bed was that thin, twisting line that looked about as wide as the average car.

She started to say "Good luck," but it didn't seem appropriate. Neither did "It was nice knowing you." In the end, all she could manage was "Okay."

It happened fast. Suddenly they were no longer skimming above the earth. The ground was *there,* and they hit it hard, so hard she pitched forward against the seat belt, then snapped back. They went briefly airborne again as the wheels bounced, then hit again even harder. She heard metal screeching in protest; then her head banged against the side window, and for a chaotic moment she didn't see or hear anything, just felt the tossing and bouncing of the plane. She was boneless, unable to hold on, flopping like a shirt in a clothes dryer.

Then there came the hardest bounce of all, jarring her teeth. The plane spun sideways in a sickening motion, then lurched to a stop. Time and reality splintered, broke apart, and for a long moment nothing made any sense; she had no grasp on where she was or what had happened.

She heard a voice, and the world jolted back into place.

"Sunny? Sunny, are you all right?" Chance was asking urgently.

She tried to gather her senses, tried to answer him. Dazed, battered, she realized that the force of the landing had turned her inside the confines of the seat belt, and she was facing the side window, her back to Chance. She felt his hands on her, heard his low swearing as he unclipped the seat belt and eased her back against his chest, supporting her with his body.

She swallowed, and managed to find her voice. "I'm okay." The words weren't much more than a croak, but if she could talk at all that meant she was alive. They were both alive. Joyful disbelief swelled in her chest. He had actually managed to land the plane!

"We have to get out. There may be a fuel leak." Even as he spoke, he shoved open the door and jumped out, dragging her with him as if she was a sack of flour. She felt rather sacklike, her limbs limp and trembling.

A fuel leak. The engine had been dead when they landed, but there was still the battery, and wiring that could short out and spark. If a spark got to any fuel, the plane and everything in it would go up in a fireball.

Everything in it. The words rattled in her brain, like marbles in a can, and with dawning horror she realized what that meant. Her bag was still in the plane.

"Wait!" she shrieked, panic sending a renewed surge of adrenaline through her system, restoring the bones to her legs, the strength to her muscles. She twisted in his grasp, grabbing the door handle and hanging on. "My bag!"

"Damn it, Sunny!" he roared, trying to break her grip on the handle. "Forget the damn bag!"

"No!"

She jerked away from him and began to climb back into the plane. With a smothered curse he grabbed her around the waist and bodily lifted her away from the plane. "I'll get the damn bag! Go on—get out of here! Run!"

She was appalled that he would risk his life retrieving her bag, while sending her to safety. "I'll get it," she said fiercely, grabbing him by the belt and tugging. "*You* run!"

For a split second he literally froze, staring at her in shock. Then he gave his head a little shake, reached in for the bag and effortlessly hefted it out. Wordlessly Sunny tried to take it, but he only gave her an incendiary look and she didn't have time to argue. Carrying the bag in his left hand and gripping her upper arm with his right, he towed her at a run away from the plane. Her shoes sank into the soft grit, and sand and scrub brush bit at her ankles, but she scrambled to stay upright and keep pace with him.

They were a good fifty yards away before he judged it safe. He dropped the bag and turned on her like a panther pouncing on fresh meat, gripping her upper arms with both hands as if he wanted to shake her. "What the hell are you thinking?" he began in a tone of barely leashed violence, then cut himself off, staring at her face. His expression altered, his golden-brown eyes darkening.

"You're bleeding," he said harshly. He grabbed his handkerchief out of his pocket and pressed it to her chin. Despite the roughness of his tone, his touch was incredibly gentle. "You said you weren't hurt."

"I'm not." She raised her trembling hand and took the handkerchief, dabbing it at her chin and mouth. There wasn't much blood, and the bleeding seemed to have stopped. "I bit my lip," she confessed. "Before you landed, I mean. To keep from screaming."

He stared down at her with an expression like flint. "Why didn't you just scream?"

"I didn't want to distract you." The trembling was growing worse by the second; she tried to hold herself steady, but every limb shook as if her bones had turned to gelatin.

He tilted up her face, staring down at her for a moment in the deepening twilight. He breathed a low, savage curse, then slowly leaned down and pressed his lips to her mouth. Despite the violence she sensed in him, the kiss was light, gentle, more of a salute than a kiss. She caught her breath, beguiled by the softness of his lips, the warm smell of his skin, the hint of his taste. She fisted her hands in his T-shirt, clinging to his strength, trying to sink into his warmth.

He lifted his head. "That's for being so brave," he murmured. "I couldn't have asked for a better partner in a plane crash."

"Landing," she corrected shakily. "It was a landing."

That earned her another soft kiss, this time on the temple. She made a strangled sound and leaned into him, a different sort of trembling beginning to take hold of her. He framed her face with his hands, his thumbs gently stroking the corners of her mouth as he studied her. She felt her lips tremble a little, but then, all of her was shaking. He touched the small sore spot her teeth had made in her lower lip; then he was kissing her again, and this time there was nothing gentle about it.

This kiss rocked her to her foundation. It was hungry, rough, deep. There were reasons why she shouldn't respond to him, but she couldn't think what they were. Instead, she gripped his wrists and went on tiptoe to slant her parted lips against his, opening her mouth for the thrust of his tongue. He tasted like man, and sex, a potent mixture that went to her head faster than hundred-proof whiskey. Heat bloomed in her loins and breasts, a desperate, needy heat that brought a low moan from her throat.

He wrapped one arm around her and pulled her against him, molding her to him from knee to breast while his kisses became even deeper, even harder. She locked her arms around his neck and arched into him, wanting the feel of his hard-muscled body against her with an urgency that swept away reason. Instinctively she pushed her hips against his, and the hard length of his erection bulged into the notch of her thighs. This time she cried out in want, in need, in a desire that burned through every cell of her body. His hand closed roughly around her breast, kneading, rubbing her nipple through the layers of blouse and bra, both easing and intensifying the ache that made them swell toward his touch.

Suddenly he jerked his head back. "I don't believe this," he muttered. Reaching up, he prised her arms from around his neck and set her away from him. He looked even more savage than he had a moment before, the veins standing out in his neck. "Stay here," he barked. "Don't move an inch. I have to check the plane."

He left her standing there in the sand, in the growing twilight, suddenly cold all the way down to the bone. Deprived of his warmth, his strength, her legs slowly collapsed, and she sank to the ground.

CHANCE SWORE TO HIMSELF, steadily and with blistering heat, as he checked the plane for fuel leaks and other damage. He had deliberately made the landing rougher than necessary, and the plane had a reinforced landing gear as well as extra protection for the fuel lines and tank, but a smart pilot didn't take anything for granted. He had to check the plane, had to stay in character.

He didn't want to stay in character. He wanted to back her against one of those big boulders and lift her skirt. Damn! What was wrong with him? In the past fifteen years he'd held a lot of beautiful, deadly women in his arms, and even though he let his body respond, his mind had always remained cool. Sunny Miller wasn't the most beautiful, not by a long shot; she was more gamine than goddess, with bright eyes that invited laughter rather than seduction. So why was he so hot to get into her pants?

"Why" didn't matter, he angrily reminded himself. Okay, so his attraction to her was unexpected; it was an advantage, something to be used. He wouldn't have to fake anything, which meant there was even less chance of her sensing anything off-kilter.

Danger heightened the emotions, destroying inhibitions. They had lived through a life-threatening situation together, they were alone and there was a definite physical attraction between them. He had arranged the first two circumstances; the third was a bonus. It was a textbook situation; studies in human nature had shown that, if a man and a woman were thrown together in a dangerous situation and they had only each other to rely on, they quickly formed both sexual and emotional bonds. Chance had the advantage, in that he knew the plane hadn't been in any danger of crashing, and that they weren't in a life-and-death situation. Sunny would think they were stranded, while he knew better. Whenever he signaled Zane, they would promptly be "rescued," but he wouldn't send that signal until Sunny took him into her confidence about her father.

Everything was under control. They weren't even in Oregon, as he'd told her. They were in Nevada, in a narrow box canyon he and Zane had scouted out and selected because it was possible to land a plane in it, and, unless one had the equipment to scale vertical rock walls, impossible to escape. They weren't close to any commercial flight pattern, he had disabled the transponder so no search plane would pick up a signal and they were far off their route. They wouldn't be found.

Sunny was totally under his control; she just didn't know it.

The growing dusk made it impossible to see very much, and it was obvious that if the plane was going to explode in flames, it would already have done so. Chance strode back to where Sunny was sitting on the ground, her knees pulled up and her arms wrapped around her legs, and that damn bag close by her side. She scrambled to her feet as he approached. "All clear?"

"All clear. No fuel leaks."

"That's good." She managed a smile. "It wouldn't do us any good for you to fix the fuel pump if there wasn't any fuel left."

"Sunny…if it's a clogged line, I can fix it. If the fuel pump has gone out, I can't."

He decided to let her know right away that they might not be flying out of here in the morning.

She absorbed that in silence, rubbing her bare arms to ward off the chill of the desert air. The temperature dropped like a rock when the sun went down, which was one of the reasons he had chosen this site. They would have to share their body heat at night to survive.

He leaned down and hefted the bag, marveling anew at its weight, then took her arm to walk with her back to the plane. "I hope you have a coat in this damn bag, since you thought it was important enough to risk your life getting it," he growled.

"A sweater," she said absently, looking up at the crystal clear sky with its dusting of stars. The black walls of the canyon loomed on either side of them, making it obvious they were in a hole in the earth. A big hole, but still a hole. She shook herself, as if dragging her thoughts back to the problem at hand. "We'll be all right," she said. "I have some food, and—"

"Food? You're carrying food in here?" He indicated the bag.

"Just some emergency stuff."

Of all the things he'd expected, food was at the bottom of the list. Hell, food wasn't even *on* the list. Why would a woman on an overnight trip put food in her suitcase?

They reached the plane, and he set the bag down in the dirt. "Let me get some things, and we'll find a place to camp for the night. Can you get anything else in there, or is it full?"

"It's full," she said positively, but then, he hadn't expected her to open it so easily.

He shrugged and dragged out his own small duffel, packed with the things a man could be expected to take on a charter flight: toiletries, a change of clothes. The duffel was unimportant, but it wouldn't look right if he left it behind.

"Why can't we camp here?" she asked.

"This is a stream bed. It's dry now, but if it rains anywhere in the mountains, we could be caught in the runoff."

As he spoke, he got a flashlight out of the dash, the blanket from the back and a pistol from the pocket in the pilot's side door. He stuck the pistol in his belt, and draped the blanket around her shoulders. "I have some water," he said, taking out a plastic gallon milk jug that he'd refilled with water. "We'll be all right tonight." Water had been the toughest thing to locate. He and Zane had found several box canyons in which he could have landed the plane, but this was the only one with water. The source wasn't much, just a thin trickle running out of the rock at the far end of the canyon, but it was enough. He would "find" the water tomorrow.

He handed her the flashlight and picked up both bags. "Lead the way," he instructed, and indicated the direction he wanted. The floor of the canyon sloped upward on one side; the stream bed was the only smooth ground. The going was rough, and Sunny carefully picked her way over rocks and gullies. She was conscientious about shining the light so he could see where he was going, since he was hampered by both bags.

Damn, he wished she had complained at least a little, or gotten upset. He wished she wasn't so easy to like. Most people would have been half-hysterical, or asking endless questions about their chances of being rescued if he couldn't get the plane repaired. Not Sunny. She coped, just as she had coped at the airport, with a minimum of fuss. Without *any* fuss, actually; she had bitten the blood out of her lip to keep from distracting him while he was bringing the plane down.

The canyon was so narrow it didn't take them long to reach the vertical wall. Chance chose a fairly flat section of sandy gray dirt, with a pile of huge boulders that formed a rough semi-circle. "This will give us some protection from the wind tonight."

"What about snakes?" she asked, eyeing the boulders.

"Possible," he said, as he set down the bags. Had he found a weakness he could use to bring her closer to him? "Are you afraid of them?"

"Only the human kind." She looked around as if taking stock of their situation, then kind of braced her shoulders. It was a minute movement, one he wouldn't have noticed if he hadn't been studying her so keenly. With an almost cheerful note she said, "Let's get this camp set up so we can eat. I'm hungry."

She squatted beside her bag and spun the combination dial of the rather substantial lock on her bag. With a quiet *snick* the lock opened, and she unzipped the bag. Chance was a bit taken aback at finding out what was in the bag this easily, but he squatted beside her. "What do you have? Candy bars?"

She chuckled. "Nothing so tasty."

He took the flashlight from her and shone it into the bag as she began taking out items. The bag was as neatly packed as a salesman's sample case, and she hadn't been lying about not having any room in there for anything else. She placed a sealed plastic bag on the ground between them. "Here we go. Nutrition bars." She slanted a look at him. "They taste like you'd expect a nutrition bar to taste, but they're concentrated. One bar a day will give us all we need to stay alive. I have a dozen of them."

The next item was a tiny cell phone. She stared at it, frozen, for a moment, then looked up at him with fragile hope in her eyes as she turned it on. Chance knew there wasn't a signal here, but he let her go through the motions, something inside him aching at the disappointment he knew she would feel.

Her shoulders slumped. "Nothing," she said, and turned the phone off. Without another word she returned to her unpacking.

A white plastic box with a familiar red cross on the top came out next. "First aid kit," she murmured, reaching back into the bag. "Water purification tablets. A couple of bottles of water, ditto orange juice. Light sticks. Matches." She listed each item as she set it on the ground. "Hairspray, deodorant, toothpaste, pre-moistened towelettes, hairbrush, curling iron, blow dryer, two space blankets—" she paused as she reached the bottom of the bag and began hauling on something bigger than any of the other items. "—and a tent."

A TENT. CHANCE STARED down at it, recognizing the type. This was survivalist stuff, what people stored in underground shelters in case of war or natural disaster—or what someone who expected to spend a lot of time in the wilderness would pack.

"It's small," she said apologetically. "Really just a one-man tent, but I had to get something light enough for me to carry. There will be enough room for both of us to sleep in it, though, if you don't mind being a little crowded."

Why would she carry a *tent* on board a plane, when she expected to spend one night in Seattle—in a hotel—then fly back to Atlanta? Why would anyone carry that heavy a bag around when she could have checked it? The answer was that she hadn't wanted it out of her possession, but he still wanted an explanation of why she was carrying it at all.

Something didn't add up here.

HIS SILENCE WAS UNNERVING. Sunny looked down at her incongruous pile of possessions and automatically emptied out the bag, removing her sweater and slipping it on, sitting down to pull on a pair of socks, then stuffing her change of clothes and her grooming items back into the bag. Her mind was racing. There was something about his expression that made a chill go down her spine, a hardness that she hadn't glimpsed before. Belatedly, she remembered how easily he had caught the cretin in the airport, the deadly grace and speed with which he moved. This was no ordinary charter pilot, and she was marooned with him.

She had been attracted to him from the first moment she saw him, but she couldn't afford to let that blind her to the danger of letting down her guard. She was accustomed to living with danger, but this was a different sort of danger, and she had no idea what form it could, or would, take. Chance could simply be one of those men who packed more punch than others, a man very capable of taking care of himself.

Or he could be in her father's pay.

The thought chilled her even more, the cold going down to her bones before common sense reasserted itself. No, there was no way her father could have arranged for everything that had happened today, no way he could have known she would be in the Salt Lake City airport. Being there had been pure bad luck, the result of a fouled-up flight schedule. *She* hadn't known she would be in Salt Lake City. If her father had been involved, he would have tried to grab her in either Atlanta or Seattle. All the zigzagging across the country she had done today had made it impossible for her father to be involved.

As her mind cleared of that silent panic, she remembered how Chance had dragged her bodily from the plane, the way he had draped the blanket around her, even the courtesy with which he had treated her in the airport. He was a strong man, accustomed to being in the lead and taking the risks. *Military training,* she thought with a sudden flash of clarity, and wondered how she had missed it before. Her life, and Margreta's, depended on how well she could read people, how prepared she was, how alert. With Chance, she had been so taken off guard by the strength of her attraction to him, and the shock of finding that interest returned, that she hadn't been thinking.

"What's this about?" he asked quietly, squatting down beside her and indicating the tent. "And don't tell me you were going to camp out in the hotel lobby."

She couldn't help it. The thought of setting up the tent in a hotel lobby was so ludicrous that she chuckled. Seeing the funny side of things was what had kept her sane all these years.

One big hand closed gently on the nape of her neck. "Sunny," he said warningly. "Tell me."

She shook her head, still smiling. "We're stranded here tonight, but essentially we're strangers. After we get out of here we'll never see each other again, so there's no point in spilling our guts to each other. You keep your secrets, and I'll keep mine."

The flashlight beam sharpened the angles of his face. He exhaled a long, exasperated breath. "Okay—for now. I don't know why it matters, anyway. Unless I can get the plane fixed, we're going to be here a long time, and the reason why you have the tent will be irrelevant."

She searched his face, trying to read his impassive expression. "That isn't reassuring."

"It's the truth."

"When we don't show up in Seattle, someone will search for us. The Civil Air Patrol, someone. Doesn't your plane have one of those beacon things?"

"We're in a canyon."

He didn't have to say more than that. Any signal would be blocked by the canyon walls, except for directly overhead. They were in a deep, narrow slit in the earth, the narrowness of the canyon limiting even more their chances of anyone picking up the signal.

"Well, darn," she said forcefully.

This time he was the one who laughed, and he shook his head as he released her neck and stood up. "Is that the worst you can say?"

"We're alive. That outcome is so good considering what *could* have happened that, in comparison, being stranded here only rates a 'darn.' You may be able to fix the plane." She shrugged. "No point in wasting the really nasty words until we know more."

He leaned down and helped her to her feet. "If I can't get us going again, I'll help you with those words. For now, let's get this tent set up before the temperature drops even more."

"What about a fire?"

"I'll look for firewood tomorrow—*if* we need it. We can get by tonight without a fire, and I don't want to waste the flashlight batteries. If we're here for any length of time, we'll need the flashlight."

"I have the lightsticks."

"We'll save those, too. Just in case."

Working together, they set up the tent. She could have done it herself; it was made for one person to handle, and she had practiced until she knew she could do it with a minimum of fuss, but with two people the job took only moments. Brushing away the rocks so they would have a smooth surface beneath the tent floor took longer, but even so, they weren't going to have a comfortable bed for the night.

When they were finished, she eyed the tent with misgivings. It was long enough for Chance, but... She visually measured the width of his shoulders, then the width of the tent. She was either going to have to sleep on her side all night long—or on top of him.

The heat that shot through her told her which option her body preferred. Her heart beat a little faster in anticipation of their enforced intimacy during the coming night, of lying against his strong, warm body, maybe even sleeping in his arms.

To his credit, he didn't make any insinuating remarks, even though when he looked at the tent he must have drawn the same conclusion as she had. Instead, he bent down to pick up the bag of nutrition bars and said smugly, "I knew you'd have dinner with me tonight."

She began laughing again, charmed by both his tact and his sense of humor, and fell a little in love with him right then.

She should have been alarmed, but she wasn't. Yes, letting herself care for him made her emotionally vulnerable, but they had lived through a terrifying experience together, and she *needed* an emotional anchor right now. So far she hadn't found a single thing about the man that she didn't like, not even that hint of danger she kept sensing. In this situation, a man with an edge to him was an asset, not a hindrance.

She allowed herself to luxuriate in this unaccustomed feeling as they each ate a nutrition bar—which was edible, but definitely not tasty—and drank some water. Then they packed everything except the two space blankets back in the bag, to protect their supplies from snakes and insects and other scavengers. They didn't have to worry about bears, not in this desertlike part of the country, but coyotes were possible. Her bag was supposedly indestructible; if any coyotes showed up, she supposed she would find out if the claim about the bag was true, because there wasn't room in the tent for both them and the bag.

Chance checked the luminous dial of his watch. "It's still early, but we should get in the tent to save our body heat, and not burn up calories trying to stay warm out here. I'll spread this blanket down, and we'll use your two blankets for cover."

For the first time, she realized he was in his T-shirt. "Shouldn't you get your jacket from the plane?"

"It's too bulky to wear in the tent. Besides, I don't feel the cold as much as you do. I'll be fine without it." He sat down and pulled off his boots, tossed them inside the tent, then crawled in with the blanket. Sunny slipped off her own shoes, glad she had the socks to keep her feet warm.

"Okay, come on in," Chance said. "Feet first."

She gave him her shoes, then sat down and worked herself feetfirst into the tent. He was lying on his side, which gave her room to maneuver, but it was still a chore keeping her skirt down and trying not to bunch up the blanket as she wiggled into place. Chance zipped the tent flaps shut, then pulled his pistol out of his waistband and placed it beside his head. Sunny eyed the big black automatic; she wasn't an expert on pistols, but she knew it was one of the heavier calibers, either a .45 or a 9mm. She had tried them, but the bigger pistols were too heavy for her to handle with ease, so she had opted for a smaller caliber.

He had already unfolded the space blankets and had them ready to pull in place. She could already feel his body heat in the small space, so she didn't need a blanket yet, but as the night grew colder, they would need all the covering they could get.

They both moved around, trying to get comfortable. Because he was so big, Sunny tried to give him as much room as possible. She turned on her side and curled her arm under her head, but they still bumped and brushed against each other.

"Ready?" he asked.

"Ready."

He turned off the flashlight. The darkness was complete, like being deep in a cave. "Thank God I'm not claustrophobic," she said, taking a deep breath. His scent filled her lungs, warm and...different, not musky, exactly, but earthy, and very much the way a man should smell.

"Just think of it as being safe," he murmured. "Darkness can feel secure."

She did feel safe, she realized. For the first time in her memory, she was certain no one except the man beside her knew where she was. She didn't have to check locks, scout out an alternate exit or sleep so lightly she sometimes felt as if she hadn't slept at all. She didn't have to worry about being followed, or her phone being tapped, or any of the other things that could happen. She did worry about Margreta, but she had to think positively. Tomorrow Chance would find the problem was a clogged fuel line, he would get it cleared, and they would finish their trip. She would be too late to deliver the package in Seattle, but considering they had landed safely instead of crashing, she didn't really care about the package. The day's outcome could have been so much worse that she was profoundly grateful they were all in one piece and relatively comfortable—"relatively" being the key word, she thought, as she tried to find a better position. The ground was as hard as a rock. For all she knew the ground *was* a rock, covered by a thin layer of dirt.

She was suddenly exhausted. The events of the day—the long flight and fouled-up connections, the lack of food, the stress of being mugged, then the almost unbearable tension of those last minutes in the plane—finally took their toll on her. She yawned and unconsciously tried yet again to find a comfortable position, turning over to pillow her head on her other arm. Her elbow collided with something very solid, and he grunted.

"I'm sorry," she mumbled. She squirmed a little more,

inadvertently bumping him with her knee. "This is so crowded I may have to sleep on top."

She heard the words and in shock realized that she had actually said them aloud. She opened her mouth to apologize again.

"Or I could be the one on top."

His words stopped her apology cold. Her breath tangled in her lungs and didn't escape. His deep voice seemed to echo in the darkness, that single sentence reverberating through her consciousness. She was suddenly, acutely, aware of every inch of him, of the sensual promise in his tone. The kiss—the kiss she could write off as reaction; danger was supposed to be an aphrodisiac, and evidently that was true. But this wasn't reaction; this was desire, warm and curious, seeking.

"Is that a 'no' I'm hearing?"

Her lungs started working again, and she sucked in a breath. "I haven't said anything."

"That's my point." He sounded faintly amused. "I guess I'm not going to get lucky tonight."

Feeling more certain of herself with his teasing, she said dryly, "I guess not. You've already used up your quota of luck for the day."

"I'll try again tomorrow."

She stifled a laugh.

"Does that snicker mean I haven't scared you?"

She should be scared, she thought, or at least wary. She had no idea why she wasn't. The fact was, she felt tempted. Very tempted. "No, I'm not scared."

"Good." He yawned. "Then why don't you pull off that sweater and let me use it as a pillow, and you can use my shoulder. We'll both be more comfortable."

Common sense said he was right. Common sense also said she was asking for trouble if she slept in his arms.

She trusted him to behave, but she wasn't that certain of herself. He was sexy, with a capital SEX. He made her laugh. He was strong and capable, with a faintly wicked edge to him. He was even a little dangerous. What more could a woman want?

That was perhaps the most dangerous thing about him, that he made her want him. She had easily resisted other men, walking away without a backward look or a second thought. Chance made her long for all the things she had denied herself, made her aware of how lonely and alone she was.

"Are you sure you can trust me to behave?" she asked, only half joking. "I didn't mean to say that about being on top. I was half-asleep, and it just slipped out."

"I think I can handle you if you get fresh. For one thing, you'll be sound asleep as soon as you stop talking."

She yawned. "I know. I'm crashing hard, if you'll pardon the terminology."

"We didn't crash, we landed. Come on, let's get that sweater off, then you can sleep."

There wasn't room to fully sit up, so he helped her struggle out of the garment. He rolled it up and tucked it under his head, then gently, as if worried he might frighten her, drew her against his right side. His right arm curled around her, and she nestled close, settling her head in the hollow of his shoulder.

The position was surprisingly comfortable, and comforting. She draped her right arm across his chest, because there didn't seem to be any other place to put it. Well, there were other places, but none that seemed as safe. Besides, she liked feeling his heartbeat under her hand. The strong, even thumping satisfied some primitive instinct in her, the desire not to be alone in the night.

"Comfortable?" he asked in a low, soothing tone.

"Um-hmm."

With his left arm he snagged one of the space blankets and pulled it up to cover her to the shoulders, keeping the chill from her bare arms. Cocooned in warmth and darkness, she gave in to the sheer pleasure of lying so close to him. Sleepy desire hummed just below the surface, warming her, softening her. Her breasts, crushed against his side, tightened in delight, and her nipples felt achy, telling her they had hardened. Could he feel them? she wondered. She wanted to rub herself against him like a cat, intensifying the sensation, but she lay very still and concentrated on the rhythm of his heartbeat.

He had touched her breasts when he kissed her. She wanted to feel that again, feel his hard hand on her bare flesh. She wanted him, wanted his touch and his taste and the feel of him inside her. The force of her physical yearning was so strong that she actually ached from the emptiness.

If we don't get out of here tomorrow, she thought in faint despair just before she went to sleep, *I'll be under him before the sun goes down again.*

SUNNY WAS ACCUSTOMED to waking immediately when anything disturbed her; once, a car had backfired out in the street and she had grabbed the pistol from under the pillow and rolled off the bed before the noise had completely faded. She had learned how to nap on demand, because she never knew when she might have to run for her life. She could count on one hand the number of nights since she had stopped being a child that she had slept through undisturbed.

But she woke in Chance's arms aware that she had slept all night long, that not only had lying next to him not disturbed her, in a very basic way his presence had been reassuring. She was safe here, safe and warm and unutterably relaxed. His hand was stroking slowly down her back, and that was what had awakened her.

Her skirt had ridden up during the night, of course, and was twisted at midthigh. Their legs were tangled together, her right leg thrown over his; his jeans were old and soft, but the denim was still slightly rough against the inside of her thigh. She wasn't lying completely on top of him, but it was a near thing. Her head lay pillowed on his chest instead of his shoulder, with the steady thumping of his heart under her ear.

The slow motion of his hand continued. "Good morning," he said, his deep voice raspy from sleep.

"Good morning." She didn't want to get up, she realized, though she knew she should. It was after dawn; the morning light seeped through the brown fabric of the tent, washing them with a dull gold color. Chance should get started on the fuel pump, so they could get airborne and in radio contact with someone as soon as possible, to let the FAA know they hadn't crashed. She knew what she should do, but instead she continued to lie there, content with the moment.

He touched her hair, lifting one strand and watching it drift back down. "I could get used to this," he murmured.

"You've slept with women before."

"I haven't slept with *you* before."

She wanted to ask how she was different, but she was better off not knowing. Nothing could come of this fast-deepening attraction, because she couldn't let it. She had to believe that he could repair the plane, that in a matter of hours they would be separating and she would never see him again. That was the only thing that gave her the strength, finally, to pull away from him and straighten her clothes, push her hair out of her face and unzip the tent.

The chill morning air rushed into their small cocoon. "Wow," she said, ignoring his comment. "Some hot coffee would be good, wouldn't it? I don't suppose you have a jar of instant in the plane?"

"You mean you don't have coffee packed in that survival bag of yours?" Taking his cue from her, he didn't push her to continue their provocative conversation.

"Nope, just water." She crawled out of the tent, and he handed her shoes and sweater out through the opening. Quickly she slipped them on, glad she had brought a heavy cardigan instead of a summer-weight one.

Chance's boots came out next, then him. He sat on the ground and pulled on his boots. "Damn, it's cold. I'm going to get my jacket from the plane. I'll take care of business there, and you go on the other side of these boulders. There shouldn't be any snakes stirring around this early, but keep an eye out."

Sunny dug some tissues out of her skirt pocket and set off around the boulders. Ten minutes later, nature's call having been answered, she washed her face and hands with one of the pre-moistened towelettes, then brushed her teeth and hair. Feeling much more human and able to handle the world, she took a moment to look around at their life-saving little canyon.

It was truly a slit in the earth, no more than fifty yards wide where he had landed the plane. About a quarter of a mile farther down it widened some, but the going was much rougher. The stream bed was literally the only place they could have safely landed. Just beyond the widest point, the canyon made a dog leg to the left, so she had no idea how long it was. The canyon floor was littered with rocks big and small, and a variety of scrub brush. Deep grooves were cut into the ground where rain had sluiced down the steep canyon walls and arrowed toward the stream.

All the different shades of red were represented in the dirt and rock, from rust to vermillion to a sandy pink. The scrub brush wasn't a lush green; the color was dry, as if it had been bleached by the sun. Some of it was silvery, a bright contrast against the monochromatic tones of the earth.

They seemed to be the only two living things there. She didn't hear any birds chirping, or insects rustling. There had to be small wildlife such as lizards and snakes, she knew, which meant there had to be something for them to eat, but at the moment the immense solitude was almost overwhelming.

Looking at the plane, she saw that Chance was already poking around in its innards. Shoving her cold hands into the sweater pockets, she walked down to him.

"Don't you want to eat something?"

"I'd rather save the food until I see what the problem is." He gave her a crooked grin. "No offense, but I don't want to eat another one of those nutrition bars unless I absolutely have to."

"And if you can fly us out of here, you figure you can hold out until we get to an airport."

"Bingo."

She grinned as she changed positions so she could see what he was doing. "I didn't eat one, either," she confessed.

He was checking the fuel lines, his face set in that intent expression men got when they were doing anything mechanical. Sunny felt useless; she could have helped if he was working on a car, but she didn't know anything about airplanes. "Is there anything I can do to help?" she finally asked.

"No, it's just a matter of taking off the fuel lines and checking them for clogs."

She waited a few more minutes, but the process looked

tedious rather than interesting, and she began getting restless. "I think I'll walk around, explore a bit."

"Stay within yelling distance," he said absently.

The morning, though still cool, was getting warmer by the minute as the sun heated the dry desert air. She walked carefully, watching where she placed each step, because a sprained ankle could mean the difference between life and death if she had to run for it. Someday, she thought, a sprain would be an inconvenience, nothing more. One day she would be free.

She looked up at the clear blue sky and inhaled the clean, crisp air. She had worked hard to retain her enjoyment of life, the way she had learned to rely on a sense of humor to keep her sane. Margreta didn't handle things nearly as well, but she already had to deal with a heart condition that, while it could be controlled with medication, nevertheless meant that she had to take certain precautions. If she were ever found, Margreta lacked Sunny's ability to just drop out of sight. She had to have her medication refilled, which meant she had to occasionally see her doctor so he could write a new prescription. If she had to find a new doctor, that would mean being retested, which would mean a lot more money.

Which meant that Sunny never saw her sister. It was safer if they weren't together, in case anyone was looking for sisters. She didn't even have Margreta's phone number. Margreta called Sunny's cell phone once a week at a set time, always from a different pay phone. That way, if Sunny was captured, she had no information her captors could get by any means, not even drugs.

She had four days until Margreta called, Sunny thought. If she didn't answer the phone, or if Margreta didn't call, then each had to assume the other had been caught. If Sunny didn't answer the phone, Margreta would bolt from her safe hiding place, because with the phone records her location could be narrowed down to the correct city. Sunny couldn't bear to think what would happen then; Margreta, in her grief and rage, might well throw caution to the wind in favor of revenge.

Four days. The problem *had* to be a clogged fuel line. It just had to be.

CHAPTER SIX

MINDFUL OF CHANCE'S WARNING, Sunny didn't wander far. In truth, there wasn't much to look at, just grit and rocks and scraggly bushes, and those vertical rock walls. The desert had a wild, lonely beauty, but she was more appreciative when she wasn't stranded in it. When rain filled the stream this sheltered place probably bloomed with color, but how often did it rain here? Once a year?

As the day warmed, the reptiles began to stir. She saw a brown lizard dart into a crevice as she approached. A bird she didn't recognize swooped down for a tasty insect, then flew back off to freedom. The steep canyon walls didn't mean anything to a bird, while the hundred feet or so were unscalable to her.

She began to get hungry, and a glance at her watch told her she had been meandering through the canyon for over an hour. What was taking Chance so long? If there was a clog in the lines he should have found it by now.

She began retracing her steps to the plane. She could see Chance still poking around the engine, which meant he probably hadn't found anything. A chilly finger of fear prodded her, and she pushed it away. She refused to anticipate trouble. She would deal with things as they happened, and if Chance couldn't repair the plane, then they would have to find some other way out of the canyon. She hadn't explored far; perhaps the other end was open, and they could simply walk out. She didn't know how far they were from a town, but she was willing to make the effort. Anything was better than sitting and doing nothing.

As she approached, Chance lifted his hand to show he saw her, then turned back to the engine. Sunny let her gaze linger, admiring the way his T-shirt clung to the muscles of his back and shoulders. The fit of his jeans wasn't bad, either, she thought, eyeing his butt and long legs.

Something moved in the sand near his feet.

She thought she would faint. Her vision dimmed and narrowed until all she saw was the snake, perilously close to his left boot. Her heart leaped, pounding against her rib cage so hard she felt the thuds.

She had no sensation or knowledge of moving; time took on the viscosity of syrup. All she knew was that the snake was getting bigger and bigger, closer and closer. Chance looked around at her and stepped back from the plane, almost on the coiling length. The snake's head drew back and her hand closed on a coil, surprisingly warm and smooth, and she threw the awful thing as far as she could. It was briefly outlined against the stark rock, then sailed beyond a bush and dropped from sight.

"Are you all right? Did it bite you? Are you hurt?" She couldn't stop babbling as she went down on her knees and began patting his legs, looking for droplets of blood, a small tear in his jeans, anything that would show if he had been bitten.

"I'm all right. I'm all right. Sunny! It didn't bite me." His voice overrode hers, and he hauled her to her feet, shaking her a little to get her attention. "Look at me!" The force of his tone snagged her gaze with his and he said more quietly, "I'm okay."

"Are you sure?" She couldn't seem to stop touching him, patting his chest, stroking his face, though logically she knew there was no way the snake could have bitten him up there. Neither could she stop trembling. "I hate snakes," she said in a shaking voice. "They terrify me. I saw it— it was right under your feet. You almost *stepped* on it."

"Shh," he murmured, pulling her against him and rocking her slowly back and forth. "It's all right. Nothing happened."

She clutched his shirt and buried her head against his chest. His smell, already so familiar and now with the faint odor of grease added, was comforting. His heartbeat was steady, as if he hadn't almost been snakebitten. *He* was steady, rock solid, his body supporting hers.

"Oh, my God," she whispered. "That was awful." She raised her head and stared at him, an appalled expression on her face. "Yuk! I *touched* it!" She snatched her hand away from him and held it at arm's length. "Let me go, I have to wash my hand. Now!"

He released her, and she bolted up the slope to the tent, where the towelettes were. Grabbing one, she scrubbed furiously at her palm and fingers.

Chance was laughing softly as he came up behind her. "What's the matter? Snakes don't have cooties. Besides, yesterday you said you weren't afraid of them."

"I lied. And I don't care what they have, I don't want one anywhere near me." Satisfied that no snake germs lingered on her hand, she blew out a long, calming breath.

"Instead of swooping down like a hawk," he said mildly, "why didn't you just yell out a warning?"

She gave him a blank look. "I couldn't." Yelling had never entered her mind. She had been taught her entire life not to yell in moments of tension or danger, because to do so would give away her position. Normal people could scream and yell, but she had never been allowed to be normal.

He put one finger under her chin, lifting her face to the sun. He studied her for a long moment, something dark moving in his eyes; then he tugged her to him and bent his head.

His mouth was fierce and hungry, his tongue probing. She sank weakly against him, clinging to his shoulders and kissing him in return just as fiercely, with just as much hunger. More. She felt as if she had always hungered, and never been fed. She drank life itself from his mouth, and sought more.

His hands were all over her, on her breasts, her bottom, lifting her into the hard bulge of his loins. The knowledge that he wanted her filled her with a deep need to know more, to feel everything she had always denied herself. She didn't know if she could have brought herself to pull away, but he was the one who broke the kiss, lifting his head and standing there with his eyes closed and a grim expression on his face.

"Chance?" she asked hesitantly.

He growled a lurid word under his breath. Then he opened his eyes and glared down at her. "I can't believe I'm stopping this a second time," he said with a raw, furious frustration. "Just for the record, I'm *not* that noble. Damn it all to hell and back—" He broke off, breathing hard. "It isn't a clogged fuel line. It must be the pump. We have other things we need to do. We can't afford to waste any daylight."

Margreta. Sunny bit her lip to hold back a moan of dismay. She stared up at him, the knowledge of the danger of their situation lying like a stark shadow between them.

She wasn't licked yet. She had four days. "Can we walk out?"

"In the desert? In August?" He looked up at the rim of the canyon. "Assuming we can even get out of here, we'd have to walk at night and try to find shelter during the day. By afternoon, the temperature will be over a hundred."

The temperature was probably already well into the seventies, she thought; she was dying of heat inside her heavy sweater, or maybe that was just frustrated lust, since she hadn't noticed how hot it was until now. She peeled off the sweater and dropped it on top of her bag. "What do we need to do?"

His eyes gleamed golden with admiration, and he squeezed her waist. "I'll reconnoiter. We can't get out on this end of the canyon, but maybe there's a way farther down."

"What do you want me to do?"

"Look for sticks, leaves, anything that will burn. Gather as much as you can in a pile."

He set off in the direction she had gone earlier, and she went in the opposite direction. The scrub brush grew heavier at that end of the canyon, and she would find more wood there. She didn't like to think about how limited the supply would be, or that they might be here for a long, long time. If they couldn't get out of the canyon, they would eventually use up their meager resources and die.

HE HATED LYING to her. Chance's expression was grim as he stalked along the canyon floor. He had lied to terrorists, hoodlums and heads of state alike without a twinge of conscience, but it was getting harder and harder to lie to Sunny. He fiercely protected a hard core of honesty deep inside, the part of him that he shared only with his family, but Sunny was getting to him. She wasn't what he had expected. More and more he was beginning to suspect she wasn't working with her father. She was too…*gallant* was the word that sprang to mind. Terrorists weren't gallant. In his opinion, they were either mad or amoral. Sunny was neither.

He was more shaken by the episode with the snake than he had let her realize. Not by the snake itself—he had on boots, and since he hadn't heard rattles he suspected the snake hadn't been poisonous—but by her reaction. He would never forget the way she had looked, rushing in like an avenging angel, her face paper-white and utterly focused. By her own admission she was terrified of snakes, yet she hadn't hesitated. What kind of courage had it taken for her to pick up the snake with her bare hand?

Then there was the way she had patted him, looking for a bite. Except with certain people, or during sex, he had to struggle to tolerate being touched. He had learned how to accept affection in his family, because Mom and Maris would *not* leave him alone. He unabashedly loved playing with all his nephews—and niece—but his family had been the only exception. Until now. Until Sunny. He not only hadn't minded, he had, for a moment, allowed himself the pure luxury of enjoying the feel of her hands on his legs, his chest. And that didn't even begin to compare to how much he had enjoyed sleeping with her, feeling those sweet curves all along his side. His hand clenched as he remembered the feel of her breast in his palm, the wonderful resilience that was both soft and firm. He ached to feel her bare skin, to taste her. He wanted to strip her naked and pull her beneath him for a long hard ride, and he wanted to do it in broad daylight so he could watch her brilliant eyes glaze with pleasure.

If she wasn't who she was he would take her to the south of France, maybe, or a Caribbean island, any place where they could lie naked on the beach and make love in the sunshine, or in a shaded room with fingers of sunlight slipping through closed blinds. Instead, he had to keep lying to her, because whether or not she was working with her father didn't change the fact that she was the key to locating him.

He couldn't change the plan now. He couldn't suddenly "repair" the plane. He thanked God she didn't know anything about planes, because otherwise she would never have fallen for the fuel pump excuse; a Skylane had a backup fuel pump, for just such an emergency. No, he had to play out the game as he had planned it, because the goal was too damned important to abandon, and he couldn't take the risk that she was involved up to her pretty ears, after all.

He and Zane had walked a fine line in planning this out. The situation had to be survivable but grim, so nothing would arouse her suspicion. There was food to be had, but not easily. There was water, but not a lot. He hadn't brought any provisions that might make her wonder why he had them, meaning he had limited himself to the blanket, the water and the pistol, plus the expected items in the plane, such as flares. Hell, she was a lot more prepared than he was, and that made him wary. She wasn't exactly forthcoming about her reason for toting a damn tent around, either. The lady had secrets of her own.

He reached the far end of the canyon and checked to make certain nothing had changed since he and Zane had been here. No unexpected landslide had caved in a wall, allowing a way out. The thin trickle of water still ran down the rock. He saw rabbit tracks, birds, things they could eat. Shooting them would be the easy way, though; he would have to build some traps, to save his ammunition for emergencies.

Everything was just as he had left it. The plan was working. The physical attraction between them was strong; she wouldn't resist him much longer, maybe not at all. She certainly hadn't done anything to call a halt earlier. And after he was her lover—well, women were easily beguiled by sexual pleasure, the bonds of the flesh. He knew the power of sex, knew how to use it to make her trust him. He wished he could trust *her*—this would be a lot easier if he could—but he knew too much about the human soul's capability of evil, and that a pretty face didn't necessarily mean a pretty person was behind it.

When he judged enough time had passed for him to completely reconnoiter the canyon, he walked back. She was still gathering sticks, he saw, going back and forth between the bushes and the growing pile next to the tent. She looked up when he got closer, hope blazing in her expression.

He shook his head. "It's a box canyon. There's no way out," he said flatly. "The good news is, there's water at the far end."

She swallowed. Her eyes were huge with distress, almost eclipsing her face. "We can't climb out, either?"

"It's sheer rock." He put his hands on his hips, looking around. "We need to move closer to the water, for convenience. There's an overhang that will give us shade from the sun, and the ground underneath is sandier, so it'll be more comfortable."

Or as comfortable as they could get, sleeping in that small tent.

Wordlessly she nodded and began folding the tent. She did it briskly, without wasted movement, but he saw she was fighting for control. He stroked her upper arm, feeling her smooth, pliant skin, warm and slightly moist from her exertion. "We'll be okay," he reassured her. "We just have to hold out until someone sees our smoke and comes to investigate."

"We're in the middle of nowhere," she said shakily. "You said so yourself. And I only have four days until—"

"Until what?" he asked, when she stopped.

"Nothing. It doesn't matter." She stared blindly at the sky, at the clear blue expanse that was turning whiter as the hot sun climbed upward.

Four days until what? he wondered. What was going to happen? Was she supposed to do something? Was a terrorist attack planned? Would it go forward without her?

THE DOGLEG OF the canyon was about half a mile long, and the angle gave it more shade than where they had landed. They worked steadily, moving their camp, with Chance hauling the heaviest stuff. Sunny tried to keep her mind blank, to not think about Margreta, to focus totally on the task at hand.

It was noon, the white sun directly overhead. The heat was searing, the shade beneath the overhang so welcome she sighed with relief when they gained its shelter. The overhang was larger than she had expected, about twelve feet wide and deep enough, maybe eight feet, that the sunshine would never penetrate its depths. The rock sloped to a height of about four feet at the back, but the opening was high enough that Chance could stand up without bumping his head.

"I'll wait until it's cooler to get the rest," he said. "I don't know about you, but I'm starving. Let's have half of one of your nutrition bars now, and I'll try to get a rabbit for dinner."

She rallied enough to give him a look of mock dismay. "You'd eat Peter Cottontail?"

"I'd eat the Easter Bunny right now, if I could catch him."

He was trying to make her laugh. She appreciated his effort, but she couldn't quite shake off the depression that had seized her when her last hope of getting out of here quickly had evaporated.

She had lost her appetite, but she dug out one of the nutrition bars and halved it, though she hid the fact that Chance's "half" was bigger than hers. He was bigger; he needed more. They ate their spartan little meal standing up, staring out at the bleached tones of the canyon. "Drink all the water you want," he urged. "The heat dehydrates you even in the shade."

Obediently she drank a bottle of water; she needed it to get the nutrition bar down. Each bite felt as if it was getting bigger and bigger in her mouth, making it difficult to swallow. She resorted to taking only nibbles, and got it down that way.

After they ate, Chance made a small circle of rocks, piled in some sticks and leaves, both fresh and dead, and built a fire. Soon a thin column of smoke was floating out of the canyon. It took him no more than five minutes to accomplish, but when he came back under the overhang his shirt was damp with sweat.

She handed him a bottle of water, and he drank deeply, at the same time reaching out a strong arm and hooking it around her waist. He drew her close and pressed a light kiss to her forehead, nothing more, just held her comfortingly. She put her arms around him and clung, desperately needing his strength right now. She hadn't had anyone to lean on in a long time; she had always had to be the strong one. She had tried so hard to stay on top of things, to plan for every conceivable glitch, but she hadn't thought to plan for this, and now she had no idea what to do.

"I have to think of something," she said aloud.

"Shh. All we have to do is stay alive. That's the most important thing."

He was right, of course. She couldn't do anything about

Margreta now. This damn canyon had saved their lives yesterday, but it had become a prison from which she couldn't
escape. She had to play the hand with the cards that had
been dealt to her and not let depression sap her strength.
She had to hope Margreta wouldn't do anything foolish,
just go to ground somewhere. How she would ever find
her again she didn't know, but she could deal with that if
she just knew her sister was alive and safe somewhere.

"Do you have family who will worry?" he asked.

God, that went to the bone! She shook her head. She
had family, but Margreta wouldn't worry; she would simply assume the worst.

"What about you?" she asked, realizing she had fallen
halfway in love with the man and didn't know a thing
about him.

He shook his head. "C'mon, let's sit down." With nothing to use for a seat, they simply sat on the ground. "I'll
take two of the seats out of the plane this afternoon, so
we'll be more comfortable," he said. "In answer to your
question, no, I don't have anyone. My folks are dead, and
I don't have any brothers or sisters. There's an uncle somewhere, on my dad's side, and my mom had some cousins,
but we never kept in touch."

"That's sad. Family should stay together." *If they could,*
she added silently. "Where did you grow up?"

"All over. Dad wasn't exactly known for his ability to
keep a job. What about your folks?"

She was silent for a moment, then sighed. "I was adopted. They were good people. I still miss them." She
drew a design in the dirt with her finger. "When we didn't
show up in Seattle last night, would someone have notified the FAA?"

"They're probably already searching. The problem is,

first they'll search the area I should have been over when I filed my flight plan."

"We were off course?" she asked faintly. It just kept getting worse and worse.

"We went off course looking for a place to land. But if anyone is searching this area, eventually he'll see our smoke. We just have to keep the fire going during the day."

"How long will they look? Before they call off the search?"

He was silent, his golden eyes narrowed as he searched the sky. "They'll look as long as they think we might be alive."

"But if they think we've crashed—"

"Eventually they'll stop looking," he said softly. "It might be a week, a little longer, but they'll stop."

"So if no one finds us within, say, ten days—" She couldn't go on.

"We don't give up. There's always the possibility a private plane will fly over."

He didn't say that the possibility was slight, but he didn't have to. She had seen for herself the kind of terrain they'd flown over, and she knew how narrow and easily missed this canyon was.

She drew up her knees and wrapped her arms around her legs, staring wistfully at the languid curls of gray smoke. "I used to wish I could go someplace where no one could find me. I didn't realize there wouldn't be room service."

He chuckled as he leaned back on one elbow and stretched out his long legs. "Nothing gets you down for long, does it?"

"I try not to let it. Our situation isn't great, but we're alive. We have food, water and shelter. Things could be worse."

"We also have entertainment. I have a deck of cards in the plane. We can play poker."

"Do you cheat?"

"Don't need to," he drawled.

"Well, I do, so I'm giving you fair warning."

"Warning taken. You know what happens to cheaters, don't you?"

"They win?"

"Not if they get caught."

"If they're any good, they don't get caught."

He twirled a finger in her hair and lightly tugged. "Yeah, but if they get caught they're in big trouble. You can take that as my warning."

"I'll be careful," she promised. A yawn took her by surprise. "How can I be sleepy? I got plenty of sleep last night."

"It's the heat. Why don't you take a nap? I'll watch the fire."

"Why aren't you sleepy?"

He shrugged. "I'm used to it."

She really was sleepy, and there was nothing else to do. She didn't feel like setting up the tent, so she dragged her bag into position behind her and leaned back on it. Silently Chance tossed her sweater into her lap. Following his example, she rolled up the sweater and stuffed it under her head. She dozed within minutes. It wasn't a restful sleep, being one of those light naps in which she was aware of the heat, of Chance moving around, of her worry about Margreta. Her muscles felt heavy and limp, though, and completely waking up was just too much trouble.

The problem with afternoon naps was that one woke feeling both groggy and grungy. Her clothes were sticking to her, which wasn't surprising considering the heat. When she finally yawned and sat up, she saw that the sun was beginning to take on a red glow as it sank, and though the temperature was still high, the heat had lost its searing edge.

Chance was sitting cross-legged, his long, tanned fingers deftly weaving sticks and string into a cage. There was something about the way he looked there in the shadow of the overhang, his attention totally focused on the trap he was building while the light reflected off the sand outside danced along his high cheekbones, that made recognition click in her brain. "You're part Native American, aren't you?"

"American Indian," he corrected absently. "Everyone born here is a native American, or so Dad always told me." He looked up and gave her a quick grin. "Of course, 'Indian' isn't very accurate, either. Most labels aren't. But, yeah, I'm a mixed breed."

"And ex-military." She didn't know why she said that. Maybe it was his deftness in building the trap. She wasn't foolish enough to attribute that to any so-called Native American skills, not in this day and age, but there was something in the way he worked that bespoke survival training.

He gave her a surprised glance. "How did you know?"

She shook her head. "Just a guess. The way you handled the pistol, as if you were very comfortable with it. What you're doing now. And you used the word 'reconnoiter.'"

"A lot of people are familiar with weapons, especially outdoorsmen, who would also know how to build traps."

"Done in by your vocabulary," she said, and smirked. "You said 'weapons' instead of just 'guns,' the way most people—even outdoorsmen—would have."

Again she was rewarded with that flashing grin. "Okay, so I've spent some time in a uniform."

"What branch?"

"Army. Rangers."

Well, that certainly explained the survival skills. She didn't know a lot about the Rangers, or any military group, but she did know they were an elite corps.

He set the finished trap aside and began work on another one. Sunny watched him for a moment, feeling useless. She would be more hindrance than help in building traps. She sighed as she brushed the dirt from her skirt. Darn, stranded only one day and here she was, smack in the middle of the old sexual stereotypes.

She surrendered with good grace. "Is there enough water for me to wash out our clothes? I've lived in these for two days, and that's long enough."

"There's enough water, just nothing to collect it in." He unfolded his legs and stood with easy grace. "I'll show you."

He led the way out of the overhang. She clambered over rocks in his wake, feeling the heat burn through the sides of her shoes and trying not to touch the rocks with her hands. When they reached more shade, the relief was almost tangible.

"Here." He indicated a thin trickle of water running down the face of the wall. The bushes were heavier here, because of the water, and the temperature felt a good twenty degrees cooler. Part of it was illusion, because of the contrast, but the extra greenery did have a cooling effect.

Sunny sighed as she looked at the trickle. Filling their water bottles would be a snap. Washing off would be easy. But washing clothes—well, that was a different proposition. There wasn't a pool in which she could soak them, not even a puddle. The water was soaked immediately into the dry, thirsty earth. The ground was damp, but not saturated.

The only thing she could do was fill a water bottle over

and over, and rinse the dust out. "This will take forever," she groused.

An irritating masculine smirk was on his face as he peeled his T-shirt off over his head and handed it to her. "We aren't exactly pressed for time, are we?"

She almost thrust the shirt back at him and demanded he put it on, but not because of his comment. She wasn't a silly prude, she had seen naked chests more times than she could count, but she had never before seen *his* naked chest. He was smoothly, powerfully muscled, with pectorals that looked like flesh-covered steel and a hard, six-pack abdomen. A light patch of black hair stretched from one small brown nipple to the other. She wanted to touch him. Her hand actually ached for the feel of his skin, and she clenched her fingers hard on his shirt.

The smirk faded, his eyes darkening. He touched her face, curving his fingers under her chin and lifting it. His expression was hard with pure male desire. "You know what's going to happen between us, don't you?" His voice was low and rough.

"Yes." She could barely manage a whisper. Her throat had tightened, her body responding to his touch, his intent.

"Do you want it?"

So much she ached with it, she thought. She looked up into those golden-brown eyes and trembled from the enormity of the step she was taking.

"Yes," she said.

CHAPTER SEVEN

SHE HAD LIVED her entire life without ever having lived at all, Sunny thought as she mechanically rinsed out his clothes and draped them over the hot rocks to dry. She and Chance might never get out of this canyon alive, and even if they did, it could take a long time. Weeks, perhaps months, or longer. Whatever Margreta did, she would long since have done it, and there wasn't a damn thing Sunny could do about the situation. For the first time in her life, she had to think only about herself and what *she* wanted. That was simple; what she wanted was Chance.

She had to face facts. She was good at it; she had been doing it her entire life. The fact that had been glaring her in the face was that they could very well die here in this little canyon. If they didn't survive, she didn't want to die still clinging to the reasons for not getting involved that, while good and valid in civilization, didn't mean spit here. She already *was* involved with him, in a battle for their very lives. She certainly didn't want to die without having known what it was like to be loved by him, to feel him inside her and hold him close, and to tell him that she loved him. She had a whole world of love dammed up inside her, drying up because she hadn't had anyone to whom she could give it, but now she had this opportunity, and she wasn't going to waste it.

A psych analyst would say this was just propinquity: the "any port in a storm" type of attraction, or the Adam and

Eve syndrome. That might be part of it, for him. If she had to guess, Sunny would say that Chance was used to having sex whenever he wanted it. He had that look about him, a bone-deep sexual confidence that would draw women like flies. She was currently the only fly available.

But it wasn't just that. He had been attracted to her before, just as she had been to him. If they had made it to Seattle without trouble, she would have been strong enough to refuse his invitation and walk away from him. She would never have allowed herself to get to know him. Maybe they had met only twenty-four hours before, but those hours had been more intense than anything else she had ever known. She imagined it was as if they had gone into battle together; the danger they had faced, and were still facing, had forged a bond between them like soldiers in a war. She had learned things about him that it would have taken her weeks to learn in a normal situation, weeks that she would never have given herself.

Of all the things she had learned about him in those twenty-four hours, there wasn't one she didn't like. He was a man willing to step forward and take a risk, get involved, otherwise he wouldn't have stopped the cretin in the airport. He was calm in a crisis, self-sufficient and capable, and he was more considerate of her than anyone else she had ever known. On top of all that, he was so sexy he made her mouth water.

Most men, after hearing something like what she had told him, would have immediately gone for the sex. Chance hadn't. Instead, he had kissed her very sweetly and said, "I'll get the rest of the things from the plane, so I can change clothes and give you my dirty ones to wash."

"Gee, thanks," she had managed to say.

He had winked at her. "Any time."

He was a man who could put off his personal pleasure in

order to take care of business. So here she was, scrubbing his underwear. Not the most romantic thing in the world to be doing, yet it was an intimate chore that strengthened the link forming between them. He was working to feed her; she was working to keep their clothes clean.

So far, Chance was everything that was steadfast and reliable. So why did she keep sensing that edge of danger in him? Was it something his army training had given him that was just *there* no matter what he was doing? She had never met anyone else who had been a ranger, so she had no means of comparison. She was just glad of that training, if it helped keep them alive.

After his clothes were as clean as she could get them, she hesitated barely a second before stripping out of her own, down to her skin. She couldn't tolerate her grimy clothes another minute. The hot desert air washed over her bare skin, a warm, fresh caress on the backs of her knees, the small of her back, that made her nipples pinch into erect little nubs. She had never before been outside in the nude, and she felt positively decadent.

What if Chance saw her? If he was overcome with lust by the sight of her naked body, nothing would happen that hadn't been going to happen, anyway. Not that it was likely he would be overcome, she thought wryly, smiling to herself, her curves were a long way from voluptuous. Still, if a man was faced with a naked, available woman—it could happen.

She poured a bottle of water over herself, then scooped up a handful of sand and began scrubbing. Rinsing off the sand was a matter of refilling the bottle several times. When she was finished she felt considerably refreshed and her skin was baby smooth. Maybe the skin-care industry should stop grinding up shells and rock for body scrubs, she thought, and just go for the sand.

Naked and wet, she could feel a slight breeze stirring the hot air, cooling her until she was actually comfortable. She didn't have a towel, so she let herself dry naturally while she washed her own clothes, then quickly dressed in the beige jeans and green T-shirt that she always carried. They were earth colors, colors that blended in well with vegetation and would make her more difficult to see if she had to disappear into the countryside. She would have opted for actual camouflage-patterned clothing, if that wouldn't have made her more noticeable in public. Her bra was wet from its scrubbing, so she hadn't put it back on, and the soft cotton of the T-shirt clung to her breasts, clearly revealing their shape and their soft jiggle when she walked, and the small peaks of her nipples. She wondered if Chance would notice.

"Hey," he said from behind her, his voice low and soft.

Startled, she whirled to face him. It was as if she had conjured him from her thoughts. He stood motionless about ten yards away, his eyes narrowed, his expression focused. His whiskey-coloured gaze went straight to her breasts. Oh, he noticed all right.

Her nipples got even harder, as if he had touched them.

She swallowed, trying to control a ridiculous twinge of her nerves. After all, he had already touched her breasts, and she had given him permission to do more. "How long have you been there?"

"Awhile." His eyelids were heavy, his voice a little rough. "I kept waiting for you to turn around, but you never did. I enjoyed the view, anyway."

Her breath hitched. "Thank you."

"You have the sweetest little ass I've ever seen."

Liquid heat moved through her. "You sweet talker, you," she said, not even half kidding. "When do I get a peep show?"

"Any time, honey." His tone was dark with sensual

promise. "Any time." Then he smiled ruefully. "Any time except now. We need to move these clothes so I can set the trap up here. Since this is where the water is, this is where the game will come. I'll set the traps now and try to catch something for supper, then wash up after I clean whatever we catch—if we catch anything at all."

He wasn't exactly swept away with lust, but there was that reassuring steadfastness again, the ability to keep his priorities straight. In this situation, she didn't want Gonad the Barbarian; she wanted a man on whom she could depend to do the smart thing.

He began gathering the wet clothes off the rocks, and Sunny moved to help him. "Let me guess," she said. "The clothes still smell like humans."

"There's that, plus they're something different. Wild animals are skittish whenever something new invades their territory."

As they walked back to the overhang she asked, "How long does it normally take to catch something in a trap?"

He shrugged. "There's no 'normal' to it. I've caught game before within ten minutes of putting out the trap. Sometimes it takes days."

She wasn't exactly looking forward to eating Peter Cottontail, but neither did she want another nutrition bar. It would be nice if some big fat chicken had gotten lost in the desert and just happened to wander into their trap. She wouldn't mind eating a chicken. After a moment of wishful thinking she resigned herself to rabbit—if they were lucky, that is. They would have to eat whatever Chance could catch.

When they reached "home," which the overhang had become, they spread their clothes out on another assortment of hot rocks. The first items she had washed were already almost dry; the dry heat of the desert was almost as efficient as an electric clothes dryer.

When they had finished, Chance collected his two handmade traps and examined them one last time. Sunny watched him, seeing the same intensity in his eyes and body that she had noticed before. "You're enjoying this, aren't you?" she asked, only mildly surprised. This was, after all, the ultimate in primitive guy stuff.

He didn't look at her, but a tiny smile twitched the corners of his mouth. "I guess I'm not all that upset. We're alive. We have food, water and shelter. I'm alone with a woman I've wanted from the first minute I saw her." He produced a badly crushed Baby Ruth candy bar from his hip pocket and opened the wrapper, then pinched off small pieces of it and put them in the traps.

Sunny was instantly diverted. "You're using a candy bar as bait?" she demanded in outraged tones. "Give me that! You can use my nutrition bar in the traps."

He grinned and evaded her as she tried to swipe the remainder of the candy bar. "The nutrition bar wouldn't be a good bait. No self-respecting rabbit would touch it."

"How long have you been hiding that Baby Ruth?"

"I haven't been hiding it. I found it in the plane when I got the rest of the stuff. Besides, it's melted from being in the plane all day."

"Melted, schmelted," she scoffed. "That doesn't affect chocolate."

"Ah." He nodded, still grinning. "You're one of those."

"One of those what?"

"Chocoholics."

"I am not," she protested, lifting her chin at him. "I'm a sweetaholic."

"Then why didn't you pack something sweet in that

damn survival bag of yours, instead of something that tastes like dried grass?"

She scowled at him. "Because the idea is to stay alive. If I had a stash of candy, I'd eat it all the first day, then I'd be in trouble."

The golden-brown gaze flicked at her, lashing like the tip of a whip. "When are you going to tell me why you packed survival gear for an overnight plane trip to Seattle?" He kept his tone light, but she felt the change of mood. He was dead serious about this, and she wondered why. What did it matter to him why she lugged that stuff everywhere she went? She could understand why he would be curious, but not insistent.

"I'm paranoid," she said, matching his tone in lightness. "I'm always certain there will be some sort of emergency, and I'm terrified of being unprepared."

His eyes went dark and flat. "Bull. Don't try to blow me off with lies."

Sunny might be good-natured almost to a fault, but she didn't back down. "I was actually trying to be polite and avoid telling you it's none of your business."

To her surprise, he relaxed. "That's more like it."

"What? Being rude?"

"Honest," he corrected. "If there are things you don't want to tell me, fine. I don't like it, but at least it was the truth. Considering our situation, we need to be able to totally rely on each other, and that demands trust. We have to be up front with each other, even when the truth isn't all sweetness and light."

She crossed her arms and narrowed her eyes, giving him an "I'm not buying this" look. "Even when you're just being nosy? I don't think so." She sniffed. "You're trying to psych me into spilling my guts."

"Is it working?"

"I felt a momentary twinge of guilt, but then logic kicked in."

She sensed he tried to fight it, but a smile crinkled his eyes, then moved down to curl the corners of that beautifully cut mouth. He shook his head. "You're going to cause me a lot of trouble," he said companionably as he picked up the traps and started back to their little water hole, if a trickle could be called a hole.

"Why's that?" she called to his back.

"Because I'm afraid I'm going to fall in love with you," he said over his shoulder as he walked around a jutting curve of the canyon wall and disappeared from sight.

Sunny's legs felt suddenly weak; her knees actually wobbled, and she reached out to brace her hand on the wall. Had he really said that? Did he mean it? Would a man admit to something like that if he wasn't already emotionally involved?

Her heart was pounding as if she had been running. She could handle a lot of things most people never even thought of having to do, such as running for her life, but when it came to a romantic relationship she was a babe in the woods—or in the desert, to be accurate. She had never let a man get close enough to her to matter, because she had to be free to disappear without a moment's notice or regret. But this time she couldn't disappear; she couldn't go anywhere. This time she was in a lot more trouble than Chance was, because she was already in love—fully, falling-down-a-mine-shaft, terrifyingly in love.

The feeling was a stomach-tightening mixture of ecstasy and horror. The last thing she wanted to do was love him, but it was way too late to worry about that now. What had already begun had blossomed into full flower when he *didn't* make love to her after she had said he could. Something very basic and primal had recognized him then as her mate. He was everything she had ever wanted in a man, everything she had ever dreamed about in those half-formed thoughts she had never let fully surface into her consciousness, because she had always known that life wasn't for her.

But those circumstances held sway up in the world, not down here in this sunlit hole where they were the only two people alive. She felt raw inside, as if all her nerve endings and emotions had been stripped of their protective coverings, leaving her vulnerable to feelings she had always before been able to keep at bay. Those emotions kept sweeping over her in exhilarating waves, washing her into unknown territory. She wanted very much to protect herself, yet all the shields she had used over the years were suddenly useless.

Tonight they would become lovers, and one last protective wall would be irrevocably breached. Sex wasn't just sex to her; it was a commitment, a dedication of self, that would be part of her for the rest of her life.

She wasn't naive about what else making love with him could mean. She wasn't on any form of birth control, and while he might have a few condoms with him, they would quickly be used. The bell couldn't be un-rung, and once they had made love they couldn't go back to a chaste relationship. What would she do if she got pregnant and they weren't rescued? She had to hold out hope that they wouldn't be down here forever, yet a small kernel of logic told her that it was possible they wouldn't be found. What would she do if she got pregnant even if they *were* rescued? A baby would be a major complication. How would she protect it? Somehow she couldn't see herself and Chance and a baby making a normal little all-American family; she would still be running, because that was the only way to be safe.

Keeping him at a distance, remaining platonic, was the only safe, sane thing to do. Unfortunately, she didn't seem to have a good grip on her sanity any longer. She felt as if those waves had carried her too far from shore for her to make it back now. For better or worse, all she could do was ride the current where it would take her.

Nevertheless, she tried. She tried to tell herself how stupidly irresponsible it was to risk getting pregnant under any circumstances, but particularly in *this* circumstance. Yes, women all over the world conceived and gave birth in primitive conditions, but for whatever reasons, cultural, economic or lack of brain power, they didn't have a choice. She did. All she had to do was say "no" and ignore all her feminine instincts shrieking "yes, yes."

When Chance returned she was still standing in the same spot she had been when he left, her expression stricken. He was instantly alert, reaching for the pistol tucked into his waistband at the small of his back. "What's wrong?"

"What if I get pregnant?" she asked baldly, indicating their surroundings with a sweep of her hand. "That would be stupid."

He looked surprised. "Aren't you on birth control?"

"No, and even if I was, I wouldn't have an unlimited supply of pills."

Chance rubbed his jaw, trying to think of a way around this one without tipping his hand. He knew they wouldn't be here for long, only until she gave him the information he needed on her father, but he couldn't tell her that. And why in the hell wasn't she on some form of birth control? All of the female agents he knew were on long-term birth control, and Sunny's circumstances weren't that different. "I have some condoms," he finally said.

She gave him a wry smile. "How many? And what will we do when they're gone?"

The last thing he wanted to do now was make her hostile. Deciding to gamble a little, to risk not being able to make love to her in exchange for keeping her trust, he put his arms around her and cradled her against his chest. She felt good in his arms, he thought, firm with muscle and yet soft in all the right places. He hadn't been able to stop thinking about the way she looked naked: her slender, graceful back and small waist, and the tight, heart-shaped—and heart-stopping—curve of her butt. Her legs were as slim and sleekly muscled as he had expected, and the thought of them wrapping around his waist brought him to full, instant arousal. He held her so close there was no way she could miss his condition, but he didn't thrust himself at her; let her think he was a gentleman. *He* knew better, but it was essential she didn't.

He kissed the top of her head and took that gamble. "We'll do whatever you want," he said gently. "I want you—you know that. I have about three dozen condoms—"

She jerked back, glaring at him. *"Three dozen?"* she asked, horrified. "You carry around three dozen condoms?"

There it was again, that urge to laugh. She could get to him faster than any other woman he knew. "I had just stocked up," he explained, keeping his tone mild.

"They have an expiration date, you know!"

He bit the inside of his jaw—hard. "Yeah, but they don't go bad as fast as milk. They're good for a couple of years."

She gave him a suspicious look. "How long will thirty-six condoms keep you supplied?"

He sighed. "Longer than you evidently think."

"Six months?"

He did some quick math. Six months, thirty-six condoms…he would have to have sex more than once a week.

If he were in a monogamous relationship, that would be nothing, but for an unattached bachelor...

"Look," he said, letting frustration creep into both his voice and his expression, "with you, three dozen might last a week."

She looked startled, and he could see her doing some quick math now. As she arrived at the answer and her eyes widened, he thrust his hand into her hair, cupping the back of her head and holding her still while he kissed her, ruthlessly using all his skill to arouse her. Her hands fluttered against his chest as if she wanted to push him away, but her hands wouldn't obey. He stroked his tongue into her mouth, slow and deep, feeling the answering touch of her tongue and the pressure of her lips. She tasted sweet, and the fresh smell of her was pure woman. He felt her nipples peak under the thin fabric of her T-shirt, and abruptly he had to touch them, feel them stabbing into his palm. He had his hand under her shirt almost before the thought formed. Her breasts were firm and round, her skin cool silk that warmed under his touch. Her nipples were hard little nubs that puckered even tighter when he touched them. She arched in his arms, her eyes closed, a low moan humming in her throat.

He had intended only to kiss her out of her sudden attack of responsibility. Instead, the pleasure of touching her went to his head like old whiskey, and suddenly he had to see her, taste her. With one swift motion he pulled her shirt up, baring her breasts, and tilted her back over his arm so the firm mounds were offered up to him in a sensual feast. He bent his dark head and closed his mouth over one tight, reddening nipple, rasping his tongue over it before pressing it against the roof of his mouth and sucking. He heard the sound she made this time, the cry of a sharply aroused woman, a wild, keening sound that went straight to his loins. He was dimly aware of her nails biting into his shoulders, but the pain was small, and nothing in comparison with the urgency that had seized him. Blood thundered in his ears, roared through his veins. He wanted her with a savage intensity that rode him with sharp spurs, urging him to take instead of seduce.

Grimly he reached for his strangely elusive self-control. Only the experience and training of his entire adulthood, spent in the trenches of a dirty, covert, on-going war, gave him the strength to rein himself in. Reluctantly he eased his clamp on her nipple, giving the turgid little bud an apologetic lick. She quivered in his arms, whimpering, her golden hair spilling back as she hung helplessly in his grasp, and he almost lost it again.

Damn it all, he couldn't wait.

Swiftly he dipped down and snagged the blanket from the ground, then hooked his right arm under her knees and lifted her off her feet, carrying her out into the sunlight. The golden glow of the lowering sun kissed her skin with a subtle sheen, deepened the glitter of her hair. Her breasts were creamy, with the delicate blue tracery of her veins showing through the pale skin, and her small nipples were a sweet rosy color, shining wetly, standing out in hard peaks. "God, you're beautiful," he said in a low, rough voice.

He set her on her feet; she swayed, her lovely eyes dazed with need. He spread out the blanket and reached for her before that need began to cool. He wanted her scorching hot, so ready for him that she would fight him for completion.

He stripped the T-shirt off over her head, dropped it on the blanket and hooked his fingers in the waistband of her jeans. A quick pop of the snap, a jerk on the tab of the zipper, and the jeans slid down her thighs.

Her hands gripped his forearms. "Chance?" She sounded strangely uncertain, a little hesitant. If she changed her mind now—

He kissed her, slow and deep, and thumbed her nipples. She made that little humming sound again, rising on her toes to press against him. He pushed her jeans down to her ankles, wrapped both arms around her and carried her down to the blanket.

She gasped, her head arching back. "Here? Now?"

"I can't wait." That was nothing more than the hard truth. He couldn't wait until dark, until they had politely crawled into the tent together as if they were following some script. He wanted her now, in the sunlight, naked and warm and totally spontaneous. He stripped her panties down and freed her ankles from the tangle of jeans and underwear.

It seemed she didn't want to wait, either. She tugged at his shirt, pushing it up. Impatiently he gripped the hem and wrenched the garment off over his head, then spread her legs and eased his weight down on her, settling into the notch of her open thighs.

She went very still, her eyes widening as she stared up at him. He fished in his pocket for the condom he'd put there earlier, then lifted himself enough to unfasten his jeans and shove them down. He donned the condom with an abrupt, practiced motion. When he came back down to her, she braced her hands against his shoulders as if she wanted to preserve some small distance between them. But any distance was too much; he grasped her hands in one of his and pulled them over her head, pinning them to the blanket and arching her breasts against him. With his free hand he reached between them and guided his hard length to the soft, wet entrance of her body.

Sunny quivered, helpless in his grasp. She had never

before felt so vulnerable, or so alive. His passion wasn't controlled and gentle, the way she had expected; it was fierce and tumultuous, buffeting her with its force. He held her down, dwarfed her with his big muscular body, and she trembled as she waited for the hard thrust of penetration. She was ready for him, oh, so ready. She ached with need; she burned with it. She wanted to beg him to hurry, but she couldn't make her lungs work. He reached down, and she felt the brush of his knuckles between her legs, then the stiff, hot length of him pushing against her opening.

Everything in her seemed to tighten, coiling, focusing on that intimate intrusion. The soft flesh between her legs began to burn and sting as the blunt pressure stretched her. He pushed harder, and the pressure became pain. Wild frustration filled her. She wanted him *now,* inside her, easing the ache and tension, stroking her back into feverish pleasure.

He started to draw back, but she couldn't let him, couldn't bear losing what his touch had promised. She had denied herself so many things, but not this, not now. She locked her legs around his and lifted her hips, fiercely impaling herself, thrusting past the resistance of her body.

She couldn't hold back the thin cry that tore from her throat. Shock robbed her muscles of strength, and she went limp on the blanket.

Chance moved over her, his broad shoulders blotting out the sun. He was a dark, massive silhouette, his shape blurred by her tears. He murmured a soft reassurance even as he probed deeper, and deeper still, until his full length was inside her.

He released her hands to cradle her in both arms. Sunny clung to his shoulders, holding as tight as she could, because without his strength she thought she might fly apart. She hadn't realized this would hurt so much, that he would feel so thick and hot inside her, or go so deep. He was invading all of her, taking over her body and commanding its responses, even her breathing, her heartbeat, the flow of blood through her veins.

He moved gently at first, slowly, angling his body so he applied pressure where she needed it most. He did things to her with his hands, stroking her into a return of pleasure. He kissed her, leisurely exploring her with his tongue. He touched her nipples, sucked them, nibbled on the side of her neck. His tender attention gradually coaxed her into response, into an instinctive motion as her hips rose and fell in time with his thrusts. She still clung to his shoulders, but in need rather than desperation. An overwhelming heat swept over her, and she heard herself panting.

He pushed her legs farther apart and thrust deeper, harder, faster. Sensation exploded in her, abruptly convulsing her flesh. She writhed beneath him, unable to hold back the short, sharp cries that surged upward, past her constricted throat. The pounding rhythm wouldn't let the spasms abate; they kept shuddering through her until she was sobbing, fighting him, wanting release, wanting more, and finally—when his hard body stiffened and began shuddering—wanting nothing.

CHAPTER EIGHT

A VIRGIN. SUNNY MILLER had been a *virgin*. He tried to think, when he could think at all, what the possible ramifications were, but none of that seemed important right now. Of far more immediate urgency was how to comfort a woman whose first time had been on a blanket spread over the rough ground, in broad daylight, with a man who hadn't even taken off his boots.

He lay sprawled on his back beside her on the blanket. She had turned on her side away from him, curling in on herself while visible tremors shook her slender, naked body. Moving was an effort—*breathing* was an effort—as he pulled off the condom and tossed it away. He had climaxed so violently that he felt dazed. And if it affected him so strongly, with his experience, what was she thinking? Feeling? Had she anticipated the pain, or been shocked by it?

He knew she had climaxed. She had been as aroused as he; when he had started to pull back in stunned realization, she had hooked her legs around his and forced the entry herself. He had seen the shock in her eyes as he penetrated her, felt the reverberations in her flesh. And he had watched her face as he carefully aroused her, holding himself back with ruthless control until he felt the wild clenching of her loins. Then nothing had been able to hold him back, and he had exploded in his own gutwrenching release.

For a woman of twenty-nine to remain a virgin, she had to have some strongly held reason for doing so. Sunny had willingly, but not lightly, surrendered her chastity to him. He felt humbled, and honored, and he was scared as hell. He hadn't been easy with her, either in the process or the culmination. At first glance the fact that she had climaxed might make everything all right with her, but he knew better. She didn't have the experience to handle the sensual violence her body and emotions had endured. She needed holding, and reassuring, until she stopped shaking and regained her equilibrium.

He put his hand on her arm and tugged her over onto her back. She didn't actively resist, but she was stiff, uncoordinated. She was pale, her eyes unusually brilliant, as if she fought tears. He cradled her head on his arm and leaned over her, giving her the attention and the contact he knew she needed. She glanced quickly up at him, then away, and a surge of color pinkened her cheeks.

He was charmed by the blush. Gently he smoothed his hand up her bare torso, stroking her belly, trailing his fingers over her breasts. The lower curves of her breasts bore the marks of his beard stubble. He soothed them with his tongue, taking care not to add more abrasions, and made a mental note to shave when he washed.

Something needed to be said, but he didn't know what. He had talked his way into strongholds, drug dens and government offices; he had an uncanny knack for making a lightning assessment of any given person and situation, and then saying exactly the right thing to get the reaction he wanted. But from the moment he had seen Sunny, lust had gotten in the way of his usual expertise. No amount of prep work could have prepared him for the impact of her sparkling eyes and bright smile, or told him he could be so disarmed by a sense of humor. "Sunny" was a very apt nickname for her.

Just now his sunshine was very quiet, almost stricken, as if she regretted their intimacy. And he couldn't bear it. He had lost count, over the years, of the women who had tried to cling to him after the sex act was finished and he slipped away, both physically and mentally, but he couldn't bear it that this one woman wasn't trying to hold him. For some reason, whether this was simply too much too soon or for some deeper reason, she was trying to hold her distance from him. She wasn't curling in his arms, sighing with repletion; she was retreating behind an invisible wall, the one that had been there from the beginning.

Everything in him rejected the idea. A primitive, possessive rage swept over him. She was his, and he would not let her go. His muscles tightened in a renewed surge of lust, and he mounted her, sliding into the tight, swollen clasp of her sheath. She inhaled sharply, the shock of his entry jarring her out of her malaise. She wedged her hands between them and sank her nails into his chest, but she didn't try to push him away. Her legs came up almost automatically, wrapping around his hips. He caught her thighs and adjusted them higher, around his waist. "Get used to it," he said, more harshly than he'd intended. "To me. To this. To us. Because I won't let you pull away from me."

Her lips trembled, but he had her full attention now. "Even for your own sake?" she whispered, distress leaching the blue undertones from her eyes and leaving them an empty gray.

He paused for a fraction of a second, wondering if she was referring to her father. "Especially for that," he replied, and set himself to the sweet task of arousing her. This time was totally for her; he wooed her with a skill that went beyond sexual experience. His extensive training in the martial arts had taught him how to cripple with a touch, kill with a single blow, but it had also taught him all the places on the human body that were exquisitely sensitive to pleasure. The backs of her knees and thighs, the delicate arches of her feet, the lower curve of her buttocks, all received their due attention. Slowly she came alive under him, a growing inner wetness easing his way. She began to move in time with his leisurely thrusts, rising up to meet him. He stroked the cluster of nerves in the small of her back and was rewarded by the reflexive arch that took him deeper into her.

She sighed, her lips parted, her eyes closed. Her cheeks glowed; her lips were puffy and red. He saw all the signs of her arousal and whispered encouragement. Her head tossed to the side, and her hardened nipples stabbed against his chest. Gently, so gently, he bit the tender curve where her neck met her shoulder.

She cried out and began climaxing, her peak catching him by surprise. So did his own. He hadn't meant to climax, but the delicate inner clench and release of her body sent pleasure roaring through him, bursting out of control.

He tried to stop, tried to withdraw; his body simply wouldn't obey. Instead, he thrust deep and shuddered wildly as his seed spurted from him into the hot, moist depths of her. He heard his own deep, rough cry; then both time and thought stopped, and all that was left of him sank down on her in a heavy sprawl.

Shadow had crept across the canyon floor when he wrapped her in the blanket and carried her back to the sheltering overhang. The surrounding rock blocked the sun during the day, but it also absorbed its heat so that at night, when the temperature dropped, it was noticeably warmer in their snug little niche than it was outside. Sunny yawned, drowsy with satisfaction, and rested her head on his shoulder. "I can walk," she said mildly, though she made no effort to slide her feet to the ground.

"Hey, I'm doing my macho act here," he protested. "Don't ruin it."

She tilted her head back to look at him. "You aren't acting, though, are you?"

"No," he admitted, and earned a chuckle from her.

Time had gotten away from him while they drifted in the sleepy aftermath of passion. The sun was so far down in the sky that only the upper rim of the canyon was lit, the reds and golds and purples of the rock catching fire in the sunset, while the sky had taken on a deep violet hue.

"I'm going to check the traps while there's still a few minutes of light left," he said as he deposited her on the ground. "Sit tight. I won't be long."

Sunny sat tight for about two seconds after he disappeared from view, then bounced to her feet. Quickly she washed and dressed, needing the protection of her clothing. She had the uneasy feeling that nothing was the same as it had been before Chance carried her out into the sunlight. She had been prepared for the lovemaking, but not for that overwhelming assault on her senses. She had hoped for pleasure, and instead found something so much more powerful that she couldn't control it.

And most of all, Chance had revealed himself for the marauder he was.

She had seen glimpses of it before, in moments when the force of his personality broke through his control. She should have realized then; one didn't bolt a steel gate on an empty room. His control had given her the rare, luxurious feeling of safety, and she had been so beguiled that she had ignored the power that gate held constrained, or what would happen if it ever broke loose. This afternoon, she had found out.

He had said he'd been in the Army Rangers. That should have told her everything she needed to know about the kind of man he was. She could only think she'd let the stress of the situation, and her worry about Margreta, blind her to his true nature.

A shiver rippled down her spine, a totally sensual reaction as she remembered the tumultuous hour—or hours— on the blanket. She had been helpless, totally blindsided by the force of her reaction. She had known from the beginning that she responded to him as she never had before to any man, but she still hadn't been prepared for such a complete upheaval of her senses. He wasn't the only one accustomed to control; her very life had depended on her control of any given situation, and with Chance, she had found that she couldn't control either him or herself.

She had never been more terrified in her life.

The way she had felt about him before was nothing compared to now. It wasn't just the sex, which had been so much more intense and harsh than she had ever imagined. No, it was the part of his character he had revealed, the part that he had tried to keep hidden, that called to her so strongly she knew only her own death would end the love she felt for him. Chance was one of a very special breed of men, a warrior. All the little pieces of him she had sensed were now settled into place, forming the picture of a man who would always have something wild and ruthless inside him, a man willing to put himself at risk, step into the line of fire, to protect what he loved. He was the complete antithesis of her father, whose life was devoted wholly to destruction.

Sunny hadn't had a choice in a lot of the sacrifices of her life. Their mother had given her and Margreta away in an effort to save them, but hadn't been able to completely sever herself from her daughters' lives. Instead, she had taught them all her hard-learned skills, taught them how to hide, to disappear—and, if necessary, how to fight. By necessity, Pamela Vickery Hauer had become an expert in her own brand of guerrilla warfare. Whenever she thought it safe she would visit, and the kindly Millers would go out of their way to give her time with her girls.

When Sunny was sixteen, Pamela's luck had finally run out. Their father's network was extensive, and he had many more resources at his disposal than his fugitive wife could command. Logically, it had been only a matter of time before he found her. And when she was finally run to ground, Pamela had killed herself rather than take the chance he would, by either torture or drugs, be able to wring their location from her.

That was Sunny's legacy, a life living in shadows, and a courageous mother who had killed herself in order to protect her children. No one had asked her if this was the life she wanted; it was the life she had, so she had made the best of it she could.

Nor had it been her choice to live apart from Margreta; that had been her sister's decision. Margreta was older; she had her own demons to fight, her own battles to wage, and she had never been as adept at the survival skills taught by their mother as Sunny had been. So Sunny had lost her sister, and when the Millers died, first Hal and then Eleanor, she had been totally alone. The calls on her cell phone from Margreta were the only contact she had, and she knew Margreta was content to leave it at that.

She didn't think she had the strength to give up Chance, too. That was why she was terrified to the point of panic, because her very presence endangered his life. Her only solace was that because he was the man he was, he was very tough and capable, more able to look after himself.

She took a deep breath, trying not to anticipate trouble.

If and when they got out of this canyon, then she would decide what to do.

Because she was too nervous to sit still, she checked the clothes she had washed out and found they were already dry. She gathered them off the various rocks where they had spread them, and though the little chore had taken only minutes, by the time she walked back to the overhang there was barely enough light for her to see.

Chance hadn't taken the flashlight with him, she remembered. It was a moonless night; if he didn't get back within the next few minutes, he wouldn't be able to see.

The fire had been kept smoldering all day, to maximize the smoke and conserve their precious store of wood, but now she quickly added more sticks to bring up a good blaze, both for her own sake and so he would have the fire as a beacon. The flickering firelight penetrated the darkness of the overhang, sending patterns dancing against the rock wall. She searched through their belongings until she found the flashlight, to have it at hand in case she had to search for him.

Total blackness came suddenly, as if Mother Nature had dropped her petticoats over the land. Sunny stepped to the front of the overhang. "Chance!" she called, then paused to listen.

The night wasn't silent. There were rustlings, the whispers of the night things as they crept about their business. A faint breeze stirred the scrub brush, sounding like dry bones rattling together. She listened carefully, but didn't hear an answering call.

"Chance!" She tried again, louder this time. Nothing. "Damn it," she muttered, and flashlight in hand set off for the deep end of the canyon where their life-giving water trickled out of a crack in the rock.

She walked carefully, checking where she put her feet.

A second encounter with a snake was more than she could handle in one day. As she walked she periodically called his name, growing more irritated by the moment. Why didn't he answer her? Surely he could hear her by now; sound carried in the thin, dry air.

A hard arm caught her around the waist and swung her up against an equally hard body. She shrieked in alarm, the sound cut off by a warm, forceful mouth. Her head tilted back under the pressure, and she grabbed his shoulders for support. He took his time, teasing her with his tongue, kissing her until the tension left her body and she was moving fluidly against him.

When he lifted his head his breathing was a little ragged. Sunny felt obliged to complain about his treatment of her. "You scared me," she accused, though her voice sounded more sultry than sulky.

"You got what you deserved. I told you to sit tight." He kissed her again, as if he couldn't help himself.

"Is this part of the punishment?" she murmured when he came up for air.

"Yeah," he said, and she felt him smile against her temple.

"Do it some more."

He obliged, and she felt the magic fever begin burning again deep inside her. She ached all over from his previous lovemaking; she shouldn't feel even a glimmer of desire so soon, and yet she did. She wanted to feel all the power of his superbly conditioned body, take him inside her and hold him close, feel him shake as the pleasure overwhelmed him just as it did her.

Finally he tore his mouth from hers, but she could feel his heart pounding against her, feel the hard ridge in his jeans. "Have mercy," he muttered. "I won't have a chance to starve to death. I'm going to die of exhaustion."

Starving reminded her of the traps, because she was very hungry. "Did you catch a rabbit?" she asked, her tone full of hope.

"No rabbit, just a scrawny bird." He held up his free hand, and she saw that he held the plucked carcass of a bird that was quite a bit smaller than the average chicken.

"That isn't the Roadrunner, is it?"

"What's this thing you have with imaginary animals? No, it isn't a roadrunner. Try to be a little more grateful."

"Then what is it?"

"Bird," he said succinctly. "After I spit it and turn it over the flames for a while, it'll be roasted bird. That's all that matters."

Her stomach growled. "Well, okay. As long as it isn't the Roadrunner. He's my favorite cartoon character. After Bullwinkle."

He began laughing. "When did you see those old cartoons? I didn't think they were on anywhere now."

"They're all on disk," she said. "I rented them from my local video store."

He took her arm, and they began walking back to camp, chatting and laughing about their favorite cartoons. They both agreed that the slick animated productions now couldn't match the older cartoons for sheer comedy, no matter how realistic the modern ones were. Sunny played the flashlight beam across their path as they walked, watching for snakes.

"By the way, why were you calling me?" Chance asked suddenly.

"It's dark, in case you didn't notice. You didn't carry the flashlight with you."

He made a soft, incredulous sound. "You were coming to *rescue* me?"

She felt a little embarrassed. Of course, a former ranger

could find his way back to camp in the dark. "I wasn't thinking," she admitted.

"You were thinking too much," he corrected, and hugged her to his side.

They reached their little camp. The fire she had built up was still sending little tongues of flame licking around the remnants of the sticks. Chance laid the bird on a rock, swiftly fashioned a rough spit from the sticks and sharpened the end of another stick with his pocket knife. He skewered the bird with that stick, and set it in the notches of the spit, then added some small sticks to the fire. Soon the bird was dripping sizzling juice into the flames, which leaped higher in response. The delicious smell of cooking meat made her mouth water.

She shoved a flat rock closer to the fire and sat down, watching him turn the bird. She was close enough to feel the heat on her arms; as chilly as the night was already, it was difficult to remember that just a few short hours ago the heat had been scorching. She had camped out only once before, but the circumstances had been nothing like this. For one thing, she had been alone.

The amber glow of the flames lit the hard angles of his face. He had washed up while he was gone, she saw; his hair was still a little damp. He had shaved, too. She smiled to herself.

He looked up and saw her watching him, and a wealth of knowledge, of sensual awareness, flashed between them. "Are you all right?" he asked softly.

"I'm fine." She had no idea how her face glowed as she wrapped her arms around her legs and rested her chin on her drawn-up knees.

"Are you bleeding?"

"Not now. And it was only a little, at first," she added hastily when his eyes narrowed in concern.

He returned his gaze to the bird, watching as he carefully turned it. "I wish I had known."

She wished he didn't know now. The reasons for her recently lost virginity weren't something she wanted to dissect. "Why?" she asked, injecting a light note into her tone. "Would you have been noble and stopped?"

"Hell, no," he said. "I'd have gone about it a little differently, is all."

Now, that was interesting. "What would have been different?"

"How rough I was. How long I took."

"You took long enough," she assured him, smiling. "Both times."

"I could have made it better for you."

"How about for you?"

His dark gaze flashed upward, and he gave a rueful smile. "Sweetheart, if it had been any better for me, my heart would have given out."

"Ditto."

He turned the bird again. "I didn't wear a condom the second time."

"I know." The evidence had been impossible to miss.

Their gazes met and locked again, and again they were linked by that silent communication. He might have made her pregnant. He knew it, and she knew it.

"How's the timing?"

She rocked her hand back and forth. "Borderline." The odds were in their favor, she figured, but it wasn't a risk she wanted to take again.

"If we weren't stuck here—" he began, then shrugged.

"What?"

"I wouldn't mind."

Desire surged through her, and she almost jumped his bones right then. She got a tight grip on herself, literally, and fought to stay seated. Hormones were sneaky devils, she thought, ready to undermine her common sense just because he mentioned wanting to make her pregnant.

"Neither would I," she admitted, and watched to see if he had the same reaction. Color flared high on his carved cheekbones, and a muscle in his jaw flexed. His hand tightened on the spit until his knuckles were white. Yep, it went both ways, she thought, fascinated by his battle to remain where he was.

When he judged the bird was done, he took the skewer off the spit and kicked another rock over to rest beside hers, then sat down on it. With his pocket knife he cut a strip of meat and held it out to her. "Careful, don't burn yourself," he warned as she reached eagerly for the meat.

She juggled the strip back and forth in her hands, blowing on it to cool it. When she could hold it, she took her first tentative bite. Her taste buds exploded with the taste of wood and smoke and roasted fowl. "Oh, that's good," she moaned, chewing slowly to get every ounce of flavor.

Chance cut off a strip for himself and took his first bite, looking as satisfied as she with their meal. They chewed in silence for a while. He was careful to divide the meat equally, until she was forced to stop eating way before she was satisfied. He was so much bigger than she was that if they each ate the same amount, he would be short-changed.

He knew what she was doing, of course. "You're taking care of me again," he observed. "You're hell on my image, you know that? I'm supposed to be taking care of you."

"You're a lot bigger than I am. You need larger portions."

"Let me worry about the food, sweetheart. We won't starve. There's more game to catch, and tomorrow I'll look for some edible plants to round out our diet."

"Bird and bush," she said lightly. "What all the trendy people are eating these days."

Her quip made him grin. He persuaded her to eat a little more of the meat, then they finished off one of the remaining nutrition bars. Their hunger appeased, they began getting ready to turn in for the night.

He banked the fire while she got the tent ready. They brushed their teeth and made one last nature call, just like old married folks, she thought in amusement. Their "home" wasn't much, really nothing more than a niche in the rock, but their preparations for the night struck her as very domestic—until he said, "Do you want to wear my shirt tonight? It would be more like a nightgown on you than the shirt you're wearing."

There was nothing the least bit tamed in the way he was looking at her. Her heartbeat picked up in speed, and the now familiar heat began spreading through her. That was all he had to do, she thought; one look and she was aroused. He had taught her body well during the short time she had been sprawled beneath him on the blanket. Now that she knew exactly how it felt to take his hard length inside her, she craved the sensation. She wanted that convulsive peak of pleasure, even though it had frightened her with its intensity. She hadn't realized she would feel as if she were flying apart, as if her soul was being wrenched from her body. In a blinding, paralyzing moment of clarity, she knew that no other man in the world would be able to do that for her, to her. He was the One for her, capital *O*, big letter, underlined and italicized. The *One*. She would never again be whole without him.

She must have looked stricken, because suddenly he was by her side, supporting her with an arm around her waist as he gently but inexorably guided her to the tent.

He would be considerate, she realized, but he didn't intend to be refused.

She cleared her throat, searching for her equilibrium. "You'll need your shirt to keep warm—"

"You're joking, right?" He smiled down at her, the corners of his eyes crinkling. "Or did you think we were through for the night?"

She couldn't help smiling back. "That never crossed my mind. I just thought you'd need it *afterward*."

"I don't think so," he said, his hands busy unsnapping her jeans.

They were both naked and inside the tent in record time. He switched off the flashlight to save the batteries, and the total darkness closed around them, just as it had the night before. Making love when one was going totally by feel somehow heightened the other senses, she found. She was aware of the calluses on his hands as he stroked her, of the heady male scent of his skin, of the powerful muscles that bunched under her own exploring hands. His taste filled her; his kisses were a feast. She reveled in the smooth firmness of his lips, the sharp edges of his teeth; she rubbed his nipples and felt them contract under her fingers. She loved the harsh groan he gave when she cupped the soft, heavy sacs between his legs, and the way they tightened even as she held them.

She was shocked when she closed her hand around his pulsing erection. How on earth had she ever taken him inside her? The long, thick column ended in a smooth, bulbous flare, the tip of which was wet with fluid. Entranced, she curled down until she could take the tip in her mouth and lick the fluid away.

He let out an explosive curse and tumbled her on her back, reversing their positions. The confines of the small tent restricted their movement, but he managed the shift with his usual powerful grace.

She laughed, full of wonder at the magic between them, and draped her arms around his neck as he settled on top of her. "Didn't you like it?"

"I almost came," he growled. "What do you think?"

"I think I'll have my way with you yet. I may have to overpower you and tie you up, but I think I can handle the job."

"I'm positive of it. Let me know when you're going to overpower me, so I can have my clothes off."

That afternoon, caught in the whirlpool of his lovemaking, she wouldn't have believed she would be so at ease with him now, that they could indulge in this sensual teasing. She wouldn't have believed how naturally her thighs parted to accommodate his hips, or how comfortable it was, as if nature had designed them to fit together just so. Actually nature had; she just hadn't realized it until now.

He gave her a taste of her own medicine, kissing his way down her body until his hair brushed the insides of her thighs and she discovered a torture so sweet she shattered. When she could breathe again, when the colored pinpoints of light stopped flashing against her closed eyelids, he kissed her belly and laid his head on the pillowing softness. "My God, you're easy," he whispered.

She managed a strangled sound that was almost a laugh. "I guess I am. For you, anyway."

"Just for me." The dark tones of masculine possessiveness and triumph underlaid the words.

"Just for you," she whispered in agreement.

He put on a condom and slid into place between her thighs. She fought back a cry; she was sore and swollen, and he was big. He moved gently back and forth until she accepted him more easily and the discomfort faded, but gradually his thrusts quickened, became harder. Even then she sensed he was holding himself back to keep from hurting her. When he climaxed, he pulled back so only half his length was inside her, and held himself there while shudders racked his strong body.

Afterward, he tugged his T-shirt on over her head, immediately enveloping her in his scent. The roomy garment came halfway to her knees—or it would have if he hadn't bunched it around her waist. He cradled her in his arms, one big hand on her bare bottom to keep her firmly against him. He used her rolled-up cardigan for a pillow, and she used him. Oh, this was wonderful.

·"Is Sunny your real name, or is it a nickname?" he asked sleepily, his lips brushing her hair.

Even as relaxed as she was, as sated, a twinge of caution made her hesitate. She never told anyone her real name. It took her a moment to remember that none of that made any difference here now. "It's a nickname," she murmured. "My real name is Sonia, but I've never used it. Sonia Ophelia Gabrielle."

"Good God." He kissed her. "Sunny suits you. So you're saddled with four names, huh?"

"Yep. I never use the middle ones, though. What about you? What's your middle name?"

"I don't have one. It's just Chance."

"Really? You aren't lying to me because it's something awful, like Eustace?"

"Cross my heart."

She settled herself more comfortably against him. "I suppose it balances out. I have four names, you have two—together, we average three."

"How about that."

She could hear a smile in his voice now. She rewarded him with a small, sneaky pinch that made him jump. His retaliation ended, a long time later, in the use of another condom.

Sunny went to sleep to the knowledge that she was happier now, with Chance, than she had ever before been in her life.

CHAPTER NINE

THE NEXT MORNING the traps were empty. Sunny struggled with her disappointment. After such an idyllic, pleasure-filled night, the day should have been just as wonderful. A nice hot, filling breakfast would have been perfect.

"Could you shoot something?" she asked as she chewed half of one of the tasteless nutrition bars. "We have eight of these bars left." If they each ate a bar a day, that meant they would be out of food in four days.

In three days, Margreta would call.

Sunny pushed that thought away. Whether or not they got out of here in time for her to answer Margreta's call was something she couldn't control. Food was a more immediate problem.

Chance narrowed his eyes as he scanned the rim of the canyon, as if looking for a way out. "I have fifteen rounds in the pistol, and no extra cartridges. I'd rather save them for emergencies, since there's no telling how long we'll be here. Besides, a 9mm bullet would tear a rabbit to pieces and wouldn't leave enough left of a bird for us to eat. Assuming I could hit a bird with a pistol shot, that is."

She wasn't worried about his marksmanship. He was probably much better with a rifle, but with his military background, he would be more than competent with the pistol. She looked down at her hands. "Would a .38 be better?"

"It isn't as powerful, so for small game, yeah, it would

be better. Not great, but better—but I have a 9mm, so it's a moot point."

"I have one," she said softly.

His head whipped around. Something dangerous flashed in his eyes. "What did you say?"

She nodded toward her bag. "I have a .38."

He looked in the direction of her gaze, then back at her. His expression was like flint. "Would you like to tell me," he said very deliberately, "just how you happen to have a pistol of any kind with you? You were on a commercial flight. How did you get past the scanners?"

She didn't like giving away all her secrets, not even to Chance. A lifetime on the run had ingrained caution into her very bones, and she had already given him more of herself than she ever had anyone else. Still, they were in this together. "I have some special containers."

"Where?" he snapped. "I saw you unpack everything in your bag and there weren't any—ah, hell. The hair spray can, right?"

Unease skittered along her spine. Why was he angry? Even if he was a stickler for rules and regulations, which she doubted, he should be glad they had an extra weapon, no matter how they came by it. She straightened her shoulders. "And the blow-dryer."

He stood over her like an avenging angel, his jaw set. "How long have you been smuggling weapons on board airplanes?"

"Every time I've flown," she said coolly, standing up. She was damned if she would let him tower over her as if she was a recalcitrant child. He still towered over, just not as much. "I was sixteen the first time."

She walked over to the bag and removed the pertinent items. Chance leaned down and snagged the can of spray from her hands. He took the cap off and examined the nozzle, then pointed it away from him and depressed it. A powder-fine mist of spray shot out.

"It's really hair spray," she said. "Just not much of it." She took the can and deftly unscrewed the bottom. A short barrel slid out of the can into her hands. Putting it aside, she lifted the hair-dryer and took it apart with the same deft twist, yielding the remaining parts of the pistol. She assembled it with the ease of someone who had done the task so often she could do it in her sleep, then fed the cartridges into the magazine, snapped it into place, reversed the pistol and presented it to him butt-first.

He took it, his big hand almost swallowing the small weapon. "What in *hell* are you doing with a weapon?" he bit out.

"The same thing you are, I imagine." She walked away from him and missed the look of shock that crossed his face. With her back to him she said, "I carry it for self-protection. Why do you carry yours?"

"I charter my plane to a lot of different people, most of whom I don't know. I fly into some isolated areas sometimes. And my weapon is licensed." He hurled the words at her like rocks. "Is yours?"

"No," she said, unwilling to lie. "But I'm a single woman who travels alone, carrying packages valuable enough that a courier service is hired to deliver them. The people I deliver the packages to are strangers. Think about it. I'd have to be a fool not to carry some means of protection." That was the truth, as far as it went.

"If your reason for carrying is legitimate, then why don't you have a license?"

She felt as if she were being interrogated, and she didn't like it. The tender, teasing lover of the night was gone, and in his place was someone who sounded like a prosecutor.

She had never applied for a license to carry a concealed

weapon because she didn't want any background checks in the national data system, didn't want to bring herself to the notice of anyone in officialdom.

"I have my reasons," she retorted, keeping her tone very deliberate.

"And you aren't going to tell me what they are, right?" He threw her a look that was almost sulfuric in its fury and stalked off in the direction of the traps. His stalking, like everything else he did, was utterly graceful—and completely silent.

"Good riddance, Mr. Sunshine," she hurled at his back. It was a childish jab, but she felt better afterward. Sometimes a little childishness was just what the doctor ordered.

With nothing better to do, she set off in the opposite direction, toward the plane, to gather more sticks and twigs for the all-important fire. If he tried to keep her pistol when they got out of here—and they *would* get out, she had to keep hoping—then it would be war.

CHANCE EXAMINED THE compact pistol in his hand. It was unlike any he had ever seen before, for the simple reason that it hadn't come from any manufacturer. A gunsmith, a skilled one, had made this weapon. It bore no serial number, no name, no indication of where or when it was made. It was completely untraceable.

He couldn't think of any good reason for Sunny to have it, but he could think of several bad ones.

After yesterday, he had been more than halfway convinced she was innocent, that she was in no way involved with her father. Stupid of him, but he had equated chastity with honor. Just because a woman didn't sleep around didn't mean she was a fine, upstanding citizen. All it meant was that, for whatever reason, she hadn't had sex.

He knew better. He was far better acquainted with the

blackness of the human soul than with its goodness, because he had chosen to live in the sewers. Hell, he came from the sewers; he should be right at home there, and most of the time he was. The blackness of his own soul was always there, hidden just a few layers deep, and he was always aware of it. He used to make his way in the dangerous world he had chosen, shaped it into a weapon to be used in defense of his country and, ultimately, his family. And being on such intimate terms with hell, with the twisted evil humans could visit on one another, he should know that golden hair and bright, sparkling eyes didn't necessarily belong on an angel. Shakespeare had hit the nail on the head when he warned the world against smiling villains.

It was just—*damn* it, Sunny got to him. She had slipped right past defenses he would have sworn were impregnable, and she had done it so easily they might as well not have been there at all. He wanted her, and so he had almost convinced himself that she was innocent.

Almost. There was just too much about her that didn't add up, and now there was this untraceable pistol that she smuggled on board airplanes, concealed in some very effective but simple containers. Airport scanners would show metal, but if a security guard was suspicious enough to check, he or she would find only the normal female styling aids. The hair spray can actually sprayed, and he didn't doubt the blow-dryer would work, too.

If Sunny could get a pistol on board a plane, then others could, too. He went cold at the thought of how many weapons must be flying around at any given time. Airport security wasn't his line of work, but damn if he wasn't going to make it a point to kick some asses over this.

He shoved his anger aside so he could concentrate on this assignment. He hoped he hadn't blown it by losing his temper with her, but his disillusionment had been too sharp for him to contain. The pleasure of the night they had just spent together should more than outweigh their first argument. Her inexperience with men worked against her; she would be easy to manipulate, where a seasoned veteran of the mattress wars would be more wary and blasé about their lovemaking. He still held all the trump cards, and soon he would be playing them.

He reached a particular point in the canyon and positioned himself so he was in the deepest morning shadows. Sunny couldn't catch him unawares here, and he had a clear line of sight to a certain rock on the rim of the canyon. He took a laser light from his pocket, a pencil-thin tube about two inches long that, when clicked, emitted an extraordinarily bright finger of light. He aimed it at the rock on the rim and began clicking, sending dashes of light in the code he and Zane had agreed on at the beginning of the plan. Every day he signalled Zane, both to let him know that everything was all right and that they shouldn't be rescued yet.

There was an answering flash, message received. No matter how closely he watched that rock, he never saw any movement, though he knew Zane would have immediately pulled back. He himself was damn good at moving around undetected, but Zane was extraordinary even for a SEAL. There was no one else on this earth Chance would rather have beside him in a fight than Zane.

That mission accomplished, Chance settled down in some cover where he could watch the trickle of water. Since the traps hadn't been productive overnight, he really did need to shoot something for supper. He was willing to starve to achieve his ends—but only if he had to. If a bunny rabbit showed its face, it was history.

AS SUNNY WALKED the canyon floor, picking up what sticks she could find, she studied the rock walls, looking for a fissure that might have escaped notice, an animal trail, anything that might point the way to freedom. If they only had some rock-climbing gear, she thought wistfully. A rope, cleats, anything. She had tried to anticipate any possible need when she packed her bag, but somehow being trapped in a box canyon hadn't occurred to her.

For the most part, the walls were perpendicular. Even when they slanted a little, the angle wasn't much off ninety degrees. Erosion from wind and rain had, over millions of years, cut grooves in the rock that looked like ripples in water. The only sign the canyon wasn't impregnable was the occasional little heap of rubble where smaller rocks had crumbled and fallen.

She had passed several of those small heaps before the light went on.

A fragile stirring of hope made her stomach tighten as she investigated one scattered pile of rock. It looked as if a larger boulder had fallen from the rim and shattered on impact. She picked up a fist-sized rock and rubbed her thumb over the surface, finding it gritty, the texture of sandpaper. Sandstone, she thought. It was a lovely pink color. It was also soft.

Just to be certain, she banged the rock down on a larger rock, and it broke into several pieces.

This site was no good; it was too steep. She walked along the wall, looking up at the rim and trying to find a place where the wall slanted back just a little. That was all she asked; just a little slant, enough that the angle wasn't so extreme.

There. One of the ripples curved backward, and when she picked her way through rocks and bushes to investigate she saw the opportunity for which she had been looking. She ran her hand over the rock, exulting in the sandpaper texture of it under her palm. Maybe, just maybe...

She ran back to the camp and grabbed the curling iron out of the bag. Chance hadn't asked, but the pistol wasn't the only weapon she carried. Quickly she unscrewed the metal barrel from the handle and removed a knife from the interior. It was a slender blade, made for slicing rather than hacking, but sharp and almost indestructible.

Her idea registered somewhere between being a long shot and just plain crazy, but it was the only idea she'd had that was even remotely possible. At least she would be doing *something*, rather than just waiting around for a rescue that might never happen.

She needed gloves to protect her hands, but she didn't have any. Hastily she opened the first-aid box and took out the roll of gauze. She wrapped the gauze around her palms and wove it in and around her fingers, then taped the loose ends. The result was crude but workable, she thought. She had seen the gloves rock climbers wore, with their fingers and thumbs left free; this makeshift approximation would have to do. She might wear blisters on her hands, anyway, but that was a small price to pay if they could get out of here.

Knife in hand, she went back to her chosen point of attack and tried to figure out the best way to do this. She needed another rock, she realized, one that wasn't soft. Anything that crumbled would be useless. She scouted around and finally found a pitted, dark gray rock that was about the size of a grapefruit, heavy enough to do the job.

Digging the point of the knife into the soft sandstone of the wall, she gripped the rock with her right hand and pounded it against the knife, driving the blade deeper. She jerked the blade out, moved it a little to the right and pounded it in again. The next time she drove the knife in at a right angle to the original gouge, and hammered it downward. A chunk of sandstone broke loose, leaving a nice little gouge in the rock.

"This just might work," Sunny said aloud, and set herself to the task. She didn't let herself think how long it would take to carve handholds out of the rock all the way to the top, or if it was even possible. She was going to try; she owed it to Margreta, and to herself, to do everything she could to get out of this canyon.

Almost two hours later, the sharp crack of a pistol shot reverberated through the canyon, startling her so much that she nearly fell. She clung to the rock, her cheek pressed against the rough surface. Her heart pounded from the close call. She wasn't that high, only about ten feet, but the canyon floor was jagged with rock, and any fall was certain to cause injuries.

She wiped the sweat from her face. The temperature was rising by the minute, and the rock was getting hotter and hotter. Standing with her toes wedged into the gouges she had hammered out of the rock, she had to lean inward against the rock to brace herself, because she had to have both hands free to wield the knife and the rock. She couldn't put nearly as much effort into it now, or the impact would jar her from her perch.

Panting, she reached over her head and blindly swung the rock. Because she had to press herself to the rock to keep her balance, she couldn't see to aim. Sometimes she hit the target and the knife bit into the rock; sometimes she hit her own hand. There had to be a better way to do this, but she couldn't think of one. She was an expert at working with what she had; she could do it this time, too. All she had to do was be careful, and patient.

"I can do this," she whispered.

CHANCE CARRIED THE skinned and cleaned rabbit back to the camp. He had also found a prickly pear cactus and cut off two of the stems, sticking himself several times as he removed the spines. The prickle pear was both edible and nutritious; it was usually fried, but he figured roasting would do just as well.

His temper had cooled. All right, so she had taken him in. He hadn't blown the plan; everything was still on track. All he had to do was remember not to be fooled by that oh-so-charming face she presented to the world and the plan would work just as he had expected. Maybe he couldn't make her love him, but he could make her think she did, and that was all he needed. A little trust, a little information, and he was in business.

He stepped beneath the overhang, grateful for the relief the shade afforded, and took off his sunglasses. Sunny wasn't here. He turned around and surveyed what he could see of the canyon but couldn't spot her. Her green T-shirt and beige jeans didn't exactly stand out in the terrain, he thought, and abruptly realized what effective camouflage her clothing was. Had she chosen it for that exact purpose? She must have; everything she carried in that bag had been geared toward survival, so why should her clothing be any different?

"Sunny!" he called. His voice echoed, then died. He listened, but there was no answer.

Damn it, where was she?

The fire had died down, which meant she hadn't tended it in quite a while. He bent down and added more sticks, then skewered the rabbit and set it on the spit, more to keep it away from insects than anything else. The fire was too low to cook it, but the smoke wafting over the meat would give it a good flavor. He wrapped the prickly pear stems in his handkerchief and walked back under the overhang to keep them out of the sun until he was ready to cook them.

The first thing he saw was the open first aid kit.

Alarm punched him in the gut. The paper wrapping

had been torn off the roll of gauze; the tape was lying in the lid of the box, and it had also been used, because the end had been left free rather than stuck back to the roll.

Another detail caught his eyes. The curling iron had been taken apart; the two halves of it lay in the sand.

He swore viciously. Damn it, he should have remembered the curling iron and not assumed the pistol was the only weapon she had. She couldn't have hidden another pistol in the curling iron, but a knife would fit.

He didn't see any blood, but she must have injured herself somehow. Where in the hell was she?

"Sunny!" he roared as he stepped back out into the sun. Only silence answered him.

He studied the ground. Her footprints were everywhere, of course, but he saw where she had walked to her bag, presumably to get the first aid kit; then the prints led back out into the canyon. She was headed toward the plane.

He wasn't aware of reaching for his pistol. He was so accustomed to it that he didn't notice the weight of it in his hand as he followed her tracks, everything in him focusing on finding her.

If it hadn't been for the tracks, he would have missed her. She was almost at the far end of the canyon, past where the plane sat baking in the sun. The rock walls were scored with hundreds of cuts, and she was tucked inside one of them, clinging to the rock about a dozen feet off the ground.

Astonishment, anxiety, relief and anger all balled together in his gut. In speechless fury he watched her reach over her head and stab a wicked-looking blade into the soft rock, then, still keeping her face pressed against the hot stone, use another rock to try to pound the knife deeper. She hit her hand instead of the knife handle, and the curse she muttered made his eyebrows rise.

Strips of gauze were wound around her hands. He didn't know if she had wrapped her hands because she had hurt them, or if the gauze was an effort to keep them from being hurt. All he knew was that if she fell she would likely maim herself on the rocks, and that he really, *really* wanted to spank her.

He ruthlessly restrained the urge to yell at her. The last thing he wanted to do was startle her off her precarious perch. Instead, he stuck the pistol in his waistband at the small of his back and worked his way over until he was standing beneath her, so he could catch her if she fell.

He forced himself to sound calm. "Sunny, I'm right beneath you. Can you get down?"

She stopped with her right hand drawn back to deliver another blow with the rock. She didn't look down at him. "Probably," she said. "It has to be easier than getting up here."

He was fairly certain what she was doing, but the sheer magnitude of the task, the physical impossibility of it, left him stunned. Just for confirmation he asked, "What are you doing?"

"I'm cutting handholds in the rock, so we can climb out of here." She sounded grim, as if she also realized the odds against success.

His hands clenched into fists as he fought for control. He looked up at the towering wall, at the expanse stretching above her. The dozen feet she had climbed was only about one tenth of the distance needed—and it was the easiest tenth.

He put his hand on the rock and almost jerked back at the heat radiating from it. A new concern gnawed at him. He didn't yell at her that this was the stupidest idea he'd ever heard of, the way he wanted. Instead, he said,

"Sweetheart, the rock's too hot. Come down before you're burned."

She laughed, but without her usual humor. "It's too late."

To hell with cajoling. "Throw the knife down and get off that damn rock," he barked in sharp command.

To his surprise, she dropped the knife, then the rock she held in her right hand, tossing both to the side so they wouldn't land near him. Every muscle in her body was taut with strain as she reached for the handholds she had cut and began to work her way down, feeling with her toes for the gouges. He stood directly beneath her, reaching up for her in case she fell. The muscles in her slender arms flexed, and he realized anew just how strong she was. One didn't get that kind of strength with a once-in-a-while jog or the occasional workout in a gym. It took dedication and time; he knew, because he kept himself in top physical condition. Her normal routine would be at least an hour of work, maybe two, every day. For all he knew, while he had been checking the traps she had been doing pushups.

For all the gut-deep burn of his anger, it was overridden by his concern as he watched her inch her way down the face of the rock. She was careful and took her time, despite the fact that he knew the rock was scorching her fingers. He didn't speak again, not wanting to distract her; he simply waited, not very patiently, for her to get within his reach.

When she did, he caught her feet and guided them to the next gouges. "Thanks," she panted, and worked her way down another foot.

That was enough. He caught her around the knees and scooped her off the rock. She shrieked, fighting for her balance, but now that he had her in his grip he wasn't about to let her go. Before she could catch her breath, he turned her and tossed her face down over his shoulder.

"Hey!" The indignant protest was muffled against his back.

"Just shut up," he said between his teeth as he dipped down to pick up her knife, then set off for the camp. "You scared the hell out of me."

"Good. You had too much hell in you, anyway." She clutched him around the waist to steady herself. He just hoped she didn't grab the pistol out of his waistband and shoot him, since it was so close to hand.

"Damn it, don't you dare joke about it!" Her upturned bottom was very close to his hand. Temptation gnawed at him. Now that he had her down, he was shaking, and he wanted some retribution for having been put through that kind of anxiety. He put his hand on her butt and indulged in a few moments of fantasy, which involved her jeans around her knees and her bent over his lap.

He realized he was stroking his palm over the round curves of her buttocks and regretfully gave up on his fantasy. Some things weren't going to happen. After he tended her hands and got through raising hell with her for taking such a risk, he fully intended to burn off his fright and anger with an hour or two on the blanket with her.

How could he still want her so much? This wasn't part of the job; he could live with it, if it had been. This was obsession, deep and burning and gut-twisting. He had tried to put a light face on it, for her benefit, but if she had been more experienced, she would have known a man didn't make love to a woman five times during the night just because she was available. At this rate, those three dozen condoms wouldn't last even a week. He had already used six, and it might take two or three more to get him settled down after the scare she had given him.

The hard fact of it was, a man didn't make love to a woman that often unless he was putting his brand on her.

This wouldn't work. Couldn't work. He had to get himself under control, stay focused on the job.

He heard her sniffing as they neared the camp. "Are you *crying?*" he demanded incredulously.

She sniffed again. "Don't be silly. What's that smell?" She inhaled deeply. "It smells like…food."

Despite himself, a smile quirked the corners of his mouth. "I shot a rabbit."

There was a small disruption on his shoulder as she twisted around so she could see the fire. Her squeal of delight almost punctured his eardrums, and his smile grew. He couldn't stop himself from enjoying her; he had never before met anyone who took such joy in life, who was so vibrantly alive herself. How she could be a part of a network devoted to taking lives was beyond his understanding.

He dumped her on the ground under the overhang and squatted beside her, taking both her hands in his and turning them up for his inspection. He barely controlled a wince. Her fingers were not only scorched from the hot rock, they were scraped raw and bleeding.

Fury erupted in him again, a flash fire of temper at seeing the damage she had done to herself. He surged to his feet. "Of all the stupid, lame-brained…! What in hell were you thinking? You weren't thinking at all, from the looks of it! Damn it, Sunny, you risked your life pulling this stupid stunt—"

"It wasn't stupid," she shouted, shooting to her feet to face him, her brilliant eyes narrowed. She clenched her bleeding hands into fists. "I know the risks. I also know it's my only hope of getting out of this damn canyon before it's too late!"

"Too late for what?" he yelled back. "Do you have a date this weekend or something?" The words were heavy with sarcasm.

"Yeah! It just so happens I do!" Breathing hard, she glared at him. "My sister is supposed to call."

CHAPTER TEN

A SISTER? CHANCE STARED at her. His investigation hadn't turned up any information about a sister. The Millers hadn't had any children of their own, and he had found adoption papers only on Sunny. His mind raced. "You said you didn't have any family."

She gave him a stony look. "Well, I have a sister."

Yeah, right. "You'd risk your life for a phone call?" Some terrorist act was being planned after all, he thought with a cold feeling in the pit of his stomach. That was why she'd been lugging the tent around. He didn't know how the tent fit into the scheme, but evidently she had been planning to drop out of sight.

"I would for this one." She wheeled away, every line of her body tense. "I have to try. Margreta calls my cell phone every week at the same time. It's how we know the other is still alive." She turned back to him and shouted, "If I don't answer that call, she'll think I'm dead!"

Whoa. Once again, the pieces of the puzzle that was Sunny had been scattered. Margreta? Was that a code name? He searched his memory, which was extensive, but couldn't find anything or anyone named Margreta. Sunny was so damned convincing....

"Why would she think you're dead?" he demanded. "You might just be in a place that doesn't have a signal— like here. What is she, some kind of nutcase?"

"I make certain I'm always somewhere that has a signal.

And, no, she isn't a *nutcase!*" She threw the words back at him like bullets, her mouth twisted with fury at him, at the situation, at her own helplessness. "Her problem is the same as mine—we're our father's daughters!"

His pulse leaped. There it was, out in the open, just like that. He hadn't needed seduction; anger had done the job. "Your father?" he asked carefully.

Tears glittered in her eyes, dripped down her cheeks. She dashed them away with a furious gesture. "Our father," she said bitterly. "We've been running from him all our lives."

The pieces of the puzzle jumped about a little more, as if a fist had slammed down and jarred them. *Easy,* he cautioned himself. *Don't seem too interested. Find out exactly what she means; she could be referring to his influence.* "What do you mean, running?"

"I mean running. Hiding." She wiped away more tears. "Father dear is a terrorist. He'll kill us if he ever finds us."

CHANCE GENTLY CLEANED her hands with the alcohol wipes from the first-aid kit, soothed the red places with burn ointment and the raw spots with antibiotic cream. The gauze she'd wrapped around her hands had protected her palms, but her fingers were a mess. Sunny felt a little bewildered. One minute they had been yelling at each other, the next she had been locked against him, his arms like a vise around her. His heart had been pounding like a runaway horse.

Since then he had been as tender as a mother with a child, rocking her in comfort, cuddling her, drying her tears. The emotional firestorm that had burned through her had left her feeling numb and disoriented; she let him do whatever he wanted without offering a protest, not that she had any reason to protest. It felt good to lean on him.

Satisfied with the care he had given her hands, he left her sitting on the rock while he added some fuel to the fire and turned the rabbit on the spit. Coming back under the overhang, he spread the blanket against the wall, scooped her into his arms and settled on the blanket with her cradled against him. He propped his back against the wall, arranged her so she was draped half across his lap and lifted her face for a light kiss.

She managed a shaky smile. "What was that? A kiss to make it better?"

He rubbed his thumb over her bottom lip, his expression strangely intent as if studying her. "Something like that."

"I'm sorry for crying all over you. I usually handle things better than this."

"Tell me what's going on," he said quietly. "What's this about your father?"

She leaned her head on his shoulder, grateful for his strength. "Hard to believe, isn't it? But he's the leader of a terrorist group that has done some awful things. His name is Crispin Hauer."

"I've never heard of him," Chance lied.

"He operates mostly in Europe, but his network extends to the States. He even has someone planted in the FBI." She was unable to keep the raw bitterness out of her voice. "Why do you think I don't have a license for that pistol? I don't know who the plant is, how high he ranks, but I do know he's in a position to learn if the FBI gets any information Hauer wants. I didn't want to be in any database, in case he found out who adopted me and what name I'm using."

"So he doesn't know who you are?"

She shook her head. She had spent a lifetime keeping all her fear and worry bottled up inside her, and now she couldn't seem to stop it from spewing out. "My mother took Margreta and left him before I was born. I've never met him. She was five months pregnant with me when she ran."

"What did she do?"

"She managed to lose herself. America's a big place. She stayed on the move, changing her name, paying with cash she had taken from his safe. When I was born, she intended to have me by herself, in the motel room she'd taken for the night. But I wouldn't come, the labor just kept on and on, and she knew something was wrong. Margreta was hungry and scared, crying. So she called 911."

He wound a strand of golden hair around his finger. "And was there something wrong?"

"I was breech. She had a C-section. While she was groggy from the drugs, they asked her the father's name and she didn't think to make up a name, just blurted out *his*. So that's how I got into the system, and how he knows about me."

"How do you know he knows?"

"I was almost caught, once." She shivered against him, and he held her closer. "He sent three men. We were in… Indianapolis, I think. I was five. Mom had bought an old car and we were going somewhere. We were always on the move. We got boxed in, in traffic. She saw them get out of their cars. She had taught us what to do if she ever told us to run. She dragged us out of the car and screamed 'Run!' I did, but Margreta started crying and grabbed Mom. So Mom took off running with Margreta. Two men went after them, and one came after me." She began shuddering. "I hid in an alley, under some garbage. I could hear him calling me, his voice soft like he was singing. 'Sonia, Sonia.' Over and over. They knew my name. I waited forever, and finally he went away."

"How did your mother find you again? Or was she caught?"

"No, she and Margreta got away, too. Mom taught herself street smarts, and she never went anywhere that she wasn't always checking out ways to escape."

He knew what that was like, Chance thought.

"I stayed in my hiding place. Mom had told us that sometimes, after we thought they were gone, the bad men would still be there watching, waiting to see if we came out. So I thought the bad men might be watching, and I stayed as still as I could. I don't think it was winter, because I wasn't wearing a coat, but when night fell I got cold. I was scared and hungry and didn't know if I'd ever see Mom again. I didn't leave, though, and finally I heard her calling me. She must have noticed where I ran and worked her way back when she thought it was safe. All I knew was that she'd found me. After that was when she decided it wasn't safe to keep us with her anymore, so she began looking for someone to adopt us."

Chance frowned. He hadn't found a record of any adoption but hers. "The same family took both of you?"

"Yes, but I was the only one adopted. Margreta wouldn't." Her voice was soft. "Margreta...remembers things. She had lost everything except Mom, so I guess she clung more than I did. She had a hard time adapting." She shrugged. "Having grown up the way I did, I can adjust to pretty much anything."

Meaning she had taught herself not to cling. Instead, with her sunny personality, she had found joy and beauty wherever she could. He held her closer, letting her cling to him. "But...you said he was trying to kill you. It sounds as if he was trying very hard to get you back."

She shook her head. "He was trying to get *Margreta* back. He didn't know me. I was just a means he could have used to force Mom to give Margreta back to him. That's all he would want with me now, to find Margreta. If I was caught, when he found out I don't know where she is, I'd be worthless to him."

"You don't know?" he asked, startled.

"It's safer that way. I haven't seen her in years." Unconscious longing for her sister was in her voice. "She has my cell phone number, and she calls me once a week. So long as I answer the call, she knows everything is all right."

"But you don't know how to get in touch with her?"

"No. I can't tell them what I don't know. I move around a lot, so a cell phone was the best way for us. I keep an apartment in Chicago, the tiniest, cheapest place I could find, but I don't live there. It's more of a decoy than anything else. I suppose if I live anywhere it's in Atlanta, but I take all the assignments I can get. I seldom spend more than one night at a time in one place."

"How would he find you now, since your name has been changed? Unless he knows who adopted you, but how could he find that out?" Chance himself had found her only because of the incident in Chicago, when her courier package was stolen and he checked her out. As soon as he said it, though, he knew that the mole in the FBI—and he would damn sure find out who *that* was—had probably done the same checking. Had he gone as deep in the layers of bureaucracy as Chance had, to the point of hacking into those sealed adoption records? Sunny's cover might have been blown. He wondered if she realized it yet.

"I don't know. I just know I can't afford to assume I'm safe until I hear he's dead."

"What about your mom? And Margreta?"

"Mom's dead." Sunny paused, and he felt her inhale as if bracing herself. "They caught her. She committed suicide rather than give up any information on us. She had told us she would—and she did."

She stopped, and Chance gave her time to deal with the bleakness he heard in her voice. Finally she said, "Margreta is using another name, I just don't know what it is. She has a heart condition, so it's better if she stays in one location."

Margreta was living a fairly normal life, he thought, while Sunny was on the move, always looking over her shoulder. That was what she had known since birth, the way she had been taught to handle the situation. But what about the years they had spent with the Millers? Had her life been normal then?

She answered those questions herself. "I miss having a home," she said wistfully. "But if you stay in one place you get to know people, form relationships. I couldn't risk someone else's life that way. God forbid I should get married, have children. If Hauer ever found me—" She broke off, shuddering at the thought of what Hauer was capable of doing to someone she loved in order to get the answers he wanted.

One thing didn't make sense, Chance thought. Hauer was vicious and crazy and cunning, and would go to any lengths to recover his daughter. But why Margreta, and not Sunny, too? "Why is he so fixated on your sister?"

"Can't you guess?" she asked rawly, and began shuddering again. "That's why Mom took Margreta and ran. She found him with her, doing…things. Margreta was only four. He had evidently been abusing her for quite a while, maybe even most of her life. By then Mom had already found out some of what he was, but she hadn't worked up the nerve to leave. After she found him with Margreta, she didn't have a choice." Her voice dropped to an agonized whisper. "Margreta remembers."

Chance felt sick to his stomach. So in addition to being a vicious, murdering bastard, Hauer was also a pervert, a child molester. Killing was too good for him; he deserved to be dismembered—slowly.

Worn out by both physical labor and her emotional storm, Sunny drifted to sleep. Chance held her, content to let her rest. The fire needed more fuel, but so what? Holding her was more important. Thinking his way through this was more important.

First and foremost, he believed every word she'd said. Her emotions had been too raw and honest for any of it to have been faked. For the first time, all the pieces of the puzzle fit together, and his relief was staggering. Sunny was innocent. She had nothing to do with her father, had never seen him, had spent her entire life running from him. That was why she lugged around a tent, with basic survival provisions; she was ready to disappear at any given moment, to literally go to ground and live out in the forest somewhere until she thought it was safe to surface and rebuild her life yet again.

She had no way of contacting Hauer. The only way to get to him, then, was to use her as bait. And considering how she felt about her father, she would never, under any circumstances, agree to any plan that brought her to his attention.

He would have to do it without her agreement, Chance thought grimly. He didn't like using her, but the stakes were too high to abandon. Hauer couldn't be left free to continue wreaking his destruction on the world. How many innocent people would die this year alone if he wasn't caught?

There was no point in staying here any longer; he'd found out what he needed to know. Zane wouldn't check in again, though, until tomorrow morning, so they were stuck until then. He adjusted Sunny in his arms and rested his face against the top of her head. He would use the time to formulate his game plan—and to use as many of those condoms as possible.

"GET AWAY FROM ME," Sunny grumbled the next morning, turning her head away from his kiss. She pried his hand off her breast. "Don't touch me, you—you *mink*."

Chance snorted with laughter.

She pulled his chest hair.

"Ouch!" He drew back as far as he could in the small confines of the tent. "That hurt."

"Good! I don't think I can walk." Quick as a snake, her hand darted out and pulled his chest hair again. "This way, you can have as much fun as I'm having."

"Sunny," he said in a cajoling tone.

"Don't 'Sunny' me," she warned, fighting her way into her clothes. Since they barely had room to move, he began dodging elbows and knees, and his hands slipped over some very interesting places. "Stop it! I mean it, Chance! I'm too sore for any more monkey business."

More to tease her than anything else, he zeroed in on an interesting place that had her squealing. She shot out of the tent, and he collapsed on his back, laughing—until she raised the tent flap and dashed some cold water on him.

"There," she said, hugely satisfied by his yelp. "One cold shower, just what you needed." Then she ran.

If she thought the fact that he was naked would hamper his pursuit, she found out differently. He snatched up a bottle of water as he passed by their cache of supplies and caught her before she had gone fifty yards. She was laughing like a maniac, otherwise she might have gotten away. He held her with one arm and poured the water over her head. It was ice-cold from having been left out all night, and she shrieked and sputtered and giggled, clinging to him when her legs went weak from so much laughter.

"Too sore to walk, huh?" he demanded.

"I w-wasn't walking," she said, giggling as she pushed her wet hair out of her face. Cold droplets splattered on him, and he shivered.

"Damn, it's cold," he said. The sun was barely up, so the temperature was probably in the forties.

She slapped his butt. "Then get some clothes on. What do you think this is, a nudist colony?"

He draped his arm around her shoulders, and they walked back to the camp. Her playfulness delighted him; hell, everything about her delighted him, from her wit to her willingness to laugh. And the sex—God, the sex was unbelievable. He didn't doubt she was sore, because *he* was. Last night had been a night to remember.

When she awakened yesterday afternoon she had been naturally melancholy, the normal aftermath of intense emotions. He hadn't talked much, letting her relax. She went with him to check the traps, which were still empty, and they had bathed together. After a quiet supper of rabbit and cactus they went to bed, and he had devoted the rest of the night to raising her spirits. His efforts had worked.

"How are your hands?" he asked. If she could pull his chest hairs and slap his butt, the antibiotic cream must have worked wonders.

She held them out, palms up, so he could see. The redness from the burns was gone, and her raw fingertips looked slick and shiny. "I'll wrap Band-Aids around them before I get started," she said.

"Get started doing what?"

She gave him a startled look. "Cutting handholds in the rock, of course."

He was stunned. He stared at her, unable to believe what

he was hearing. "You're not climbing back on that damn wall!" he snapped.

Her eyebrows rose in what he now recognized as her "the-hell-you-say" look. "Yes, I am."

He ground his teeth. He couldn't tell her they would be "rescued" today, but no way was he letting her wear herself out hacking holes in rock or put herself at that kind of risk.

"I'll do it," he growled.

"I'm smaller," she immediately objected. "It's safer for me."

She was trying to protect him again. He felt like beating his head against a rock in frustration.

"No, it isn't," he barked. "Look, there's no way you can cut enough handholds for us to climb out of here in the next two days. You got, what, twelve feet yesterday? If you managed twelve feet a day—and you wouldn't get that much done today, with your hands the way they are—it would take you over a week to reach the top. That's if—*if*—you didn't fall and kill yourself."

"So what am I supposed to do?" she shot back. "Just give up?"

"Today you aren't going to do a damn thing. You're going to let your hands heal if I have to tie you to a rock, is that clear?"

She looked as if she wanted to argue, but he was a lot bigger than she was, and maybe she could tell by his expression that he meant exactly what he said. "All right," she muttered. "Just for today."

He hoped she would keep her word, because he would have to leave her alone while he went to the spot where he signaled Zane. He would just have to risk it, but there would be hell to pay if he came back to find her on that rock.

He quickly dressed, shivering, and they ate another cold

breakfast of water and nutrition bar, since there wasn't anything left of the rabbit from the night before. Tomorrow morning, he promised himself, breakfast would be bacon and eggs, with a mountain of hash browns and a pot of hot coffee.

"I'm going to check the traps," he said, though he knew there wouldn't be anything in them. When he'd checked them the afternoon before, knowing they would be leaving here today, he had quietly released them so they couldn't be sprung. "Just tend to the fire and keep it smoking. You take it easy today, and I'll wash our clothes this afternoon." That was a safe promise to make.

"It's a deal," she said, but he could tell she was thinking about Margreta.

He left her sitting by the fire. It was a good ten-minute walk to the designated spot, but he hurried, unwilling to leave her to her own devices for so long. Taking the laser light from his pocket, he aimed it toward the rock on the rim and began flashing the pickup signal. Immediately Zane flashed back asking for confirmation, to make certain there wasn't an error. After all, they hadn't expected this to happen so fast. Chance flashed the signal again and this time received an okay.

He dropped the light back in his pocket. He didn't know how long it would take for Zane to arrange the pickup, but probably not long. Knowing Zane, everything was already in place.

He was walking back to the camp when the small twin-engine plane flew over. A grin spread across his face. That was Zane for you!

He began running, knowing Sunny would be beside herself. He heard her shrieking before he could see her; then she came into view, jumping in her glee as she came to meet him. "He saw me!" she screamed, laughing and crying at the same time. "He waggled the wings! He'll come back for us, won't he?"

He caught her as she hurled herself into his arms and couldn't stop himself from planting a long, hard kiss on that laughing mouth. "He'll come back," he said. "Unless he thought you were just waving hello at him." The opportunity to tease her was too great to resist, considering she had pulled his chest hair and poured cold water on him. He'd retaliated for the cold water; this was for the hair-pulling.

She looked stricken, the laughter wiped from her face as if it had never been. "Oh, no," she whispered.

He didn't have the heart to keep up the pretense. "Of course he'll come back," he chided. "Waggling the wings was the signal that he saw you and would send help."

"Are you sure?" she asked, blinking back tears.

"I promise."

"I'll get you for this."

He had to kiss her again, and he didn't stop until she had melted against him, her arms locked around his neck. He hadn't thought he would be interested in sex for quite a while, not after last night, but she proved him wrong.

He huffed out a breath and released her. "Stop manhandling me, you hussy. We have to get packed."

The smile she gave him was brilliant, like the sun rising, and it warmed him all the way through.

They gathered their belongings. Chance returned her pistol to her, and watched her break it down and store the pieces in their hiding places. Then they walked back to the plane and waited.

Rescue came in the form of a helicopter, the blades beating a thumping rhythm in the desert air, the canyon echoing with the sound. It hovered briefly over them, then lowered itself like a giant mosquito. Sand whipped into their air, stinging them, and Sunny hid her face against his shirt.

A sixtyish man with a friendly face and graying beard hopped out of the bird. "You folks need some help?" he called.

"Sure do," Chance answered.

When he was closer, the man stuck out his hand. "Charlie Jones, Civil Air Patrol. We've been looking for you for a couple of days. Didn't expect to find you this far south."

"I veered off course looking for a place to land. Fuel pump went out."

"In that case, you're mighty lucky. That's rough territory out there. This might be the only spot in a hundred miles when you could have landed. Come on. I expect you folks are ready for a shower and some food."

Chance held out his hand to Sunny, and she gave him that brilliant smile again as she put her hand in his and they walked to the helicopter.

CHAPTER ELEVEN

SUNNY WAS ALMOST dizzy with mingled relief and regret; relief because she wouldn't miss Margreta's call, regret because this time with Chance, even under such trying conditions, had been the happiest, most fulfilling few days of her life and they were now over. She had known from the beginning that their time together was limited; once they were back in the regular world, all the old rules came back into play.

She couldn't, wouldn't risk his life by letting him be a part of hers. He had given her two nights of bliss, and a lifetime of memories. That would have to be enough, no matter how much she was already aching at the thought of walking away from him and never seeing him again. At least now she knew what it was to love a man, to revel in his existence, and she was richer for it. She wouldn't have traded these few days with him for any amount of money, no matter the price in loneliness she would have to pay.

So she held his hand all during the helicopter flight to a small, ramshackle air field. The only building was made of corrugated metal, rounded at the top like a Quonset hut, with a wooden addition, housing the office, added to one side. If the addition had ever seen a coat of paint, the evidence of it had long since been blasted off by the wind-driven sand. After living under a rock for three days, Sunny thought the little field looked like heaven.

Seven airplanes, of various makes and vintage, were

parked with almost military precision along one side of the air strip. Charlie Jones landed his helicopter on a concrete pad behind the corrugated building. Three men, one wiping his greasy hands on a stained red rag, left the building by the back door and walked toward them, ducking their heads against the turbulence of the rotor blades.

Charlie took off his headset and hopped out of the chopper, smiling. "Found 'em," he called cheerfully to the approaching trio. To Chance and Sunny he said, "The two on the left fly CAP with me. Saul Osgood, far left, is the one who spotted your smoke this morning and radioed in your position. Ed Lynch is the one in the middle. The one with the greasy hands is Rabbit Warren, the mechanic here. His real name's Jerome, but he'll fight you if you call him that."

Sunny almost laughed aloud. She controlled the urge, but she was careful not to look at Chance as they shook hands with the three men and introduced themselves.

"I couldn't believe it when I saw your bird in that little bitty narrow canyon," Saul Osgood said, shaking his head after Chance told them what had happened. "How you ever found it is a miracle. And to make a dead stick landing—" He shook his head again. "Someone was sure looking out for you, is all I can say."

"So you think it was your fuel pump went out, huh?" Rabbit Warren asked as they walked into the hangar.

"Everything else checked out."

"It's a Skylane, right?"

"Yeah." Chance told him the model, and Rabbit stroked his lean jaw.

"I might have a pump for that. There was a feller in here last year flying a Skylane. He ordered some parts for it, then left and never did come back for 'em. I'll check while you folks are refreshing yourselves."

If "refreshing" themselves had anything to do with a

bathroom, Sunny was more than ready. Chance gave her the first turn, and she almost crooned with delight at the copious water that gushed from the faucet at a turn of the handle. And a flush toilet! She was in heaven.

After Chance had his turn, they indulged in ice-cold soft drinks from a battered vending machine. A snack machine stood beside it, and Sunny surveyed the offerings with an eager eye. "How much change do you have?" she asked Chance.

He delved his hand into his front pocket and pulled out his change, holding it out for Sunny to see. She picked out two quarters and fed them into the machine, punched a button, and a pack of cheese and crackers fell to the tray.

"I thought you'd go for a candy bar," Chance said as he fed more quarters into the machine and got a pack of peanuts.

"That's next." She raised her eyebrows. "You didn't think I was going to stop with cheese and crackers, did you?"

Ed Lynch opened the door to the office. "Is there anyone you need to call? We've notified the FAA and called off the search, but if you have family you want to talk to, feel free to use the phone."

"I need to call the office," Sunny said, pulling a wry face. She had a good excuse—a very good one—for not making her delivery, but the bottom line was that a customer was unhappy.

Chance waited until she was on the phone, then strolled over to where Rabbit was making a show of looking for a fuel pump. His men were good, Chance thought; they had played this so naturally they should have been on the stage. Of course, subterfuge was their lives, just as it was his.

"Everything's good," Chance said quietly. "You guys can clear out after Charlie takes us back to the canyon with the fuel pump."

Rabbit pulled a greasy box from a makeshift shelf that was piled with an assortment of parts and tools. Over Chance's shoulder he eyed Sunny through the windowed door to the office. "You pulled a real hardship assignment this time, boss," he said admiringly. "That's the sweetest face I've seen in a while."

"There's a sweet person behind it, too," Chance said as he took the box. "She's not part of the organization."

Rabbit's eyebrows went up. "So all this was for nothing."

"No, everything is still a go. The only thing that's changed is her role. Instead of being the key, she's the bait. She's been on the run from Hauer her entire life. If he knows where she is, he'll come out of hiding." He glanced around to make certain she was still on the phone. "Spread the word that we're going to be extra careful with her, make sure she doesn't get hurt. Hauer has already caused enough damage in her life."

And he himself was going to cause more, Chance thought bleakly. As terrified as she was of Hauer, when she learned Chance had deliberately leaked her location to the man she was going to go ballistic. That would definitely be the end of *this* relationship, but he'd known from the beginning this was only temporary. Like her, he wasn't in any position for permanent ties. Sunny's circumstances would change when her father was gone, but Chance's wouldn't; he would move on to another crisis, another security threat.

Just because he was her first lover didn't mean he would be her last.

The idea shot a bolt of pure rage through him. Damn it, she was *his*—he caught the possessive thought and strangled it. Sunny wasn't his; she was her own person, and if she found happiness in her life with some other man, he should be happy for her. She more than deserved anything good that came her way.

He wasn't happy. Her laughter, her passion—he wanted it all for himself. Knowing he couldn't have her was already eating a huge hole out of his insides, but she deserved far better than a mongrel with blood on his hands. He had chosen his world, and he was well-suited for it. He was accustomed to living a lie, to pretending to be someone he wasn't, to always staying in the shadows. Sunny was… sunny, both by name and by nature. He would enjoy her while he had her—by God, he'd enjoy her—but in the end he knew he would have to walk away.

Sunny ended the call and left the office. Hearing the door close, he turned to watch her approach, and he let himself savor the pleasure of just watching her.

She wrinkled her nose. "Everyone's glad the plane didn't crash, that I'm alive—but the fact that I didn't die makes it a little less forgivable that I didn't deliver the package on time. The customer still wants it, though, so I still have to go to Seattle."

She came to him as naturally as if they had been together for years, and just as naturally he found himself slipping his arm around her slender waist. "Screw 'em," he said dismissively. He lifted the box. "Guess what I have."

She beamed. "The keys to the kingdom."

"Close enough. Charlie's going to take me back to the plane so I can swap out the fuel pump. Do you want to go with me, or stay here and rest until I get back?"

"Go with you," she said promptly. "I don't know anything about airplanes, but I can keep you company while you work. Are we coming back here, anyway?"

"Sure. This is as good a place to refuel as any." Plus she wouldn't find out they weren't in Oregon as he'd told her.

"Then I'll leave my bag here, if that's all right with

Rabbit." She looked inquiringly at Rabbit, who nodded his head.

"That'll be just fine, ma'am. Put it in the office and it'll be as safe as a baby in the womb."

Sunny walked away to get the bag. She felt safe, Chance realized, otherwise she would never let the bag out of her possession. Except for her worry for Margreta, these last few days she must have felt free, unburdened by the need to constantly look over her shoulder.

He had enjoyed their little adventure, too, every minute of it, because he had known they weren't in any danger. Sunny made him feel more alive than he ever had before, even when he was angry at her because she had just scared him half to death. And when he was inside her—then he was as close to heaven as he was ever likely to get. The pleasure of making love to her was so intense it was almost blinding.

He grinned to himself as he hefted his own overnight bag. No way was he leaving it here; after all, the condoms were in it. No telling what might happen when he and Sunny were alone.

The afternoon was wearing on when Charlie set the helicopter down in the canyon again. He looked up at the light with an experienced pilot's eye. "You think you have enough time to get that fuel pump put on before dark?"

"No problem," Chance said. After all, as he and Charlie both knew, there was nothing wrong with the fuel pump, anyway. He would tinker around for a while, make it look realistic. Sunny wasn't likely to stand at his elbow the entire time, and if she did he would distract her.

He and Sunny jumped out of the helicopter, and he leaned in to get his bag. "See you in a few hours."

"If you don't make it back to the airfield, we know where you are," Charlie said, saluting.

They ducked away from the turbulence as the helicopter lifted away. Sunny pushed her hair away from her face and looked around the canyon, smiling. "Home again," she said, and laughed. "Funny how it looks a lot more inviting now that I know we aren't stuck here."

"I'm going to miss it," he said, winking at her. He carried his bag and the box containing the fuel pump over to the plane. "But we'll find out tonight if a bed is more fun than a tent."

To his surprise, sadness flashed in her eyes. "Chance… once we're away from here…" She shook her head. "It won't be safe."

He checked for a moment, then very deliberately put down the bag and box. Turning back to her, he put his hands on his hips. "If you're saying what I think you're saying, you can just forget about it. You aren't dumping me."

"You know what the situation is! I don't have a choice."

"*I* do. You're not just a fun screw who was available while we were here. I care about you, Sunny," he said softly. "When you look over your shoulder, you're going to see my face. Get used to it."

Tears welled in her brilliant eyes, filling them with diamonds. "I can't," she whispered. "Because I love you. Don't ask me to risk your life, because I can't handle it."

His stomach muscles tightened. He had set out to make her love him, or at least get involved in a torrid affair with him. He had succeeded at doing both. He felt humbled, and exhilarated—and sick, because he was going to betray her.

He had her in his arms before he was aware of moving, and his mouth was on hers. He felt desperate for the taste of her, as if it had been days since he'd kissed her instead of just hours. Her response was immediate and wholehearted, as she rose on her tiptoes to fit her hips more intimately to his. He tasted the salt of her tears and drew back, rubbing his thumbs across her wet cheeks.

He rested his forehead against hers. "You're forgetting something," he murmured.

She sniffed. "What?"

"I was a ranger, sweetheart. I'm a little harder to kill than your average guy. You need someone watching your back, and I can do it. Think about it. We probably made the news. When we get to Seattle, don't be surprised if there's a television camera crew there. Both our faces will be on television. Besides that, we were reported missing to the FAA, which is federal. Information would have been dug up on both of us. Our names our linked. If the mole in the FBI tumbles to who you are, your father's goons will be after me, anyway—especially if they can't find you."

She went white. "Television?" She looked a lot like her mother; Chance had seen old photos of Pamela Vickery Hauer. Anyone familiar with Pamela would immediately notice the resemblance. As sharp as she was, Sunny also knew the danger of being on television, even a local newscast.

"We're in this together." He lifted her hand to his mouth and kissed her knuckles, then grinned down at her. "Lucky for you, I'm one mean son of a bitch when I need to be— lucky for you, unlucky for them."

NOTHING SHE SAID would sway him, Sunny thought with despair late that night as she showered in the hotel suite he had booked them into for the night—a suite because it had more than one exit. He had been exactly right about the television news crew. Crews, she corrected herself. News had been slow that day, so every station in Seattle had jumped on the human-interest story. The problem was, so had both national news channels.

She had evaded the cameras as much as possible, but the reporters had seemed fixated on her, shouting questions at her instead of Chance. She would have thought the female reporters, at least, would be all over Chance, but he'd worn such a forbidding expression that no one had approached him. She hadn't answered any questions on camera, though at Chance's whispered suggestion she had given them a quick comment off-camera, for them to use as a filler on their broadcast.

Her one break was that, since it had been so late when they landed, the story didn't make even the late news. But unless something more newsworthy happened soon, the story would air in just a few hours over millions of breakfast tables countrywide.

She had to assume her cover had been blown. That meant leaving the courier service, moving—not that she had much to move; she had never accumulated many possessions—even changing her name. She would have to build a new identity.

She had always known it could happen, and she had prepared for it, both mentally and with actual paperwork. Changing her name wouldn't change who she was; it was just a tool to use to escape her father.

The real problem was Chance. She couldn't shake him, no matter how she tried, and she knew she was good at that kind of thing. She had tried to lose him at the airport, ducking into a cab when his back was turned. But he seemed to have a sixth sense where she was concerned, and he was sliding in the other door before she could give the driver the address where she had to deliver the courier package. He had remained within touching distance of her until they walked into the hotel room, and she had no doubt that, if she opened the bathroom door, she would find him sprawled across the bed, watching her.

In that, she underestimated him. Just as she began lathering her hair, the shower curtain slid back and he stepped naked into the tub with her. "I thought I'd conserve water and shower with you," he said easily.

"Hah! You're just afraid I'll leave if you shower by yourself," she said, turning her back on him.

A big hand patted her bottom. "You know me so well."

She fought a smile. Damn him, why did he have to be so well-matched to her in every way? She could, and had, run rings around most people, but not Chance.

She hogged the spray, turning the nozzle down to rinse her hair. He waited until she was finished with that, at least, then adjusted the nozzle upward so the water hit him in the chest. It also hit her full in the face. She sputtered and elbowed him. "This is *my* shower, and I didn't invite you. I get control of the nozzle, not you."

She knew challenging him was a mistake. He said, "Oh, yeah?" and the tussle was on. Before she knew it she was giggling, he was laughing, and the bathroom was splattered with water. She had played more with Chance than she had since she'd been a little girl; she felt lighthearted with him, despite her problems. Their wet, naked bodies slid against each other, and neither of them could get a good grasp on any body part. At least, she couldn't. She suspected he could have won the tussle at any time simply by using his size and strength and wrapping his arms around her, but he held back and played at her level, as if he were used to restraining his strength to accommodate someone weaker than himself.

His hands were everywhere: on her breasts, her bottom, sliding between her legs while she laughed and batted them away. One long finger worked its way inside her and she squealed, trying to twist away while excitement spiraled wildly through her veins. Their naked wrestling match was having a predictable effect on both of them. She grabbed for the nozzle and aimed the blast of water at his face, and while he was trying to deflect the spray she made her escape, hopping out of the tub and snatching up a towel to wrap around her.

He vaulted out of the tub and slammed the door shut just as she reached for it. "You left the shower running," she accused, trying to sidetrack him.

"I'm not the one who turned it on." He grinned and hooked the towel away from her.

"Water's getting all over the floor." She tried to sound disapproving.

"It needed mopping, anyway."

"It did not!" She pushed a strand of dripping wet hair out of her eyes. "We're going to be kicked out. Water will drip through the floor into the room below and we'll be kicked out."

He grabbed her and swung her around so she was facing the shower. "Turn it off, then, if you're worried."

She did, because she hated to waste the water, and it was making such a mess. "There, I hope you're satisfied."

"Not by a long shot." He turned her to face him, holding her lips against his and angling her torso away from him, so he could look his fill at her. "Have I told you today how damn sexy you are?"

"Today? You've never told me at all!"

"Have so."

"Have not. When?"

"Last night. Several times."

She tried not to be entranced by the way water droplets were clinging to his thick dark lashes. "That doesn't count. Everyone knows you can't believe anything a man says when he's in...uh—"

"You?" he supplied, grinning.

She managed a haughty look. "I was going to say 'extremis,' but I think that applies only to dying."

"Close enough." He looked down at her breasts, his expression altering and the laughter fading. Still holding her anchored to him with one arm, he smoothed a hand up her torso to cup her breasts, and they both watched his long brown fingers curve around the pale globes. "You're sexy," he murmured, a slow, dark note entering his voice. She knew that note well, having heard it many times over the past two nights. "And beautiful. Your breasts are all cream-and-rose colored, until I kiss your nipples. Then they pucker up and turn red like they're begging me to suck them."

Her nipples tightened at his words, the puckered tips flushing with color. He groaned and bent his dark head, water dripping from his hair onto her skin as he kissed both breasts. She was leaning far back over his arm, supported by his arm around her hips and her own desperate grasp on his shoulders. She didn't know how much longer she would be able to stand at all. Her loins throbbed, and she gasped for breath.

"And your ass," he growled. "You have the sweetest little ass." He turned her around so he could stroke the aforementioned buttocks, shaping his palms to the full, cool curves. Sunny's legs trembled, and she grabbed the edge of the vanity for support. The cultured marble slab was a good six feet long, and a mirror covered the entire wall behind it. Sunny barely recognized herself in the naked woman reflected there, a woman whose wet hair dripped water down her back and onto the floor. Her expression was etched with desire, her face flushed and her eyes heavy-lidded.

Chance looked up, and his gaze met hers in the mirror. Electricity sparked between them. "And here," he whispered, sliding one hand around her belly and between her legs. His muscled forearm looked unbelievably powerful against her pale belly, and his big hand totally covered her mound. She felt his fingers sliding between her folds, rubbing her just as she liked. She moaned and collapsed against him, her legs going limp.

"You're so soft and tight," the erotic litany continued in her ear. "I can barely get inside you. But once I do—my heart stops. And I can't breathe. I think I'm going to die, but I can't, because it feels too good to stop." His fingers slid farther, and he pressed two of them inside her.

She arched under the lash of sensation, soaring close to climax as his fingers stretched her. She heard herself cry out, a strained cry that told him exactly how near she was to fulfillment.

"Not yet, not yet," he said urgently, sliding his fingers out of her and bending her forward. He braced her hands on the vanity. "Hold on, sweetheart."

She didn't know if he meant to the vanity, or to her control. Both were impossible. "I can't," she moaned. Her hips moved, undulating, searching for relief. "Chance, I can't—please!"

"I'm here," he said, and he was, dipping down and pushing his muscled thighs between her legs, spreading them. She felt his lower belly against her buttocks, then the smooth, hard entry of his sex. Instinctively she bent forward to aid his penetration, taking all of him deep within her. He began driving, and on the second hard thrust she convulsed, crying out her pleasure. His climax erupted a moment later, and he collapsed over her back, holding himself as deep as he could while he groaned and shook.

Sunny closed her eyes, fighting for breath. Oh, God, she loved him so much she ached with it. She wasn't strong enough to send him away, not even for his own protection.

If she had been really trying, she could have gotten away from him, but deep down she knew she couldn't give him up. Not yet. Soon. She would have to, to keep him safe.

Just one more day, she thought as tears welled. One more. Then she would go.

CHAPTER TWELVE

TEN DAYS LATER, Sunny still hadn't managed to shake him. She didn't know if she was losing her touch or if army rangers, even ex ones, were very, very good at not being shaken.

They had left Seattle early the next morning. Sunny was too cautious to fly back to Atlanta; as she had feared, the morning newscasts had been splashed with the "real-life romantic adventure" she and Chance had shared. His name was mentioned, but by some perverse quirk his face was never clearly shown; the camera would catch the back of his head, or while he was in a quarter profile, while hers was broadcast from coast to coast.

One of the a.m. news shows even tracked them down at the hotel, awakening them at three in the morning to ask if they would go to the local affiliate studios for a live interview.

"Hell, no," Chance had growled into the phone before he slammed it down into the cradle.

After that, it had seemed best they remove themselves from the reach of the media. They checked out of the hotel and took a taxi to the airport before dawn. The plane was refueled and ready to go. By the time the sun peeked over the Cascades they were in the air. Chance didn't file a flight plan, so no one had any way of finding out where they were going. Sunny didn't know herself until they landed in Boise, Idaho, where they refurbished their wardrobes. She always carried a lot of cash, for just such a situation, and Chance seemed to have plenty, too. He still had to use his credit card for refueling, so she knew they were leaving a trail, but those records would show only where they had last been, not where they were going.

Chance's presence threw her off her plan. She knew how to disappear by herself; Chance and his airplane complicated things.

From a pay phone in Boise, she called Atlanta and resigned her job, with instructions to deposit her last paycheck into her bank. She would have the money wired to her when she needed it. Sometimes, adrift from the familiar life she had fashioned for herself, she wondered if she was overreacting to the possibility anyone would recognize her. Her mother had been dead for over ten years; there were few people in the world able to see the resemblance. The odds had to be astronomical against one of those few people seeing that brief human-interest story that had been shown for only one day.

But she was still alive because her mother had taught her that any odds at all were unacceptable. So she ran, as she had learned how to do in the first five years of her life. After all, the odds were also against her getting pregnant, yet here she was, waiting for a period that hadn't materialized. They had slipped up twice, only twice: once in the canyon, and in the hotel bathroom in Seattle. The timing hadn't been great for her to get pregnant even if they hadn't used protection at all, so why hadn't her period started? It was due two days ago, and her cycle was relentlessly regular.

She didn't mention it to Chance. She might just be late, for one of the few times in her life since she'd starting having menstrual periods. She had been terrified when she thought they were going to crash; maybe her emotions had disrupted her hormones. It happened.

She might sprout wings and fly, too, she thought in quiet desperation. She was pregnant. There were no signs other than a late period, but she knew it deep down in her bones, as if on some level her body was communicating with the microscopic embryo it harbored.

It would be so easy just to let Chance handle everything. He was good at this, and she had too much on her mind to be effective. She didn't think he'd noticed how easily distracted she'd been these past few days, but then, he didn't know when her period had been due, either.

She had talked to Margreta twice, and told her she was going underground. She would have to arrange for a new cellular account under a different name, with a new number, and do it before the service she now had was disconnected. She had tried to tell Margreta everything that was going on, but her sister, as usual, kept the calls short. Sunny understood. It was difficult for Margreta to handle anything having to do with their father. Maybe one day they would be able to live normal lives, have a normal sisterly relationship; maybe one day Margreta would be able to get past what he had done to her and find some happiness despite him.

Then there was Chance. He had brought sunshine into her life when she hadn't even known she was living in shadows. She had thought she managed quite well, but it was as if B.C., Before Chance, had been in monochrome. Now, A.C., was in vivid technicolor. She slept in his arms every night. She ate her meals with him, quarreled with him, joked with him, made plans with him—nothing long term, but plans nevertheless. Every day she fell more and more in love with him, when she hadn't thought it possible.

Sometimes she actually pinched herself, because he was too good to be true. Men like him didn't come along every day; most women lived their entire lives without meeting a man who could turn their worlds upside down with a glance.

This state of affairs couldn't last much longer, this aimless drifting. For one thing, it was expensive. Chance wasn't earning any money while they were flying from one remote airfield in the country to another, and neither was she. She needed to get the paperwork for her new name, get a job, get a new cellular number—and get an obstetrician, which would cost money. She wondered how her mother had managed, with one frightened, traumatized child in tow, pregnant with another, and without any of the survival skills Sunny possessed. Pamela must have spent years in a state of terror, yet Sunny remembered her mother laughing, playing games with them and making life fun even while she taught them how to survive. She only hoped she could be half as strong as her mother had been.

She was full of wild hopes these days. She hoped she hadn't been recognized. She hoped her baby would be healthy and happy. Most of all, she hoped she and Chance could build a life together, that he would be thrilled about the baby even though it was unplanned, that he truly cared about her as much as he appeared to. He never actually said he loved her, but it was there in his voice, in his actions, in his eyes and his touch as he made love to her.

Everything had to be all right. It had to. There was too much at stake now.

SUNNY SLEPT THROUGH the landing as Chance set the plane down in Des Moines. He glanced at her, but she was soundly asleep, like a child, her breathing deep and her cheeks flushed. He let her sleep, knowing what was coming to a head.

The plan was working beautifully. He had arranged for Sunny's face to be broadcast worldwide, and the bait had been taken immediately. His people had tracked two of Hauer's men into the country and maintained discreet but constant surveillance on them. Chance hadn't made it easy for anyone to follow him and Sunny; that would have been too obvious. But he had left a faint trail that, if the bloodhounds were good, they would be able to follow. Hauer's bloodhounds were good. They had been about a day behind them for about a week now, but until Hauer himself showed up, Chance made sure the hounds never caught up with him.

The news he'd been waiting for had finally come yesterday. Word in the underground of terrorist organizations was that Hauer had disappeared. He hadn't been seen in a few days, and there was a rumor he was in the States planning something big.

Somehow Hauer had slipped out of Europe and into America without being spotted, but now that Chance knew there was a mole in the FBI helping Hauer, he wasn't surprised.

Hauer was too smart to openly join his men, but he would be nearby. He was the type who, when Sunny was captured, would want to interrogate this rebellious daughter himself.

Chance would take him apart with his bare hands before he let that happen.

But he would have to let them think they had her, not knowing they were surrounded at all times, at a distance, by his men. Chance just hoped he himself wasn't shot at the beginning, to get him out of the way. If Hauer's men were smart, they would realize they could use threats to Chance to keep Sunny in line, and they had proven they were smart. This was the risky part, but he had taken all the safeguards he could without tipping his hand.

His interlude with Sunny would end tonight, one way or another. If all went well, they would both live through it, and she would be free to live her life out in the open. He just hoped that one day she wouldn't hate him, that she would realize he had done what he had to do in order to capture Hauer. Who knows? Maybe one day he would meet her again.

He guided the Cessna to a stop in its designated spot and killed the engine. Sunny slept on, despite the sudden silence. Maybe he'd cost her too much sleep and it had finally caught up with her, he thought, smiling despite his inner tension. He had glutted himself with sex for the past two weeks, as if subconsciously he had been trying to stockpile memories and sensations for the time when she was no longer there. But as often as he'd had her, he still wanted her. Again. More. He was half hard right now, just thinking about her.

Gently he shook her, and she opened her sleepy eyes with a look of such trust and love that his heart leaped. She sat up, stretching and looking around. "Where are we?"

"Des Moines." Puzzled, he said, "I told you where we were going."

"I remember," she said around a yawn. "I'm just groggy. Wow! That was some nap. I don't usually sleep during the daytime. I must not be getting enough sleep at night." She batted her eyelashes at him. "I wonder why."

"I have no idea," he said, all innocence. He opened the door and climbed out, turning around to hold his hands up for her. She clambered out, and he lifted her to the ground.

Looking up at the wide, cerulean-blue sky, he stretched, too, twisting his back to get out the kinks. "It's a pretty day. Want to have a picnic?"

"A what?" She looked at him as if he were speaking a foreign language.

"A picnic. You know, where you sit on the ground and eat with your hands, and fight wild animals for your food."

"Sounds like fun. But haven't we already done that?"

He laughed. "This time we'll do it right—checkered tablecloth, fried chicken, the works."

"All right, I'm game. Where are we going to have this picnic? Beside the runway?"

"Smart-ass. We'll rent a car and go for a drive."

Her eyes began to sparkle as she realized he meant it. That was what he loved best about Sunny, her ability to have fun. "How much time do we have? What time are we leaving?"

"Let's stay for a couple of days. Iowa's a nice place, and my tail could use some time away from that airplane seat."

He handled his business with the airport, then went to a rental car desk and walked away with the keys to a sport utility.

"You rented a *truck?*" Sunny teased when she saw the green Ford Explorer. "Why didn't you get something with style, like a red sports car?"

"Because I'm six-three," he retorted. "My legs don't fit in sports cars."

She had bought a small backpack that she carried instead of the bulky carry-on she had been lugging around. She could get her toiletries and a change of clothes into the backpack, and that was enough for the single night they usually spent in a place. That meant her pistol was always with her, fully assembled when they weren't having to go through X-ray scanners, and he didn't protest. He always carried his own pistol with him, too, tucked into his waistband under his loose shirt. She put the backpack on the floorboard and climbed into the passenger seat, and began pushing buttons and turning knobs, every one she could reach.

Chance got behind the wheel. "I'm afraid to start this thing now. There's no telling what's going to happen."

"Chicken," she said. "What's the worst that could happen?"

"I'm just thankful Explorers don't have ejection seats," he muttered as he turned the key in the ignition. The engine caught immediately. The radio blared, the windshield wipers flopped back and forth at high speed and the emergency lights began blinking. Sunny laughed as Chance dived for the radio controls and turned the volume down to an acceptable level. She buckled herself into the seat, smiling a very self-satisfied smile.

He had a map from the rental car company, though he already knew exactly where he was going. He had gotten very specific directions from the clerk at the rental agency, so the clerk would remember where they had gone when Hauer's men asked. He had personally scouted out the location before putting the plan into motion. It was in the country, to cut the risk of collateral damage to innocent civilians. There was cover for his men, who would be in place before he and Sunny arrived. And, most important, Hauer and his men couldn't move in without being observed. Chance had enough men in place that an ant couldn't attend this picnic unless he wanted it there. Best of all, he knew Zane was out there somewhere. Zane didn't usually do fieldwork, but in this instance he was here guarding his brother's back. Chance would rather have Zane looking out for him than an entire army; the man was unbelievable, he was so good.

They stopped at a supermarket deli for their picnic supplies. There was even a red-checkered plastic cloth to go on the ground. They bought fried chicken, potato salad, rolls, cole slaw, an apple pie and some green stuff Sunny called pistachio salad. He knew he wasn't about to touch it. Then he had to buy a small cooler and ice, and some soft drinks to go in it. By the time he got Sunny out of the supermarket, over an hour had passed and he was almost seventy bucks lighter in the wallet.

"We have apple pie," he complained. "Why do we need apples?"

"I'm going to throw them at you," she said. "Or better yet, shoot them off your head."

"If you come near me with an apple, I'll scream," he warned. "And pickled beets? Excuse me, but who eats pickled beets?"

She shrugged. "Someone does, or they wouldn't be on the shelves."

"Have *you* ever eaten pickled beets?" he asked suspiciously.

"Once. They were nasty." She wrinkled her nose at him.

"Then why in hell did you buy them?" he shouted.

"I wanted you to try them."

He should be used to it by now, he thought, but sometimes she still left him speechless. Muttering to himself, he stowed the groceries—including the pickled beets—in the back of the Explorer.

God, he was going to miss her.

She rolled down the window and let the wind blow through her bright hair. She had a happy smile on her face as she looked at everything they passed. Even service stations seemed to interest her, as did the old lady walking a Chihuahua that was so fat its belly almost kept its feet from touching the ground. Sunny giggled about the fat little dog for five minutes.

If it made her laugh like that, he thought, he would eat the damn pickled beets. But he'd damn sure eat something else afterward, because if he got shot, he didn't want pickled beets to be the last thing he tasted.

The late August afternoon was hot when he pulled off the road. A tree-studded field stretched before them. "Let's walk to those trees over there," he said, nodding to a line of trees about a hundred yards away. "See how they're growing, in a line like that? There might be a little creek there."

She looked around. "Shouldn't we ask permission?"

He raised his eyebrows. "Do you see a house anywhere? Who do we ask?"

"Well, all right, but if we get in trouble, it's your fault."

He carried the cooler and most of the food. Sunny slung her backpack on her shoulders, then took charge of the ground cloth and the jar of pickled beets. "I'd better carry these," she said. "You might drop them."

"You could take something else, too," he grunted. This stuff was heavy.

She stretched up to peek in the grocery bag. The apple pie was perched on top of the other stuff. "Nah, you won't drop the pie."

He grumbled all the way to their picnic site, more because she enjoyed it than any other reason. This was the last day she would ever tease him, or he would see that smile, hear that laugh.

"Oh, there *is* a creek!" she exclaimed when they reached the trees. She carefully set the jar of beets down and unfolded the ground cloth, snapping it open in that brisk, economical movement all women seemed to have and letting it settle on the thick, overgrown grass. A light breeze was blowing, so she anchored the cloth with her backpack on one corner and the jar of beets on the another.

Chance set the cooler and food down and sprawled out on the cloth. "I'm too tired now to enjoy myself," he complained.

She leaned over and kissed him. "You think I don't know what you're up to? Next thing I know you'll get something in your eye, and I'll have to get really, really close to see it. Then your back will need scratching, and you'll have to take off your shirt. Before I know it, we'll both be naked and it'll be time to leave, and we won't have had a bite to eat."

He gave her a quizzical look. "You have this all planned out, don't you?"

"Down to the last detail."

"Suits me." He reached for her, but with a spurt of laughter she scooted out of reach. She picked up the jar of beets and looked at him expectantly.

He flopped back with a groan. "Oh, man. Don't tell me you expect me to try them *now*."

"No, I want you to open the jar so *I* can eat them."

"I thought you said they were nasty."

"They are. I want to see if they're as nasty as I remember." She handed him the jar. "If you'll open them for me, I'll let you eat fried chicken and potato salad to build up your strength before I wring you out and hang you up to dry."

He sat up and took the jar. "In your dreams, little miss 'don't-touch-me-again-you-lech.'" He put some muscle behind the effort, twisting the lid free.

"I've been sandbagging," she said. "This time, don't even bother begging for mercy."

She reached for the jar. The loosened lid came off, and

the jar slipped from her hands. He dived for it, not wanting beets all over everything. Just as he moved, the tree beside him exploded, and a millisecond later he heard the blast of the shot.

He twisted in midair, throwing himself on top of Sunny and rolling with her behind the cover of the tree.

CHAPTER THIRTEEN

"STAY DOWN!" CHANCE BARKED, shoving her face into the grass.

Sunny couldn't have moved even if she had wanted to, even if his two hundred-plus pounds hadn't been lying on top of her. She was paralyzed, terror freezing in her veins as she realized her worst nightmare had come true; her father had found them, and Chance was nothing more than an obstacle to be destroyed. That bullet hadn't been aimed at *her*. If she hadn't dropped the jar of beets, if Chance hadn't lunged for it, the slug that blew chunks of wood out of the tree would have blown off half his head.

"Son of a bitch," he muttered above her, his breath stirring her hair. "Sniper."

The earth exploded two inches from her head, clods of dirt flying in her face, tiny pieces of gravel stinging her like bees. Chance literally threw her to the side, rolling with her again; the ground dropped out from beneath her, and her stomach gave a sickening lurch. As suddenly as the fall began, it stopped. She landed hard in three inches of sluggish water.

He had rolled them into the creek, where the banks afforded them more cover. A twist of his powerful body and he was off her, his big pistol in his hand as he flattened himself against the shallow bank. Sunny managed to get to her knees, slipped on the slimy creek bottom, and clambered on her hands and knees to a spot beside him. She felt numb, as if her arms and legs didn't belong to her, yet they were working, moving.

This wasn't real. It couldn't be. How had he found them?

She closed her eyes, fighting the terror. She was a liability to Chance unless she got herself under control. She'd had close calls before and handled herself just fine, but she had never before seen the man she loved almost get killed in front of her. She had never before been pregnant, with so much to lose.

Her teeth were chattering. She clamped her jaw together.

Silence fell over the field. She heard a car drive by on the road, and for a wild moment she wondered why it didn't stop. But why would it? There was nothing the average passerby would notice, no bodies lying around on the highway, no haze of gun smoke hanging over the green grass. There was only silence, as if even the insects had frozen in place, the birds stopped singing; even the breeze had stopped rustling the leaves. It was as if nature held its breath, shocked by the sudden violence.

The shot had come from the direction of the road, but she hadn't seen anyone drive up. They had only just arrived themselves; it was as if whoever had shot at them had already been here, waiting. But that was impossible, wasn't it? The picnic was an impulse, and the location sheer chance; they could just as well have stopped at a park.

The only other explanation that occurred to her was if the shooter had nothing to do with her father. Maybe it was a crazy landowner who shot at trespassers.

If only she had brought her cell phone! But Margreta wasn't due to call her for several more days, and even if she had brought the phone, it would be in her backpack, which was still lying on the ground cloth. The distance of a few yards might as well be a mile. Her pistol was also in the pack; though a pistol was useless against a sniper, she would feel better if she had some means of protection.

Chance hadn't fired; he knew the futility of it even more than she did. His dark gold eyes were scanning the countryside, looking for anything that would give away the assailant's position: a glint of sunlight on the barrel, the color of his clothing, a movement. The extreme angle of the late afternoon sun picked out incredible detail in the trees and bushes, but nothing that would help them.

Only nightfall would help, she thought. If they could just hold out for…how long? Another hour? Two hours, at most. When it was dark, then they could belly down in the little creek and work their way to safety, either upstream or down, it didn't matter.

If they lived that long. The sniper had the advantage. All they had was the cover of a shallow creek bank.

She became aware that her teeth were chattering again. Again she clamped her jaw together to still the movement. Chance spared a glance at her, a split-second assessment before he returned to once again scanning the trees for the sniper. "Are you all right?" he asked, though he obviously knew she was all in one piece. He wasn't asking about her physical condition.

"S-scared spitless," she managed to say.

"Yeah. Me, too."

He didn't look scared, she thought. He looked coldly furious.

He reached out and rubbed her arm, a brief gesture of comfort. "Thank God for those beets," he said.

She almost cried. The beets. She had thoroughly enjoyed teasing him about the beets, but the truth was, when she saw them in the supermarket she had been overcome by an almost violent craving for them. She wanted those beets. She felt as if she could eat the entire jar of them.

Could cravings start this early in a pregnancy? If so, then he should thank God not for the beets, but for the beginnings of life forming inside her.

She wished she had told him immediately when her period didn't come. She couldn't tell him now; the news would be too distracting.

If they lived through this, she thought fervently, she wouldn't keep the secret to herself a minute longer.

"It can't be Hauer's men," she blurted. "It's impossible. They couldn't be here ahead of us, because we didn't know we were coming here. It has to be a crazy farmer, or a—a jerk who thought it would be funny to shoot at someone."

"Sweetheart." He touched her arm again, and she realized she was babbling. "It isn't a crazy farmer, or a trigger-happy jerk."

"How do you know? It could be!"

"The sniper's too professional."

Just four words, but they made her heart sink. Chance would know; he had training in this sort of thing.

She pressed her forehead against the grassy bank, fighting for the courage to do what she had to do. Her mother had died protecting her and Margreta; surely she could be as brave? She couldn't tell Hauer anything about Margreta, so her sister was safe, and if she could save Chance, then dying would be worth it....

Her child would die with her.

Don't make me choose, she silently prayed. *The child or the father.*

If it were just her, she wouldn't hesitate. In the short time she had known Chance—was it really just two weeks?—he had given her a lifetime of happiness and the richness of love. She would gladly give her life in exchange for his.

The life inside her wasn't really a child yet; it was still just a rapidly dividing cluster of cells. No organs or bones had formed, nothing recognizable as a human. It was maybe the size of a pin head. But the potential…oh, the potential. She loved that tiny ball of cells with a fierceness that burned through every fiber of her being, had loved it from the first startled awareness that her period was late. It was as if she had blinked and said, "Oh. Hello," because one second she had been totally unaware of its existence, and the next she had somehow known.

The child or the father. The father or the child.

The words writhed in her brain, echoing, bouncing. She loved them both. How could she choose? She couldn't choose; no woman should have to make such a decision. She hated her father even more for forcing her into this situation. She hated the chromosomes, the DNA, that he had contributed to her existence. He wasn't a father, he had never been a father. He was a monster.

"Give me your pistol." She heard the words, but the voice didn't sound at all like hers.

His head snapped around. "What?" He stared at her as if she had lost her mind.

"Give me the pistol," she repeated. "He—they—don't know we have it. You haven't fired back. I'll tuck it in the back of my jeans and walk out there—"

"The hell you will!" He glared at her. "If you think I—"

"No, listen!" she said urgently. "They won't shoot me. He wants me alive. When they get close enough for me to use the pistol I—"

"No!" He grabbed her by the shirt and hauled her close so they were almost nose to nose. His eyes were almost shooting sparks. "If you make one move to stand up, I swear I'll knock you out. Do you understand me? *I will not let you walk out there.*"

He released her, and Sunny sank back against the creek

bank. She couldn't overpower him, she thought bleakly. He was too strong, and too alert to be taken by surprise.

"We have to do something," she whispered.

He didn't look at her again. "We wait," he said flatly. "That's what we do. Sooner or later, the bastard will show himself."

Wait. That was the first idea she'd had, to wait until dark and slip away. But if Hauer had more than one man here, the sniper could keep them pinned down while the other worked his way around behind them—

"Can we move?" she asked. "Up the creek, down the creek—it doesn't matter."

He shook his head. "It's too risky. The creek's shallow. The only place we have enough cover is flat against the bank on this side. If we try to move, we expose ourselves to fire."

"What if there's more than one?"

"There is." He sounded positive. A feral grin moved his lips in a frightening expression. "At least four, maybe five. I hope it's five."

She shook her head, trying to understand. Five to two were deadly odds. "That makes you happy?"

"Very happy. The more the merrier."

Nausea hit the back of her throat, and she closed her eyes, fighting the urge to vomit. Did he think sheer guts and fighting spirit would keep them alive?

His lean, powerful hand touched her face in a gentle caress. "Chin up, sweetheart. Time's on our side."

Now wasn't the time for explanations, Chance thought. The questions would be too angry, the answers too long and complicated. Their situation was delicately balanced between success and catastrophe; he couldn't relax his guard. If he was correct and there were five men out there hunting them—and that was the only explanation, that one of his own men was a traitor and had given Hauer the location of their supposedly impromptu picnic—then they could, at any time, decide to catch him in a pincer movement. With only one pistol, and Sunny to one side of him, he couldn't handle an attack from more than two directions. The third one would get him—and probably Sunny, too. In a fire fight, bullets flew like angry hornets, and most of them didn't hit their target. If a bullet didn't hit its target, that meant it hit something—or someone—else.

His own men would have been stood down, or sent to a bogus location. That was why there hadn't been any return fire when he and Sunny were fired on—no one was there. For that to have happened, the traitor had to be someone in a position of authority, a team leader or higher. He would find out. Oh, yeah, he'd find out. There had been several betrayals over the years, but they hadn't been traceable. One such breach had almost cost Barrie, Zane's wife, her life. Chance had been trying to identify the bastard for four years now, but he'd been too smart. But this time it was traceable. This time, his men would know who had changed their orders.

The traitor must have thought it was worth blowing his cover, to have this opportunity to kill Chance Mackenzie himself. And he should be here in person, to see the job done. Hauer's two men would bring the count to three. Hauer made it four. The only way Hauer could have gotten into the country and moved about as freely and undetected as he had was with inside help—the FBI mole. If Chance were really lucky, the mole was here, too, bringing the count to five.

But they'd made a big mistake. They didn't know about his ace in the hole: Zane. They didn't know he was out there; that was an arrangement Chance had made totally off the record. If Zane wasn't needed, no one would ever know he was there. Chance's men were damn good, world class, but they weren't in Zane's class. No one was.

Zane was a superb strategist; he always had a plan, and a plan to back up his plan. He would have seen in an instant what was going down and been on the phone calling the men back into position from wherever they'd been sent. How long it took them to get here depended on how far away they were, assuming they could get here at all. And after the call Zane would have started moving, ghosting around, searching out Hauer and his men. Every minute that passed increased the odds in Chance's favor.

He couldn't explain any of that to Sunny, not now, not even to ease the white, pinched expression that made him ache to hold her close and reassure her. Her eyes were haunted, their sparkle gone. She had worked her entire life to make certain she was never caught off guard, and yet she had been; he himself had seen to it.

The knowledge was bitter in his mouth. She was terrified of the monster who had relentlessly hunted her all her life, yet she had been willing to walk out there and offer herself as a sacrifice. How many times in the short two weeks he'd known her had she put herself on the line for him? The first time had been when she barely knew him, when she swooped down to grab the snake coiled so close to his feet. She was terrified of snakes, but she'd done it. She was shaking with fear now, but he knew that if he let her, she would do exactly what she'd offered. That kind of courage amazed him, and humbled him.

His head swiveled restlessly as he tried to keep watch in all directions. The minutes trickled past. The sun slid below the horizon, but there was still plenty of light; twilight wouldn't begin deepening for another fifteen, twenty minutes. The darker it was, the more Zane was in his element. By now, he should have taken out at least one, maybe two—

A man stepped out from behind the tree under which Chance and Sunny had intended to have their picnic and aimed a black 9mm automatic at Sunny's head. He didn't say "Drop it" or anything else. He just smiled, his gaze locked with Chance's.

Carefully Chance placed his pistol on the grass. If the gun had been aimed at his own head, he would have taken the risk that his reflexes were faster. He wouldn't risk Sunny's life. As soon as he moved his hand away from the pistol, the black hole in the man's weapon centered between his eyes.

"Surprised?" the man asked softly. At his voice Sunny gasped and whirled, her feet sliding on the slippery creek bottom. Chance reached out and steadied her without taking his gaze from a man he knew very well.

"Not really," he said. "I knew there was someone."

Sunny looked back and forth between them. "Do you *know* him?" she asked faintly.

"Yeah." He should have been prepared for this, he thought. Knowing one of his own men was involved, he should have realized the traitor would have the skill to approach silently, using the same tree that helped shield them as his own cover. Doing so took patience and nerve, because if Chance had happened to move even a few inches to one side, he would have seen the man's approach.

"H-how?" she stammered.

"We've worked together for years," Melvin Darnell said, still smiling. Mel the Man. That was what the others called him, because he would volunteer for any mission, no matter how dangerous. What better way to get inside information? Chance thought.

"You sold out to Hauer," Chance said, shaking his head. "That's low."

"No, that's lucrative. He has men everywhere. The FBI, the Justice Department, the CIA…even here, right under your nose." Mel shrugged. "What can I say? He pays well."

"I misjudged you. I never thought you'd be the type to get a kick out of torture. Or are you chickening out and leaving as soon as he gets his hands on her?" Chance nodded his head toward Sunny.

"Nice try, Mackenzie, but it won't work. He's her father. All he wants is his little girl." Mel smirked at Sunny.

Chance snorted. "Get a clue. Do you think she'd be so terrified if all he wanted was to get to know her?"

Mel spared another brief glance in her direction. She was absolutely colorless, even her lips. There was no mistaking her fear. He shrugged. "So I was wrong. I don't care what he does with her."

"Do you care that he's a child molester?" Keep him talking. Buy time. Give Zane time to work.

"Give it up," Mel said cheerfully. "He could be Hitler's reincarnation and it still wouldn't change the color of his money. If you think I'm going to develop a conscience— well, you're the one who needs to get a clue."

There was movement behind Mel. Three men approaching, walking openly now, as if they had nothing to fear. Two were dressed in suits, one in slacks and an open-necked shirt. The one in slacks and one of the suits carried hand guns. The suit would be the FBI informant, the one in slacks one of Hauer's bloodhounds. The man in the middle, the one wearing the double-breasted Italian silk suit, his skin tanned, his light brown hair brushed straight back—that was Hauer. He was smiling.

"My dear," he said jovially when he reached them. He stepped carefully around the spilled beets, his nose wrinkling in distaste. "It is so good to finally meet you. A father should know his children, don't you think?"

Sunny didn't speak for a moment. She stared at her father with unconcealed horror and loathing. Beside her, Chance felt the fear drain out of her, felt her subtly relax. Extreme terror was like that, sometimes. When one feared that something would happen, it was the dread and anxiety, the anticipation, that was so crippling. Once the thing actually happened, there was nothing left to fear. He took a firm grip on her arm, wishing she had remained petrified. Sunny was valiant enough when she was frightened; when she thought she had nothing left to lose, there was no telling what she would do.

"I thought you'd be taller," she finally said, looking at him rather dismissively.

Crispin Hauer flushed angrily. He wasn't a large man, about five-eight, and slender. The two men flanking him were both taller. Chance wondered how Sunny had known unerringly how to prick his ego. "Please get out of the mud—if you can bring yourself to leave your lover's side, that is. I recommend it. Head shots can be nasty. You wouldn't want his brains on you, would you? I hear the stain never comes out of one's clothes."

Sunny didn't move. "I don't know where Margreta is," she said. "You might as well kill me now, because I can't tell you anything."

He shook his head in mock sympathy. "As if I believe that." He held out his hand. "You may climb out by yourself, or my men will assist you."

There wasn't much light left, Chance thought. If Sunny could keep delaying her father without provoking him into violence, Zane should be here soon. With Hauer out in the open, Zane must be positioning himself so he could get all four men in his sights.

"Where's the other guy?" he asked, to distract them. "There *are* five of you, aren't there?"

The FBI man and the bloodhound looked around, in the direction of the trees on the opposite side of the road. They seemed vaguely surprised that no one was behind them.

Mel didn't take his attention from Chance. "Don't let him spook you," he said sharply. "Keep your mind on business."

"Don't you wonder where he is?" Chance asked softly.

"I don't give a damn. He's nothing to me. Maybe he fell out of the tree and broke his neck," Mel said.

"Enough," Hauer said, distaste for this squabbling evident in his tone. "Sonia, come out now. I promise you won't like it if my men have to fetch you."

Sunny's contemptuous gaze swept him from head to foot. Unbelievably, she began singing. And the ditty she sang was a cruel little song of the sort gradeschoolers sang to make fun of a classmate they didn't like. "Monkey man, monkey man, itty bitty monkey man. He's so ugly, he's so short, he needs a ladder to reach his butt."

It didn't rhyme, Chance thought in stunned bemusement. Children, crude little beasts that they were, didn't care about niceties such as that. All they cared about was the effectiveness of their taunt.

It was effective beyond his wildest expectation.

Mel Darnell smothered a laugh. The two other men froze, their expressions going carefully blank. Crispin Hauer flushed a dark, purplish red and his eyes bulged until white showed all around the irises. "You bitch!" he screamed, spittle flying, and he grabbed for the gun in the FBI mole's hand.

A giant red flower bloomed on Hauer's chest, accompanied by a strange, dull splat. Hauer stopped as if he had run into a glass wall, his expression going blank.

Mel had excellent reflexes, and excellent training. In that nanosecond before the sound of the shot reached them, Chance saw Mel's finger begin tightening on the trigger, and he grabbed for his own weapon, knowing he wouldn't be fast enough. Then Sunny hit him full force, her entire body crashing into him and knocking him sideways, her scream almost drowning out the thunderous boom of Mel's big-caliber pistol. She clambered off him almost as fast as she had hit him, trying to scramble up the grassy bank to get to Mel before he could fire another round, but Mel never had another opportunity to pull the trigger. Mel never had anything else, not even a second, because Zane's second shot took him dead center of the chest just as his first had taken Hauer.

Then all hell broke loose. Chance's men, finally back in position and with the threat to Chance and Sunny taken care of, opened fire on the remaining two men. Chance grabbed Sunny and flattened her in the creek again, covering her with his own body, holding her there until Zane roared a cease fire and the night was silent.

SUNNY SAT OFF to the side of the nightmarish scene, brightly lit now with battery-operated spotlights that picked out garish detail and left stark black shadows. From somewhere, one of the small army of men who suddenly swarmed the field had produced a bucket that he turned upside down for her, providing her with a seat. She was wet and almost unbearably cold, despite the warmth of the late August night. Her muddy clothes were clammy, so the blanket she clutched around her with nerveless fingers didn't do much to help, but she didn't release it.

She hurt, with an all-consuming agony that threatened to topple her off the bucket, but she grimly forced herself to stay upright. Sheer willpower kept her on that bucket.

The men around her were professionals. They were quiet and competent as they dealt with the five bodies that were laid out on the ground in a neat row. They were courteous with the local law enforcement officers who arrived *en force,* sirens blasting, blue lights strobing the night, though there was never any doubt who held jurisdiction.

And Chance was their leader.

That man, the one who had first held a gun on them, had called him "Mackenzie." And several times one or another of the locals had referred to him as Mr. Mackenzie; he had answered, so she knew there was no mistake in the name.

The events of the night were a chaotic blur in her mind, but one fact stood out: this entire scene was a setup, a trap—and she had been the bait.

She didn't want to believe it, but logic wouldn't let her deny it. He was obviously in charge here. He had a lot of men on site, men he commanded, men who could be here only if he had arranged it in advance.

Viewed in the light of that knowledge, everything that had happened since she met him took on a different meaning. She even thought she recognized the cretin who had stolen her briefcase in the Salt Lake City airport. He was cleaned up now, with the same quiet, competent air as the others, but she was fairly certain he was the same man.

Everything had been a setup. Everything. She didn't know how he'd done it, her mind couldn't quite grasp the sphere of influence needed to bring all of this off, but somehow he had manipulated her flights so that she was in the Salt Lake City airport at a certain time, for the cretin to grab her briefcase and Chance to intercept him. It was a hugely elaborate play, one that took skill and money and more resources than she could imagine.

He must have thought she was in cahoots with her father, she thought with a flash of intuition. This had all happened after the incident in Chicago, which was undoubtedly what had brought her to Chance's notice. What had his plan been? To make her fall in love with him and use her to infiltrate her father's organization? Only it hadn't worked out that way. Not only was she not involved with her father, she desperately feared and hated him. So Chance, knowing why Hauer really wanted her, had adjusted his plan and used her as bait.

What a masterful strategy. And what a superb actor he was; he should get an Oscar.

There hadn't been anything wrong with the plane at all. She didn't miss the significance of the timing of their "rescue." Charlie Jones had just happened to find them first thing in the morning after she spilled her guts about her father to Chance the night before. He must have signaled Charlie somehow.

How easy she had been for him. She had been completely duped, completely taken in by his lovemaking and charm. He had been a bright light to her, a comet blazing into her lonely world, and she had fallen for him with scarcely a whisper of resistance. He must think her the most gullible fool in the world. The worst of it was, she was an even bigger fool than he knew, because she was pregnant with his child.

She looked across the field at him, standing tall in the glaring spotlights as he talked with another tall, powerful man who exuded the deadliest air she had ever seen, and the pain inside her spread until she could barely contain it.

Her bright light had gone out.

CHANCE LOOKED AROUND at Sunny, as he had been doing periodically since the moment she sank down on the overturned bucket and huddled deep in the blanket someone had draped around her. She was frighteningly white, her face drawn and stark. He couldn't take the time to comfort her, not now. There was too much to do, local authorities to soothe at the same time that he let them know he was the one in control, not they, the bodies to be handled, sweeps initiated at the agencies Mel had listed as having Hauer's moles employed there.

She wasn't stupid; far from it. He had watched her watching the activity around her, watched her expression become even more drawn as she inevitably reached the only conclusion she *could* reach. She had noticed when people called him Mackenzie instead of McCall.

Their gazes met, and locked. She stared at him across the ten yards that separated them, thirty feet of unbridgeable gulf. He kept his face impassive. There was no excuse he could give her that she wouldn't already have considered. His reasons were good; he knew that. But he had used her and risked her life. Being the person she was, she would easily forgive him for risking her life; it was the rest of it, the way he had used her, that would strike her to the core.

As he watched, he saw the light die in her eyes, draining away as if it had never been. She turned her head away from him—

And gutted him with the gesture.

Shaken, pierced through with regret, he turned back to Zane and found his brother watching him with a world of knowledge in those pale eyes. "If you want her," Zane said, "then don't let her go."

It was that simple, and that difficult. Don't let her go. How could he not, when she deserved so much better than what he was?

But the idea was there now. Don't let her go. He couldn't resist looking at her again, to see if she was still watching him.

She wasn't there. The bucket still sat there, but Sunny was gone.

Chance strode rapidly across to where she had been, scanning the knots of men who stood about, some working, some just observing. He didn't see that bright hair. Damn it, she was just here; how could she disappear so fast?

Easily, he thought. She had spent a lifetime practicing.

Zane was beside him, his head up, alert. The damn spotlights blinded them to whatever was behind them. She could have gone in any direction, and they wouldn't be able to see her.

He looked down to see if he could pick up any tracks, though the grass was so trampled by now that he doubted he would find anything. The bucket gleamed dark and wet in the spotlight.

Wet?

Chance leaned down and swiped his hand over the bucket. He stared at the dark red stain on his fingers and palm. Blood. Sunny's blood.

He felt as if his own blood was draining from his body. My God, she'd been shot, and she hadn't said a word. In the darkness, the blood hadn't been noticeable on her wet clothing. But that had been…how long ago? She had sat there all that time, bleeding, and not told anyone.

Why?

Because she wanted to get away from him. If they had known she was wounded, she would have to be bundled up and taken to a hospital, and she wouldn't be able to escape without having to see him again. When Sunny walked, she did it clean. No scenes, no excuses, no explanations. She just disappeared.

If he had thought it hurt when she turned away from him, that was nothing to the way he felt now. Desperate fear seized his heart, froze his blood in his veins. "Listen up!" he boomed, and a score of faces, trained to obey his every command, turned his way. "Did anyone see where Sunny went?"

Heads shook, and men began looking around. She was nowhere in sight.

Chance began spitting out orders. "Everyone drop what you're doing and fan out. Find her. She's bleeding. She was shot and didn't tell anyone." As he talked, he was striding out of the glare of the spotlights, his heart in his mouth. She couldn't have gone far, not in that length of time. He would find her. He couldn't bear the alternative.

CHAPTER FOURTEEN

CHANCE BLINDLY PACED the corridor outside the surgical waiting room. He couldn't sit down, though the room was empty and he could have had any chair he wanted. If he stopped walking, he thought, he might very well fall down and not be able to stand again. He hadn't known such crippling fear existed. He had never felt it for himself, not even when he looked down the barrel of a weapon pointed at his face—and Mel's hadn't been the first—but he felt it for Sunny. He'd been gripped by it since he found her lying facedown in the grassy field, unconscious, her pulse thready from blood loss.

Thank God there were medics on hand in the field, or she would have died before he could get her to a hospital. They hadn't managed to stop the bleeding, but they had slowed it, started an IV saline push to pump fluid back into her body and raise her plummeting blood pressure, and gotten her to the hospital still alive.

He had been shouldered aside then, by a whole team of gowned emergency personnel. "Are you any relation to her, sir?" a nurse had asked briskly as she all but manhandled him out of the treatment room.

"I'm her husband," he'd heard himself say. There was no way he was going to allow the decisions for her care to be taken out of his hands. Zane, who had been beside him the entire time, hadn't revealed even a flicker of surprise.

"Do you know her blood type, sir?"

Of course he didn't. Nor did he know the answers to any of the other questions posed by the woman they handed him off to, but he was so numb, his attention so focused on the cubicle where about ten people were working on her, that he barely knew anyone was asking the questions, and the woman hadn't pushed it. Instead, she had patted his hand and said she would come back in a little while when his wife was stabilized. He had been grateful for her optimism. In the meantime, Zane, as ruthlessly competent as usual, had requested that a copy of their file on Sunny be downloaded to his wireless Pocket Pro, so Chance would have all the necessary information when the woman returned with her million and one questions. He was indifferent to the bureaucratic snafu he was causing; the organization would pay for everything.

But the shocks had kept arriving, one piling on top of the other. The surgeon came out of the cubicle, his green paper gown stained red with her blood. "Your wife regained consciousness briefly," he'd said. "She wasn't completely lucid, but she asked about the baby. Do you know how far along she is?"

Chance had literally staggered and braced his hand against the wall for support. "She's pregnant?" he asked hoarsely.

"I see." The surgeon immediately switched gears. "I think she must have just found out. We'll do some tests and take all the precautions we can. We're taking her up to surgery now. A nurse will show you where to wait." He strode away, paper gown flapping.

Zane had turned to Chance, his pale blue eyes laser sharp. "Yours?" he asked briefly.

"Yes."

Zane didn't ask if he was certain, for which Chance

was grateful. Zane took it for granted Chance wouldn't be mistaken about something that important.

Pregnant? How? He pinched the bridge of his nose, between his eyes. He knew how. He remembered with excruciating clarity how it felt to climax inside her without the protective sheath of a condom dulling the sensation. It had happened twice—just twice—but once was enough.

A couple of little details clicked into place. He'd been around pregnant women most of his life, with first one sister-in-law and then another producing a little Mackenzie. He knew the symptoms well. He remembered Sunny's sleepiness this afternoon, and her insistence on buying the beets. Those damn pickled beets, he thought; her craving for them—for he was certain now that was why she'd wanted them—had saved his life. Sometimes the weird cravings started almost immediately. He could remember when Shea, Michael's wife, had practically wiped that section of Wyoming clean of canned tuna, a full week before she missed her first period. The sleepiness began soon in a pregnancy, too.

He knew the exact day when he'd gotten her pregnant. It had been the second time he'd made love to her, lying on the blanket in the late afternoon heat. The baby would be born about the middle of May...if Sunny lived.

She had to live. He couldn't face the alternative. He loved her too damn much to even think it. But he had seen the bullet wound in her right side, and he was terrified.

"Do you want me to call Mom and Dad?" Zane asked.

They would drop everything and come immediately if he said yes, Chance knew. The whole family would; the hospital would be inundated with Mackenzies. Their support was total, and unquestioning.

He shook his head. "No. Not yet." His voice was raw, as if he had been screaming, though he would have sworn all his screams had been held inside. If Sunny…if the worst happened, he would need them then. Right now he was still holding together. Just.

So he walked, and Zane walked with him. Zane had seen a lot of bullet wounds, too; he'd taken his share. Chance was the lucky one; he'd been cut a few times, but never shot.

God, there had been so much blood. How had she stayed upright for so long? She had answered questions, said she was all right, even walked around a little before one of the men had found that bucket for her to sit on. It was dark, she had a blanket wrapped around her—that was why no one had noticed. But she should have been on the ground, screaming in pain.

Zane's thoughts were running along the same path. "I'm always amazed," he said, "at what some people can do after being shot."

Contrary to what most people thought, a bullet wound, even a fatal one, didn't necessarily knock the victim down. All cops knew that even someone whose heart had been virtually destroyed by a bullet could still attack and kill *them,* and die only when his oxygen-starved brain died. Someone crazed on drugs could absorb a truly astonishing amount of damage and keep on fighting. On the other side of the spectrum were those who suffered relatively minor wounds and went down as if they had been poleaxed, then screamed unceasingly until they reached the hospital and were given enough drugs to quiet them. It was pure mind over matter, and Sunny had a will like titanium. He only hoped she applied that will to surviving.

It was almost six hours before the tired surgeon approached, the six longest hours of Chance's life. The surgeon looked haggard, and Chance felt the icy claw of dread. No. No—

"I think she's going to make it," the surgeon said, and smiled a smile of such pure personal triumph that Chance knew there had been a real battle in the O.R. "I had to remove part of the liver and resection her small intestine. The wound to the liver is what caused the extensive hemorrhage. We had to replace almost her complete blood volume before we got things under control." He rubbed his hand over his face. "It was touch and go for a while. Her blood pressure bottomed out and she went into cardiac arrest, but we got her right back. Her pupil response is normal, and her vitals are satisfactory. She was lucky."

"Lucky," Chance echoed, still dazed by the combination of good news and the litany of damage.

"It was only a fragment of a bullet that hit her. There must have been a ricochet."

Chance knew she hadn't been hit while he'd had her flattened in the creek. It had to have happened when she knocked him aside and Darnell fired. Evidently Darnell had missed, and the bullet must have struck a rock in the creek and fragmented.

She had been protecting him. Again.

"She'll be in ICU for at least twenty-four hours, maybe forty-eight, until we see if there's a secondary infection. I really think we have things under control, though." He grinned. "She'll be out of here in a week."

Chance sagged against the wall, bending over to clasp his knees. His head swam. Zane's hard hand gripped his shoulder, lending his support. "Thank you," Chance said to the doctor, angling his head so he could see him.

"Do you need to lie down?" the doctor asked.

"No, I'm all right. God! I'm great. She's going to be okay!"

"Yeah," said the doctor, and grinned again.

SUNNY KEPT SURFACING to consciousness, like a float bobbing up and down in the water. At first her awareness was fragmented. She could hear voices in the distance, though she couldn't make out any words, and a soft beeping noise. She was also aware of something in her throat, though she didn't realize it was a tube. She had no concept of where she was, or even that she was lying down.

The next time she bobbed up, she could feel smooth cotton beneath her and recognized the fabric as sheets.

The next time she managed to open her eyes a slit, but her vision was blurry and what seemed like a mountain of machinery made no sense to her.

At some point she realized she was in a hospital. There was pain, but it was at a distance. The tube was gone from her throat now. She vaguely remembered it being removed, which hadn't been pleasant, but her sense of time was so confused that she thought she remembered the tube being there after it was removed. People kept coming into the small space that was hers, turning on bright lights, talking and touching her and doing intimate things to her.

Gradually her dominion over her body began to return, as she fought off the effects of anesthesia and drugs. She managed to make a weak gesture toward her belly, and croak out a single word. "Baby?"

The intensive care nurse understood. "Your baby's fine," he said, giving her a comforting pat, and she was content.

She was horribly thirsty. Her next word was "Water," and slivers of ice were put in her mouth.

With the return of consciousness, though, came the pain. It crept ever nearer as the fog of drugs receded. The pain was bad, but Sunny almost welcomed it, because it meant she was alive, and for a while she had thought she might not be.

She saw the nurse named Jerry the most often. He came into the cubicle, smiling as usual, and said, "There's someone here to see you."

Sunny violently shook her head, which was a mistake. It set off waves of agony that swamped the drugs holding them at bay. "No visitors," she managed to say.

It seemed as if she spent days, eons, in the intensive care unit, but when she asked Jerry he said, "Oh, about thirty-six hours. We'll be moving you to a private room soon. It's being readied now."

When they moved her, she was clearheaded enough to watch the ceiling tiles and lights pass by overhead. She caught a glimpse of a tall, black-haired man and quickly looked away.

Settling her into a private room was quite an operation, requiring two orderlies, three nurses and half an hour. She was exhausted when everything, including herself, had been transferred and arranged. The fresh bed was nice and cool; the head had been elevated and a pillow tucked under her head. Sitting up even that much made her feel a hundred percent more normal and in control.

There were flowers in the room. Roses, peach ones, with a hint of blush along the edges of their petals, dispensed a spicy, peppery scent that overcame the hospital scents of antiseptics and cleaning fluids. Sunny stared at them but didn't ask who they were from.

"I don't want any visitors," she told the nurses. "I just want to rest."

She was allowed to eat Jell-O, and drink weak tea. On the second day in the private room she drank some broth, and she was placed in the bedside chair for fifteen minutes. It felt good to stand on her own two feet, even for the few seconds it took them to move her from bed to chair. It felt even better when they moved her back to the bed.

That night, she got out of bed herself, though the process was slow and unhappy, and walked the length of the bed. She had to hold on to the bed for support, but her legs remained under her.

The third day, there was another delivery from a florist. This was a bromeliad, with thick, grayish green leaves and a beautiful pink flower blooming in its center. She had never had houseplants for the same reason she had never had a pet, because she was constantly on the move and couldn't take care of them. She stared at the bromeliad, trying to come to grips with the fact that she could have all the houseplants she wanted now. Everything was changed. Crispin Hauer was dead, and she and Margreta were free.

The thought of her sister sent alarm racing through her. What day was it? When was Margreta due to call? For that matter, where was her cell phone?

On the afternoon of the fourth day, the door opened and Chance walked in.

She turned her head to look out the window. In truth, she was surprised he had given her this long to recover. She had held him off as long as she could, but she supposed there had to be a closing act before the curtain could fall.

She had held her inner pain at bay by focusing on her physical pain, but now it rushed to the forefront. She fought it down, reaching for control. There was nothing to be gained by causing a scene, only her self-respect to lose.

"I've kept your cell phone with me," he said, walking around to place himself between her and the windows, so she had to either look at him or turn her head away again. His conversational opening had guaranteed she wouldn't turn away. "Margreta called yesterday."

Sunny clenched her fists, then quickly relaxed her right hand as the motion flexed the IV needle taped to the back of it. Margreta would have panicked when she heard a man's voice answer instead of Sunny's.

"I talked fast," Chance said. "I told her you'd been shot but would be okay, and that Hauer was dead. I told her I'd bring the phone to you today, and she could call again tonight to verify everything I said. She didn't say anything, but she didn't hang up on me, either."

"Thank you," Sunny said. He had handled the situation in the best possible way.

He was subtly different, she realized. It wasn't just his clothing, though he was now dressed in black slacks and a white silk shirt, while he had worn only jeans, boots and casual shirts and T-shirts before. His whole demeanor was different. Of course, he wasn't playing a raffish, charming charter pilot any longer. He was himself now, and the reality was what she had always sensed beneath the surface of his charm. He was the man who led some sort of commando team, who exerted enormous influence in getting things done his way. The dangerous edge she had only glimpsed before was in full view now, in his eyes and the authority with which he spoke.

He moved closer to the side of the bed, so close he was leaning against the rail. Very gently, the touch as light as gossamer, he placed his fingertips on her belly. "Our baby is all right," he said.

He knew. Shocked, she stared at him, though she realized she should have known the doctor would tell him.

"Were you going to tell me?" he asked, his golden-brown eyes intent on her face, as if he wanted to catch every nuance of expression.

"I hadn't thought about it one way or the other," she said honestly. She had just been coming to terms with the knowledge herself; she hadn't gotten around to forming any plans.

"This changes things."

"Does it really," she said, and it wasn't a question. "Was *anything* you told me the truth?"

He hesitated. "No."

"There was nothing wrong with the fuel pump."

"No."

"You could have flown us out of the canyon at any time."

"Yes."

"Your name isn't Chance McCall."

"Mackenzie," he said. "Chance Mackenzie."

"Well, that's one thing," she said bitterly. "At least your first name was really your own."

"Sunny…don't."

"Don't what? Don't try to find out how big a fool I am? Were you really an army ranger?"

He sighed, his expression grim. "Navy. Naval Intelligence."

"You arranged for all of my flights to be fouled up that day."

He shrugged an admittance.

"The cretin was really one of your men."

"A good one. The airport security people were mine, too."

She creased the sheet with her left hand. "You knew my father would be there. You had it set up."

"We knew two of his men were trailing us, had been since the television newscast about you aired."

"You arranged that, too."

He didn't say anything.

"Why did we fly all over the country? Why didn't we just stay in Seattle? That would have been less wear and tear on the plane."

"I had to make it look good."

She swallowed. "That day…the picnic. Would you have made love—I mean, had sex—with me with your men watching? Just to make it look good?"

"No. Having an affair with you was necessary, but… private."

"I suppose I should thank you for that, at least. Thank you. Now get out."

"I'm not going anywhere." He sat down in the bedside chair. "If you've finished with the dissection, we need to make some decisions."

"I've already made one. I don't want to see you again."

"Sorry about that, but you aren't getting your wish. You're stuck with me, sweetheart, because that baby inside you is mine."

CHAPTER FIFTEEN

SUNNY WAS RELEASED from the hospital eight days after the shooting. She could walk, gingerly, but her strength was almost negligible, and she had to wear the nightgown and robe Chance had bought her, because she couldn't stand any clothing around her middle. She had no idea what she was going to do. She wasn't in any condition to catch a flight to Atlanta, not to mention that she would have to travel in her nightgown, but she had to find somewhere to stay. Once she knew she was being released, she got the phone book and called a hotel, made certain the hotel had room service and booked herself a room there. The hotel had room service; until she was able to take care of herself again, a hotel was the best she could do.

In the hospital she had, at first, entertained a fragile hope that Margreta would come to stay with her and help her until she was recovered. With their father dead, they didn't have to hide any longer. But though Margreta had sounded happy and relieved, she had resisted Sunny's suggestion that she come to Des Moines. They had exchanged telephone numbers, but that was all—and Margreta hadn't called back.

Sunny understood. Margreta would always have problems relating to people, forming relationships with them. She was probably very comfortable with the long-distance contact she had with Sunny, and wanted nothing more. Sunny tried to fight her sadness as she realized she would never have the sister she had wanted, but melancholy too easily overwhelmed her these days.

Part of it was the hormonal chaos of early pregnancy, she knew. She found herself tearing up at the most ridiculous things, such as a gardening show she watched on television one day. She lay in her hospital bed and began thinking how she had always wanted a flower garden but had never been able to have one, and presto, all of a sudden she was feeling sorry for herself and sitting there like an idiot with tears rolling down her face.

Depression went hand in glove with physical recovery, too, one of the nurses told her. It would pass as she got stronger and could do more.

But the biggest part of her depression was Chance. He visited every day, and once even brought along the tall, lethal-looking man she had noticed him talking to the night she was injured. To her surprise, Chance introduced the man as his brother, Zane. Zane had shaken her hand with exquisite gentleness, shown her photos of his pretty wife and three adorable children, and spent half an hour telling her yarns about the exploits of his daughter, Nick. If even half of what he said about the child was true, the world had better brace itself for when she was older.

After Zane left, Sunny was even more depressed. Zane had what she had always wanted: a family he loved, and who loved him in return.

When he visited, Chance always avoided the subject that lay between them like a coiled snake. He had done what he had done, and no amount of talking would change reality. She had to respect, reluctantly, his lack of any attempt to make excuses. Instead, he talked about his family in Wyoming, and the mountain they all still called home, even though only his parents lived there now. He had four brothers and one sister, a dozen nephews—and one niece, the notorious Nick, whom he obviously adored. His sister was a horse trainer, who was married to one of his agents; one brother was a rancher who had married the grand-daughter of an old family enemy; another brother was an ex-fighter pilot who was married to an orthopedic surgeon; Zane was married to the daughter of an ambassador; and Joe, his oldest brother, was General Joseph Mackenzie, chairman of the Joint Chiefs of Staff.

That couldn't all be true, she thought, yet the tales had a ring of truth to them. Then she remembered that Chance was a consummate actor, and bitterness would swamp her again.

She couldn't seem to pull herself out of the dismals. She had always been able to laugh, but now she found it difficult to even smile. No matter how she tried to distract herself, the knowledge was always there, engraved on her heart like a curse that robbed her life of joy: Chance didn't love her. It had all been an act.

It was as if part of her had died. She felt cold inside, and empty. She tried to hide it, tried to tell herself the depression would go away if she just ignored it and concentrated on getting better, but every day the grayness inside her seemed to spread and deepen.

The day she was released, the escort finally arrived with a wheelchair and Sunny called a taxi to meet them at the entrance in fifteen minutes. She gingerly lowered herself into the wheelchair, and the escort obligingly placed the small bag containing her few articles of clothing and her backpack on her lap, then balanced the bromeliad on top.

"I'm sure I have to sign some papers before I'm released," Sunny said.

"No, I don't think so," the woman said, checking her orders. "According to this, you're all ready to go. Your husband probably handled it for you."

Sunny bit back the urge to snap that she wasn't married. He hadn't mentioned it, and in truth she hadn't given a thought to how she would pay for her hospital care, but now that she thought about it, she realized Chance had indeed handled all of that. Maybe he thought the least he could do was pick up her tab.

She was surprised he wasn't here, since he'd been so adamant about being a part of the baby's life, and persistent in visiting. For all she knew, she thought, he had been called away on some mysterious spy stuff.

She underestimated him. When the escort rolled her to the doors of the patient discharge area, she saw a familiar dark green Ford Explorer parked under the covered entrance. Chance unfolded his long length from behind the steering wheel and came to meet her.

"I've already called a taxi," she said, though she knew it was a waste of breath.

"Tough," he said succinctly. He took her clothes and the bromeliad and put them in the back of the Explorer, then opened the passenger door.

Sunny began to inch herself forward in the wheelchair seat, preparatory to standing; she had mastered the art when seated in a regular chair, but a wheelchair was trickier. Chance gave her an exasperated look, then leaned down and scooped her up in his powerful arms, handling her weight with ease as he deposited her in the Explorer.

"Thank you," she said politely. She would at least be civil, and his method had been much less painful and time-consuming than hers.

"You're welcome." He buckled the seat belt around her, making certain the straps didn't rub against the surgical incision, then closed the door and walked around to slide under the steering wheel.

"I've booked a room in a hotel," she said. "But I don't know where it is, so I can't give you directions."

"You aren't going to a hotel," he growled.

"I have to go somewhere," she pointed out. "I'm not able to drive, and I can't handle negotiating an airport, so a hotel with room service is the only logical solution."

"No it isn't. I'm taking you home with me."

"No!" she said violently, everything in her rejecting the idea of spending days in his company.

His jaw set. "You don't have a choice," he said grimly. "You're going—even if you kick and scream the whole way."

It was tempting. Oh, it was tempting. Only the thought of how badly kicking would pull at the incision made her resist the idea.

The dime didn't drop until she noticed he was driving to the airport. "Where are we going?"

He gave her an impatient glance. "I told you. Hell, Sunny, you know I don't live in Des Moines."

"All right, so I know where you don't live. But I *don't* know where you *do* live." She couldn't resist adding, "And even if you had told me, it would probably be a lie."

This time his glance was sulfuric. "Wyoming," he said through gritted teeth. "I'm taking you home to Wyoming."

SHE WAS SILENT during the flight, speaking only when necessary and then only in monosyllables. Chance studied her when her attention was on the landscape below, his sunglasses hiding his eyes. They had flown around so much during the time they'd been together that it felt natural to once again be in the plane with her, as if they were where they belonged. She had settled in with a minimum of fussing and no complaints, though he knew she had to be exhausted and uncomfortable.

She looked so frail, as if a good wind would blow her away. There wasn't any color in her cheeks or lips, and she had dropped a good ten pounds that she didn't need to lose. The doctor had assured him that she was recovering nicely, right on schedule, and that while her pregnancy was still too new for any test to tell them anything about the baby's condition, they had taken all precautions and he had every confidence the baby would be fine.

As thrilled as he was about the baby, Chance was more worried that the pregnancy would sap her strength and slow her recovery. She needed all the resources she could muster now, but nature would ensure that the developing child got what it needed first. The only way he could be confident she was getting what *she* needed was if he arranged for her to be watched every minute, and coddled and spoiled within an inch of her life. The best place for that was Mackenzie's Mountain.

He had called and told them he was bringing Sunny there, of course. He had told them the entire situation, that she was pregnant and he intended to marry her, but that she was still mad as hell at him and hadn't forgiven him. He had set quite a task for himself, getting back in Sunny's good graces. But once he had her on the mountain, he thought, he could take his time wearing her down.

Mary, typically, was ecstatic. She took it for granted Sunny would forgive him, and since she had been prodding him about getting married and giving her more grandchildren, she probably thought she was getting everything she wanted.

Chance was going to do everything he could to see that she did, because what she wanted was exactly what he wanted. He'd always sworn he would never get married and have children, but fate had stepped in and arranged things otherwise. The prospect of getting married scared him—no, it terrified the hell out of him, so much so that he hadn't even broached the subject to Sunny. He didn't know how to tell her what she needed to know about him, and he didn't know what she would do when she found out, if she would accept his proposal or tell him to drop dead.

The only thing that gave him hope was that she'd said she loved him. She hadn't said it since she found out how he'd set her up, but Sunny wasn't a woman who loved lightly. If there was a spark of love left in her, if he hadn't totally extinguished it, he would find a way to fan it to life.

He landed at the airstrip on Zane's property, and his heart gave a hard thump when he saw what was waiting for them. Even Sunny's interest was sparked. She sat up straighter, and for the first time since she'd been shot he saw a hint of that lively interest in her face. "What's going on?" she asked.

His spirits lifting, he grinned. "Looks like a welcoming party."

The entire Mackenzie clan was gathered by the airstrip. Everyone. Josh and Loren were there from Seattle with their three sons. Mike and Shea and their two boys. Zane and Barrie, each holding one of the twins. And there was Joe, decked out in his Air Force uniform with more rows of fruit salad on it than should be allowed. How he had carved time out of his schedule to come here, Chance didn't know—but then, Joe could do damn near anything he wanted, since he was the highest ranking military officer in the nation. Caroline, standing beside him and looking positively chic in turquoise capri pants and white sandals—and also looking damn good for her age—had probably had a harder time getting free. She was one of the top-ranked physicists in the world. Their five sons were with him, and John, the oldest, wasn't the only one this time who had a girlfriend with him. Maris and

Mac stood together; Mac had his arm draped protectively around Maris's slight frame. And Mom and Dad were in the middle of the whole gang, with Nick perched happily in Wolf's arms.

Every last one of them, even the babies, held a balloon.

"Oh, my," Sunny murmured. The corners of her pale mouth moved upward in the first smile he had seen in eight days.

He cut the motor and got out, then went to the other door and carefully lifted Sunny out. She was so bemused by the gathering that she put her arm around his neck.

That must have been the signal. Wolf leaned down and set Nick on her feet. She took off toward Chance like a shot, running and skipping and shrieking his name in the usual litany. "UncaDance, UncaDance, Unca*Dance!*" The balloon she was holding bobbed like a mad thing. The whole crowd started forward in her wake.

In seconds they were surrounded. He tried to introduce everyone to Sunny, but there was too much of a hubbub for him to complete a sentence. His sisters-in-law, bless them, were laughing and chattering as if they had known her for years; the men were flirting; Mary was beaming; and Nick's piping voice could be heard above everyone. "Dat's a weally, weally pwetty dwess." She fingered the silk robe and beamed up at Sunny.

John leaned down and whispered something in Nick's ear. *"Dress,"* she said, emphasizing the *r*. "Dat's a weally, weally pwetty *dress*."

Everyone cheered, and Nick glowed.

Sunny laughed.

Chance's heart jumped at the sound. His throat got tight, and he squeezed his eyes shut for a second. When he opened them, Mary had taken control.

"You must be exhausted," she was saying to Sunny in

her sweet, Southern-accented voice. "You don't have to worry about a thing, dear. I have a bed all ready for you at the house, and you can sleep as long as you want. Chance, carry her along to the car, and be careful with her."

"Yes, ma'am," he said.

"Wait!" Nick wailed suddenly. "I fordot de sign!"

"What sign?" Chance asked, gently shifting Sunny so he could look down at his niece.

She fished in the pocket of her little red shorts and pulled out a very crumpled piece of paper. She stretched up on her tiptoes to hand it to Sunny. "I did it all by myself," she said proudly. "Gamma helped."

Sunny unfolded the piece of paper.

"I used a wed cwayon," Nick informed her. "Because it's de pwettiest."

"It certainly is," Sunny agreed. She swallowed audibly. Chance looked down to see the paper shaking in her hand.

The letters were misshapen and wobbly and all different sizes. The little girl must have labored over them for a long time, with Mary's expert and patient aid, because the words were legible. "'Welcome home Sunny,'" Sunny read aloud. Her face began to crumple. "That's the most beautiful sign I've ever seen," she said, then buried her face against Chance's neck and burst into tears.

"Yep," Michael said. "She's pregnant, all right."

IT WAS DIFFICULT to say who fell more in love with whom, Sunny with the Mackenzies, or the Mackenzies with her. Once Chance placed her in the middle of the king-sized bed Mary had made up for her—he didn't tell her it was his old bedroom—Sunny settled in like a queen holding court. Instead of lying down to sleep, she propped herself up on pillows, and soon all of the women and most of the younger kids were in there, sitting on the bed and on the floor, some even in chairs. The twins were working their way from one side of the bed to the other and back again, clutching the covers for support and babbling away to each other in what Barrie called their "twin talk." Shea had Benjy down on the floor, tickling him, and every time she stopped he would shriek, "More! More!" Nick sat cross-legged on the bed, her "wed cwayon" in hand as she studiously worked on another sign. Since the first one had been such a resounding success, this one was for Barrie, and she was embellishing it with lopsided stars. Loren, being a doctor, wanted the details of Sunny's wound and present condition. Caroline was doing an impromptu fashion consultation, brushing Sunny's hair and swirling it on top of her head, with some very sexy tendrils curling loose on her slender neck. Maris, her dark eyes glowing, was telling Sunny all about her own pregnancy, and Mary was overseeing it all.

Leaving his family to do what they did best, weave a magic spell of warmth and belonging, Chance walked down to the barn. He felt edgy and worried and a little panicked, and he needed some peace and quiet. When everything quieted down tonight, he had to talk to Sunny. He couldn't put it off any longer. He prayed desperately that she could forgive him, that what he had to tell her didn't completely turn her against him, because he loved her so much he wasn't certain he could live without her. When she had buried her face against him and cried, his heart had almost stopped because she had turned *to* him instead of away from him.

She had laughed again. That sound was the sweetest sound he'd ever heard, and it had almost unmanned him. He couldn't imagine living without being able to hear her laugh.

He folded his arms across the top of a stall door and rested his head on them. She had to forgive him. She had to.

"It's tough, isn't it?" Wolf said in his deep voice, coming up to stand beside Chance and rest his arms on top of the stall door, too. "Loving a woman. And it's the best thing in the world."

"I never thought it would happen," Chance said, the words strained. "I was so careful. No marriage, no kids. It was going to end with me. But she blindsided me. I fell for her so fast I didn't have time to run."

Wolf straightened, his black eyes narrowed. "What do you mean, 'end with you'? Why don't you want kids? You love them."

"Yeah," Chance said softly. "But they're Mackenzies."

"You're a Mackenzie." There was steel in the deep voice.

Tiredly, Chance rubbed the back of his neck. "That's the problem. I'm not a real Mackenzie."

"Do you want to walk in the house and tell that little woman in there that you're not her son?" Wolf demanded sharply.

"*Hell*, no!" No way would he hurt her like that.

"You're my son. In all the ways that matter, you're mine."

The truth of that humbled Chance. He rested his head on his arms again. "I never could understand how you could take me in as easily as you did. You know what kind of life I led. You may not know the details, but you have a good general idea. I wasn't much more than a wild animal. Mom had no idea, but you did. And you still brought me into your home, trusted me to be around both Mom and Maris—"

"And that trust was justified, wasn't it?" Wolf asked.

"But it might not have been. You had no way of knowing." Chance paused, looking inward at the darkness inside him. "I killed a man when I was about ten, maybe eleven," he said flatly. "That's the wild kid you brought home with you. I stole, I lied, I attacked other kids and beat them up, then took whatever it was they had that I wanted. That's the kind of person I am. That kid will always live inside me."

Wolf gave him a sharp look. "If you had to kill a man when you were ten, I suspect the bastard deserved killing."

"Yeah, he deserved it. Kids who live in the street are fair game to perverts like that." He clenched his hands. "I have to tell Sunny. I can't ask her to marry me without her knowing what she'll be getting, what kind of genes I'll be passing on to her children." He gave a harsh laugh. "Except I don't know what kind of genes they are. I don't know what's in my background. For all I know my mother was a drugged-out whore and—"

"Stop right there," Wolf said, steel in his voice.

Chance looked up at him, the only father he had ever known, and the man he respected most in the world.

"I don't know who gave birth to you," Wolf said. "But I do know bloodlines, son, and you're a thoroughbred. Do you know what I regret most in my life? Not finding you until you were fourteen. Not feeling your hand holding my finger when you took your first step. Not getting up with you in the night when you were teething, or when you were sick. Not being able to hold you the way you needed holding, the way all kids need holding. By the time we got you I couldn't do any of that, because you were as skittish as a wild colt. You didn't like for us to touch you, and I tried to respect that.

"But one thing you need to know. I'm more proud of you than I've ever been of anything in my life, because you're one of the finest men I've ever known, and you had to work a lot harder than most to get to where you are. If

I could have had my pick of all the kids in the world to adopt, I still would have chosen you."

Chance stared at his father, his eyes wet. Wolf Mackenzie put his arms around his grown son and hugged him close, the way he had wanted to do all these years. "I would have chosen you," he said again.

CHANCE ENTERED THE bedroom and quietly closed the door behind him. The crowd had long since dispersed, most to their respective homes, some spending the night here or at Zane's or Michael's. Sunny looked tired, but there was a little color in her cheeks.

"How do you feel?" he asked softly.

"Exhausted," she said. She looked away from him. "Better."

He sat down beside her on the bed, taking care not to jostle her. "I have some things I need to tell you," he said.

"If it's an explanation, don't bother," she shot back. "You used me. Fine. But *damn* you, you didn't have to take it as far as you did! Do you know how it makes me feel that I was such a fool to fall in love with you, when all you were doing was playing a game? Did it stroke your ego—"

He put his hand across her mouth. Above his tanned fingers, her gray eyes sparked pure rage at him. He took a deep breath. "First and most important thing is: I love you. That wasn't a game. I started falling the minute I saw you. I tried to stop it but—" He shrugged that away and got back to the important part. "I love you so much I ache inside. I'm not good enough for you, and I know it—"

She swatted his hand aside, scowling at him. "What? I mean, I agree, after what you did, but—what do you mean?"

He took her hand and was relieved when she didn't pull away from him. "I'm adopted," he said. "That part's fine. It's the best. But I don't know who my biological parents are or anything about them. They—she—tossed me into the street and forgot about me. I grew up wild in the streets, and I mean literally in the streets. I don't remember ever having a home until I was about fourteen, when I was adopted. I could come from the trashiest people on the planet, and probably do, otherwise they wouldn't have left me to starve to death in the gutter. I want to spend the rest of my life with you, but if you marry me, you have to know what you'll be getting."

"What?" she said again, as if she couldn't understand what he was telling her.

"I should have asked you to marry me before," he said, getting it all out. "But—hell, how could I ask anyone to marry me? I'm a wild card. You don't know what you're getting with me. I was going to let you go, but then I found out about the baby and I couldn't do it. I'm selfish, Sunny. I want it all, you and our baby. If you think you can take the risk—"

She drew back, such an incredulous, outraged look on her face that he almost couldn't bear it. "I don't believe this," she sputtered, and slapped him across the face.

She wasn't back to full strength, but she still packed a wallop. Chance sat there, not even rubbing his stinging jaw. His heart was shriveling inside him. If she wanted to hit him again, he figured he deserved it.

"You fool!" she shouted. "For God's sake, my father was a *terrorist!* That's the heritage *I'm* carrying around, and you're worried because you *don't know who your parents were?* I wish to hell I didn't know who my father was! I don't believe this! I thought you didn't love me! Everything would have been all right if I'd known you love me!"

Chance uttered a startled, profound curse, one of Nick's really, really bad words. Put in those terms, it did sound incredibly trivial. He stared at her lovely, outraged face, and the weight lifted off his chest as if it had never been. Suddenly he wanted to laugh. "I love you so much I'm half crazy with it. So, will you marry me?"

"I have to," she said grumpily. "You need a keeper. And let me tell you one thing, Chance Mackenzie, if you think you're still going to be jetting all over the world getting stabbed and shot at while you get your adrenaline high, then you'd better think again. You're going to stay home with me and this baby. Is that understood?"

"Understood," he said. After all, the Mackenzie men always did whatever it took to keep their women happy.

EPILOGUE

SUNNY WAS ASLEEP, exhausted from her long labor and
then the fright and stress of having surgery when the baby
wouldn't come. Her eyes were circled with fatigue, but
Chance thought she had never been more beautiful. Her
face, when he laid the baby in her arms, had been exalted.
Until he died, he would never forget that moment. The
medical personnel in the room had faded away to nothing, and it had been just him and his wife and their child.

He looked down at the wrinkled, equally exhausted little face of his son. The baby slept as if he had run a mara-
thon, his plump hands squeezed into fierce little fists. He
had downy black hair, and though it was difficult to judge
a newborn's eye color, he thought they might turn the same
brilliant gray as Sunny's.

Zane poked his head in the door. "Hi," he said softly.
"I've been sent to reconnoiter. She's still asleep, huh?"

Chance looked at his wife, as sound asleep as the baby.
"She had a rough time."

"Well, hell, he weighs ten pounds and change. No wonder she needed help." Zane came completely into the room,
smiling as he examined the unconscious little face. "Here,
let me hold him. He needs to start meeting the family." He
took the baby from Chance, expertly cradling him to his
chest. "I'm your uncle Zane. You'll see me around a lot. I
have two little boys who are just itching to play with you,
and your aunt Maris—you'll meet her in a minute—has

one who's just a little older than you are. You'll have plenty of playmates, if you ever open your eyes and look around."

The baby's eyelids didn't flicker open, even when Zane rocked him. His pink lips moved in an unconscious sucking motion.

"You forget fast how little they are," Zane said softly as he smoothed his big hand over the baby's small round skull. He glanced up at Chance and grinned. "Looks like I'm still the only one who knows how to make a little girl."

"Yeah, well, this is just my first try."

"It'll be your last one, too, if they're all going to weigh ten pounds," came a voice from the bed. Sunny sighed and pushed her hair out of her eyes, and a smile spread across her face as she spied her son. "Let me have him," she said, holding out her arms.

There was a protocol to this sort of thing. Zane passed the baby to Chance, and Chance carried him to Sunny, settling him in her arms. No matter how often he saw it, he was always touched by the communion between mother and new baby, that absorbed look they both got as if they recognized each other on some basic, primal level.

"Are you feeling well enough for company?" Zane asked. "Mom's champing at the bit, wanting to get her hands on this little guy."

"I feel fine," Sunny said, though Chance knew she didn't. He had to kiss her, and even now there was that flash of heat between them, even though their son was only a few hours old. She pulled back, laughing a little and blushing. "Get away from me, you lech," she said, teasing him, and he laughed.

"What are you going to name him?" Zane demanded. "We've been asking for months, but you never would say. It can't stay a secret much longer."

Chance trailed his finger down the baby's downy cheek,

then he put his arms around both Sunny and the baby and held them close. Life couldn't get much better than this.

"Wolf," he said. "He's little Wolf."

* * * * *

LOVING EVANGELINE

CHAPTER ONE

DAVIS PRIESEN DIDN'T think of himself as a coward, but he would rather have had surgery without anesthesia than face Robert Cannon and tell him what he had to tell him. It wasn't that the majority stockholder, CEO and president of Cannon Group would hold him responsible for the bad news; Cannon had never been known to shoot the messenger. But those icy green eyes would become even colder, even more remote, and Davis knew from experience that he would feel the frigid touch of fear along his spine. Cannon had a reputation for scrupulous fairness, but also for unmatched ruthlessness when someone tried to screw him. Davis couldn't think of anyone he respected more than Robert Cannon, but that didn't relieve his dread.

Other men in Cannon's position, with his power, insulated themselves behind layers of assistants. It was a measure of his own control and personal remoteness that only Cannon's personal assistant guarded the gates to his inner sanctum. Felice Koury had been Cannon's PA for eight years and ran his office with the precision of a Swiss watch. She was a tall, lean, ageless woman with iron-gray hair and the smooth complexion of a twenty-year-old. Davis knew that her youngest child was in his mid-twenties, putting Felice at least in her mid-forties, but it was impossible to guess her age from her appearance. She was cool under fire, frighteningly efficient and had never shown a hint of nervousness around her boss. Davis wished he had a little of that last ability.

He had called beforehand to make certain Cannon could see him, so Felice wasn't surprised when he entered her office. "Good morning, Mr. Priesen." She reached immediately for the phone and punched a button. "Mr. Priesen is here, sir." She replaced the receiver and stood. "He'll see you now." With the smooth efficiency that always intimidated him, she was at the door of the inner office before he could reach it, opening it for him, then firmly closing it when he was inside. There was nothing subservient in Felice's attention; rather, he felt as if she controlled even his entrance into Cannon's office. Which, of course, she did.

Cannon's office was huge, luxurious and exquisitely decorated. It was a tribute to his taste that the effect was relaxing, rather than overwhelming, even though original oil paintings hung on the walls and a two-hundred-year-old Persian rug was underfoot. To the right was a large sitting area, complete with entertainment center, though Davis doubted that Cannon ever used the large-screen television or VCR for anything other than business. Six Palladian windows marched along the wall, framing the matchless views of New York City as if they were six paintings. The windows were works of art in themselves, beautifully fashioned panes of cut glass that took the light streaming through them and splintered it into diamonds.

Cannon's massive desk was another antique, a masterpiece of carved black wood that supposedly had belonged to the eighteenth-century Romanovs. He looked very at home behind it.

He was a tall, lean man, with the elegant grace and power of a panther. There was something pantherish about his coloring, too, with his sleek black hair and pale green eyes. One might even think of Robert Cannon as indolent. One would be dangerously mistaken.

He rose to his feet to shake hands, his long, well-shaped fingers gripping Davis's with surprising strength. Davis was always taken aback by the steeliness of that grip.

On some occasions Cannon had invited him to the sitting area and asked if he would like coffee. This was not one of those occasions. Cannon hadn't reached his position by misreading people, and his eyes narrowed as he examined the tension in Davis's face. "I would say it's good to see you, Davis," he remarked, "but I don't think you're here to tell me something I'm going to like."

His voice had been easy, almost casual, but Davis felt his tension go up another ten notches. "No, sir."

"Is it your fault?"

"No, sir." Then, scrupulously honest, he admitted, "Though I probably should have caught it sooner."

"Then relax and sit down," Robert said gently as he reseated himself. "If it isn't your fault, you're safe. Now, tell me what the problem is."

Davis nervously took a seat, but relaxing was out of the question. He perched on the edge of a soft leather chair. "Someone in Huntsville is selling our software for the space station," he blurted.

Cannon was never a restless man, but now he became even more still, and those green eyes took on the glacial look that Davis dreaded. "Do you have proof?" he asked.

"Yes, sir."

"Do you know who?"

"I think so, sir."

"Fill me in." With those abrupt words, Cannon leaned back, his gaze focused on Davis like a pale green laser.

Davis did, stumbling several times as he tried to explain how he had become suspicious and done a bit of investigating on his own to verify his suspicions before he accused anyone. Cannon listened in silence, and Davis wiped the sweat from his brow as he described the results of his sleuthing. The Cannon Group company, PowerNet, located in Huntsville, Alabama, was currently working on highly classified software developed for NASA. That software was definitely showing up in the hands of a company affiliated with another country. This wasn't just industrial espionage, which would have been enough; this was treason.

His suspicions had centered on Landon Mercer, the company manager. Mercer had divorced the year before, and his style of living had gone noticeably upward. His salary was very good, but not good enough to support a family and live the way he had been living. Davis had discreetly hired an investigation service that had discovered large deposits into Mercer's bank account. After following him for several weeks, they had reported that he regularly visited a marina in Guntersville, a small town nearby, situated on Guntersville Lake, an impoundment of the Tennessee river.

The owner/operator of the marina was a woman named Evie Shaw; the investigators hadn't yet been able to find out anything substantive from her bank accounts or spending habits, which could mean only that she was smarter than Mercer. On at least two occasions, however, Mercer had rented a motorboat at the marina, and shortly after he had left in the boat, Evie Shaw had closed the marina, gotten into her own boat and followed him. They had returned separately, some fifteen minutes apart. It looked as if they were meeting somewhere on the big lake, where they would find it very easy both to conceal their actions, and to see and hear anyone approaching them. It was much safer than trying to conduct clandestine business in the busy marina; in fact, the popularity of the marina made it all the odder that she would close it down in the middle of the day.

When Davis had finished and sat nervously cracking his knuckles, Cannon's face was hard and expressionless. "Thank you, Davis," he said calmly. "I'll notify the FBI and take it from here. Good work."

Davis flushed as he got to his feet. "I'm sorry I didn't catch it sooner."

"Security isn't your area. Someone was falling down on the job. I'll take care of that, too. We're lucky that you're as sharp as you are." Robert made a mental note to both increase Davis's salary, which was already healthy, and begin grooming him for more responsibility and power. He had shown a sharpness and initiative that shouldn't go unrewarded. "I'm sure the FBI will want to speak with you, so stay available for the rest of the day."

"Yes, sir."

As soon as Davis had left, Robert used his private line to call the FBI. The bureau maintained a huge force in the city, and he had had occasion to work with them before. He was put through immediately to the supervisory agent. His control was such that none of his rage was revealed in his voice as he requested that the two best agents come to his office as soon as possible. His influence was such that no questions were asked; he was simply given the quiet assurance that two agents would be there within the half hour.

That done, he sat back and considered all the options open to him. He didn't allow his cold fury to cloud his thinking. Uncontrolled emotion was not only useless, it was stupid, and Robert never allowed himself to do anything stupid. He took it personally that someone at one of his companies was selling classified computer programs; it was a blemish on his own reputation. He had nothing but contempt for someone who would sell out his own country merely for the money involved, and he would stop at nothing to halt the theft and put the perpetrator behind bars. Within fifteen minutes, he had formulated his plan of action.

The two agents arrived in twenty minutes. When Felice buzzed him, he told her to send them in, and that he wanted no interruptions of any kind until the gentlemen had left. A perfect secretary to the bone, she asked no questions.

She ushered the two conservatively dressed men into his office and firmly closed the door behind them. Robert stood to welcome them, but all the while he was assessing them with his cool, unreadable gaze. The younger man, about thirty, was immediately recognizable as a midlevel civil servant, but there was also a certain self-assurance in the man's eyes that Robert approved of. The older man, perhaps in his early fifties, had light brown hair that had gone mostly gray. He was not quite of average height, and was stocky of build. The blue eyes, behind metal-framed glasses, were tired, but nevertheless sparkled with intelligence and authority. No junior agent, this.

The older man held out his hand to Robert. "Mr. Cannon?" At Robert's nod, he said, "I'm William Brent, senior agent with the Federal Bureau of Investigation. This is Lee Murray, special agent assigned to counterespionage."

"Counterespionage," Robert murmured, his eyes cool. The presence of these two particular agents meant that the FBI had already been investigating PowerNet. "Good guess, gentlemen. Please sit down."

"It wasn't much of a guess," Agent Brent replied ruefully, as they took the offered seats. "A corporation such as yours, which handles so many government contracts, is unfortunately a prime target for espionage. I'm also aware that you have some experience in that area yourself, so it followed that you might need our particular talents, so to speak."

He was good, Robert thought. Just the type of person to inspire trust. They wanted to know if he knew anything, but they weren't going to tip their own hand if he didn't mention PowerNet. That little charade was a screen of innocence, behind which they could exhibit surprise and consternation if he informed them that he had discovered a leak at the company, or hide their own knowledge if he didn't mention the matter.

He didn't let them get away with it. "I see you've picked up some disquieting information yourselves," he said remotely. "I'm interested in knowing why you didn't contact me immediately."

William Brent grimaced. He had heard that nothing got by Robert Cannon, but still, he hadn't expected the man to be so acute.

Cannon was looking at him with a slight, cool lift of his eyebrow that invited explanations, an expression most people found difficult to resist.

Brent managed to control the inclination to rush into speech, mingling explanation with apology; he was astonished that the impulse even existed. It made him study Robert Cannon even more closely. He already knew a lot about the man, as he had made it his business to find out. Cannon came from a cultured, moneyed background, but had made himself much wealthier with his own astute business sense, and his reputation was impeccable. He also had a lot of friends in both the State and Justice departments, powerful men in their own right, who held him in the greatest respect. "Look, here," one of those men had said. "If something crooked is going on with any of the Cannon Group companies, I'd take it as a personal favor if you'd let Robert Cannon know about it before you do anything."

"I can't do that," Brent had replied. "It would compromise the investigation."

"Not at all," the man had said. "I would trust Cannon with the country's most sensitive intelligence. As a matter of fact, I already have, on several occasions. He's done some…favors for us."

"It's possible he could be in on it," Brent had warned, still resisting the idea of briefing a civilian outsider on the situation developing down in Alabama.

But the other man had shaken his head. "No. Not Robert Cannon."

After learning something about the nature and magnitude of the "favors" Cannon had done, and the dangers involved, Brent had reluctantly agreed to apprise Cannon of the situation before they put any plans into operation. Cannon had derailed that by calling first, and they hadn't been certain if he already knew, or not. The plan had been to keep quiet until they found out why he had called. It hadn't worked. He'd seen through them immediately.

Brent was used to reading men, but he couldn't read Cannon. His persona was that of a wealthy, cultured, sophisticated man, and Brent supposed he was all that, but nevertheless, it was only the first layer. The other layers, whatever they were, were so well hidden that he only sensed their existence, and even that was due only to his own access to privileged information. Watching Cannon's leanly handsome face, he couldn't catch so much as a flicker of expression; there were only those remote eyes watching him with unlimited patience.

Making a swift decision, William Brent leaned forward. "Mr. Cannon, I'm going to tell you a lot more than I had originally planned. We have a definite problem at one of your companies, a software company down in Alabama—"

"Suppose I tell you what I know?" Robert interrupted

in an even tone. "Then you can tell me if you have anything to add."

With calm, precise sentences, he recounted what Davis Priesen had told him. The two agents shared one startled, involuntary glance that revealed they hadn't discovered as much as Davis had, which upped that young man's stock with Robert even more.

When he had finished, William Brent cleared his throat and leaned forward. "Congratulations. You're a bit ahead of us. This will help us considerably in our investigation—"

"I'm flying down there tomorrow morning," Robert said.

Brent looked disapproving. "Mr. Cannon, I appreciate your desire to help, but this is best handled by the bureau."

"You misunderstand. I don't intend to *help*. This is my company, my problem. I'll take care of it myself. I'm merely apprising you of the situation and my intentions. I don't have to take the time to set up a cover and get inside the operation, because I own it. I will, of course, keep you informed."

Brent was already shaking his head. "No, it's out of the question."

"Who better? I not only have access to everything, my presence wouldn't be as alarming as that of federal investigators." He paused, then said gently, "I'm not a rank amateur."

"I'm aware of that, Mr. Cannon."

"Then I suggest you talk this over with your superiors." He glanced at his watch. "In the meantime, I have arrangements to make."

He had no doubt that when Brent took this to his superiors, he would be surprised and chagrined to be told to back off and let Robert Cannon handle this problem on his own. They would provide every assistance, of course, and have backup in place if he needed it, but Agent Brent would find that Robert was calling the shots.

He spent the rest of the day clearing his calendar. Felice made the open-ended flight arrangements and his hotel reservation in Huntsville. Just before leaving that night, he checked his watch and took a chance. Though it was eight o'clock in New York, it was only six in Montana, and the long summer daylight hours meant ranch work went on for much longer than during the winter.

To his delight, the phone was picked up on the third ring and his sister's lazy drawl came over the line. "Duncans' Madhouse, Madelyn speaking."

Robert chuckled. He could hear in the background the din his two young nephews were making. "Had a busy day, honey?"

"Robert!" Pleasure warmed her voice. "You might say that. Would you be interested in having your nephews for a prolonged visit?"

"Not until they're housebroken. I won't be at home, anyway."

"Where are you off to this time?"

"Huntsville, Alabama."

She paused. "It's hot down there."

"I'm aware of that."

"You might even *sweat*," she warned him. "Think how upset you'd be."

His firm mouth twitched at the amusement in her voice. "That's a chance I'll have to take."

"It must be serious, then. Trouble?"

"A few glitches."

"Take care."

"I will. If it looks as though I'll be down there for any length of time, I'll call you and give you my number."

"All right. Love you."

"Love you, too." He smiled a bit as he hung up. It was typical of Madelyn that she hadn't asked questions but had immediately sensed the seriousness of the situation awaiting him in Alabama. In six words she had given him her blessing, her support and her love. Though she was actually only his stepsister, the affection and understanding between them were as strong as if they had been connected by blood.

Next he called the woman he had been escorting rather regularly lately, Valentina Lawrence. The relationship hadn't progressed far enough that he would expect her to wait until his return, so the easiest thing for both of them was if he made it clear that she was free to see anyone she wished. It was a pity; Valentina was too popular to remain unattached for long, and he suspected he would be in Alabama for several weeks.

She was just the sort of woman Robert had always been most attracted to: the thoroughbred racehorse type—tall, lean, small-breasted. Her makeup was always impeccable and understated, her clothing both stylish and tasteful. She had a genuinely pleasant personality, and enjoyed the theater and opera as much as he did. She would have been a wonderful companion, if this problem hadn't interfered.

It had been several months since he had ended his last relationship, and he was feeling restless. He much preferred living with a woman to living alone, though he was perfectly content with his own company. He deeply enjoyed women, both mentally and physically, and he normally preferred the steadiness of a long-term relationship. He didn't do one-nighters and disdained those who were so stupid. He refrained from making love to a woman until she had committed herself to a relationship with him.

Valentina accepted the news of his prolonged absence with grace; after all, they weren't lovers and had no claim on each other. He could hear the gentle regret in her voice, but she didn't ask him to call when he returned.

That final piece of business concluded, he sat for several minutes, frowning as he allowed himself to think about the relationship that hadn't quite developed into intimacy, and how long it would be before he had time to attend to the sexual part of his life again. He wasn't pleased at the prospect of a long wait.

He wasn't casual about sex in any way. His intense sexuality was always under strict control; with the difference between a man's strength and a woman's, a man who *wasn't* in control could easily brutalize a woman, something that disgusted him. He tempered both his sexual appetite and his steely strength, reining them in with the icy power of his intellect. He never pressured a woman, though he always made it clear when he was attracted, so she would know where she stood. But he let his lady set the pace, let the intimacy progress at her speed. He respected a woman's natural caution about opening her tender, vulnerable body to a much bigger, stronger male. When it came to sex, he treated women gently and took his time so they could become fully aroused. Such control was no hardship; he could spend hours caressing soft, feminine skin and intriguing curves. Lingering over the lovemaking helped satisfy his own hunger, while intensifying his partner's.

There was nothing like making love that first time with a new partner, he mused. Never again was the experience so intense and hungry. He always tried to make it special for his lady, to make *her* feel special. He never stinted on the little details that made a woman feel treasured: romantic dinners for two, candlelight, champagne, thoughtful gifts, his complete attention. When the time finally came to retire to the bedroom, he would use all of his skill and control to satisfy her again and again before he allowed release for himself.

Thinking about what the problem in Alabama was causing him to miss made him irritated.

He was roused by a knock on his door. He looked up as Felice stuck her head in. "You should have gone home," he reproved. "You didn't have to stay."

"A messenger brought this envelope for you," she said, approaching to place it on his desk. She ignored his comment. No matter how late, she seldom left before he did.

"Go home," he said calmly. "That's an order. I'll call you tomorrow."

"Do you need anything before I go? A fresh pot of coffee?"

"No, I won't be staying much longer myself."

"Then have a good trip." She smiled and left the room. He could hear her in the outer office gathering together her possessions and locking everything up for the night.

He doubted that anything about the trip would be good. He was in a vengeful mood and out for blood.

He noticed that the manila envelope had no return address. He opened it and slid several pages out. There was one grainy, photostated picture, a recap of the situation and what they already knew about it, and a brief message from Agent Brent, identifying the woman in the picture and informing Robert that the bureau would cooperate with him in all matters, which was only what he had expected.

He picked up the reproduced photograph and studied it. It was of very poor quality, but pictured a woman standing on a dock, with motorboats in the background. So this was Evie Shaw. She was wearing sunglasses, so it was difficult to tell much about her, other than she had blondish, untidy hair and seemed to be rather hefty. No Mata Hari there, he thought, his fastidious taste offended by her poor choice of clothes and her general hayseed appearance. She looked more like a female mud wrestler, a coarse hick who was selling out her country for greed.

Briskly he returned the papers to the envelope. He looked forward to bringing both Landon Mercer and Evie Shaw to justice.

CHAPTER TWO

IT WAS A typically hot, sultry Southern summer day. The sky overhead was a deep, rich blue, dotted with fat white clouds that lazily sailed along on a breeze so slight it barely rippled the lake's surface. Gulls wheeled overhead and boats bobbed hypnotically in their slips. A few diehard fishermen and skiers dotted the water, ignoring the heat, but most of the fishermen who had gone out that morning had returned before noon. The air was heavy and humid, intensifying the odors of the lake and the surrounding lush, green mountains.

Evangeline Shaw looked out over her domain from the big plate-glass windows at the rear of the main marina building. Everyone on earth needed his own kingdom, and hers was this sprawling skeletal maze of docks and boat slips. Nothing within these few square acres escaped her attention. Five years ago, when she had taken over, it had been run-down and barely paying expenses. A sizable bank loan had been required to give it the infusion of capital it had needed, but within a year she had had it spruced up, expanded and bringing in more money than it ever had before. Of course, it took more money to run it, but now the marina was making a nice profit. With any luck she would have the bank loan paid off in another three years. Then the marina would be completely hers, free and clear of debt, and she would be able to expand even more, as well as diversify her holdings. She only hoped business would hold up; the fishing trade had slacked off a lot, due to the Tennessee Valley Authority's "weed management" program that had managed to kill most of the water plants that had harbored and protected the fish.

But she had been careful, and she hadn't overextended. Her debt was manageable, unlike that of others who had thought the fishing boom would last forever and had gone deeply into debt to expand. Her domain was secure.

Old Virgil Dodd had been with her most of the morning, sitting in the rocking chair behind the counter and entertaining her and her customers with tales of his growing-up days, back in the 1900s. The old man was as tough as shoe leather, but almost a century weighed on his inceasingly frail shoulders, and Evie was afraid that another couple of years, three at the most, would be too much for him. She had known him all her life; he had been *old* all her life, changing little, as enduring as the river and the mountains. But she knew all too well how fleeting and uncertain human life was, and she treasured the mornings that Virgil spent with her. He enjoyed them, too; he no longer went out fishing, as he had for the first eighty years of his life, but at the marina he was still close to the boats, where he could hear the slap of the water against the docks and smell the lake.

They were alone now, just the two of them, and Virgil had launched into another tale from his youth. Evie perched on a tall stool, occasionally glancing out the windows to see if anyone had pulled up to the gas pump on the dock, but giving most of her attention to Virgil.

The side door opened, and a tall, lean man stepped inside. He stood for a moment before removing his sunglasses, helping his eyes adjust to the relative dimness, then moved toward her with a silent, pantherish stroll.

Evie gave him only a swift glance before turning her

attention back to Virgil, but it was enough to make her defenses rise. She didn't know who he was, but she recognized immediately *what* he was; he was not only a stranger, he was an outsider. There were a lot of Northerners who had retired to Guntersville, charmed by the mild winters, the slow pace, low cost of living and natural beauty of the lake, but he wasn't one of them. He was far too young to be retired, for one thing. His accent would be fast and hard, his clothes expensive and his attitude disdainful. Evie had met his kind before. She hadn't been impressed then, either.

But it wasn't just that. It was the other quality she had caught that made her want to put a wall at her back.

He was dangerous.

Though she smiled at Virgil, instinctively she analyzed the stranger. She had grown up with bad boys, daredevils and hell-raisers; the South produced them in abundance. This man was something different, something...more. He didn't embrace danger as much as he *was* danger. It was a different mind-set, a will and temperament that brooked no opposition, a force of character that had glittered in those startlingly pale eyes.

She didn't know how or why, but she sensed that he was a threat to her.

"Excuse me," he said, and the deepness of his voice ran over her like velvet. A strange little quiver tightened her belly and ran up her spine. The words were courteous, but the iron will behind them told her that he expected her to immediately attend to him.

She gave him another quick, dismissive glance. "I'll be with you in a minute," she said, her tone merely polite, then she turned back to Virgil with real warmth. "What happened then, Virgil?"

No hint of emotion showed on Robert's face, though he

was a bit startled by the woman's lack of response. That was unusual. He wasn't accustomed to being ignored by anyone, and certainly not by a woman. Women had always been acutely aware of him, responding to the intense masculinity he kept under ruthless control. He wasn't vain, but his effect on women was something he largely took for granted. He couldn't remember ever wanting a woman and not having her, eventually.

But he was willing to wait and use the opportunity to watch this woman. Her appearance had thrown him a little off balance, also something unusual for him. He still hadn't adjusted his expectations to the reality.

This was Evie Shaw, no doubt about it. She sat on a stool behind the counter, all her attention on an old man who sat in a rocking chair, his aged voice gleeful as he continued to recount some tall tale from his long-ago youth. Robert's eyes narrowed fractionally as he studied her.

She wasn't the thick-bodied hayseed he had expected. Or rather, she wasn't thick-bodied; he reserved judgment on the hayseed part. The unflattering image he'd formed must have been caused by the combination of bad photography and poorly fitting clothes. He had walked in looking for a woman who was coarse and ill-bred, but that wasn't what he'd found.

Instead, she…glowed.

It was an unsettling illusion, perhaps produced by the brilliant sunlight streaming in through the big windows, haloing her sunny hair and lighting the tawny depths of her hazel eyes. The light caressed her golden skin, which was as smooth and unblemished as a porcelain doll's. Illusion or not, the woman was luminous.

Her voice had been surprisingly deep and a little raspy, bringing up memories of old Bogie and Bacall movies and making Robert's spine prickle. Her accent was lazy and liquid, as melodious as a murmuring creek or the wind in the trees, a voice that made him think of tangled sheets and long, hot nights.

Watching her, he felt something inside him go still.

The old man leaned forward, folding his gnarled hands over the crook of his walking cane. His faded blue eyes were full of laughter and the memories of good times. "Well, we'd tried ever way we knowed to get John H. away from that still, but he weren't budging. He kept an old shotgun loaded with rat shot, so we were afeard to venture too close. He knowed it was just a bunch of young'uns aggravating him, but *we* didn't know he knowed. Ever time he grabbed that shotgun, we'd run like jackrabbits, then we'd come sneakin' back…."

Robert forced himself to look around as he tuned out the rest of Virgil's tale. Ramshackle though the building was, the business seemed to be prospering, if the amount of tackle on hand and the number of occupied boat slips were any indication. A pegboard behind the counter held the ignition keys to the rental boats, each key neatly labeled and numbered. He wondered how she kept track of who had which boat.

Virgil was well into his tale, slapping his knee and chortling. Evie Shaw threw back her head with a shout of pure enjoyment, her laughter as deep as her speaking voice. Robert was suddenly aware of how accustomed he had become to carefully controlled social laughter, how shrill and shallow it was compared to her unabashed mirth, with nothing forced or held back.

He tried to resist the compulsion to stare at her, but, to his surprise, it was like resisting the need to breathe. He could manage it for a little while, but it was a losing battle from the start. With a mixture of fury and curiosity, he gave in to the temptation and let his gaze greedily drink her in.

He watched her with an impassive expression, his self-control so absolute that neither his posture nor his face betrayed any hint of his thoughts. Unfortunately, that self-control didn't extend to those thoughts as his attention focused on Evie Shaw with such intensity that he was no longer aware of his surroundings, that he no longer heard Virgil's cracked voice continuing with his tale.

She wasn't anything like the women he had always found most attractive. She was also a traitor, or at least was involved in industrial espionage. He had every intention of breaking her, of bringing her to justice. Yet he couldn't take his eyes off her, couldn't control his wayward thoughts, couldn't still the sudden hard thumping in his chest. He had been sweating in the suffocating heat, but suddenly the heat inside him was so blistering that it made the outer temperature seem cool in comparison. His skin felt too tight, his clothing too restrictive. A familiar heaviness in his loins made the last two sensations all too real, rather than products of his imagination.

The women he had wanted in the past, for all the differences in their characters, had shared a certain sense of style, of sophistication. They had all looked—and been—expensive. He hadn't minded, and had enjoyed spoiling them more. They had all been well dressed, perfumed, exquisitely turned out. His sister, Madelyn, had disparagingly referred to a couple of them as mannequins, but Madelyn herself was a clotheshorse of the highest order, so he had been amused rather than irritated by the comment.

Evie Shaw, in contrast, evidently paid no attention to her clothes. She wore an oversize T-shirt that she had knotted at the waist, a pair of jeans so ancient that they were threadbare and almost colorless and equally old docksiders.

Her hair, a sun-streaked blond that ranged in color from light brown to the palest flax, and included several different shades of gold, was pulled back and confined in an untidy braid that was as thick as his wrist and hung halfway down her back. Her makeup was minimal and probably a waste of time in this humidity, but with her complexion, she didn't really need it.

Damn it, how could she glow like that? It wasn't the sheen of perspiration, but the odd impression that light was attracted to her, as if she forever stood in a subtle spotlight. Her skin was lightly tanned, a creamy golden hue, and it looked like warm, living satin. Even her eyes were the golden brown hazel of dark topaz.

He had always preferred tall, lean women; as tall as he was himself, he had felt better matched with them on the dance floor and in bed. Evie Shaw was no more than five-four, if that. Nor was she lean; rather, the word that came to mind was *luscious,* followed immediately by *delicious.* Caught off guard by the violence of his reaction, he wondered savagely if he wanted to make love to her or eat her, and the swift mental answer to his own question was a flat, unequivocal "yes." To both choices.

She was a symphony of curves, not quite full-figured, but sleek and rounded, the absolute essence of femaleness. No slim, boyish hips there, but a definite flare from her waist, and she had firm, round buttocks. He had always adored the delicacy of small breasts but now found himself entranced by the soft globes that shaped the front of the annoyingly loose T-shirt. They weren't big, heavy breasts, though they had a slight bounce that riveted his attention whenever she moved; they weren't exactly voluptuous, but were just full enough to be maddeningly tempting. Their soft, warm weight would fill his hands,

hands that he tightened into fists in an effort to resist the urge to reach out and touch her.

Everything about her was shaped for a man's delight, but he wasn't delighted by his reaction. If *he* could respond to her like this, maybe Mercer was her pawn rather than the other way around. It was a possibility he couldn't ignore.

Not only was she nothing like the women he had previously desired, he was furious with himself for wanting her. He was down here to gather evidence that would send her to prison, and he couldn't let lust make him lose sight of that. This woman was wading hip-deep in the sewer of espionage, and he shouldn't feel anything for her except disgust. Instead he was struggling with a physical desire so intense that it was all he could do to simply stand there, rather than act. He didn't want to court her, seduce her; he wanted to grab her and carry her away. His lair was a hideously expensive Manhattan penthouse, but the primitive instinct was the same one that had impelled men to the same action back when their lairs were caves. He wanted her, and there was nothing civilized or gentle about it. The urge made a mockery of both his intellect and his self-control.

He wanted to ignore the attraction, but he couldn't; it was too strong, the challenge too great. Evie Shaw was not just ignoring him, she was totally oblivious to the pure male intent that was surging through him. He might as well have been a post for all the attention she was paying to him, and every aggressive cell in his body was on alert. By God, he *would* have her.

The door behind him opened, and he turned, grateful for the interruption. A young woman, clad in shorts, sandals and a T-shirt, smiled at him and murmured, "Hello," as she approached. Both the smile and the look lingered for just a moment before she turned her attention to the two people behind the counter. "Have you enjoyed your visit, PawPaw? Who all has been in today?"

"Had a good time," Virgil said, slowly getting to his feet with a lot of help from the cane. "Burt Mardis spent some time with us, and both of the Gibbs boys came by. Have you got the young'uns rounded up?"

"They're in the car with the groceries." She turned to Evie. "I hate to run, but it's so hot I want to get the food put up before it spoils."

"Everything I can, I put off until night," Evie said. "Including buying groceries. Bye, Virgil. You take care of that knee, all right? And come back soon."

"The knee feels better already," he assured her. "Getting old ain't no fun, but it's better than dying." He winked and steadily made his way down the aisle, using the cane but otherwise not making much allowance for his noticeable limp.

"See you later, Evie," the young woman said as she turned to go. She gave Robert another smile in passing.

When the old man and young woman had left and the door had closed behind them, Robert leaned negligently against the counter and said in a mild tone, "I assume she's his granddaughter."

Evie shook her head and turned away to check the gas pumps again. She was too aware of being alone with him, which was ridiculous; she was alone with male customers several times a day and had never felt the least hint of uneasiness—until now. She had felt a subtle alarm the second he had walked in the door. He hadn't said or done anything untoward, but still, she couldn't shake that feeling of wariness. "Great-granddaughter. He lives with her. I apologize for making you wait, but I'll have other customers, while Virgil is ninety-three, and he may not be around much longer."

"I understand," he said calmly, not wanting to antagonize her. He held out his hand, a gesture calculated to force her to look at him, truly acknowledge him, *touch* him. "I'm Robert Cannon."

She put her hand in his, just slowly enough to let him know that she was reluctant to shake hands with him and did it only to be polite. Her fingers were slim and cool and gripped his with surprising strength. "Evie Shaw," she said. He made certain his own grip was firm, but not enough to hurt, and promptly released her. The contact was brief, impersonal…and not enough.

Immediately she turned away and said briskly, "What is it you need, Mr. Cannon?"

He came up with several graphic ideas but didn't give voice to them. Instead he thoughtfully eyed her slim back, rapidly adjusting his impressions. He had thought her oblivious to him, but she was too studiously ignoring him for that; no, quite the contrary, she was very aware of him, and very on edge. In a flash, all of his plans changed.

He had entered the marina wanting only to look around a little, get an idea of the security and layout of the place, maybe buy a fishing license or map, but all of that had changed in the past few minutes. Rather than shadow Mercer, he now intended to stick to Evie Shaw like glue.

Why was she so wary of him? She had been, right from the beginning, even before he had introduced himself. The only explanation that came to mind was that she had already known who he was, had somehow recognized him, and she could only have done that if she had been briefed. If so, this operation was more sophisticated than he had expected. It wouldn't be beyond his capabilities, but it would certainly be more of a challenge. With one of his lightning-fast decisions, he changed the base of his investigation from Huntsville to Guntersville. Before the fall of the Soviet Union, he had, on a couple of memorable occasions, found himself attracted to female operatives; taking them to bed had been a risk, but a delightful one. Danger certainly added to the excitement. Bedding Evie Shaw, he suspected, would be an event he would never forget.

"First, I need information," he said, irritated because she still wasn't looking at him, but not a hint of it sounded in his voice. He needed to lull her suspicions, make her comfortable with him. Gentling women had never been difficult for him before, and he didn't expect it to be now. As far as anyone outside a few government officials knew, he was nothing more than a very wealthy businessman; if she was as smart as he now suspected her to be, she would soon see the benefits in becoming close to him, not only for what he could give her but for the information she could get from him. A summer fling would be perfect for her needs, and he intended to give her just that.

"Perhaps you should go to the Visitors' Center," she suggested.

"Perhaps," he murmured. "But I was told that you can help me."

"Maybe." Her tone was reluctant. She certainly wasn't committing herself to anything. "What kind of information do you need?"

"I'm taking a long vacation here, for the rest of the summer," he said. "My second reason for coming here is to rent a boat slip, but I also want someone to show me around the lake. I was told that you know the area as well as anyone."

She faced him, her gaze hooded. "That's true, but I don't guide. I can help you with the boat, but that's all."

She had thrown up a wall as soon as she had seen him, and she had no intention of being cooperative about anything. He gave her a gentle smile, one that had been soothing nervous women for years. "I understand. You don't know me."

He saw the involuntary reaction to that smile in the way her pupils flared. Now she looked uncertain. "It isn't that. I don't know a lot of my customers."

"I believe the going rate for guides is a hundred a day, plus expenses. I'm willing to pay twice that."

"It isn't a matter of money, Mr. Cannon. I don't have the time."

Pushing her now wouldn't accomplish anything, and he had a lot to get in place before he could really pursue her. He had made certain she wouldn't forget him, which was enough for a first meeting. "Can you recommend a guide, then?" he asked, and saw her relax a little.

She reeled off several names, which he committed to memory, for he fully intended to learn the river. Then she said, "Would you like to look at the boat slips that are available now?"

"Yes, of course." It would give him a chance to inspect her security arrangements, too.

She picked up a portable phone and clipped it to a belt loop, then came out from behind the counter. Robert fell into step slightly behind her, his heavy-lidded gaze wandering over her curvy hips and heart-shaped bottom, clearly outlined by the snug jeans. Her sun-streaked head barely reached the top of his shoulder. His blood throbbed warmly through his veins as he thought of cupping her bottom in his hands. It was an effort to wrench his attention away from the image that thought provoked.

"Do you just leave the store unattended?" he asked as they walked down the dock. The sunlight was blinding as it reflected off the water, and he slipped his sunglasses into place again. The heat was incredible, like a sauna.

"I can see from the docks if anyone drives up," she replied.

"How many others work here?"

She gave him a curious glance, as if wondering why he would ask. "I have a mechanic, and a boy who works mornings for me during the summer, then shifts to afternoons during the school year."

"How many hours a day are you open?"

"From six in the morning until eight at night."

"That's a long day."

"It isn't so bad. During the winter, I'm only open from eight until five."

Four of the docks were covered, and most of the slips were occupied. A variety of crafts bobbed in the placid water: houseboats, cabin cruisers, pontoon boats, ski boats, sailboats. The four covered docks were on the left, and the entrance to them was blocked by a locked gate. To the right were two uncovered docks, for use by general traffic. The rental boats were in the first row of boat slips on the secured dock closest to the marina building.

Evie unlocked the padlock that secured the gate, and they stepped onto the floating dock, which bobbed gently on the water. Silently she led him down the rows of boats, indicating which of the empty slips were available. Finally she asked, "What size boat do you have?"

He made another instant decision. "I intend to buy a small one. A speedboat, not a cabin cruiser. Can you recommend a good dealership in the area?"

She gave him another of those hooded looks, but merely said in a brisk tone, "There are several boat dealerships in town. It won't be hard to find what you want." Then she turned and started back toward the marina office, her steps sure and graceful on the bobbing dock.

Again Robert followed her, enjoying the view just as

much as he had before. She probably thought she was rid of him, but there was no way that would happen. Anger and anticipation mingled, forming a volatile aggression that made him feel more alert, more on edge, than he ever had before. She would pay for stealing from him, in more ways than one.

"Will you have dinner with me tonight?" he asked, using a totally unaggressive tone. She halted so abruptly that he bumped into her. He could have prevented the contact, but deliberately let his body collide with hers. She staggered off balance, and he grabbed her waist to steady her, easing her back against him before she regained control. He felt the shiver that ran through her as he savored the heat and feel of her under his hands, against his thighs and loins and belly. "Sorry," he said with light amusement. "I didn't realize having dinner with me was such a frightening concept."

She should have done a number of things. If reluctant, she should have moved away from the subtle sexuality of his embrace. If compliant, she should have turned to face him. She should have hastened to assure him that his invitation hadn't frightened her at all, then accepted to prove that it hadn't. She did none of those things. She stood stock-still, as if paralyzed by his hands clasping her waist. Silence thickened between them, growing taut. She shivered again, a delicately sensual movement that made his hands tighten on her, made his male flesh quiver and rise. Why didn't she move, why didn't she say something?

"Evie?" he murmured.

"No," she said abruptly, her voice raspier than usual. She wrenched away from him. "I'm sorry, but I can't go out to dinner with you."

Then a boat idled into the marina, and he watched her golden head turn, her face light with a smile as she recognized her customer. Sharp fury flared through him at how easily she smiled at others, but would scarcely even glance at him.

She lifted her left arm to wave, and with shock Robert focused on that slim hand.

She was wearing a wedding ring.

CHAPTER THREE

EVIE TRIED TO concentrate on the ledgers that lay open on her desk, but she couldn't keep her mind on posting the day's income and expenses. A dark, lean face kept forming in her mind's eye, blotting out the figures. Every time she thought of those pale, predatory eyes, the bottom would drop out of her stomach and her heart would begin hammering. Fear. Though he had been polite, Robert Cannon could no more hide his true nature than could a panther. In some way she could only sense, without being able to tell the exact nature of it, he was a threat to her.

Her instincts were primitive; she wanted to barricade herself against him, wall him out. She had fought too long to put her life on an even keel to let this dark stranger disrupt what she had built. Her life was placid, deliberately so, and she resented this interruption in the even fabric of days she had fashioned about herself.

She looked up at the small photograph that sat on the top shelf of her old-fashioned rolltop desk. It wasn't one of her wedding photos; she had never looked at any of those. This photo was one that had been taken the summer before their senior year in high school; a group of kids had gotten together and spent the whole day on the water, skiing, goofing off, going back on shore to cook out. Becky Watts had brought her mother's camera and taken photos of all of them that golden summer day. Matt had been chasing Evie with an ice cube, trying to drop it down her blouse, but when he finally caught her, she had struggled and made him drop it. Matt's hands had been on her waist, and they had been laughing. Becky had called, "Hey, Matt!" and snapped the photo when they both automatically looked over at her.

Matt. Tall, just outgrowing the gangliness of adolescence and putting on some of the weight that came with maturity. That shock of dark hair falling over his brow, crooked grin flashing, bright blue eyes twinkling. He'd always been laughing. Evie didn't spare any looks for the girl she had been then, but she saw the way Matt had held her, the link between them that had been obvious even in that happy-go-lucky moment. She looked down at the slim gold band on her left hand. *Matt.*

In all the years since, there hadn't been anyone. She hadn't wanted anyone, had been neither interested nor tempted. There were people she loved, of course, but in a romantic sense her emotional isolation had been so complete that she had been totally unaware if any man had been attracted to her...until Robert Cannon had walked into her marina and looked at her with eyes like green ice. Though his expression had been impassive, she had felt his attention focus on her like a laser, had felt the heated sexual quality of it. That, and something else. Something even more dangerous.

He had left immediately after looking at the boat slips, but he would be back. She knew that without question. Evie sighed as she got up and walked to the French doors. She could see starlight twinkling on the water and stepped out onto the deck. The warm night air wrapped around her, humid, fragrant. Her little house sat right on the riverfront, with steps leading down from the deck to her private dock and boathouse. She sat in one of the patio chairs and propped her feet on the railing, calmed by the peacefulness of the river.

The summer nights weren't quiet, what with the constant chirp of insects, frogs and night birds, the splash of fish jumping, the rustle of the trees, the low murmur of the river itself, but there was a serenity in the noise. There was no moon, so the stars were plainly visible in the black bowl of the sky, the fragile, twinkling light reflected in millions of tiny diamonds on the water. The main river channel curved through the lake not sixty feet from her dock, the current ruffling the surface into waves.

Her nearest neighbors were a quarter of a mile away, out of sight around a small promontory. The only houses she could see from her deck were on the other side of the lake, well over a mile away. Guntersville Lake, formed when the TVA had dammed the Tennessee River back in the thirties, was both long and wide, irregularly shaped, curving back and forth, with hundreds of inlets. Numerous small, tree-covered islands dotted the lake.

She had lived here all her life. Here was home, family, friends, a network of roots almost two hundred years old that spread both wide and deep. She knew the pace of the seasons, the pulse of the river. She had never wanted to be anywhere else. The fabric of life here was her fortress. Now, however, her fortress was being threatened by two different enemies, and she would have to fight to protect herself.

The first threat was one that made her furious. Landon Mercer was up to no good. She didn't know the man well, but she had a certain instinct about people that was seldom wrong. There was a slickness to his character that had put her off from the start, when he had first begun renting one of her boats, but she hadn't actually become suspicious of him for a couple of months. It had been a lot of little things that had gradually alerted her, like the way he always carefully looked around before leaving the dock; it would have made sense if he'd been looking at the river traffic, but instead he'd looked at the parking lot and the highway. And there was always a mixture of triumph and relief in his expression when he returned, as if he'd done something he shouldn't have and gotten away with it.

His clothes were wrong, somehow. He made an effort to dress casually, the way he thought a fisherman would dress, but never quite got it right. He carried a rod and reel and one small tackle box, but from what Evie could tell, he never used them. He certainly never came back with any fish, and the same lure had been tied onto the line every time he went out. She knew it was the same one, because it was missing the back set of treble hooks. No, Mercer wasn't fishing. So why carry the tackle? The only logical explanation was that he was using it as a disguise; if anyone saw him, they wouldn't think anything about it.

But because Evie was alert to anything that threatened her domain, she wondered why he would need a disguise. Was he seeing a married woman? She dismissed that possibility. Boats were noisy and obvious; using them wasn't a good way to sneak around. If his lover's house was isolated, a car would be better, because then Mercer wouldn't have to worry about the vagaries of the weather. If the house had neighbors within sight, then a boat would attract attention when it pulled up to the dock; river people tended to notice strange boats. Nor was an assignation in the middle of the lake a good idea, given the river traffic.

Drugs, maybe. Maybe the little tackle box was full of cocaine, instead of tackle. If he had a system set up, selling in the middle of the river would be safe; the water patrol couldn't sneak up on him, and if they did approach, all he had to do was drop the evidence over the side. His most dangerous time would be before he got out on the water, while he could be caught carrying the stuff. That was why he never examined the parking lot when he returned; the evidence was gone. For all intents and purposes, he had just been enjoying a little fishing.

She had no hard evidence. Twice she had tried to follow him, but had lost him in the multitude of coves and islands. But if he was using one of her boats to either sell or transfer drugs, he was jeopardizing her business. Not only could the boat be confiscated, the publicity would be terrible for the marina. Boat owners would pull out of the slips they rented from her; there were enough marinas in the Guntersville area that they could always find another place to house their boats.

Both times Mercer had headed toward the same area, the island-dotted area around the Marshall County Park, where it was easy to lose sight of a boat. Evie knew every inch of the river; eventually she would be able to narrow down the choices and find him. She didn't have any grandiose scheme to apprehend him, assuming he *was* doing something illegal. She didn't even intend to get all that close to him; she carried a pair of powerful binoculars with her in the boat. All she wanted to do was satisfy her suspicions; if she was correct, then she would turn the matter over to the sheriff and let him work it out with the water patrol. That way, she would have protected both her reputation and the marina. She might still lose the boat, but she didn't think the sheriff would confiscate it if she were the one who put him onto Mercer to begin with. All she wanted was to be certain in her own mind before she accused a man of something as serious as drug dealing.

The problem with following Mercer was that she never knew when to expect him; if she had customers in the marina, she couldn't just drop everything and hop in a boat.

But she would handle that as the opportunity presented itself. Robert Cannon was something else entirely.

She didn't want to handle him. She didn't want anything to do with him—this man with his cold, intense eyes and clipped speech, this stranger, this Yankee. He made her feel like a rabbit facing a cobra: terrified, but fascinated at the same time. He tried to hide his ruthlessness behind smooth, cosmopolitan manners, but Evie had no doubts about the real nature of the man.

He wanted her. He intended to have her. And he wouldn't care if he destroyed her in the taking.

She touched her wedding ring, turning it on her finger. Why couldn't Matt have lived? So many years had passed without him, and she had survived, had gotten on with her life, but his death had irrevocably changed her. She was stronger, yes, but also set apart, isolated from other men who might have wanted to claim her. Other men had respected that distance; *he* wouldn't.

Robert Cannon was a complication she couldn't afford. At the very least, he would distract her at a time when she needed to be alert. At the worst, he would breach her defenses and take what he wanted, then leave without any thought for the emotional devastation he left behind. Evie shuddered at the thought. She had survived once; she wasn't sure she could do it again.

Today, when he had put his hands on her waist and pulled her against his lean, hard body, she had been both shocked and virtually paralyzed by the exquisite pleasure of the contact. It had been so many years since she had felt that kind of joy that she had forgotten how enthralling, how potent, it was to feel hard male flesh against her. She had been startled by the heated strength of his hands and the subtle muskiness of his scent. She had been swamped by the sensations, by her memories. But her memories were old ones, of two young people who no longer existed. The hands holding her had been Matt's; the eager, yearning kisses had been from Matt's lips. Time had dulled those memories, the precious ones, but the image of Robert Cannon was sharp, almost painful, in its freshness.

The safest thing would be to ignore him, but that was the one thing she was sure he wouldn't allow.

ROBERT STROLLED INTO the offices of PowerNet the next morning and introduced himself to the receptionist, a plump, astute woman in her thirties who immediately made a phone call and then personally escorted him to Landon Mercer's office. He was in a savage mood, had been since he'd seen the wedding ring on Evie Shaw's hand, but he gave the receptionist a gentle smile and thanked her, making her blush. He never took out his temper on innocents; in fact, his self-control was so great that the vast majority of his employees didn't know he even *had* a temper. The few who knew otherwise had learned it the hard way.

Landon Mercer, however, was no innocent. He came swiftly out of his office to meet Robert halfway, heartily greeting him. "Mr. Cannon, what a surprise! No one let us know you were in Huntsville. We're honored!"

"Hardly that," Robert murmured as he shook hands with Mercer, deliberately modifying his grip to use very little strength. His mood deteriorated even further to find that Mercer was tall and good-looking, with thick blond hair and a very European sense of style. Expertly Robert assessed the cost of the Italian silk suit Mercer was wearing, and mentally he raised his eyebrows. The man had expensive tastes.

"Come in, come in," Mercer urged, inviting Robert into his office. "Would you like coffee?"

"Please." The acceptance of hospitality, Robert had

found, often made subordinates relax a little. Landon Mercer would be edgy at his sudden appearance, anyway; it wouldn't hurt to calm him down.

Mercer turned to his secretary, who was making herself very busy. "Trish, would you bring in two coffees, please?"

"Of course. How do you take yours, Mr. Cannon?"

"Black."

They went on into Mercer's office, and Robert took one of the comfortable visitors' chairs, rather than automatically taking Mercer's big chair behind the desk to show his authority. "I apologize for just dropping in on you without warning," he said calmly. "I'm in the area on vacation and thought I'd take the opportunity to see the operation, since I've never personally been down here."

"We're pleased to have you anytime," Mercer replied, still in that hearty tone of voice. "Vacation, you say? Strange place to take a vacation, especially in the middle of summer. The heat is murderous, as I'm sure you've noticed."

"Not so strange." Robert could almost hear Mercer's furiously churning, suspicious thoughts. Why was Robert here? Why now? Were they on to Mercer? If they were, why hadn't he been arrested? Robert didn't mind Mercer being suspicious; in fact, he was counting on it.

There was a light knock on the door; then Trish entered with two cups of steaming coffee. She passed Robert's to him first, then gave the other cup to Mercer. "Thank you," Robert said. Mercer didn't bother with the courtesy.

"About your vacation?" Mercer prompted, when Trish had closed the door behind her.

Robert leaned back in the chair and indolently crossed his legs. He could feel Mercer sharply studying him and knew what he would see: a lean, elegantly dressed man with cool, slightly bored eyes, certainly nothing to alarm him, despite this unexpected visit. "I have a house on the lake in Guntersville," he said in a lazy, slightly remote tone. It was a lie, but Mercer wouldn't know that. "I bought it and some land several years ago. I've never been down here before, but I've let several of my executives use the place, and they've all returned with the usual exaggerated fishing stories. Even allowing for that, they've all been enthusiastic about coming back, so I thought I'd try out the fishing for myself."

"I've heard it's a good lake," Mercer said politely, but the mental wheels were whirling faster than before.

"We'll see." Robert allowed himself a slight smile. "It seems like a nice, quiet place. Just what the doctor ordered."

"Doctor?"

"High blood pressure. Stress." Robert shrugged. "I feel fine, but the doctor insisted that I needed a long vacation, and this seemed like the perfect place to avoid stress."

"That's for sure," Mercer said. Suspicion still lingered in his eyes, but now it was tempered with relief at the plausible explanation for Robert's presence.

"I don't know how long I'll stay," Robert continued in an indifferent tone. "I won't be dropping in on you constantly, though. I'm supposed to forget about work for a while."

"We'll be glad to see you anytime, but you really should listen to your doctor," Mercer urged. "Since you're here, would you like a tour of the place? There isn't much to see, of course, just a lot of programmers and their computers."

Robert glanced at his watch, as if he had somewhere else to go. "I believe I have time, if it wouldn't be too much trouble."

"No, not at all." Mercer was already on his feet, anxious to complete the tour and send Robert on his way.

Even if he hadn't already known about Mercer, Robert thought, he would have disliked him; there was a slickness to him that was immediately off-putting. Mercer tried to disguise it with a glib, hearty attitude, but the man thought he was smarter than everyone else, and the contempt slipped through every so often. Did he treat Evie with the same attitude? Or was she, despite her relative lack of sophistication, cool and discerning enough that Mercer watched his step with her?

They were probably lovers, he thought, even though she was married. When had marital vows ever prevented anyone from straying, if they were so inclined? And why would a woman involved in espionage hesitate at cheating on her husband? Odd that her marital status hadn't been included in the information he'd received on her, but then, why would it be, unless her husband was also involved? Evidently he wasn't, but nevertheless, as soon as Robert had returned to his hotel room in Huntsville the afternoon before, he had called his own investigative people and asked for information concerning the man. He was coldly furious; he had never, under any circumstances, allowed himself to become involved with a married woman, and he wasn't going to lower his standards now. But neither had he ever wanted another woman as violently as he wanted Evie Shaw, and knowing that he had to deprive himself made his temper very precarious.

Mercer was all smooth bonhomie as he escorted Robert through the offices, pointing out the various features and explaining the work in progress. Robert made use of the tour to gather information. Calling on his ability to totally concentrate on one thing at a time, he pushed Evie Shaw out of his mind and ruthlessly focused on the business at hand. PowerNet was housed in a long, one-story brick building. The company offices were in front, while the

real work, the programming, was done in the back, with
computer geniuses working their peculiar magic. Robert
quietly noted the security setup and approved; there were
surveillance cameras, and motion and thermal alarms. Access to the classified material could be gained only by a
coded magnetic card, and the bearer still had to have the
necessary security clearance. No paperwork or computer
disks were allowed to leave the building. All work was
logged in and placed in a secure vault when the programmers left for the day.

For Robert, the security measures made things simple;
the only way the system could have been breached without detection was by someone in a position of authority,
someone who had access to the vault: Landon Mercer.

He made a point of checking his watch several times
during the tour, and as soon as it was completed, he
said, "I've enjoyed this very much, but I'm supposed
to meet with a contractor to do a few repairs on the
house. Perhaps we could get together for a round of
golf sometime."

"Of course, anytime," Mercer said. "Just call."

Robert allowed himself a brief smile. "I'll do that."

He was satisfied with the visit; his intention hadn't
been to do any actual snooping but rather to let Mercer
know he was in town and to see for himself the security
measures at PowerNet. He had the security layout from
the original specs, of course, but it was always best to
check out the details and make certain nothing had been
changed. He might have to slip into the building at night,
but that wasn't his primary plan, merely a possibility.
Catching Mercer on-site with classified data didn't prove
anything; the trick was to catch him passing it to someone else. Let his presence make Mercer nervous. Nervous
people made mistakes.

AN ENVELOPE FROM his personal investigators was waiting for him at the desk when he returned to the hotel. Robert stepped into the empty elevator and opened the envelope as the car began moving upward. He quickly scanned the single sheet. The information was brief. Matt Shaw, Evie's husband, had been killed in a car accident the day after their wedding, twelve years before.

He calmly slid the sheet back into the envelope, but a savage elation was rushing through him. She was a widow! She was available. And, though she didn't know it yet, she was his for the taking.

Once in his hotel room, he picked up the phone and began making calls, sliding the chess pieces of intrigue into place.

CHAPTER FOUR

EVIE STUCK HER head out the door. "Jason!" she bellowed at her fourteen-year-old nephew. "Stop horsing around. *Now!*"

"Aw, okay," he grudgingly replied, and Evie pulled her head back inside, though she kept an eye on him, anyway. She adored the kid but never forgot that he *was* just a kid, with an attention span that leaped around like a flea and all the ungovernable energy and awkwardness that went with early adolescence. Her niece, Paige, was content to sit inside with her, in the air-conditioning, but a couple of Jason's buddies had come by, and now they were out on the docks, clowning around. Evie expected any or all of the boys to fall into the water at any time.

"They're so jerky," Paige said with all the disdain a thirteen-year-old could muster, which was plenty.

Evie smiled at her. "They'll improve with age."

"They'd better," Paige said ominously. She pulled her long, coltish legs up into the rocking chair and returned to the young-adult romance she was reading. She was a beautiful girl, Evie thought, studying the delicate lines of the young face, which still wore some of the innocence of childhood. Paige had dark hair, like her father, and a classic bone structure that would only improve with age. Jason was more outgoing than his sister, but then, Jason was more outgoing than just about everyone.

A boat idled into the marina and pulled up to the gas

pumps. Evie went outside to take care of her customers, two young couples who had already spent too much time on the water, judging by their sunburns. After they had paid and left, she checked on Jason and his friends again, but for the time being they were ambling along one of the docks and refraining from any rough horseplay. Knowing teenage boys as she did, she didn't expect that state of affairs to last long.

The day was another scorcher. She glanced up at the white sun in the cloudless sky; no chance of rain to cool things off. Though she had been outside for only a few minutes, she could already feel her hair sticking to the back of her neck as she opened the door to the office and stepped inside. How could the boys stand even being outside in this heat, much less doing anything as strenuous as their energetic clowning around?

She paused as she entered, momentarily blinded by the transition from bright sunlight into relative dimness. Paige was chatting with someone, her eager tone unusual in a girl who was normally quiet except with family members. Evie could see a man standing in front of the counter, but it was another minute before her vision cleared enough for her to make out his lean height and the width of his shoulders. She still couldn't see his features clearly, but nevertheless a tiny alarm of recognition tingled through her, and she drew a controlled breath. "Mr. Cannon."

"Hello." His pale green gaze slipped downward, leisurely examined her legs, which were exposed today, because the heat had been so oppressive that she had worn shorts. The once-over made her feel uncomfortable, and she slipped behind the counter to ring up the gas sale and put the money in the cash drawer.

"What may I do for you?" she asked, without looking at him. She was aware of Paige watching them with open

interest, alerted perhaps by the difference in Evie's manner from the way she usually treated customers.

He ignored the distance in her tone. "I've brought my
boat." He paused. "You *do* still have an available slip?"

"Of course." Business was business, Evie thought. She
opened a drawer and pulled out a rental agreement. "If
you'll complete this, I'll show you to your slip. When you
were here the other day, did you see any particular location that you'd like?"

He glanced down at the sheet in his hand. "No, any one
of them will do," he absently replied as he rapidly read the
agreement. It was straightforward and simple, stating the
rental fee and outlining the rules. At the bottom of the sheet
was a place for two signatures, his and hers. "Is there an
extra copy?" he asked, the businessman in him balking at
signing something without keeping a record of it.

She shrugged and pulled out an extra copy of the rental
agreement, took the one he held from his hands and slipped
a sheet of carbon paper between the two sheets. Briskly
she stapled them together and handed them back to him.
Controlling a smile, Robert swiftly filled out the form,
giving his name and address and how long he intended to
rent the slip. Then he signed at the bottom, returned the
forms to her and pulled out his wallet. The small sign taped
to the counter stated that the marina accepted all major
credit cards, so he removed one and laid it on the counter.

She still didn't look at him as she prepared a credit-
card slip. Robert watched her with well-hidden greed. In
the three days since he'd first met her, he had decided
that she couldn't possibly have been as lovely as he had
first thought or have such an impact on his senses. He had
been wrong. From the moment he had entered the marina
and watched her through the plate-glass window as she
pumped gas, tension had twisted his guts until he could

barely breathe. She was still as sleek and golden and sensual as a pagan goddess, and he wanted her.

He had accomplished a lot in those three days. In addition to making the first chess move with Mercer, he had bought a boat, a car and a house on the river. It had taken two days for the dealership to rig the boat, but he had taken possession of the house faster than that, having moved in the afternoon before. The Realtor still hadn't recovered from his blitzing style of decision making. But Robert wasn't accustomed to being thwarted; in record time the utilities had been turned on, the paperwork completed, a cleaning service from Huntsville dragooned into giving the place a thorough cleaning, and new furniture both selected and delivered. He had also put another plan into progress, one that would force Evie Shaw and Landon Mercer into a trap.

Silently Evie handed him the credit-card slip to sign. He scrawled his signature and returned it to her just as shouts from outside made her whirl.

Robert glanced out the window and saw several teenage boys roughhousing on the docks. "Excuse me," Evie said, and went over to open the door.

"They're going to get it now," Paige piped up with obvious satisfaction, getting to her knees in the rocking chair.

Just as Evie reached the door, Jason laughingly pushed one of his buddies, who immediately returned the shove, with interest. Jason had already turned away, and the motion propelled him forward; his sneakers skidded on a wet spot perilously close to the edge of the dock. His gangly arms began windmilling comically as he tried to reverse direction, but his feet shot out from under him and he flew into the air, over the water.

"Jason!"

He was too close to the dock. Evie saw it even as she

raced through the door, her heart in her mouth. She heard
the sickening crack as his head hit the edge of the dock.
His thin body went limp in midair, and a half second later
he hit the water, immediately slipping beneath the surface.

One of the boys yelled, his young voice cracking. Evie
caught only a glimpse of their bewildered, suddenly terrified faces as she fought her way through the thick, over-
heated air. The dock looked so far away, and she didn't
seem to be making any progress, even though she could
feel her feet thudding on the wood. Frantically she searched
the spot where Jason had gone under, but there was nothing, nothing....

She hit the water in a long, flat dive, stroking strongly
for where she had last seen him. She was dimly aware of
a distant splashing, but she ignored it, all her attention on
reaching Jason in time. *Don't let it be too late. Dear God,
don't let it be too late.* She could still hear the sodden *thunk*
of his head hitting the dock. He could already be dead, or
paralyzed. No. Not Jason. She refused to lose him; she
couldn't lose him. She couldn't go through that again.

She took a deep breath and dived, pushing her way
through the water, her desperately searching hands reaching out. Visibility in the river wasn't good; she would have
to locate him mostly by touch. She reached the muddy bottom and clawed her way along it. He had to be here! There
was the dark pillar of the dock, telling her that she wasn't
too far away from where he had gone in.

Her lungs began to ache, but she refused to surface.
That would use precious seconds, seconds that Jason didn't
have.

Maybe the wave motion had washed him *under* the
dock.

Fiercely she kicked, propelling herself into the darker

water under the dock. Her groping hands swept the water in front of her. *Nothing.*

Her lungs were burning. The need to inhale was almost impossible to resist. Grimly she fought the impulse as she forced her way down to feel along the bottom again.

Something brushed her hand.

She grabbed, and clutched fabric. Her other hand, groping blindly, caught an arm. Using the last of her strength, she tugged her limp burden out of the shadow of the docks and feebly kicked upward. Progress was frustratingly, agonizingly slow; her lungs were demanding air, her vision fading. Dear God, had she found Jason only to drown with him, because she lacked the strength to get them to the surface?

Then strong hands caught her, gripping her ribs with bruising force, and she was propelled upward in a mighty rush. Her head broke the surface, and she inhaled convulsively, choking and gasping.

"I have you," a deep, calm voice said in her ear. "I have both of you. Just relax against me."

She could hardly do anything else. She was supported by an arm as unyielding as iron as he stroked the short distance to the dock. The boys were on their knees, reaching eager hands down toward him. "Just hold him," she heard Cannon order. "Don't try to pull him out of the water. Let me do it. And one of you go call 911."

"I already have," Evie heard Paige say, the girl's voice wavery and thin.

"Good girl." His tone changed to brisk command, the words close by her ear. "Evie. I want you to hang on to the edge of the dock. Can you do that?"

She was still gasping, unable to talk, so she nodded.

"Let go of Jason. The boys are holding him, so he'll be okay. Do it now."

She obeyed, and he placed her hands on the edge of the dock. Grimly she clung to the wood as he heaved himself out of the water. She pushed her streaming hair out of her eyes with one hand as he knelt down and slipped both hands under Jason's arms. "He might have a spinal-cord injury," she croaked.

"I know." Robert's face was grim. "But he isn't breathing. If we don't get him up here and do CPR, he won't make it."

She swallowed hard and nodded again. As gently as possible, Robert lifted Jason out of the water, the muscles in his arms and shoulders cording under the wet shirt. Evie took one agonized look at Jason's still, blue face, and then she hauled herself out of the water, using strength she hadn't known she still possessed. She collapsed on the dock beside Jason, then struggled to her knees. "Jason!"

Robert felt for a pulse in the boy's neck and located a faint throb. Relieved, he said, "He has a heartbeat," then bent over the sprawled, limp body, pinching the boy's nostrils shut and using his other hand to press on his chin, forcing his mouth open. He placed his own mouth on the chill blue lips and carefully, forcefully, blew his breath outward. The thin chest rose. Robert lifted his mouth, and the air sighed out of the boy, his chest falling again.

Evie reached out, then forced herself to draw back. She couldn't do anything that Robert wasn't already doing, and she was still so weak and shaky that she couldn't do it nearly as well. She felt as if she were choking on her pain and desperation, on the overwhelming need to do *something,* anything. Her ears were buzzing. She would rather die herself than helplessly watch someone else she loved slowly die before her eyes.

Robert repeated the process again and again, silently counting. Fiercely he focused on what he was doing, ignoring the terrified kids grouped around them, not letting himself think about Evie's silence, her stillness. The kid's chest was rising with each breath forced into him, meaning oxygen was getting into his lungs. His heart was beating; if he didn't have a serious head or spinal injury, he should be okay, if he would just start breathing on his own. The seconds ticked by. One minute. Two. Then abruptly the boy's chest heaved, and he began choking. Quickly Robert drew back.

Jason suddenly convulsed, rolling to his side and knocking against Evie as he choked and gagged. She lurched sideways, off balance, unable to catch herself. Robert's hand shot out across Jason to steady her, the lean fingers catching her arm and preventing her from going into the water a second time. With effortless strength, he dragged her across Jason's legs, pulling her to him.

Water streamed from Jason's nostrils and open mouth. He gulped and coughed again, then abruptly vomited up a quantity of river water.

"Thank God," Robert said quietly. "No paralysis."

"No." Evie pulled loose from his grip. Tears burned her eyes as she crouched once again by Jason's side. Gently she touched the boy, soothing him, and noticed that the back of his head was red with blood. "You'll be okay, honey," she murmured as she examined the cut. "Nothing that a few stitches won't fix." She glanced up and saw Paige's white, tear-streaked face. "Paige, get a towel for me, please. And be careful! Don't run."

Paige gulped and headed back toward the marina. She didn't exactly run, but it was close.

Jason's coughing fit subsided, and he lay exhausted on his side, gulping in air. Evie stroked his arm, repeating that he was going to be all right.

Paige returned with the towel, and gently Evie pressed it

to the deep cut, stanching the flow of blood. "A-aunt Evie?" Jason croaked, his voice so hoarse it was almost soundless.

"I'm here."

"Can I sit up?" he asked, beginning to be embarrassed by the attention.

"I don't know," she replied neutrally. "Can you?"

Slowly, cautiously, he eased himself into a sitting position, but he was weak, and Robert knelt down to support him, shifting so that one strong thigh was behind Jason's back. "My head hurts," Jason groaned.

"I imagine so," Robert said in a calm, almost genial voice. "You hit it on the edge of the dock." Sirens wailed, swiftly coming closer. Jason's eyes flickered as he realized a further fuss was going to be made.

Gingerly he reached back and touched his head. Wincing, he let his hand fall to his side. "Mom's going to be peed off," he said glumly.

"Mom isn't the only one," Evie replied. "But we'll settle that between ourselves later."

He looked abashed. He tried to move away from Robert's support but didn't quite make it. Then the paramedics were there, hurrying down the dock, carrying their tackle boxes of medical equipment. Robert drew back and pulled Evie with him, giving the paramedics room to work. Paige sidled over and slipped her arms around Evie's waist, burrowing close and hiding her face against Evie's wet shirt in a child's instinctive bid for reassurance. It was a simple thing for Robert to put his arms around both of them, and Evie was too tired, too numb, to resist. She stood docilely in his embrace. His strength enfolded her; his heat comforted her. He had saved Jason's life, and maybe even her own, because she wasn't certain she could have gotten Jason to the surface without his help. If so, she would simply have drowned with him rather than let him go and try to save her own life at the expense of his.

Jason was quickly checked; then the paramedics began preparations to transport him to the hospital. "That cut will have to be stitched," one of them said to Evie. "He probably has a concussion, too, so I wouldn't be surprised if they keep him overnight, at least."

Evie stirred in Robert's embrace. "I have to call Rebecca," she said. "And I want to ride with him to the hospital."

"I'll drive you," he said, releasing her. "You'll need a way back."

"Rebecca can bring me," she said as she hurried to the office, Robert and Paige both following her inside. She reached for the phone, then halted, rubbing her forehead. "No, she'll stay with Jason. Never mind. I can drive myself."

"Of course you can," he said gently. "But you won't, because I'm driving you."

She gave him a distracted look as she dialed her sister's number. "That isn't necessary—Becky. Listen, Jason slipped on the dock and cut his head. He's going to be okay, but he needs stitches, and the paramedics are taking him to the hospital. They're leaving now. I'll meet you there. Yes, I'm bringing Paige with me. Okay. Bye."

She hung up, then lifted the receiver and dialed another number. "Craig, this is Evie. Can you take over the marina for a couple of hours? Jason's had an accident, and I'm going with him to the hospital. No, he'll be okay. Five minutes? Great. I'm leaving now."

Then, moving swiftly, she got her purse from under the counter and fished out her keys. Like lightning, Robert caught her hand and calmly removed the keys from her grasp. "You're too shaky," he said in a gentle, implacable tone. "You came close to drowning yourself. Don't fight me on this, Evie."

It was obvious that she lacked the strength to physically fight him for the keys. Frustrated, she gave in rather than waste more time. "All right."

She drove a sturdy, serviceable four-wheel-drive pickup, handy for pulling boats up a launch ramp. Paige raced ahead to scramble inside, as if afraid she would be left behind if she didn't beat them to the vehicle. Evie was only grateful that the child automatically slid to the middle of the seat, positioning herself between Evie and Robert and hastily buckling herself in.

"It's a straight shift," she blurted unnecessarily as she buckled her own seat belt.

He gave her a gentle smile as he started the engine. "I can manage."

Of course, he did more than manage. He shifted gears with the smooth expertise of someone who knew exactly what he was doing. Evie's heart gave a little thump as she tried to imagine Robert Cannon being awkward at anything.

She forced herself to watch the road, rather than him, as she gave directions to the hospital. She didn't want to look at him, didn't want to feel that primal pull deep inside her. He was dripping wet, of course, his black hair plastered to his head and his white silk shirt clinging to his muscled torso like a second skin. His leanness was deceptive; the wet shirt revealed the width of his shoulders and chest, and the smooth, steely muscles of his abdomen and back. She thought the image of him, the outline of his body, was probably branded on her mind for all eternity, as was everything else that had happened in the last fifteen minutes. Only fifteen minutes? It felt like a lifetime.

He drove fast, pulling into the hospital parking lot right

behind the ambulance. The hospital was small but new, and he couldn't fault the staff's response. Jason was whisked into an examining room before Evie could reach his side to speak to him.

Firmly Robert took her arm and ushered both her and Paige to seats in the waiting area. "Sit here," he said, and though his voice was mild, that implacable tone was in it again. "I'll get coffee for us. How about you, sweetheart?" he asked Paige. "Do you want a soft drink?"

Dumbly Paige nodded, then shook her head. "May I have coffee, too, Aunt Evie?" she whispered. "I'm cold. Or maybe hot chocolate."

Evie nodded her agreement, and Robert strode to the vending machines. She put her arm around Paige and gathered her close, knowing that the girl had suffered a shock at seeing her brother almost die. "Don't worry, honey. Jason will be home by tomorrow, probably, griping about his headache and driving you up the wall."

Paige sniffed back tears. "I know. I'll get mad at him then, but right now I just want him to be okay."

"He will be. I promise."

Robert returned with three cups, one filled with hot chocolate and the other two with coffee. Evie and Paige took theirs from him, and he settled into the chair on Evie's other side. When she sipped the hot brew, she found that he had liberally dosed it with sugar. She glanced at him and found him watching her, gauging her reaction. "Drink it," he said softly. "You're a little shocky, too."

Because he was right, she obeyed without argument, folding her cold fingers around the cup in an effort to warm them. Her wet clothes were uncomfortably chilly here in the air-conditioned hospital, and she barely restrained a shiver. He should be cold, too, she thought, but knew that he wasn't. His arm touched hers, and she felt heat radiating through his wet clothing.

As slight as it was, he felt the shiver that raced through her. "I'll get a blanket for you," he said, rising to his feet.

She watched him approach the desk and speak to the nurse. He was courteous, restrained, but in about thirty seconds he was returning with a blanket in his hands. He had an air of natural command, she thought. One look into those icy green eyes and people scurried to do his bidding.

He bent over her to tuck the blanket around her, and she let him. Just as he finished, the emergency room doors swung open and her sister, Rebecca, hurried inside, looking tense and scared. Seeing Evie and Paige, she changed her direction to join them. "What's happening?" she demanded.

"He's in the treatment room now," Robert answered for Evie, his deep voice as soothing as when he'd talked to Paige. "He'll have a few stitches in the back of his head, and a bad headache. They'll probably keep him overnight, but his injuries are relatively minor."

Rebecca turned her shrewd brown eyes on him and bluntly demanded, "Who are you?"

"This is Robert Cannon," Evie said, making an effort to appear calm as she made the introductions. "He dragged both Jason and me out of the water. Mr. Cannon, this is my sister, Rebecca Wood."

Rebecca took in Robert's wet clothes, then looked at Evie, seeing the strain on her sister's pale face. "I'll see about Jason first," she said in her usual decisive manner. "Then I want to know exactly what happened." She turned and marched toward a nurse, identified herself and was directed to the treatment room where Jason was located.

Robert sat down beside Evie. "What branch of the military was your sister in?" he asked, provoking a nervous giggle from Paige.

"I think it's called motherhood," Evie replied. "She began practicing on me at an early age."

"She's older, I presume."

"Five years."

"So you've always been 'baby sister' to her."

"I don't mind."

"I'm sure you don't. Drink your coffee," he admonished, lifting the cup himself and holding it to her lips.

Evie drank, then gave him a wry glance. "You aren't bad at the mother-hen routine yourself."

He allowed himself a slight smile. "I take care of my own." The words were a subtle threat—and a warning, if she were astute enough to hear it.

She didn't make the obvious retort, that she wasn't "his"; instead she withdrew, sinking back in her chair and staring straight ahead. Jason's close call had brought too many old memories to the surface, making it difficult for her to deal with anything just now, much less Robert Cannon. Right now, what she wanted most of all was to crawl into bed and pull the covers over her head, shutting out the world until she felt capable of facing it again. Maybe by the time night came, certainly by tomorrow, she would be all right. Then she would worry about the way he had taken over and about the gentle possessiveness that she couldn't fight. With Cannon, Evie was beginning to link gentleness with an implacable force of will that let nothing stand in his way. He would be tender and protective, but he would not be thwarted.

They sat in silence until Rebecca came out of the treatment room to rejoin them. "They're keeping him overnight," she said. "He has a slight concussion, a big shaved spot on the back of his head and ten stitches. He also won't say exactly what happened, other than mumbling that he fell. What's he trying to hide from me?"

Evie hesitated, trying to decide exactly what to tell Rebecca, and that gave Paige enough time to pipe up. "Scott and Jeff and Patrick came by the marina, and they were all acting silly out on the docks. Aunt Evie yelled at Jason to settle down, but they didn't. Jason pushed Patrick, and Patrick pushed him back, and Jason slipped and fell, and hit his head on the dock, then went into the water. Aunt Evie went in after him, and she was under forever and ever, and Mr. Cannon tried to find both of them. Then Aunt Evie came up, and she had Jason, and Mr. Cannon pulled them to the dock. Jason wasn't breathing, Mom, and Aunt Evie nearly drowned, too. Mr. Cannon had to do that artificial breathing stuff on Jason, and then Jason started coughing and puking, and the paramedics came. I called 911," she finished in a rush.

Rebecca looked a bit bemused at this flood of words from her quiet child but heard the fear still lurking under the loquaciousness. She sat down beside Paige and hugged her. "You did exactly right," she praised, and Paige gave a little sigh of relief.

Rebecca examined Evie's pale, drawn face. "He's all right," she said reassuringly. "At least for now. As soon as he's recovered, I'm going to kill him. Better yet, I think I'll ground him for the rest of the summer. *Then* I'll kill him."

Evie managed a smile. "If he lives through all that, I want a turn at him."

"It's a deal. Now, I want you to go home and get out of those wet clothes. You look worse than Jason does."

The smile, this time, was easier. "Gee, thanks." But she knew that Rebecca's sharp eyes had seen below the surface and recognized the strain that she was under.

"I'll see to her," Robert said, standing and urging Evie

to her feet. She wanted to protest, she really did, but she was so tired, her nerves so strained, that it was too much effort. So she managed to say goodbye to Rebecca and Paige, and tell them to kiss Jason for her; then she gave in and let him usher her out of the building and across the parking lot to the truck. She had left the blanket behind, but the searing afternoon heat washed over her like a glow, and she shivered with delight.

Robert's arm tightened around her waist. "Are you still cold?"

"No, I'm fine," she murmured. "The heat feels good."

He opened the truck door and lifted her onto the seat. The strength in his hands and arms, the ease with which he picked her up, made her shiver again. She closed her eyes and let her head rest against the window, as much from a desire to shut him out as from an almost overpowering fatigue.

"You can't go to sleep," he said as he got in on the driver's side, amusement lacing his tone. "You have to give me directions to your house."

She forced herself to open her eyes and sit up, and gave him calm, coherent directions. It didn't take long to get anywhere in Guntersville, and less than fifteen minutes later he stopped the truck in her driveway. She fumbled with the door but was so clumsy that he was there before she managed it, opening it and supporting her with a firm hand under her elbow. She got out, reluctant to let him inside her house but accepting the inevitable. Best just to go shower and change as fast as she could, and get it over with.

He entered right behind her. "Have a seat," she invited automatically as she headed toward her bedroom. "I'll be out in about fifteen minutes."

"I'm still too wet to sit down," he said. "But take your time. I'll go out on the deck, if that's okay with you."

"Of course," she said, giving him a polite smile without really looking at him, and escaped into the privacy of her bedroom.

Robert eyed the closed door thoughtfully. She was so wary of him that she wouldn't even look at him if she could help it. It wasn't a response he was accustomed to from a woman, though God knew she had reason to be wary, given his assumption that she knew of his connection to PowerNet. She couldn't have acted any more guilty if he had caught her red-handed. He could opt for patience and let time disarm her, but he already had plans in motion that would force the issue, so he decided to allay her suspicions in another manner, by making a definite, concerted effort to seduce her. He had planned to seduce her, anyway; he would simply intensify the pressure.

He heard the shower start running. He couldn't have asked for a better opportunity to look around, and he took advantage of it. The house was probably forty years old, he thought, but had been remodeled so the interior was open and more modern, with exposed beams and gleaming hardwood floors. She had a green thumb; indoor plants of all sizes occupied every available flat surface. He could see into the kitchen from where he stood in the living room, and beyond that was the deck, with double French doors opening onto it. A dock led from the deck down to a boathouse.

Her furnishings were neat and comfortable, but certainly not luxurious. Without haste, he went over to the big, old-fashioned rolltop desk and methodically searched it, unearthing nothing of any great interest, not that he had expected to find anything. It wasn't likely she would have been fool enough to leave him in the room with an unlocked desk if the desk contained anything incriminating. He looked through her bank statement but found no unusually large deposits, at least at this particular bank or on this particular statement.

There was a small, framed photograph on the desk. He picked it up and examined the two people pictured. Evie, defintiely—a very young Evie, but already glowing with seductiveness. The boy, for he was nothing more than that, was probably her husband, dead now for twelve years. Robert studied the boy's face more closely, seeing laughter and happiness and yes, devotion. But had the boy any idea how to handle the sensual treasure that the girl in his arms represented? Of course not; what teenage boy would? Still, Robert felt an unexpected and unpleasant twinge of jealousy for this long-dead boy, for the riches that had so briefly been his. Evie had loved him, enough that she still wore his wedding ring after all these years.

He heard the shower shut off and replaced the photograph, then quietly walked out onto the deck. She had a nice place here, nothing extravagant, but cozy and homey. There was plenty of privacy, too, with no houses visible except for those on the far side of the lake. The water was very blue, reflecting both the green of the mountains and the deep blue bowl of the sky. The afternoon was slipping away, and the sun was lower now, but still white and searing. Soon it would begin to turn bronze, and the lush scents of the heavy greenery would grow stronger. By the time purple twilight brought a respite from the heat, the air would be redolent with honeysuckle and roses, pine and fresh-cut grass. Time was slower here; people didn't rush from one occupation to another. He had actually seen people sitting on their front porches, reading newspapers or shelling peas, occasionally waving to passersby. Of course, people from New York and other large cities would say that the locals here had nothing to rush *to,* but from what he'd seen they stayed busy enough; they just didn't get in any great hurry.

He heard Evie come to the open French door. "I'm ready," she said.

He turned and looked at her. Her newly washed hair was still wet, but she had braided it and pinned the braids up so they wouldn't get her shirt damp. She had exchanged the shorts for jeans, and had on a pink T-shirt that made her golden skin glow. But her cheeks were still a bit pale, and her expression was strained.

"You have a nice place," he said.

"Thanks. I inherited it from my in-laws."

Though he knew the answer, now was the time to ask for information; it would be odd if he didn't. "You're married?" he asked.

"Widowed." She turned and retreated into the house, and Robert followed her.

"Ah. I'm sorry. How long has it been?"

"Twelve years."

"I saw the picture on the desk. Is that your husband?"

"Yes, that's Matt." She stopped and looked toward the photograph, and an ineffable sadness darkened her eyes. "We were just kids." Then she seemed to gather herself and walked briskly to the door. "I need to get back to the marina."

"My house is about five miles from here," he said. "It won't take long for me to shower and change."

She carried a towel out to the truck and dried the seat before she got inside. She didn't even bother protesting his continued possession of her keys; it would be pointless, though she was now obviously calm enough to drive safely.

His clothes had dried enough that they were merely damp now, rather than dripping wet, but she knew they had to be uncomfortable. Hers certainly had been. Her conscience twinged. He had not only saved Jason's life but likely hers, as well, and had put himself to a great deal of trouble to see that she was taken care of. No matter how he alarmed her, she knew that she would never forget his quick actions or his cool decisiveness.

"Thank you," she said softly, staring straight ahead. "Jason and I probably wouldn't have made it without you."

"The likelihood was unnerving," he said, his tone cool and even. "You'd pushed yourself so far that you couldn't have gotten him out of the water. Didn't it occur to you to let go of him and come up for another breath?"

"No." The single word was flat. "I couldn't have done that."

He glanced at her profile, saw the deepening strain in her expression and deftly changed the subject. "Will your sister really ground him for the rest of the summer?"

Evie was startled into a laugh, a rusty little sound that went right to his gut. "I'd say he'll be lucky if that's all she does. It isn't that he was fooling around, but that I'd already told him to stop and he disobeyed me."

"So he broke a cardinal rule?"

"Just about."

Robert intended to have a few words with the young man himself, about acting responsibly and the possible consequences of reckless actions, but he didn't mention it to Evie. She was obviously very protective of her niece and nephew, and though she couldn't say that it wasn't any of his business, she wouldn't like it. His conversation with Jason would be private.

When he stopped in the driveway of his new house, Evie looked around with interest. "This place has been on the market for almost a year," she said.

"Then I'm lucky no one beat me to it, aren't I?" He got

out and walked around the truck to open the door for her. Though she hadn't waited for him to perform the service at the hospital, that had been an emergency; nor would she have waited when they had reached her house, if she had been able to get the door open in time. He'd had the strong impression then that she had wanted to bolt inside and lock him out. Now, however, she waited with the natural air of a queen, as if he were only doing what he should. She might be dressed in jeans, sneakers and a T-shirt, but that didn't lessen her femininity one whit; she *expected* that male act of servitude. Robert had always preferred to treat women with the small courtesies but hadn't insisted on them when his partner had protested. He was both amused and charmed by Evie's rather regal, very Southern attitude.

He mused about this subtle signal as he ushered her into the house. Though she was still very wary of him, obviously on some level her resistance had weakened. Anticipation tightened his muscles, but he deliberately resisted it. Now was not the time. Not quite yet.

"Make yourself at home while I shower," he invited, smiling faintly as he walked toward his bedroom, which was down the hallway to the right. He had no doubt that she would do exactly as he had done, take full advantage of the opportunity to do a quick search.

Evie stood in the middle of the living room after he had gone, too tense to "make herself at home." She looked around, trying to distract herself. The house was sprawling and modern, one story of brick and redwood, easily three times the size of her own. A huge rock fireplace dominated the left wall, the chimney soaring upward to the cathedral ceiling. Twin white ceiling fans stirred a gentle breeze. The furniture was chic but comfortable-looking, sized to fit a man of his height.

The living room was separated from the dining room by a waist-high planter in which luxurious ferns flourished. Huge double windows revealed a deck, furnished with comfortable chairs, an umbrella table and even more plants. Hesitantly she walked into the dining room for a better view. The kitchen opened up to the right, an immaculate oasis gleaming with the most modern appliances available. Even the coffeemaker looked as if the user would need a degree in engineering to work the thing. There was a breakfast nook on the far side of the kitchen, occupied by a smallish table with a white ceramic tile top. She could see him sitting there in the mornings, reading a newspaper and drinking coffee. Double French doors, far more ornate and stylish than her own, led from the breakfast nook onto the deck. She would have liked to explore further but felt too constrained here on his territory. Instead she retreated to the living room once more.

Robert took his time showering and dressing. Let her look around all she wanted; the fact that she wouldn't find anything alarming would help allay her suspicions. She would begin to relax, which was exactly what he wanted.

A lot of men, maybe most of them, would have made a move while they had been at her house; she had been more off-balance, vulnerable. He had even had the opportunity, had he chosen to take it, of walking in on her while she was unclothed. But he had elected to wait, knowing she would be more at ease now that the most provocative and dangerous circumstances were past. He hadn't made a pass at her then, so she wouldn't be expecting him to do so now. And since she wouldn't be mentally prepared to handle an advance, her response would be honest, unguarded.

Finally he stopped dawdling and returned to the living room. To his surprise, she was still standing almost exactly where he had left her, and little of the strain had

faded from her face. She turned to watch him. Her lovely
golden brown eyes were still dark with some inner distress
that went far deeper than the episode with Jason, traumatic
as that had been.

Robert paused while still several feet from her, studying those somber eyes. Then he simply moved forward
with a graceful speed that gave her no time to evade him,
and took her in his arms. He heard her instinctive intake
of breath, saw the alarm widening her eyes as she lifted
her head to protest, a protest that was smothered when his
mouth covered hers.

She jerked in his arms, and he gently controlled the action, pulling her even more firmly against him. He took
care not to hurt her but deepened the insistent pressure
of his mouth until he felt her own mouth yield and open.
The sweetness of her lips sent an electrical thrill along his
nerves, tightening his muscles and swelling his sex. He
took her mouth with his tongue, holding her still for the
imitative sexual possession, repeating the motion again
and again, until she shivered and softened in his arms, her
lips beginning to cling to his.

Her tentative response made his head swim, and to his
surprise he had to struggle to maintain his control. But
she felt perfect in his arms, damn her, all those soft, luscious curves molding to the hard, muscled planes of his
body. Her mouth was sweeter than any he had ever tasted
before, and the simple act of kissing her was arousing him
to an unbelievable degree.

He didn't want to stop. He hadn't planned to do more
than kiss her, but he hadn't expected the intensity of his
own response. His mouth crushed fiercely down on hers,
demanding even more. He heard the soft, helpless sound
she made in her throat; then her arms lifted around his
neck, and she pressed full length against him. Pure, prim-

itive male triumph roared through him at this evidence
of her own arousal. He could feel her breasts, round and
firm, the nipples hard against his chest, and he slipped
his hand under her shirt to cup one of them, his thumb
rubbing across the peaked nipple through the thin lace of
her bra. Her body arched, her hips pressing hard against
his…and then suddenly she was fighting, panicked, trying to squirm free.

He let her go, though every cell in his body was screaming for more. "Easy," he managed to say, but the word was
low and rough and his breath was uneven. He tried for a
more controlled reassurance. "I won't hurt you, sweetheart."

Evie had backed away from him, her face pale but her
lips swollen and red from his kisses. She forced herself
to stop retreating, to stand her ground and face him. The
sensual pull of his masculinity was almost overwhelming, tempting her to go back into those arms, to yield to
that fierce domination. She felt a sense of doom; he was
far more dangerous to her than she had first suspected.

"Yes, you will," she whispered. Her teeth were chattering. "Why are you doing this? What do you want from
me?"

CHAPTER FIVE

SHE LOOKED READY to bolt. To soothe her, he moved back a few paces and let his hands relax at his sides. His eyes gleamed with faint irony. "You're a lovely woman, sweetheart. Surely you aren't surprised that I'm attracted to you? As for what I want from you, I was holding you closely enough that the answer to that question should have been obvious."

She didn't respond to his gentle teasing. Instead her somber gaze remained locked on his face, trying to probe beneath that smooth, urbane sophistication. He was very cosmopolitan, beyond a doubt, but he used that slick surface as a shield to hide the real man, the man who had kissed her with such ruthless passion. There were many hidden layers to him, his motives complex and unfathomable. Yes, he was attracted to her, as she was to him. It would be foolish to deny her own participation, and Evie wasn't a foolish woman. But she always had the feeling that he was studying her, manipulating her in some subtle manner. From the very first she had sensed his determination to force himself into her life, and he was doing exactly that with a calm force of will that refused to be denied. Whatever his motive, it was something that went beyond the physical.

"I don't have casual sex," she said.

He almost smiled. It was merely an expression in those pale eyes, rather than an actual movement of his mouth.

"My dear, I promise you there wouldn't be anything *casual* about it." He paused. "Are you involved with someone else?"

She shook her head. "No."

He wasn't surprised that she had denied any involvement with Mercer. "Then we don't have a problem, do we? You can't say that you aren't attracted to me, too."

She lifted her chin, and his pale eyes gleamed at that proud motion. "That velvet glove covers an iron fist, doesn't it?" she commented neutrally. "No, I can't say that I'm not attracted to you."

Her perception disturbed him, a reaction that he didn't allow to surface. "I can be determined when I want something…or someone."

She made an abrupt motion, as if tiring of the verbal jousting. "I phrased it wrong. I don't have affairs, either."

"A wise decision, but in this case too restrictive." He approached her now, and she didn't retreat. Gently he cupped her face with one long-fingered hand, his fingers stroking over the velvety texture of her cheek. God, she was lovely, not classically beautiful, but glowing with an intensely female seductiveness that made him think her name was very apt indeed. So must Eve have been, glorious in her nudity. No wonder Adam had been so easily led, a weakness he wouldn't allow himself, though he intended to fully enjoy Evie's sensuality. Her sweet, warm scent wafted up to him. "I won't force you," he murmured. "But I will have you."

"If you won't use force, how do you intend to go about it?" she asked.

His eyebrows lifted. "You think I should warn you?"

"Yes."

"An interesting notion, but one I'm going to leave untried." He rubbed his thumb over her lower lip. "For now, sweetheart, we'd better get back to the marina. You have a business to run, and I have a boat to get into a slip."

He let his hand drop as he spoke, and Evie turned from him with relief, as if she had been released from a force field. Her face tingled where he had touched her, and she remembered the electric sensation when he had put his hand on her breast. His boldness spoke of vast experience and self-confidence with women, something that put her at a disadvantage.

They were both silent on the drive back to the marina. She was vaguely surprised to see how late it was, the sun dipping low even for these long summer days. The sultry heat hadn't abated, though there was a hint of purple on the horizon that gave the promise of a cooling rain shower.

Robert's speedboat, a sleek, dark eighteen-footer, was still where he had left it, hitched to a black Jeep Renegade. Thank heavens it hadn't been blocking the launch ramps, or Craig would have had a mess on his hands. She hurried into the marina office, and Craig looked up from the sports magazine he was reading. "Is everything okay?" he asked, getting to his feet. "The kids said that Jason nearly drowned."

"He has a concussion, but he'll go home tomorrow," she said. "Thanks for coming in. I'm sorry for wrecking your day."

"No problem," he said cheerfully. He was seventeen, a tall, muscular, dark-haired kid who would be a senior when the new school year started. He had been working part-time for her for almost two years and was so steady that she had no qualms about leaving him in charge. "Say, what about that new boat outside?"

"It's mine," Robert said, stepping inside. "I'll be renting a slip here." He held out his hand. "I'm Robert Cannon."

Craig took his hand with a firm grip. "Craig Foster.

Glad to meet you, Mr. Cannon. You must be the guy who pulled Evie and Jason out of the water. The kids said it was a tall Yankee."

"I'm the guy," Robert affirmed, amusement in his eyes.

"Thought so. Want me to help you get the boat into a slip?"

"I can do it," Evie said. "I've taken enough time out of your day."

"You pay me for it," Craig replied, grinning. "I might as well, since I'm already here. Mom won't be expecting me back until supper, anyway." He and Robert left, chatting companionably.

Kids seemed to like Robert, Evie thought, watching them from the window. Even shy Paige had been at ease with him. He didn't treat kids as equals—he was the adult, his was the authority—but at the same time he didn't dismiss them. Authority and responsibility sat easily on those broad shoulders, she mused. He was obviously accustomed to command.

For her own sake, her own protection, she had to hold him at bay, and she didn't know if she could. Today, with a few kisses and frightening ease, he had shown her that he could arouse her beyond her own control. She could love him, and that was the most terrifying prospect of all. He was a strong man, in mind and soul as well as body, a man worthy of love. He would steal her heart if she weren't careful, if she didn't keep her guard up at all times.

She turned away from the window. Twelve years ago, love had almost destroyed her, leaving only a forlorn heap of ashes from which she had laboriously rebuilt a controlled, protected life. She couldn't do that again; she didn't have the strength to once more live through that hell and emerge victorious. She had already lost too many people to believe that love, or life, lasted forever. She couldn't do anything about the people she already loved, the ones already in her heart: her family, old Virgil, a very few close friends, but she hadn't allowed anyone new to stake a claim on her emotions. She had already paid out too much in pain and had precious little reserve of spirit left. She had almost lost Jason today, and the pain had been overwhelming. Rebecca knew, had realized that if Evie hadn't been able to find Jason, she would now be mourning a sister as well as a son. That was the real basis for her sister's fury with Jason.

And Evie knew that Robert Cannon planned to force his way into her life. He would be here for the summer, he'd said; he wouldn't be looking for anything more than a pleasant affair, companionship during the long, lazy weeks. If she fell in love with him, that would make the affair sweeter. But at the end of summer he would go back to his real life, and Evie would have to continue here, with one more wound on a heart that had barely survived the last blow. Emotionally, she couldn't afford him.

There were always a hundred and one things to be doing around the marina, but suddenly she couldn't think of a single one. She felt oddly disoriented, as if the world had been turned upside down. Maybe it had.

She called the hospital and was put through to Jason's room. Her sister answered the phone on the first ring. "He's grouchy and has a throbbing headache," Rebecca cheerfully announced when Evie asked his condition. "I have to wake him every couple of hours tonight, but if he does okay, then he can go home in the morning. Paul left just a few minutes ago to take Paige to his mother's, then he's coming back here. How about you? Nerves settled down yet?"

"Not quite," Evie said truthfully, though Jason's close

call wasn't all that had unsettled her. "But I'm over the shakes."

"Are you at home, I hope?"

"You know better than that."

"You should have taken it easy for the rest of the day," Rebecca scolded. "I had hopes that Mr. Cannon would take you in hand. He seems good at giving orders."

"World-class champion," Evie agreed. "I'll come by to see Jason after the marina closes. Do you want me to bring you anything? A pillow, a book, a hamburger?"

"No, I don't need anything. Don't come here. Jason's okay, and you need to go home and rest. I mean it, Evie."

"I'm okay, too," Evie calmly replied. "And I want to see Jason, even if just for a few minutes—" She cried out in surprise as the phone was plucked from her hand. She whirled as Robert lifted the receiver to his ear.

"Mrs. Wood? Robert Cannon. I'll see that she goes straight home. Yes, she's still a little wobbly."

"I am not," Evie said, narrowing her eyes at him. He reached out and gently stroked her cheek. Deliberately she stepped back, out of his reach.

"I'll take care of her," he firmly assured Rebecca, never moving his gaze from Evie's face. "On second thought, I'll take her out to dinner before I take her home. I think so, too. Goodbye."

As he hung up, Evie said in a cold voice, "I despise being treated as if I'm a helpless idiot."

"Hardly that," he murmured.

She didn't relent. "I suppose you thought that I would feel safe and protected, to have you take over and make my decisions for me. I don't. I feel insulted."

Robert lifted an inquisitive brow, hiding his true reaction. He had indeed hoped to provoke exactly that response from her and felt an uneasy surprise that she had so easily gone straight to the truth of the matter. She was proving to be uncomfortably astute. "What I think," he said carefully, "is that you were in more danger than you want your sister to know, and that you're still shaky. If you go to the hospital again, you'll have to put up a front to keep from scaring both her and Jason, and that will put even more strain on you."

"What *I* think," she replied, standing with her fists clenched at her sides, "is that I'm in far more danger from you than I ever was from the water." Her golden brown eyes were cool and unwaveringly level.

Again he felt a twinge of discomfort at her insight. Still, he was certain he could soften her stand, and his tone turned gently cajoling. "Even if I offer you a truce for tonight? No kisses, not even any hand-holding. Just dinner, then I'll see you safely home, and you can get a good night's rest."

"No, thank you. I won't have dinner with you, and I can get home by myself."

He gave her a considering look. "In that case, the offer of a truce is null and void."

His tone was so calm that she listened to it first, rather than to the actual words. She hesitated only a split second, but that was enough for him to have her in his arms again, and again she felt overcome by his steely, deceptive strength. His body was unyielding, his grip careful but unbreakable. The male muskiness of his clean, warm skin made her head swim. She had the dizzy impression that his mouth was lowering to hers and quickly ducked her head to rest it against his chest. It was disconcerting to hear a quiet chuckle over her head.

"Such a cowardly act, from one who isn't," he murmured, the words rich with amusement. "But I don't mind simply holding you. It has its own compensations."

She *was* a coward, though, Evie thought. She was terrified of him, not in a physical way, but emotional fear was just as weighty a burden to carry. She was handling him all wrong; he wouldn't be accustomed to rejection, so every time she turned him down it made him just that much more determined to have his way. If she had played up to him from the beginning, gushed over him, he would have been bored and left her alone. Hindsight, though, despite its acuity, was depressingly useless.

His hand moved soothingly over her back, subtly urging her closer. It was so easy to let him take more of her weight, so easy to give in to the strain and fatigue she had been successfully fighting until now. She resisted the urge to put her arms around him, to feel the heated vibrancy of his body under her hands, but she could hear the strong, steady thumping of his heartbeat beneath her ear, feel the rise and fall of his chest as he breathed, and that was enough to work its own seduction. The forces of life were strong in him, luring women to that intense strength. She was no different from all those countless, nameless others.

"Robert," she whispered. "Don't." A cowardly, shameless, useless plea.

That hand stroked up to her shoulder blades, rubbed the sensitive tendons that ran from her neck to her shoulders, massaged her tender nape. "Evie," he whispered in return. "Don't what?" He continued without waiting for a reply. "Is Evie your real name, or is it a nickname for Eve? Or possibly Evelyn? No matter, it suits you."

Her eyes drifted shut as his warmth and strength continued to work their black magic on her nerves, her will. Oh God, it would be so foolishly easy just to give in to him. His skill was nothing short of diabolical. "Neither. It's short for Evangeline."

"Ah." The short sigh was one of approval. He truly

hadn't known her full name; none of the reports he had seen had called her anything except Evie. "Evangeline. Feminine, spiritual, sensual...sad."

Evie didn't respond outwardly to that analysis of her name, but the last word shook her. Sad...yes. So sad that for several long, bleak years she couldn't have said if the sun ever shone or not, because with her heart she had seen only gray. She could see the sunshine now; the relentless current of life as a whole had swept her out of the darkness, but there was never a day when she didn't realize how closely the shadows lurked. They were always there, a permanent counterpoint to life. If there was light, there had to be darkness; joy was balanced by pain, intimacy by loneliness. No one sailed through life untouched.

He was subtly rocking her with his body, a barely perceptible swaying that nevertheless urged her deeper and deeper into his embrace. He was aroused again; there was no mistaking that. She thought she should move away, but somehow in the past few minutes that had ceased to be an option. She was so tired, and the gentle motion of his body was soothing, like the swaying of a boat at anchor. The ancient rhythms were difficult to resist, linked as they were to instincts aeons beyond her control.

After several minutes he murmured, "Are you going to sleep?"

"I could," she replied, not opening her eyes. Beyond the danger, there was deep comfort in his embrace.

"It's almost six-thirty. Under the circumstances, I'm sure your customers would understand if you closed a little early."

"An hour and a half isn't a 'little' early. No, I'll stay until eight, as usual."

"Then so will I." He stifled his surge of annoyance. He himself let very few things interfere with his work—

in actuality, only Madelyn and her family—but he didn't like the idea of Evie pushing herself into exhaustion at the marina.

"It isn't necessary."

"I rather believe it is," he replied thoughtfully.

"I still won't go out to dinner with you."

"Fair enough. I'll bring dinner to you. Do you have any preferences?"

She shook her head. "I'm not very hungry. I was going to have a sandwich when I got home."

"Leave it all to me."

She said against his chest, "You take charge very naturally. I suppose this is normal behavior for you."

"I'm decisive, yes."

"Don't forget autocratic."

"I'm sure you'll remind me if I forget."

She heard the undertone of amusement in his voice. Damn him, why couldn't he be nasty in his bullying, rather than relentlessly, gently cosseting? She never allowed herself to rely on anyone, though Rebecca had been trying to take care of her for years, but Robert simply ignored her resistance.

"I realize I'm rushing you," he murmured into her hair. "Today is only the second time we've met. I'll back off, sweetheart, and give you time to get to know me better and feel more comfortable around me. Okay?"

Her head moved up and down. She didn't want to agree to have anything to do with him, but right now she would grasp at any offer to cool down the situation. He had knocked her off balance, and she still hadn't regained it. Yes, she needed time, a lot of it.

Robert cupped her chin in his hand and forced her to lift her head away from the shelter of his chest. His pale green eyes were glittering with intensity. "But I won't go away," he warned.

Evie slept heavily that night, exhausted by the stress of the day. When she woke at dawn at the far-off roar of an early fisherman's outboard motor, she didn't rise immediately as was her habit but lay watching the pearly light spread across the sky.

For twelve years she had kept herself safe inside her carefully constructed fortress, but Robert was storming the walls. *Had* stormed them, if she was honest with herself. He was already in the inner court, though he hadn't yet managed to breach the defenses of the keep. Since Matt's death, she hadn't really *seen* any man, but Robert had forced her to see him. She was attracted to him, mentally as well as physically; it was only with effort that she had kept her emotions still safely locked away. She didn't want to love him and knew she risked doing exactly that if she continued to see him.

But she *would* see him, time and again. He had warned her—or was it a promise?—that he wasn't going to leave her alone, and he wasn't a man who could be easily distracted from his purpose.

He would kiss her, hold her, caress her. Eventually, she knew, all of her caution would vanish under the sheer force of physical desire, and she wouldn't be able to stop him—or herself.

She closed her eyes and relived the way he had kissed her the afternoon before, the way he had tasted, the calm expertise with which he had deepened the kiss. She thought of his lean fingers on her breast, and her nipples throbbed. For the first time since Matt, she wondered about making love in relation to herself. She thought of the feel of Robert's hard weight pressing down on her, of his hands and mouth moving over her bare skin, of his muscled thighs spreading hers apart as he positioned himself to take her. The appeal of her fantasy was strong enough to make her entire body clench with desire. Yes, she wanted him, as much as she feared the pain he would leave behind when he walked out of her life.

A prudent woman would immediately see a doctor about birth control, and Evie was a prudent woman. She could protect herself in that way, at least.

CHAPTER SIX

EVIE SLID TWO food-filled plates onto the table, one in front of Rebecca and the other in front of her own seat, then refilled their coffee cups. "Thanks." Rebecca sighed, picking up her fork. Her eyes were dark-circled after the long, sleepless night spent with Jason in the hospital.

Evie sat down. After making a doctor's appointment for the next day, she had called the hospital to check on Jason. He was fine, but Rebecca had some definitely frayed edges. Not only had she been awake all night to keep watch on him and wake him regularly, evidently Jason had become as fractious and ill-tempered as he'd been as a baby whenever he was ill. He had complained about everything, griping about being woken every hour, even though both the doctor and Rebecca had explained the reason for it. In short, his mother's wrath was about to come down hard on his sore head.

So Evie had gone up to the hospital to take care of the myriad details involved in releasing Jason. Then she'd followed them home, helped get the restless teenager settled, pushed Rebecca into a chair and set about making breakfast for them all. She knew her way around Rebecca's kitchen as well as she did her own, so the work went smoothly, and in no time at all they were digging into scrambled eggs, bacon and toast. Jason was enthroned on the couch with a tray on his lap and the television blaring.

The coffee revived Rebecca enough that her big-sister

instincts kicked in. She gave Evie a shrewd look over the rim of her cup. "Where did you have dinner last night?"

"At the marina. Sandwiches," Evie clarified.

Rebecca sat back, looking disgruntled. "He said he would take you out to dinner, then make sure you got home okay."

"I didn't want to go out."

"Really," Rebecca grumbled, "I'd thought the man was made of stronger stuff than that."

If he'd been any stronger, Evie thought wryly, she would have slept in *his* bed last night. "I was too tired to go out, so he brought sandwiches there. It was kind of him to do everything he did yesterday."

"Especially hauling both you and my brat out of the river," Rebecca said judiciously as she demolished a slice of bacon. "I need to thank him again for you. I'm reserving judgment on the wisdom of saving Jason."

Evie chuckled at Rebecca's sardonic statement. A sharp turn of phrase was a family trait that she shared with her sister, and even Paige had been exhibiting it for some time now.

"However," Rebecca continued in the same tone, "I know a man on the hunt when I see one, so don't try to throw me off the subject by telling me how *kind* he was. Kindness was the last thing on his mind."

Evie looked down at her eggs. "I know."

"Are you going to give him a chance, or are you going to look straight through him, like all the others?"

"What others?" Evie asked, puzzled.

"See what I mean? They were invisible to you. You've never even noticed all the guys who would have liked to go out with you."

"No one's ever asked me out."

"Why would they, when you never notice them? But I'll bet Robert asked you out, didn't he?"

"No." He'd *told* her that she was going out to dinner with him, and he had told her that he intended to make love to her, but he'd never actually asked her out.

Rebecca looked disbelieving. "You're pulling my leg."

"I am not. But he'll probably ask the next time he comes to the marina, if that's any consolation to you."

"The real question," her sister said shrewdly, "is if you'll go with him."

"I don't know." Evie propped her elbows on the table, the coffee cup cradled in her palms as she sipped the hot liquid. "He excites me, Becky, but he scares me, too. I don't want to get involved with anyone, and I'm afraid I wouldn't be able to stop myself with him."

"This is bad?" asked her sister with some exasperation. "Honey, it's been twelve years. Maybe it's time you became interested in men again."

"Maybe," Evie said in qualified agreement, though privately she didn't think so at all. "But Robert Cannon isn't the safest choice I could make, not by a long shot. There's something about him… I don't know. I just get the feeling that he's coming on to me for another reason besides the obvious. There's a hidden agenda there somewhere. And he puts up a good front, but he's *not* a gentleman."

"Good. A gentleman would probably take you at your word and never bother you again, after a hundred or so refusals. I have to admit, though, he struck me as being both gentle and protective."

"Possessive," Evie corrected. "And ruthless." No, he wasn't a gentleman. That cold force of will in his green diamond eyes was the look of an adventurer with a predator's heart. A hollow look of fear entered her own eyes.

Rebecca leaned forward and touched Evie's arm. "I

know," she said gently. And she did, because Rebecca had been there and seen it all. "I don't want to push you into doing something you'll regret, but you never know what's going to happen. If Robert Cannon is someone you could love, can you afford to pass up that chance?"

Evie sighed. Rebecca's arguments to the contrary, could she afford to *take* that chance? And was she going to have the choice?

To HER RELIEF, Robert wasn't at the marina when she arrived to relieve Craig. Huge, black-bellied clouds were threatening overhead, and a brisk, cool wind began to blow, signaling one of the tempestuous thunderstorms so common during summer. Both pleasure-boaters and fishermen began coming in off the lake, and for an hour she didn't have a moment's rest. Lightning forked downward over the mountains, a slash of white against the purplish black background. Thunder boomed, echoing over the water, and the storm broke with blinding sheets of rain blowing across the lake.

With all of the fishermen who had put in at the marina safely off the water and the other boats snugly in their slips, Evie gladly retreated to the office, where she could watch the storm from behind the protection of the thick, Plexiglas windows. She hadn't quite escaped all the rain, though, and she shivered as she rubbed a towel over her bare arms. The temperature had dropped twenty degrees in about ten minutes; the break from the heat was welcome, but the abrupt contrast was always chilling.

She loved the energy and drama of thunderstorms, and settled contentedly into her rocking chair to watch this one play out against the background of lake and mountains. Listening to the rain was unutterably soothing. Inevitably she became drowsy and got up to turn on the small televi-

sion she kept to entertain Paige and Jason. A small logo at
the bottom of the television screen announced "T'storm
watch."

"I'm watching, I'm watching," she told the television,
and returned to the rocking chair.

Eventually the violence of the storm dissipated, but the
welcome rain continued, settling down to a steady soaker,
the kind farmers loved. The marina was deserted, except
for the mechanic, Burt Mardis, who was contentedly
working on an outboard motor in the big metal building
where he did all the repairs. She could see him occasionally through the open door as he moved back and forth.
There wouldn't be any more business until the weather
cleared, which it showed no signs of doing. At the top of
the hour the local television meteorologist broke in on the
normal programming to show the progression of the line
of thunderstorms that were marching across the state, as
well as the solid area of rain they had left behind, stretching all the way back into Mississippi. Rain was predicted
well into the night, tapering off shortly before midnight.

It looked like a long, lazy afternoon ahead of her. She
always kept a book there for such times and pulled it out
now, but so much time had lapsed since she had started
the thing that she didn't remember much about it, so she
had to start over. Actually, this was the third time she had
started over; she would have to carry it home if she ever
hoped to finish it.

But she was already fighting drowsiness and after ten
minutes she knew that reading was going to tip the scales
in favor of sleep. Regretfully she put the book aside and
looked around for some chores to do. Craig, however, had
cleaned up that morning; the floors were freshly swept
and mopped, the merchandise impeccably straight on the
shelves or hanging on pegboard hooks.

She yawned and desperately turned the television channel to rock music videos. That should jar her awake.

When Robert walked in half an hour later, she was standing in front of the television, watching with a sort of amazed disbelief. Turning to him, she said in bemusement, "I wonder why bird-legged, sunken-chested musicians feel compelled to show their bodies to the audience?"

He was startled into a deep chuckle. He almost never laughed aloud, his amusement normally expressed, at most, by a twinkle in his eyes. This was twice, though, that Evie had charmed him into laughter. No one would ever suspect her of espionage, he thought suddenly, perhaps because of that very charm. It would be almost impossible for anyuone who knew her at all to think ill of her. Even he, who was well aware of her activities, couldn't keep himself from wanting her with a violence that both angered him and made him uneasy, because he couldn't control it.

He pushed those thoughts away as he walked toward her. If he let himself think about it now he would become enraged all over again, and Evie was so astute that he might not be able to hide it from her. When he reached her, though, and encircled her with his arms, forgetting about the other was laughably easy.

She blinked up at him, startled. Automatically she put her hands against his chest in a defensive movement. "You said you were going to back off and give me time," she accused.

"I am," Robert replied, lifting her left hand and pressing his warm, open mouth to the tender flesh on the inside of her wrist. Her pulse fluttered and raced beneath his lips. The scent of her skin was fresh and elusively, lightly fragrant, teasing him far more than if she had dabbed herself with perfume, no matter how expensive. He touched the tip of his tongue to the delicate blue veins that traced just under her skin and felt the throb of her blood beneath his touch.

Evie trembled at the subtle caress, her knees weakening. He felt that betraying quiver and gathered her more firmly against him, then lightly bit the pad at the base of her thumb. She swallowed a gasp; dear God, she hadn't known that could be so erotic.

"Will you go out to dinner with me tonight?" he murmured as his lips traveled on to her palm. Again his tongue flicked out, tasting her. Her hand trembled at the sensation.

"No, I can't." The instinctive denial was out before she could stop it, the habits of a dozen years firmly ingrained. Stunned, she realized that she *had* wanted to accept, much as a moth yearned toward the flame.

"Do you have another date?"

"No. It—it's difficult." He had no idea how difficult. She took a deep breath. "I haven't dated since my husband died."

Robert lifted his head, a slight frown drawing the black wings of his eyebrows together. "What did you say?"

She flushed and tugged her hand free. She started to wipe her palm against her jeans but instead tightly closed her fingers to hold the feel of his kiss. "I haven't gone out with anyone since Matt died."

He was silent, digesting this information, weighing it for truth. It was difficult to believe of anyone, but especially of a woman who looked like Evie. It was possible, of course, that she wasn't having an affair with Mercer after all, but to have lived like a nun for twelve years just didn't seem feasible. Still, he wasn't about to infuriate her by suggesting she was a liar.

Instead he gently stroked the underside of her jaw with the back of one finger and was immediately absorbed with the velvety texture of her skin. "Why is that?" he murmured a bit absently. "I know all the men down here can't be blind."

She bit her lip. "It was my choice. I…wasn't interested, and it didn't seem fair to waste a man's time under those circumstances."

"Reasonable, for a while. But twelve years?"

Restlessly she tried to pull away from him, but he stilled the movement, tightening the arm that remained around her. They were pressed firmly together from waist to knees, his muscled thighs hard and warm against hers. A man's strength was wonderful, she thought, inviting a woman to relax against him. Until Robert had taken her in his arms, she hadn't realized how very much she needed to be held. But not by just any man; only by him. In that moment Evie knew for certain that she had lost the battle. There was no use trying to evade him; not only would he refuse to let her get away with it, but she didn't *want* to get away with it, not any longer. For better or worse, and with dizzying speed, she had gotten herself involved with Robert Cannon. Dear God, she didn't know if she had the strength to do this, but she knew she had to try.

She didn't try to explain those twelve years. Instead she said, to his chest, "All right. I'll go out with you. Now what?"

"For starters, you could raise your head."

Slowly she did, mentally bracing herself as she met his crystalline eyes. She had expected to see amusement in them, but it was triumph glittering there rather than mirth. She shivered, more from sudden alarm than from the coolness brought by the steady rain.

"Cold?" he asked softly, rubbing his warm hands up the length of her arms.

"No. Afraid," she admitted, with painful candor. "Of

you, of getting involved with you." Her eyes were deep and mysterious with shadows as she looked up at this man who had so inexplicably forced himself into her life. If he insisted on establishing some kind of romantic relationship with her, he should know up front how she felt about a few things. "I'm not good at games, Robert. Don't kiss me unless it's for real. Don't come around unless you mean to stay."

"Do you mean marriage?" he asked coolly, his expressive eyebrows lifting.

Her cheeks burned at his tone. Of course it was ridiculous to think of marriage; that wasn't at all what she had meant. At least, not the legality of marriage, the institution itself. Mentally she shied from the notion, unable to even think of it. "Of course not! I never want to get married again. But the stability, the emotional security, what I had with Matt…well, I won't settle for anything less than that, so if you're looking for a summer affair, I'm not your woman."

His mouth twisted as an unreadable expression crossed his face. "Oh, but you are. You just haven't admitted it to yourself yet."

She shivered again, but her gaze didn't waver. "I want emotional commitment. Under those terms, if you're still willing to get involved with me, I'll go out with you. I'm not comfortable with you, but I expect that will change as we get to know each other. And I don't want to sleep with you. That would just be too risky." He probably thought she meant physically, but for her the emotional risk was by far more dangerous.

He studied her face for a long moment before saying calmly, "All right, we'll take our time and get to know each other. But I *do* want to make love with you, and I'm not going to take a vow of chastity." He cupped her face

in his hands, and the glitter in his eyes became more pro-
nounced as his head began to slowly descend. "All you
have to do to stop me, at any time," he whispered as his
mouth touched hers, "is say no."

Her breath sighed out of her, as soft as a night breeze.
The freedom to enjoy him was glorious; it felt as if she had
long been frozen and was now thawing, growing warm
with life again. For the first time her mouth opened wel-
comingly beneath his, and he took it with a calm mastery
that liquefied her bones. He could give lessons in kissing,
she thought hazily. His tongue probed and stroked, enticing her into a like response, so that their tongues touched
and curled and petted. It was surprisingly sweet, and totally erotic.

It seemed as if he kissed her like that for a long time,
simply holding her face between his palms, her body still
pressed full against his. The play of his lips and tongue
was both lulling and arousing. Her anxiety faded even
as warmth slowly spread through her breasts and loins,
making her feel as soft as butter. Her left hand was closed
around his right wrist, but her right hand was leisurely
stroking his back, feeling the firm, hard layers of muscle,
the hollow of his spine, instinctively learning some of the
details of how he was made.

The television played on unnoticed. No one came to
the door on this rainy day; they stood alone in the office,
oblivious to the music and the steady patter of the rain,
hearing only each other's breathing and the soft, unconscious sounds of pleasure. Like a morning glory opening
its shy face to the sun, Evie slowly bloomed in his arms,
her golden sensuality growing in confidence. He was painfully aroused but held himself under strict control, ignoring his own condition so that she didn't feel pressured. She
felt…safe, free to relax, and let herself feel the new sensa-

tions, explore the limits of her own desire. It was very different from the way it had been with Matt. She had been a girl then, and now she was a woman, with a woman's deeper and richer passion.

Though he had kissed her before, she had been distracted by the dangerous desire she felt for this man. Now, having given in, she could concentrate on the little details. She reveled in his taste, as the coolness of his lips rapidly became warm, then hard and hot. She measured the broadness of his shoulders, her palms smoothing over the curve of the joint and feeling the hardness of his solid bones covered by pads of muscle. She touched his hair, feeling it thick and silky and cool, warmer underneath, where it lay close to his skull. She felt the rasp of his five o'clock stubble against her cheeks. She inhaled the clean, musky scent of his maleness, a faint odor of soap, the fresh smell of rain on his clothes and skin.

"God." Abruptly he drew away, letting his head fall back as he drew in a deep breath. Her response had been hesitant at first, but then she had come alive in his arms, and he felt singed, as if he had been holding the sweetest of fires. His own response to her shook him with its violence. It was difficult to think of anything but taking her, and only their present location kept him from trying. "I'm the one calling a halt this time, sweetheart. We either have to stop or find a more private place."

She felt bereft, suddenly deprived of his touch. Her heart was pounding, and her skin felt as if it glowed with heat. Still, he was right. This wasn't the place for making out like teenagers. "There isn't a more private place," she said as she reached out to turn the television from rock to a country video station. The music abruptly changed from rap to a hauntingly passionate love song, and that was even more jarring to her nerves. She punched the Off button,

and in the sudden quiet the rain sounded heavier than before. She looked out the window at the gray curtain that
veiled the lake, obscuring the far bank.

"No one will be using their boats for the rest of the day,"
Robert said. "Why don't you close early and we'll go to
Huntsville for dinner."

She considered how his questions and suggestions
sounded like statements and demands. Had no one before
her ever said no to this man? "I can't close early."

"The rain is supposed to last halfway through the
night," he said reasonably.

"But that won't stop people from coming in to buy
tackle. Granted, there probably won't be many, maybe not
any, but the sign says that I'm open until eight."

And she would be, he thought, exasperated by the difficulty of courting a woman who refused to make time for
him. He had certainly never had that problem before. In
fact, he couldn't say that he'd ever had a problem with a
woman at all—until Evie. Getting close to her presented
him with as many obstacles as a mine field. Ruefully he
thought that if he was going to spend any time with her,
most of it would obviously be here at the marina.

Rather than become angry, which would only make her
more obstinate, he said, "Could Craig swap shifts with you
occasionally, if we give him advance notice?"

A tiny smile lifted the corners of her mouth, telling him
that he was learning. "I suppose he could. He's generally
accommodating."

"Tomorrow?"

This time she almost laughed aloud. "I can't tomorrow."
She had an appointment with her doctor at ten in the morning. Though she had told Robert that she didn't want to
sleep with him, he had said only that he would stop if she
told him to. The "if" told her that she should be prudent,

because his physical effect on her was potent. Of course, she wasn't going to tell Robert that she was arranging birth control; he would consider it a green light to making love.

He sighed. "The day after tomorrow?"

"I'll ask him."

"Thank you," he said with faint irony.

ROBERT RECEIVED TWO phone calls the next morning. He was out on the deck, reading a sheaf of papers that Felice had faxed to him; it was remarkably easy, he'd found, to keep abreast of things by way of phone, computer and fax. The first call was from Madelyn. "How are things in Alabama?"

"Hot," he replied. He was wearing only gym shorts. The rain of the day before had made everything seem even more green and lush, the scents more intense, but it hadn't done anything to ease the heat. If anything, the heat was worse. The morning sun burned on his bare chest and legs. Luckily, with his olive complexion, he didn't have to worry about sunburn.

"The weather is perfect here, about seventy-five degrees. Why don't you fly up for the weekend?"

"I can't," he said, and realized how much he sounded like Evie. "I don't know how long I'll be down here, but I can't leave until everything is tied up."

"The invitation stands," Madelyn said in her lazy drawl. A funny pang went through him as he realized how similar Madelyn's accent was to Evie's. "If you do happen to find a couple of days free, we'd love to see you."

"I'll try to get up there before I go back to New York," he promised.

"Try really hard. We haven't seen you since spring. Take care."

The phone rang again almost immediately. This time it

was the man he had hired to keep watch on Landon Mercer. "He had a visitor last night. We followed the visitor when he left, and we're working on identifying him. There hasn't been anything of interest on the phones."

"All right. Keep watching and listening. Has he spotted his tail yet?"

"No, sir."

"Anything in his house?" Robert was briefly thankful that he was a civilian and didn't have to follow the same tortuous rules and procedures that cops did, though it could have been sticky if his men had been caught breaking and entering. They hadn't seized any evidence, merely looked for it. Information was power.

"Clean as a whistle. Too clean. There's not even a bank statement lying around. We found out that he has a safety deposit box, so he might keep his paperwork in it, but we haven't been able to get into it yet. I'm working on getting a copy of his bank statement."

"Keep me informed," Robert said, and hung up. In a few days Mercer would start feeling a slight squeeze. He wouldn't think much of it at first, but soon it would become suffocating. Robert's plans for Evie, both personal and financial, were moving along nicely, too.

CHAPTER SEVEN

ROBERT DIDN'T INTEND to see Evie at all that day. He was an expert strategist in the eternal battle between men and women; after his determined pursuit of her, she would be expecting him to either call or come to the marina, and the lack of any contact with him would knock her slightly off balance, further weakening her defenses. He had often thought that seduction was similar to chess, in that the one who could keep the other guessing was the one in control of the game.

He was in control of the seduction. His instincts in that part of the game were infallible. It might take him a few weeks of gentling, but Evie would end up in his bed. Not long after that, he would have this entire mess cleaned up; Mercer and Evie would be arrested, and he would go back to New York.

Damn.

That was the problem, of course. He didn't want Evie in jail. He had been furious when he had come down here, determined to put both her and her lover away for a very long time. But that was before he had met her, before he had held her and tasted the heady sweetness of her. Before he had seen the underlying sadness in those golden brown eyes, and wondered if he would cause that expression to deepen. The thought made him uneasy.

Was she even guilty? At first he had been convinced that she was; now, even after such a short acquaintance, he was no longer certain. No criminal was untouched by his deeds. There was always a mark left behind, perhaps in a certain coldness in the eye, a lack of moral concern in certain matters. He hadn't been able to find any such mark in Evie. He had often thought that those who dealt in espionage, in the betrayal of their own country, were some of the coldest people ever born. They lacked the depth of emotion that others had. That lack of feeling wasn't evident in Evie; if anything, he would say that she felt far too much.

She hadn't hesitated at all in going into the river after Jason. That in itself wasn't unusual; any number of strangers would have done the same thing, much less a relative. But, knowing that every second counted, she had stayed down far too long herself in the effort to find the boy. He knew as surely as he knew the sun was in the sky that she would not have been able to make it back to the surface without his help…and that she had been willing to die rather than release Jason and save herself. Even now, the memory made his bones turn cold.

He had gone inside to work at the computer, but now he got up and restlessly walked out onto the deck, where the burning sun could dispel his sudden chill.

Only a person of deep emotion was capable of that kind of sacrifice.

He braced his hands on the top railing and stared out at the river. It wasn't green today, but rather a rich blue, reflecting the deep blue of the cloudless sky. There was little, if any, breeze, and the water's surface was calm. It lapped gently against the dock and the bank with a sound that tugged at something deep within him. All life had originated in the sea; perhaps it was an echo of that ancient time that made people respond so to water. But this river, peaceful as it was now, had almost taken Evie's life.

He shivered from another chill. He couldn't remember,

he thought absently, when he had been so enraged…or so afraid. He had ruthlessly controlled both emotions, allowing no hint of them to surface, but they had roiled deep within him. It hadn't been an intellectual anger, but rather a gut-level rage at fate, at chance, which had seemed to be snatching Evie out of his grasp before he could…what? Have her indicted? He snorted mirthlessly at that idea. The thought hadn't entered his mind. No, he had been furious that he wouldn't be able to hold her, make love to her, that the endless stretch of his days wouldn't have her in them.

Was Evie the type of person who could betray her country? He was beginning to doubt his own information.

Indecision wasn't normally part of Robert's makeup, and he was impatient with himself now. He couldn't allow his doubts about Evie's guilt to alter his plans. If she was innocent, then she wouldn't be harmed. She would have some uncomfortable moments, she would be worried, but in the end he would take care of the situation, and she would be okay.

Thinking about her made him edgy. He glanced at his watch; it was a little after noon. She should be at the marina now, and he should already have heard from the tail that he had assigned to follow her every move.

Right on cue, the phone rang, and he stepped inside to pick it up.

"She went to Huntsville this morning," a quiet female voice reported. "Her destination was an office building. The elevator closed before I could get on it with her, so I don't know where she went. I waited, and she returned to the lobby after an hour and twenty-three minutes. She drove straight home, changed clothes and then went to the marina. Mercer was in his office at PowerNet the entire time, and they didn't talk on the phone. There was no contact between them at all."

"What kind of tenants are in the office building?"

"I made a list. There are two insurance firms, a real estate office, four medical doctors, four lawyers, three dentists, an office temp company and two computer programming firms."

Damn, Robert thought bleakly. Aloud he said, "Find out where she went. Concentrate first on the two programming firms."

"Yes, sir."

He swore as he hung up. Why couldn't she have spent the morning shopping, or paying bills?

He wanted to see her. He wanted to shake her until her teeth rattled. He wanted to whisk her away to some secluded place and keep her locked up there until he had this mess settled. He wanted to ride her until she wept with submission. The violence of all those longings was alien to him, but he couldn't deny it. She had definitely gotten under his skin in a way no other woman had ever done.

Temper and frustration merged, and with a muttered curse he gave in. After swiftly dressing, he left the house and climbed in the black Jeep. Damn it, he wanted to see her, so he would.

VIRGIL WAS VISITING with Evie again that day. His knee was better, he said, and indeed, he was walking with less effort. The day had been fairly busy, with customers in and out on a regular basis, and Virgil had passed the time with several old friends and casual acquaintances.

She was busy ringing up a fisherman's purchase of gas, a soft drink and a pack of crackers when the door opened. Without looking, she knew Robert had entered. Her skin tingled, and she felt an instant of panic. She had hoped, foolishly, that she wouldn't see him that day, that her frazzled nerves would have a chance to recover somewhat before she actually went out with him the next night. On the other hand, she thought wryly, time and distance probably wouldn't help at all. Even if he wasn't there personally, he was in her mind, dominating both her thoughts and dreams.

Her customer taken care of, she allowed herself to look at him as he genially introduced himself to Virgil, who remembered him, of course. Very little got by that old man.

Robert was wearing jeans and a loose, white cotton shirt. A khaki baseball cap covered his black hair, and a pair of expensive sunglasses dangled from one hand. Her blood raced through her veins in excitement; even in such casual dress, there was something elegant and dangerous about him. The jeans were soft and faded with age, and he was as at home in them as he was in his silk shirts.

Then he was touching her on the arm, and it was like being burned with a tiny spark of electricity. "I'm going to take the boat out for a while, run the river and learn something about it."

So he wasn't going to be hanging around the marina all day. She was both relieved and disappointed. "Have you hired a guide?"

"No, but the river channel's marked, isn't it?"

"Yes, there shouldn't be any problem, unless you want to explore out of the channel. I'll give you a map."

"Okay." Thoughtfully Robert looked at Virgil. "Would you like to show me around the lake, Mr. Dodd? That is, if you don't have plans for the afternoon."

Virgil cackled, his faded eyes suddenly gleaming with enthusiasm. "Plans?" he snorted. "I'm ninety-three years old! Who in tarnation makes plans at my age? I could stop breathin' any minute now."

Amusement danced in Robert's eyes, making them look like pale green diamonds. "I'm willing to take the chance if you are, but I warn you, a corpse in the boat would be a real inconvenience."

Virgil hauled himself out of the rocking chair. "Tell you what, son. For the chance to park myself in a boat again, I'll try real hard not to put you to the trouble of havin' to call the coroner."

"It's a deal." Robert winked at Evie as he turned away.

Evie shook her head as she smiled at Virgil. She knew better than to try talking him out of going. Besides, he deserved to enjoy an hour or so on the river he loved, and she had faith that Robert would be as skillful at handling a boat as he was at everything else he did. How had he guessed, on such short acquaintance, that Virgil would dearly love getting out on the water again?

"Both of you be careful," she admonished. "Virgil, don't forget your cap."

"I won't, I won't," he said testily. "Think I'm fool enough to go out without somethin' on my head?"

"I'll bring the boat around to the dock," Robert said, and she was grateful to him for sparing Virgil the longer walk to the boat slip. He reached the door, stopped and came back to her. "I forgot something."

"What?"

He cupped her chin in one hand, leaned down and calmly kissed her. It wasn't a passionate kiss; it was almost leisurely. Still, when he lifted his head, her heart was pounding and her thoughts scattered. "That," he murmured.

She heard Virgil's cracked laughter and became aware of the interested gazes of the two customers who were browsing among the hooks and spinner baits. Her cheeks burned with a blush, and she turned away to fiddle with some papers until she could regain her composure.

Virgil patted her on the arm. Though stooped under the

weight of nine decades, he was still taller than she, and he grinned at her. "Heard tell that young feller made hisself useful the other day, when Becky's boy fell in."

She cleared her throat. "Yes. If he hadn't been there, Jason and I both would probably have drowned."

"Fast mover, is he?"

She found herself blushing again and waved Virgil off with shooing motions. Why on earth had Robert kissed her in public? She would never have thought that he was given to public displays of affection; there was something too contained about him. But he had certainly done just that!

She watched out the window as he idled the sleek black boat around to the dock, the powerful motor rumbling like thunder. The sunglasses were in place on the high-bridged nose, giving him a remote, lethal air. She had seen soldiers with that exact expression, and she wondered at it. With a start, she realized how little she knew about Robert Cannon. What did he do for a living? She knew he had to have some money to be able to afford that house, a new boat and the new Jeep. Where was he from? Did he have family, had he been married before, was he married *now,* did he have children? A chill went through her as she thought of all she didn't know about him.

And yet, in a way, she knew the man. He was cool and complicated, a private man who kept a subtle but permanent distance between himself and everyone else. The distance wasn't physical, God knows; he was the most physical, *sensual* man she'd ever met. Emotionally, though, he always held something back, keeping the inner man untouched. Probably most people thought of him as very controlled and unemotional; Evie agreed with the controlled part, but there was a ferocity lurking beneath the control that alarmed her even as it called to her own inner fire. He was ruthless, he was autocratic...and he had seen, al-

most at a glance, how much an old man would love to take
a boat ride on his beloved river once more.

Her breath caught, and there was a pain in her chest.
Panic filled her as she watched Virgil hobble out to the
dock as Robert brought the boat alongside. Robert held out
a strong hand, and Virgil gripped it and stepped aboard
the craft. There was a wide smile on his face as he settled
onto the seat. Robert handed him a life jacket, and obediently Virgil slipped it on, though Evie was fairly certain
he'd never worn one before in his life.

The panic that almost suffocated her was comprised of
equal parts terror and tenderness. She *couldn't* feel this
much for him, not so soon. You had to know someone
for that, and she had just been thinking how little she
knew about him. She was fascinated by him, that was all.
It was understandable. He was the first man in her life
since Matt's death, twelve long, desolate years ago. He
had brought passion alive in her again, with his skillful
kisses and determined pursuit.

She had never felt so violently attracted to a man before.

With Matt…they had grown up together, they'd been in
the same class in school, from first grade through gradu-
ation. She had known Matt as well as she knew herself;
they'd been like two halves of a whole. The love had grown
gradually between them, pure and steady, like a candle
flame. Robert… Robert was an inferno, and the heat between them could leave her in ashes.

ROBERT AND VIRGIL had been gone for over an hour when
Landon Mercer strolled into the marina. "Hi, doll," he
said jovially. "How's the prettiest woman in this part of
the state?"

Evie's expression was impassive as she glanced at him.
Unfortunately, business had slowed down and she was

there alone. She always preferred to have company around when she had to deal with him. Of course, being alone meant that she would have the opportunity to follow him again. Her thoughts began to hum. "Hello, Mr. Mercer."

"Landon," he said, as he always did. He leaned against the counter in a negligent pose, one designed to show off his physique. Mercer was a good-looking man, she admitted, but he left her cold.

"Do you want to rent a boat today?" she asked, turning to check which ones were available, though she knew without looking. She had quickly discovered that the best way to deflect his attention was to appear oblivious to it.

"Sure do. It's been a while since I've done any fishing, so I decided to play hooky from work this afternoon." He laughed at his own pun.

Evie managed a polite smile. He had brought in a small tackle box and one rod and reel, the same rig he always carried. The same lure was tied to the line.

"Do you want any particular boat?"

"No, any of them will do." He leaned closer. "When I get back, why don't we go out to dinner tonight? Not anywhere here. We'll go someplace nice, maybe in Birmingham."

"Thanks, but I'm busy tonight," she replied, her tone conveying no interest at all. Unfortunately, he was so taken with his own charm that he was oblivious to her lack of response to him.

"Tomorrow night, then. It's Saturday night. We can even go to Atlanta for some real fun, since we wouldn't have to be back for work."

"The marina's open seven days a week."

"Oh. Okay, we'll go to Birmingham."

"No, thank you, Mr. Mercer. I'm busy tomorrow night, too."

"C'mon, how busy can you be? Whatever it is, you can put it off."

Her teeth were on edge. She barely managed to be polite as she said, "I have a date tomorrow night."

"Now I'm jealous. Who's the lucky man?"

"No one you know." She took an ignition key from the pegboard and slid it across the counter to him. "There you go. Number five, the one at the end of the dock."

He took out his wallet and extracted a couple of twenties. "I'll have it back in two hours." He picked up the ignition key.

"Fine." She mustered a smile. "Have a good time. Hope you catch a lot."

"I never do, but it's fun to try," he said breezily as he picked up his tackle and went out the door.

Evie put the money into the cash drawer and locked it, all the while eyeing Mercer as he walked down the dock. He was looking around, studying the parking lot and the traffic on the street out front, as well as on the bisecting causeway.

Swiftly she picked up the phone and buzzed Burt in the maintenance building. He picked up just as Mercer was getting into the boat.

"Burt, I'm taking the boat out for a while," Evie said swiftly. "I'm locking the store, but keep an eye on the gas pumps while I'm gone."

"Sure," he said, as unquestioning as ever. Burt Mardis didn't have a curious bone in his body.

Mercer was idling away from the dock. Evie jammed a ball cap on her head, grabbed her sunglasses and hurried from the building. She locked the door behind her, then sprinted for her own boat.

He was beyond the wave breakers by the time she reached her boat, and she heard the roar as he opened up the throttle. She all but threw herself into the boat and turned the key in the ignition. The motor coughed to life with a satisfying roar. Her boat was faster than any of the rentals, but on the water, and at speed, it was difficult to distinguish one vessel from another.

She had to idle away from the marina, because a fast takeoff would make waves large enough to violently rock the boats in their slips, possibly damaging them. Swearing at every lost second, she waited until she was past the wave breakers before pushing the throttle forward. The motor roared, and the front end of the boat lifted in the air as the vessel shot forward. It planed off almost immediately, the nose dropping into the running position.

She scanned the water for Mercer; unfortunately, he had gained enough distance that she couldn't positively identify him, and there were three boats speeding away from her, small specks that bobbed slightly as they cut through the waves. Which one was Mercer?

The sun wasn't far past its apex, and the glare turned the lake into a mirror. Hot air hit her, pulling tendrils of hair loose around her face. The scent of the river filled her head and lungs, and a quiet exultation spread through her. This was a part of her life that she loved—the wind in her face, the sense of speed, the feel of the boat as it glided over calm water and bumped over waves. Though there were other boats on the lake, and houses visible all along the shoreline, when she was speeding across the water it was like being alone with God. She would have been perfectly content, if only she knew what Mercer was up to.

After a minute one boat slowed and turned toward another marina. As she neared, she could tell that it held two passengers.

That left two. The throttle was full forward, and she was gaining on one, while the other, probably a speedy bass boat, was pulling away. Since her boat was faster than the rental, the one she was overtaking had to be Mercer. Cautiously she throttled back, enough to stay at a pace with him but not so close that he would see and identify her. Just about everyone on the water would be wearing a ball cap and sunglasses, and her hair was pulled back in a braid rather than flying loose, so she felt fairly confident that he wouldn't recognize her.

He was heading toward the same area, where there were a lot of small islands dotting the lake. She wouldn't be able to get very close, because once he cut his speed he would be able to hear other boats. Her best bet, she thought, was to stop some distance away and pretend to be fishing.

The boat ahead slowed and cut between two islands. Evie kept her speed steady and cruised on past. There was a distance of over two hundred yards between them, but she could tell that now he was idling closer to the bank of the island on the right.

She turned in the opposite direction, away from him. A barge was coming downriver, heavily loaded and settled deep into the water, pushing out a wave as it plowed forward. If she let the barge come between her and Mercer, it would block his activities for almost half a minute, plenty long enough for her to lose him. But if she moved inside the barge's path, it would put her closer to him than she wanted to be.

There was no help for it. She tucked her long braid inside her shirt to hide that identifying detail and turned the boat to angle back across the river ahead of the barge.

"GUNTERSVILLE LAKE'S EASY to learn," Virgil stated. "'Course, I was fishin' the river back before the TVA built the dam, so I knowed the lay of the land before the water backed up and covered it. Not many of us around now remembers the way it used to be. River used to flood a lot. So Roosevelt's boys decided we needed us a dam, so there wouldn't be no more floods. Well, hell, 'course there ain't, 'cause now the land that flooded ever now an' then is permanently under water. The government calls it flood control. They throwed around words like eminent domain, but what they did is take people's land, turn them off their farms and put a lot of good land under water."

"The TVA brought electricity to the Tennessee River Valley, didn't it?" Robert asked. He was holding the boat to around twenty miles an hour, not much more than idling speed to the powerful motor behind them, but the slow speed made conversation possible. They had to raise their voices, but they could hear each other.

Virgil snorted. "Sure it did. Glad to have it, too. But nobody ever thought the TVA built that dam to make our lives easier. Hell, we knew what was goin' on. It was the Depression, and Roosevelt would have built the second Tower of Babel to make jobs for folks, for all the good it did to the economy. It took the war to kick-start things again."

"Did you fight in the war?"

"Too old for that one." Virgil cackled with glee. "Imagine that! Over fifty years ago, they said I was too old! But I was in the first one. Lied about my age to get in. Not that they checked too close, 'cause they needed men could hit the broad side of a barn with a rifle slug. During the second one, I volunteered to help train the younger fellers with their rifles, but that was all stateside. Suited me. My wife weren't none too pleased with me, anyway, leavin' her to handle five young'uns on her own. She'd have been mad as hell if I'd gone overseas. Our oldest boy, John Edward, was seventeen when it all started, and he joined the navy. It fretted her enough that he was gone. He made it back fine, though. Imagine that. The boy went through a war in the Pacific without a scratch, then come home and died two years later with the pneumonia. Life's got a lotta strange turns in it. Don't guess I'll see too many more of them, but then, I didn't plan on hangin' around this long to begin with."

The old man lapsed into silence, perhaps remembering all the people who had come and gone through his life. After a minute he roused himself. "Got a lot of creeks emptyin' into the lake. We passed Short Creek a ways back. This here's Town Creek."

Robert had studied maps of the lake, so when Virgil identified the creeks he was able to pinpoint their location. Since the river channel was marked, staying in safely deep water was no problem. It was when he ventured out of the river channel that Virgil's expertise came in handy, because he knew where it was shallow, where the hidden stump rows were lurking just under the surface, ready to tear the bottom out of a boat if the driver wasn't careful. For several more minutes, Virgil devoted himself to his appointed task, pointing out quirks of the lake.

Then he said, "I've lost a lot of folks over the years. My own mama and pa, of course, and all my brothers and sisters. There were sixteen of us, and I'm the only one left. Got a piss pot full of nieces and nephews, though, and all of their kids, and their kids' kids. My wife passed on in sixty-four. Lord, it don't seem like it's been that long. I've lost three of my own kids. Parents ought not to outlive their kids. It ain't right. And all my friends that I growed up with, they're long gone.

"Yep, I've had to bury many a loved one, so I get right protective of the ones I got left." Faded blue eyes were suddenly piercing as he turned them on Robert. "Evie's a special woman. She's had enough sorrow in her young life, so if you don't mean to do right by her, it would be a kindness if you'd leave her alone and haul your ass back up north."

Robert's face was impassive. "Evie's related to you?" he asked neutrally, ignoring Virgil's rather combative statement. He wasn't about to get into an argument with a ninety-three-year-old man.

Virgil snorted. "Not by blood. But I've knowed her all her life, watched her grow up, and there's not a finer woman in this town. Now, I watch television, so I know times have changed from when I was young enough to court a woman. Back then we had enough respect for womenfolk not to do nothing to cause them harm. But, like I said, times have changed. I know young folks now get serious about things without tyin' the knot proper, and that ain't what I'm talkin' about. Thing is, if you're just lookin' for a good time, then find some other woman. Evie ain't like that."

Robert had to struggle with several conflicting emotions. Foremost was his cold, instinctive anger at Virgil's scolding interference. In neither his business nor his personal life was he accustomed to being taken to task. Right after that, though, was amusement. He was thirty-six and, moreover, an extremely wealthy man who wielded a great deal of power in both financial and political circles. He almost smiled at Virgil lumping him in with "young folks."

What took most of his attention, though, was this second warning that Evie wasn't a good-time girl. Evie herself had issued the first warning: *Don't kiss me unless it's for real.* After Virgil's little speech, the underlying meaning of those warnings was clear, though the reason wasn't.

"I don't usually discuss my relationships," he finally said in a faintly distant tone, just enough to signal his displeasure. "But my interest in Evie isn't casual." *In any way.*

"What did you mean, she's had enough sorrow in her life?" Because that had been the basis of the talk: *Don't hurt her.*

"I mean, life ain't been easy on her. Grief comes to everybody, if they live long enough. Some folks, though, it hits harder than others. Losin' Matt the way she did, the day after they got married…well, it changed her. There ain't no sunshine in her eyes now, the way there used to be. She never looked at another man since Matt died, until you. So don't disappoint her, is what I'm sayin'."

Robert was knocked off balance by the surge of jealousy that seared through him. Jealousy? He'd never been jealous in his life, especially where a woman was concerned. Either his women were faithful to him or the relationship ended. Period. How could he be jealous of a boy who had been dead for a dozen years? But Evie still wore Matt Shaw's wedding ring on her finger and had evidently remained faithful to him even after all this time. Forget Mercer; that had obviously been an error. An understandable one, but still an error. He was both glad that she wasn't involved with Mercer, at least on that level, and furious that she was determined to waste herself on a memory. *I don't want to sleep with you,* she'd said. She was still trying to be faithful to a dead husband.

"What kind of person was Matt?" he asked. He didn't want to know, didn't want to talk about the boy, but he felt compelled to find out.

"He was a fine boy. Would have been a good man, if he'd had the chance. Good-natured, honest. Kindhearted, too. Can't say that about too many folks, but Matt didn't have a mean bone in his body. He never dated anybody but Evie, and it was the same with her. They planned to marry each other from the time they started high school together. Never saw two kids love each other the way they did. It was a shame that they didn't have no more time together than what they had. She didn't even have his child to keep part of him alive. Damn shame. She needed somthing to live for, back then."

Robert had had enough. He couldn't listen to much more about how wonderful Matt Shaw had been, and how much Evie had loved him, without losing his temper. He couldn't remember the last time he had lost control, but there was a deep-seated fury in him now that was surging forward. He didn't try to analyze his anger; he simply and ruthlessly contained it, shoving it down as he turned the boat downriver and headed back toward the marina. He eased the throttle forward so the noise would make conversation impossible.

Fifteen minutes later they were idling up to the docks. At the sound of the motor, a man wearing grease-covered coveralls came out of the maintenance building and walked out on the dock. He nodded a greeting to Robert and said to Virgil, "Come in outta the sun and keep me company for a while. Evie closed the office and took her boat out for a while." As he talked, he extended a muscular arm to steady Virgil as he climbed out of the boat onto the dock.

"When was this?" Robert asked sharply.

The mechanic shrugged. "An hour, maybe. I didn't pay no attention to the time."

She had refused to close the marina early one rainy late afternoon, when there had been no customers, but now she had closed it not long after lunch on a beautiful, sunny, *busy* day. Robert's eyes narrowed. He looked at the parking lot. He knew the make, model and color of Mercer's car, and there it sat.

Damn her. She had left to meet with the traitorous bastard.

CHAPTER EIGHT

ROBERT WAS STANDING on the dock when Evie eased her boat into its regular slip. He was wearing those extra dark sunglasses that completely hid his eyes, but she didn't need to see them to know that they were icy with rage. Maybe it was the way he moved, very deliberately, every action contained, that alerted her to his mood. An uncontrollable shiver ran over her, despite the heat. There was something far more alarming about that cold, ruthless control than if he had been violent. Again she had the thought that he was the most dangerous man she'd ever seen. But what had put him in such a menacing mood?

She tied off and leapt up onto the dock. "Did Virgil enjoy himself?" she asked as she stepped around Robert, heading toward the office. He wasn't the only one who had self-control. Right now she had other concerns besides dealing with his temper. She could hear the roar of a boat coming closer; that might or might not be Mercer, but she wasn't taking any more chances. When Mercer returned to the marina, she intended to be inside the office building, doing business as usual.

"Just a minute," Robert said, his tone clipped, and reached for her.

Evie evaded his grasp. "Later," she said, and hurried up the dock.

He was right behind her when she unlocked the door, but he didn't have a chance to say anything. Virgil had seen her boat and was slowly making his way across the lot. Robert eyed the old man's progress; he wouldn't have time to get any answers out of her before Virgil was there, so it would be better to wait, as she'd said, until later. Once more he controlled his anger and frustration, but the fury in him remained hot. If anything, he was becoming even angrier.

Virgil reached the doorway and gave a sigh of pleasure as the cool air-conditioning washed over him. "Got spoiled in my old age," he griped. "The heat didn't used to bother me none."

"No point in letting it bother you back then," Evie pointed out, smiling at him. "There wasn't any air-conditioning, so we all had to put up with it."

The old man eased into the rocking chair. "Spoiled," he repeated contentedly.

She went over to a vending machine and fed in the change for three soft drinks. She kept the machine's temperatre set low enough to form ice crystals in the drinks, to the delight of her customers. She popped the tops off the bottles and thrust one into Robert's hands, then gave another to Virgil. The third she drank herself, turning up the bottle for a long, cold swallow of the crisp, biting liquid.

She saw Robert eye the hourglass bottle in his hand with a less-than-thrilled expression; then he, too, took a drink. His tastes were probably too sophisticated to run to soft drinks, she thought, but if he was going to live here for the summer, he should do as the natives did. One of the front lines of defense against the heat was to consume cola every day as coolant for the insides.

A boat was idling in past the wave breakers. A quick glance told Evie that it was the rental boat. Mercer had seen her, she knew, but she didn't think he had recognized her. Wearing the universal ball cap and sunglasses, with her hair tucked in, she could have been anyone. It was doubtful that he had even been able to tell she was a woman.

Robert hitched one hip onto the counter, a sockless, docksider-clad foot swinging as he nursed the soft drink. His expression didn't give anything away, but she had the strong impression that he was...waiting. Until they could talk? No. It was more immediate than that.

She watched Mercer tie up the boat and walk jauntily along the dock, tackle box in one hand and useless tackle in the other. Then the door opened and he breezed in, all ego and self-satisfaction. "Nothing today, doll," he said in his obnoxious, too-hearty manner. "Maybe I'd have better luck if you went along. What do you say?"

"I'm not much for fishing," she lied without compunction, causing Virgil to almost choke on his drink.

Robert's back, as he sat on the counter, had been half-turned toward Mercer. Now he shifted around to face the other man. "Hello, Landon," he said coolly. "I'd like to go fishing with you the next time you take the afternoon off."

Evie was startled to hear Robert call Mercer by his first name, and a mental alarm began clanging. *How did Robert know the man?*

But if she was startled, the effect on Mercer was electric. He froze in place, his face draining of color as he gaped at Robert. "M-Mr. Cannon," he stuttered. "I—uh, how—w-what are you doing here?"

The black slashes of Robert's eyebrows rose in that sardonic way of his. Mercer was totally aghast at having run into him, Evie saw, and the tension in her relaxed. Whatever the connection, Robert wasn't in league with Mercer, or the other man wouldn't have been so taken aback at his presence.

The most obvious answer to Mercer's question would have been that he kept his boat here; that wasn't, however, what Robert said. Instead he looked deliberately at Evie and said, "The place has a certain attraction."

She felt silly, but she couldn't stop the color from heating her face. Mercer looked even more aghast, for some reason.

"Oh," he mumbled. "Yeah, sure." With an effort, he regained a bit of control and managed a sickly smile. "It's getting late. I should be going. Call me when you're free, Mr. Cannon, and we'll get in that game of golf we talked about."

"Or some fishing," Robert suggested, his voice like silk.

"Uh…yeah. Yes, we'll do that. Anytime." Mercer tossed the boat keys onto the counter and hastily left.

"Wonder what set his britches on fire," Virgil mused.

"Perhaps it was his bad luck in taking an afternoon off from work to go fishing and running into his employer at the marina," Robert suggested, his eyes hooded.

Virgil leaned back in the rocker, wheezing with laughter. "Well, I'll be! He works for you, eh? Bet that ruined his fun for the day."

"I'm certain it did."

Evie stood motionless, absorbing all the nuances of the brief scene with Mercer, and also the silkiness of Robert's murmured reply. He had taken a great deal of pleasure in watching Mercer squirm. He had also made that remark about her being the reason for his presence for the same reason: to make Mercer squirm. After all, what man would feel comfortable to find out he had just come on to the boss's woman…in front of the boss? This was in addition to being caught playing hooky from work.

Mercer probably didn't realize it, but it had been plain to Evie that Robert disliked him. He had been perfectly cordial, but the dislike had been there, underlying every word. She was enormously relieved. For a horrible moment she had been afraid that Robert was involved with whatever crooked deal Mercer had going on, but Mercer's manner certainly hadn't been that of someone who had met a friend. She was worried, though, to find that Mercer worked for Robert. Just as she didn't want his dirty waves to touch the marina, she also didn't want him to somehow harm Robert.

She hadn't been successful in finding out any more about what Mercer was up to; he had idled a twisting path around several of the islands, finally stopping for a moment on the back side of one of the larger ones. She hadn't been able to see what, if anything, he was doing. If she had had a trolling motor, she would have been able to get much closer without him hearing her, but her boat wasn't equipped with one. Then Mercer had started his motor again and resumed his weaving in and out of the islands. She had watched him as best she could, but there was no way to keep him in sight all the time. When he had finally left the islands, it had taken all the speed her boat was capable of to outpace him and reach the marina far enough in advance that he wouldn't see her.

So she still had nothing but suspicion. While she was wondering whether or not to confide in Robert when she had nothing of substance to tell him, Virgil's great-grand-daughter came in. This time she was carrying a wide-eyed, eleven-month-old girl on her hip, and was followed by two towheaded boys, ages four and six. "PawPaw, PawPaw," both boys yelled. They ran toward the rocking chair, climbing up on Virgil's lap with a naturalness that suggested they had been doing it all their lives.

"Well, how'd it go?" Virgil asked, gathering both small bodies against him. "Did the dentist give you a sucker?"

"Yep," said the oldest one, pulling a bright red lollipop from his pocket. "Mom says it's okay, because it's sugarless. You want it?" His expression said that he was disappointed by the sugarless state of the candy.

"It's tempting," Virgil allowed, "but you keep it."

Evie smiled as she watched Virgil with his great-great-grandchildren, then turned back to their mother. "Sherry, this is Robert Cannon. He and Virgil have been out running the river today. Robert, Virgil's great-granddaughter, Sherry Ferguson."

"Pleased to meet you," Sherry said with her friendly smile. She obviously remembered Robert from the first time he had come to the marina. She shifted the baby onto her other hip and held out her hand.

Robert reached to shake Sherry's hand, and the baby evidently thought he was reaching for her; with a gurgle of pleasure she released her grip on Sherry's blouse and lunged forward, both dimpled little arms outstretched. Sherry made a startled grab for the child, but Robert was faster, scooping the baby into his arms almost before she had left the safety of her mother's.

"Allison Rose!" Sherry gasped, staring at the baby. "I'm sorry," she apologized to Robert as she reached to retrieve her child. "I don't know what got into her. She's never gone to a stranger like that before."

Allison Rose wouldn't have any of it; she shrieked and turned away from her mother's hands, clinging to Robert's shirt with all her might.

"She's all right," Robert said, his wonderful deep voice now holding a soothing tone to calm both mother and daughter. One powerful hand steadied the baby's back as his eyes smiled at Sherry. "I've always had a way with women."

That was nothing less than the truth, Evie thought, her blood moving in a slow throb through her veins as she watched him cradle the baby as comfortably as if he had a dozen of his own. Was there anything the man couldn't do? Sherry was all but melting under that smiling look, and tiny Allison was in heaven.

Perched on his arm, Allison looked around with a beatific expression, as if she were a queen surveying her subjects. Robert bent his head to brush his nose against the soft blond curls and reflected that girls were different from boys even at this young age. He had rocked Madelyn's two boys when they were infants and played with them as toddlers, but they hadn't been quite as soft as the baby girl in his arms, and her scent was indefinably sweeter. He found himself enchanted by the tiny sandals on her feet and the ruffled sundress she wore. The feel of her chubby, dimpled arms clinging to him was strangely satisfying.

Oh, God, Evie thought. Her chest was so tight she could barely breathe. She had to turn away to hide the shattered look in her eyes. Why couldn't he have been uncomfortable with babies? Why did he have to cradle Allison so tenderly and close his eyes with delight at her sweet baby scent? The emotion swelling in her was so overwhelming that she couldn't think, couldn't function.

For the rest of her life she would remember the exact moment when she fell in love with Robert Cannon.

She busied herself fiddling with papers, though she couldn't have said what those papers were. As if from a distance, she could hear Sherry asking about Virgil's excursion on the river, could hear the enthusiasm in Virgil's reply and Robert's comments. The calm, soothing tone was still there, she noticed. How could Sherry fail to be reassured about the safety of the outing when his utter placidity and self-confidence said that he had taken every care without appearing to fuss over Virgil's safety?

He did it deliberately, she realized as she listened to them talk. She felt oddly detached, not really hearing words, but rather the way things were said, the underlying emotion. Robert was a master at reading people, then using his voice and manner with uncanny accuracy to manipulate them into the response he desired. It was almost as if he were a puppeteer, pulling everyone's strings so subtly that they never noticed they were being directed by his will.

And if he manipulated *them,* then it followed that he manipulated *her.*

There was a dull roaring in her ears, as if she might faint. Evie flatly refused to do something that silly and concentrated on breathing deeply. As she sucked in the first breath, she discovered that it was the first time she had done so for some time, judging by the acute relief in her lungs. She had simply stopped breathing, probably about the time Robert had rubbed his face against Allison's curls. No wonder she had felt faint.

Emotionally she had been groping for solid ground, had felt her fingers finally brush against something to which she had thought she could hold. Now she felt as if that lifeline had been jerked away from her and she was lost again, swirling away. Had anything Robert said to her been the truth, or had every word been a subtle manipulation, designed to…what? Get her into his bed? Was the thrill, for him, in the chase? The problem was that he could just as easily be sincere. How was she to tell the difference?

The answer, she thought painfully, was that she couldn't. Only time would tell if she could depend on him, entrust her heart to him, and she doubted that the time was there. He'd said he was here for the rest of the summer, and summer was half-over. He would be here another six, maybe seven, weeks.

"Evie." Her name was spoken quietly, almost in her ear. She felt his heat against her back, smelled the fresh, clean sweat on his body. His hand touched her arm. "Sherry and Virgil are leaving."

She turned, summoning both a smile and self-control. No one else had noticed her preoccupation, she saw, but Robert had, another disturbing example of his acute perception. Allison had been enticed, with one of the red suckers as bait, back into Sherry's arms, where she was engrossed with turning the cellophane-wrapped candy around and around, trying to find access. Finally she simply popped it into her mouth, cellophane and all. Virgil was standing, and the boys were already at the door, shouting that they wanted a Blizzard before they went home, while Sherry insisted that she wasn't driving all the way to Boaz to get one, at which Virgil added that he wouldn't mind having a Blizzard, himself. That, of course, settled the issue.

Evie added her voice to all the rowdy commotion, telling them goodbye, telling Virgil to take care. The boys raced out the door and headed toward the docks. Sherry stepped out and said, "Y'all get back here, *now!*" in a tone that stopped them in their tracks and brought them, pouting, back to her. It took another few minutes to get everyone settled in the station wagon, and through it all Evie was acutely aware of Robert standing very close behind her, his hand on the small of her back. Neither Sherry nor Virgil would have missed the body language, much less the touch, that stated his claim on her.

The silence after their departure was almost deafening. She closed the door and tried to slide past him, but his hands closed on her waist, and, with a dizzy whirl, she found herself plunked down on the counter with him standing between her legs to prevent her from getting down. She stared at the center of his chest, refusing to look up at him. She didn't want this, didn't want to confront him when she was still reeling from the jolting realization that she loved him and could trust him even less than she had thought.

"Damn it," he said very softly. Then, "Look at me."

"Why?"

"Because I don't want to talk to the top of your head."

"I can hear you just fine the way I am."

He hissed a curse just under his breath and caught her face between his hands, tilting it up. He was careful not to hurt her, but there was no resisting the easy strength of that grip. She tried to concentrate on his nose, but the pale green glitter of his eyes dominated his face, drawing her attention. There was no way *not* to see the cold fury there.

"Where did you go?"

The question was deceptively calm, almost idle. If she hadn't been able to see his eyes, if she hadn't been able to feel the roiling anger in him, she might have been fooled. "I had an errand to run."

"Ah." His hands tightened on her face. "Were you meeting Landon Mercer?" he asked abruptly. "Are you having an affair with him?"

She stared at him, stupefied. For several moments she was unable to formulate a single thought, her mind a total blank. How on earth had he managed to link her to Mercer? He had been gone when she had left, and she and Mercer had not come back at the same time. But she *had* left because of Mercer, even though she hadn't been with him. She could feel her cheeks heating and knew that she looked guilty, but she still couldn't seem to manage a coherent reply. Then the last question sank in, and she snapped, "No, I'm not having an affair with him! I *detest* the man!"

Robert's lips were thin. "Then why did you sneak off to meet with him?"

"I didn't sneak anywhere," she flared. "And I did *not* meet him!"

"But you closed the office in the middle of a busy day," he said relentlessly. "When you wouldn't close it a little early on a rainy afternoon when there weren't any customers at all."

"I told you, I had an errand."

"So you went in a boat?"

"I live on the water," she pointed out, light brown eyes glowing more golden by the second. "I can cross the lake faster than I can drive to my house. Sometimes, if the weather is good and I'm in the mood, I use the boat, anyway, rather than driving."

The dangerous look hadn't faded from his eyes. "Are you saying that you went home?"

Very deliberately she caught his wrists and removed his hands from her face. "I had an errand," she repeated. "I didn't meet Mercer. I'm not having an affair with him. And what in hell makes you think you have the right to interrogate me?" The last sentence was shouted as she tried to shove him away.

He didn't move, not an inch. "This," he said in a stifled tone, then moved forward as he bent his head to her.

She caught her breath at the heat of his mouth, the ravaging pressure. His movement had forced her thighs even wider, and he settled his hips in the notch. Evie quivered at the hard thrust of his sex against the vulnerable softness of her private body, alarmed by the contact even through several layers of cloth. The passion in him was as overwhelming as his anger had been, buffeting her, bending her under his will. His arms were painfully tight, and she tried to push him away once more, with the same result. "Stop it," he muttered against her mouth, and one arm dropped to encircle her bottom and pull her closer against him, rubbing her against the ridge beneath his jeans.

Unexpected, acute, the pleasure that shot through her loins made her cry out, the sound muffled by his lips. He repeated the motion, rocking his pelvis against her in a fury of jealousy and desire. The jolt was even stronger, and she arched in his arms, her hands lifting to cling to his shoulders. The transition from anger to desire was so swift that she couldn't control it, and the current of pleasure leaped within her. Every move he made increased the sensation, pushed her higher, as if she were being forced up a mountain and the purpose, once she reached the peak, was to hurl her over. The dizzying, panicked sensation was the same, and she clutched at him as the only anchor.

It had never been like this with Matt, she thought dimly. Their youthful passion had been shy, untutored, sweet but hesitant. Robert was a man who knew exactly what he was doing.

Though he hadn't touched them, her breasts were throbbing, the nipples tightly drawn and aching. She arched again, a soft, frantic sound in her throat as she tried to ease the ache by rubbing them against his chest. He knew, and whispered, "Easy," just as his hand closed over one firm, jutting mound.

She whimpered at the heat, the delicious pressure. She knew she should stop him, but putting an end to this ecstasy was the last thing she wanted to do. Her body was pliant, voluptuous with need, glowing with heat. He put his hand under her shirt and deftly opened the front snap of her bra. The cups slid apart, and then his fingers were on her naked flesh. He stroked the satin curves, then circled the tight nipples until she writhed in an agony of unfulfillment. "Is this what you want?" he murmured, and lightly pinched the distended tips. She moaned as a river of heat ran through her, gathering moisture to deposit between her thighs.

He bent her backward over his arm, the position thrusting her breasts upward. Her shirt was pulled up to completely bare them, she realized, wondering when that had happened. She saw her nipples, as red as berries; then his mouth closed over one, and her eyes closed as her head fell back.

He was going to take her right here, on the counter. She felt his determination, his own rampant desire. Panic surged through her, combating the heat that undermined her own will and common sense. He would take her here, where anyone could walk in and see them. He would take her without any thought for birth control. And she, besides risking her reputation and the chance of pregnancy, would lose the last bit of protection she retained for her heart.

His mouth was tugging at her nipple, drawing strongly on it before moving to the other one. And his hands were working at the waistband of her jeans, unsnapping and unzipping.

Desperately she wedged her arms between their bodies and stiffened them. "No," she said. The word was hoarse, barely audible. "Robert, no! Stop it!"

He froze, his muscled body taut as he held himself motionless for a long moment. Then, very slowly, he lifted his hands from her and moved back, one step, then two. His breathing was fast and audible.

Evie couldn't look at him as she slid from the counter and hastily fumbled her clothing back into presentable shape, fastening her bra, smoothing her shirt down, snapping and zipping her jeans. Her own breath was coming light and fast.

"Don't look so scared," he said calmly. "I gave you my word that I'd stop, and I did."

No, the problem wasn't with his willpower, she thought wildly, but with hers. Had they been anywhere else but in the marina, she didn't know if she could have made herself say no.

"Nothing to say?" he asked a moment later, when she remained silent.

She cleared her throat. "Not yet."

"All right." He still sounded far too calm and in control. "We'll talk tomorrow. I'll pick you up at seven o'clock."

"Seven," she echoed as he left.

ROBERT WAS ON the secure mobile phone in the Jeep by the time he had pulled out of the marina's parking lot. "Did you follow him from the time he left work?" he asked as soon as the phone was answered.

"Yes, sir, we did. We saw your Jeep at the marina and pulled back."

"Damn. I was out in my boat. He rented a boat and met someone out on the lake, possibly Evie, because she left the marina in her boat, too. Was he carrying anything when he left work?"

"Not that we could tell, but he could easily have had a disk in his coat pocket."

"He didn't fish in his suit. Where did he change clothes?"

"At his house. He was there for not quite five minutes, then came out carrying a tackle box and a fishing rod."

"If he had a disk at all, it would have been in the tackle box."

"Yes, sir. We didn't have a chance to get to it."

"I know. It wasn't your fault. First thing, though, I'm going to have a secure phone put in the boat. That way, if I'm out on the water, you can get in touch with me."

"Good idea. We went through his house again while we had the chance. Nothing."

"Damn. Okay, continue to watch him. And send some-one out to Evie's house tonight."

"The matter we discussed?"

"Yes," Robert replied. It was time for the pressure to begin.

CHAPTER NINE

THE NEXT MORNING was awful. Evie hadn't slept well—had scarcely slept at all. She had set the alarm for four-thirty, and when it went off she had been asleep for less than two hours. Dreaming about Robert was one thing, but she had been wide-awake and hadn't been able to get him out of her mind. Her thoughts had darted from the seething passion of his lovemaking, incomplete as it had been, to the unease she felt every time she thought of how he so skillfully manipulated people. She tried to analyze what he did and couldn't find any time when he had been malicious, but that didn't reassure her.

Sometime after midnight, lying in the darkness and staring at the ceiling, she realized what it was that so bothered her. It was as if Robert allowed people to see and know only a part of him; the other part, probably the closest to being the real man, was standing back, inviolate, carefully watching and analyzing, gauging reactions, deciding which subtle pressures to apply to gain the results he wanted. Everyone was shut away from that inner man, the razor-sharp intelligence functioning almost like a computer, isolated in a sterile environment. What was most upsetting was to realize that this was how he wanted it, that he had deliberately fashioned that inner isolation and wasn't about to invite anyone inside.

What place could she hope to have in his life? He desired her; he would be perfectly willing to make her the center of his attention for a time, in order to gain what he wanted: a carnal relationship. But unless she could break through into that fiercely guarded inner core, she would never reach his emotions. He would be fine, but she would break her heart battering against his defenses.

She, better than others, knew how important emotional barriers were. She had propped herself up with her own defenses for many years, until she had slowly healed to the point where she could stand on her own. How could she condemn him for staying within his own fortress? She didn't know if she should even try to get inside.

The thing was, she didn't know if she had a choice any longer. For better or worse, this afternoon he had slipped through her defenses. Such a little thing: playing with a baby. But it was the little things, rather than the watershed events, on which love was built. She had softened toward him when he had saved her and Jason's lives, but her heart had remained her own. Today she had fallen in love; it wasn't something she could back away from and ignore. It might be impossible to breach Robert's defenses and reach his heart, but she had to try.

Finally she drifted into sleep, but the alarm too soon urged her out of bed. Heavy-eyed, she put on the coffee and showered while it was brewing. Then, as she absently munched on a bowl of cereal and poured in the caffeine, a dull cramp knotted her lower belly. "Damn it," she muttered. Just what she needed; she was going out with Robert for the first time that night, and her period was starting. She had thought she had another couple of days before it was due. She made a mental note that in a few days she should begin taking the birth-control pills the doctor had just prescribed.

Normally her period didn't bother her, but the timing of this one, added to lack of sleep, made her cranky as she left the house in the predawn darkness and climbed into the truck.

The sturdy pickup, usually so reliable despite its high mileage, made some unfamiliar noises as she drove along the dark, deserted side road. "Don't you dare break down on me now," she warned it. She was just getting on a firm financial footing; a major repair job right now was just what she didn't need.

She reached U.S. 431 and turned onto it. The truck shuddered and began making loud clanging noises. Startled, she slowed and swept the gauges with a quick glance. The temperature was fine, the oil— Oh, God, the oil gauge was red-lining. She slammed on the brakes and started to veer toward the shoulder, and that was when the engine blew. There were more clanging and grinding noises, and smoke boiled up around the hood, obscuring her vision. She steered the truck off the highway, fighting the heavy wheel as, deprived of power, the vehicle lurched to a halt.

Evie got out and stood looking at the smoking corpse as it pinged and rattled, the sounds of mechanical death. Her language was usually mild, but there were some occasions that called for swear words, and this was one of them. She used every curse word she had ever heard, stringing them together in rather innovative ways. That didn't bring life back to the motor, and it didn't make her bank account any healthier, but it relieved some of her frustration. When she ran out of new ways to say things, she stopped, took a deep breath and looked up and down the highway. Dawn was lightening the sky, and traffic was picking up; maybe someone she knew would come by and she wouldn't have to walk the full two miles to a pay phone. With a sigh she got the pistol out from under the truck seat, slipped it into her purse, then locked the truck—though obviously anyone who stole it would have to haul it away—and began walking.

It was less than a minute when another pickup rolled to a stop beside her. She glanced around and saw the boat hitched up behind. Two men were in the truck, and the one on the passenger side rolled down his window. "Havin' trouble?" Then he said, a bit uncertainly, "Miss Evie?"

With relief she recognized Russ McElroy and Jim Haynes, two area fisherman whom she had known casually for several years. "Hi, Russ. Jim. The motor in my truck just blew."

Russ opened the door and hopped out. "Come on, we'll give you a ride to the marina. You don't need to be out by yourself like this. There's too much meanness goin' on these days."

Gratefully she climbed into the cab of the truck and slid to the middle of the seat. Russ got back in and closed the door, and Jim eased the rig onto the highway. "You got a good mechanic?" Jim asked.

"I thought I'd have Burt, the mechanic at the marina, take a look at it. He's good with motors."

Jim nodded. "Yeah, I know Burt Mardis. He's real good. But if he can't get to it, there's another guy, owns a shop just off Blount, who's just as good. His name's Roy Simms. Just look it up in the phone book, Simms' Automotive Repair."

"Thanks, I'll remember that."

Jim and Russ launched into a discussion of other good mechanics in the area, and soon they reached the marina. She thanked them, and Russ got out again to let her out. They probably hadn't intended to put in at her marina, but since they were there they decided they might as well. As she unlocked the gate that blocked the launch ramp, Jim began to maneuver the truck so he could back the boat into the water. Next she unlocked the office and turned on the lights. Just as Jim and Russ were idling away from the dock, Burt drove up, and she went to tell him about the demise of her truck.

IT WASN'T LONG after dawn when the phone rang. Robert opened one eye and examined the golden rose of the sky as he reached for the receiver. "Yes."

"The truck didn't make it into town. It blew just as she reached the highway. She caught a ride to the marina."

Robert sat up in bed. He could feel the fine hairs on the back of his neck prickling with mingled anger and alarm. "Damn it, she hitchhiked?"

"Yeah, I was a little worried about that, so I followed to make certain she didn't have any trouble. No problem. It was a couple of fishermen who picked her up. I guess she knew them."

That wasn't much better. Guntersville wasn't exactly a hotbed of crime, but anything could happen to a woman alone. Neither did it soothe him that she had been followed, that help was right behind if she'd needed it. The situation shouldn't have arisen in the first place. "Why was the timing off?"

"The hole in the oil line must have been bigger than West thought. Probably there's a big oil puddle in her driveway. She would have seen it if it hadn't still been dark when she left the house."

In a very calm, remote voice Robert said, "If anything had happened to her because of his mistake, I wouldn't have liked it."

There was a pause on the other end of the line. Then, "I understand. It won't happen again."

Having made his point, Robert didn't belabor it. He

moved on. "Be careful when you're in the house tonight. I don't want her to notice anything out of place."

"She won't. I'll see to it myself."

After hanging up the phone, Robert lay back down and hooked his hands behind his head as he watched the sun peek over the mountains. The day before had made him more uncertain than ever of Evie's connection with Mercer. He was fairly certain she had rendezvoused with Mercer out on the water, but either she hadn't told Mercer of his presence, or she had been unaware of his own connection with PowerNet. This appeared to be an efficient espionage ring, to have escaped notice and capture for as long as they had; given that, Evie should have known of him. At the very least, Mercer should have notified her of his presence. What reason could they have had for keeping her in the dark about his identity, unless her participation was very peripheral and no one had thought she needed to know?

The other possibility was that Evie had indeed recognized his name, or been notified, but for reasons of her own had chosen not to pass on the information that he had leased a slip at her marina and appeared to have formed an intense personal interest in her.

Either way, it followed that Evie wasn't on good terms with the others in the espionage ring. On the one hand, it gave him a weakness he could exploit. On the other, her life could be in danger.

EVIE MADE ARRANGEMENTS to have a wrecker tow the truck to the marina. That accomplished, Burt stuck his head under the hood to begin the examination. Next he lay down on a dolly and rolled underneath for another view. When he emerged, he wasn't optimistic about rebuilding the motor. "Too much damage," he said. "You'd be better off just buying another motor."

She had been expecting that, and she had already been mentally juggling her finances. The payment on the bank loan for the marina would be late this month, and then she would have to put off other payments to make the one on the loan. She could get by without transportation for a few days by using the boat to go back and forth from home to the marina. If she absolutely needed to go somewhere, she could borrow Becky's car, though she didn't like to.

"I'll call around and try to find one," she said. "Will you have time to put it in for me?"

"Sure," Burt said easily. "It's a little slow right now, anyway."

By the time Craig arrived to relieve her, it was all arranged. She had located an engine, and Burt would begin work putting it in as soon as it arrived. Depending on how much marina work came in, she might be driving home the next afternoon.

In Evie's experience, things didn't generally work that well. She wouldn't be surprised if Burt was suddenly flooded with a lot of boats needing attention.

The trip across the lake was enjoyable, despite her worries. The water was green, the surrounding mountains a misty blue, and fat, fluffy clouds drifted lazily across the sky, offering an occasional brief respite from the blazing sun. Gulls wheeled lazily over the water, and an eagle soared high in the distance. It was the kind of day when being inside was almost intolerable.

With that thought in mind, once she arrived home she put her financial worries on hold and got out the lawn mower to give her yard a trimming. She glared at the big black oil stain on the driveway where the truck had been parked. If it had been daylight when she'd left this morning, if she hadn't swapped shifts with Craig, she would have seen the oil and not have driven the truck; the motor would still be intact, and the repair bill would be much smaller.

Just simple bad timing.

The yard work finished, she went inside to cool off and tackle the housework, which was minimal. By three o'clock she was back outside, sitting on the dock with her feet in the water and a sweat-dewed glass of ice tea beside her. Fretting about the truck wouldn't accomplish anything. She would handle this just as she had handled every other money crisis that had arisen over the years, by strict economizing until all bills were paid. She couldn't do anything more than that, since it wasn't likely a good fairy would drop the money into her lap. Though there might be the possibility of taking a part-time job in the mornings at one of the fast-food restaurants serving breakfast. Forty dollars a week was a hundred and sixty dollars a month, enough to pay the power bill, with a little left over for the gas bill. But for now all she wanted was to sit on the dock with her feet in the water and gaze at the mountains, feeling contentment spread through her.

That was how Robert found her. He came around the side of the house and paused when he saw her sitting on the weathered dock, her eyes closed, face lifted to the sun. The long, thick, golden braid had been pulled forward over one shoulder, revealing the enticing, delicate furrow of her nape. She was wearing faded denim shorts and a white chemise top, hardly a sophisticated outfit, but his pulse began to throb as he studied the graceful curve of her shoulders, the delectable roundness of her slender arms, the shapeliness of her legs. Her skin glowed with a warm, pale gold luminescence, like a succulent peach. His eyes, his entire body, burned as he stared at her. His mouth was literally watering, and he had to swallow. He had never felt such urgent lust for any other woman. What he wanted was to simply throw himself on her and have her right here, right now, without thought or finesse.

She was unaware of his presence until the dock vibrated when he stepped onto it. There was no alarm in her eyes as she turned her head to see who had come visiting, only lazy curiosity followed by a warm look of welcome. Even the average five-year-old in a large city was more wary than the people around here, he thought as he sat down beside her and began taking off his shoes.

"Hi," she said, a sort of smiling serenity in that one word, which was drawled so that it took twice as long for her to say than it did for him.

He found himself smiling back, actually smiling, his mouth curved into a tender line as his heart pounded inside his chest. He had wanted her from the moment he'd first seen her; he'd been, several times, unexpectedly charmed by her. Both reactions were acute at this moment, but even more, he was enchanted.

He had whirled across countless dance floors with countless beautiful women in his arms, women who could afford to pamper themselves and wear the most expensive gowns and jewelry, women whom he had genuinely liked. He had made love to those women gently, slowly, in luxurious surroundings. He had taken women when the added fillip of danger made each encounter more intense. But never had he felt more enthralled than he was right now, sitting beside Evie on a weathered old dock, with a blazing afternoon sun, almost brutal in its clarity, bathing everything in pure light. Sweat trickled down his back and chest from the steamy heat, and his entire body pulsed with life. Even his fingertips throbbed. It took all of his formidable self-control to prevent himself from pushing her down on the dock and spreading her legs for his entry.

And yet, for all the intensity of his desire, he was oddly

content to wait. He would have her. For now he was caught in the enchantment of her slow smile, in the luminous sheen of her skin, in her warm, female scent that no perfume could match. Simply to sit beside her was to be seduced, and he was more than willing.

Having removed his shoes, he rolled up the legs of his khaki pants and stuck his feet into the water. The water was tepid, but refreshing in contrast to the heat of his skin. It made him feel almost comfortable.

"It isn't seven o'clock yet," she pointed out, but she was smiling.

"I wanted to make sure you hadn't chickened out."

"Not yet. Give me a couple of hours."

Despite the teasing, he was certain she wouldn't have stood him up. She might be nervous, even a little reluctant, but she had agreed, and she would keep her word. Her lack of enthusiasm in going out with him might have been insulting if he hadn't known how potent her physical reaction to him was. Whatever reasons she had for being wary of him, her body was oblivious to them.

She lazily moved her feet back and forth, watching the water swirl around her ankles. After a minute of wondering about the advisability of bringing up the subject that had been bothering her so much, she decided to do so, anyway. "Robert, have you ever let anyone really get close to you? Has anyone ever truly known you?"

She felt his stillness, just for a split second. Then he said in a light tone, "I've been trying to get close to you from the moment I first saw you."

She turned her head and found him watching her, his ice-green eyes cool and unreadable. "That was a nice evasion, but you just demonstrated what I meant."

"I did? What was that?" he murmured indulgently, leaning forward to press his lips to her bare shoulder.

She didn't let that burning little caress distract her. "How you deflect personal questions without answering them. How you keep everyone at arm's length. How you watch and manipulate and never give away anything of your real thoughts or feelings."

He looked amused. "You're accusing *me* of being difficult to get to know, when you're as open as the Sphinx?"

"We both have our defenses," she admitted readily.

"Suppose I turn your questions around?" he said, watching her intently. "Have you ever let anyone get close to you and really get to know you?"

A pang went through her. "Of course. My family…and Matt."

She lapsed into silence then, and Robert saw the sadness move over her face, like a cloud passing over the sun. Matt again! What had been so special about an eighteen-year-old boy that twelve years later just the mention of his name could make her grieve? He didn't like himself for the way he felt, violently jealous and resentful of a dead boy. But at least Matt's memory had diverted Evie from her uncomfortable line of questioning.

She seemed content to sit in silence now, dabbling her feet in the water and watching the sunlight change patterns as it moved lower in the sky. Robert left her to her thoughts, suddenly preoccupied with his own.

Her perception was disturbing. She had, unfortunately, been dead on the money. He had always felt it necessary to keep a large part of himself private; the persona he presented to the world, that of a wealthy, urbane businessman, was not false. It was merely a small part of the whole, the part that he chose to display. It worked very well; it was perfect for doing business, for courting and seducing the women he wanted, and was an entrée into those parts of the world where his business was not quite what it seemed.

None of his closest associates suspected that he was anything other than the cool, controlled executive. They didn't know about his taste for adventure, or the way he relished danger. They didn't know about the extremely risky favors he had done, out of sheer patriotism, for various government departments and agencies. They didn't know about all the ongoing, specialized training he did to keep himself in shape and his skills sharp. They didn't know about his volcanic temper, because he kept it under ruthless control. Robert knew himself well, knew his own lethal capabilities. It had always seemed better to keep the intense aspects of his personality to himself, to never unleash the sheer battering force of which he was capable. If that meant no one ever really *knew* him, he was content with that. There was a certain safety in it.

No woman had ever reached the seething core of his emotions, had ever made him lose control. He never wanted to truly love a woman in the romantic sense, to find himself open to her, vulnerable to her. He planned to marry someday, and his wife would be supremely happy. He would treat her with every care and consideration, pleasing her in bed and cosseting her out of it. She would never want for anything. He would be a tender, affectionate husband and father. And she would never know that she had never truly reached him, that his heart remained whole, in his isolated core.

Madelyn, of course, knew that there were fiercely guarded depths to him, but she had never probed. She had known herself to be loved, and that was enough for her. His sister was a formidable person in her own right, her lazy manner masking an almost frightening determination, as her husband had discovered to his great surprise.

But how could Evie, on such short acquaintance, so clearly see what others never did? It made him feel exposed, and he didn't like it one damn bit. He would have to be more careful around her.

The sun was shining full on his back now, and his spine was prickling with sweat. Deciding that the silence had gone on long enough, he asked in an idle tone, "Where's your truck?"

"I'm having a new motor put in it," she replied. "I might have it back by tomorrow afternoon, but until then I'm using the boat to get to the marina and back."

He waited, but there was no additional explanation. Surprised, he realized that she wasn't going to tell him about the motor blowing, wasn't going to broadcast her troubles in any way. He was accustomed to people bringing their problems to him for deft handling. He had also thought it possible that Evie would ask him for a loan to cover the repairs. They hadn't discussed his financial status, but she had seen the new boat, the new Jeep, the house on the waterfront, and she was far from stupid; she had to know he had money. He wouldn't have given her a loan, of course, because that would have defeated his subtle maneuvering to put financial pressure on her, but still, he wouldn't have been surprised if she'd asked. Instead, she hadn't even planned to tell him that her truck had broken down.

"If you need to go anywhere, call me," he finally offered.

"Thanks, but I don't have any errands that can't be put off until I get the truck back."

"There's no need to put them off," he insisted gently. "Just call me."

She smiled and let the subject drop, but he knew she wouldn't call. Even if he installed himself at the marina until her truck was repaired, she wouldn't tell him if she needed anything.

He took her hand and gently stroked her fingers. "You haven't asked me where we're going tonight."

She gave him a surprised look. "I hadn't thought about it." That was the truth. Where they went was inconsequential; the fact that she would be with *him* was what had occupied her mind.

"That isn't very flattering," he said with a faint smile.

"I didn't say I hadn't thought about going out with you. It's just that the *where* never entered my mind."

The sophisticated socialites he normally squired about New York and the world's other major cities would never have made such an artless confession. Or rather, if they had, it would have been in an intimately flirtatious manner. Evie wasn't flirting. She had simply stated the truth and let him take it as he would. He wanted to kiss her for it but refrained for now. She would be more relaxed if she didn't have to deal with a seduction attempt every time she saw him.

Then she turned to him, brown eyes grave and steady. "I answered your question," she said. "Now answer mine."

"Ah." So she had been delayed but not diverted. Swiftly he decided on an answer that would satisfy her but not leave him open. It had the advantage of being the truth, as far as it went. "I'm a private person," he said quietly. "I don't blurt out my life story to anyone who asks. You don't either, so you should understand that."

Those golden brown eyes studied him for another long moment; then, with a sigh, she turned away. He sensed that his answer hadn't satisfied her, but that she wasn't going to ask again. The sensation of being given up on wasn't a pleasant one, but he didn't want her to keep prying, either.

He checked his watch. There were a few calls he had to make before picking her up for the evening, not to mention showering and changing clothes. He kissed her shoulder again and got to his feet. "I have to leave or I'll be late to an appointment. Don't stay out much longer or you'll get a sunburn. Your shoulders are already hot."

"All right. I'll see you at seven." She remained sitting on the dock, and Robert looked down at her streaked tawny head with stifled frustration. Just when he thought he was finally making serious progress with her, she mentally retreated again, like a turtle withdrawing into its shell. But this afternoon's mood was an odd blend of contentment, melancholy and resignation. Maybe she was worried about the truck; maybe she was nervous about their first date, though why she should be, when he'd already had her half-naked, was beyond his comprehension.

The truth was that she was as opaque to him as he was to others. He had always had the ability to read people, but Evie's mind was either closed to him or she reacted in a totally unexpected way. He couldn't predict what she would do or tell what she was thinking, and it was slowly driving him mad. He forced himself to walk away, rather than stand there waiting for her to look up at him. What would that accomplish? It was likely that she would figure out why he was waiting and look up just to get it over with, so he would go. Little mind games were only for the insecure, and Robert didn't have an insecure bone in his body. Nevertheless, he was reluctant to leave her. The only time he wasn't worried about what she was doing was when he was with her.

As he climbed into the Jeep, he wryly reflected that it was a sad state of affairs when he was so obsessed with a woman he couldn't trust out of his sight.

Evie remained where she was until long after the sound of the Jeep's engine had faded in the distance. Robert had stonewalled her questions, and sadly she realized that he simply wasn't going to allow her to get close to him. She supposed she could make a pest of herself and keep yammering at him, but that would only make him close up more. No, if she wanted a relationship with him, she would have to content herself with the litte he was comfortable in giving. She had known Matt to the bone and loved him as deeply. How ironic it was that now she had fallen in love with a man who allowed her to touch only the surface.

Finally she pulled her feet out of the water and stood. This had been a day of fretting, though she had tried not to. She would be better off getting ready for her big date. She had the feeling she would need every bit of preparation she could manage.

CHAPTER TEN

A WOMAN COULDN'T have asked for a more perfect escort, she realized about halfway through the evening. For all his sophistication, or perhaps because of it, there was something very old-fashioned in the courtesy and protectiveness with which he treated her. Everything was arranged for *her* pleasure, *her* comfort, and she herself was old-fashioned enough, Southern enough, to accept it as the way things should be. Robert Cannon was courting her, so of course he should make certain she was pleased by the evening.

His attention was solely on her. He didn't eye other women, though she noticed other women watching him. He held her chair for her whenever she got up or sat down, poured wine for her and asked the maître d' to turn up the thermostat when he noticed her shivering. It was a matter of his own presence that his request was instantly honored. Whenever they walked, his hand rested warmly on the small of her back in a protective, possessive touch.

In no time, he had put her at ease. It was only natural that she had been nervous about the evening; after all, she hadn't been on a date in twelve years, and there was a great deal of difference between eighteen and thirty. Back then a date had been a hamburger and a movie, or just getting together with a bunch of friends at the skating rink. She wasn't at all certain what one did on a date with a man who was used to the most cosmopolitan of entertainments.

As she watched his dark, lean face, she realized how

truly sophisticated he was. He had brought her to a very nice restaurant in Huntsville, but she was well aware that it didn't compare to the sort of establishments available in New York or Paris or New Orleans. Not by even a hint, though, did he indicate that the standards were less than those to which he was accustomed. Others, worldly but less sophisticated—and certainly less polite—would have subtly tried to impress by describing the *truly* good restaurants where they'd eaten. Not Robert. She doubted that he even thought of it, for he had the true sophisticate's knack of being at home in any surrounding. He didn't rate or compare; he simply enjoyed. He would have been as happy eating barbecue with his fingers as he was dining with gold flatware and blotting his mouth with a starched linen napkin.

Oh, God. Not only did he play with babies, he was totally comfortable in her world. Just one more thing to love.

He waved his fingers in front of her face. "You've been watching me and smiling for about five minutes," he said with amusement coloring his tone. "Ordinarily I'd be flattered, but somehow it makes me uneasy."

Her mouth quirked as she picked up her fork. "It shouldn't, because actually it was flattering. I was thinking how comfortable you are down here, despite how different things are."

He shrugged and said gently, "The differences are mostly good ones, though I admit I wasn't prepared for the heat. Somehow, ninety degrees in New York is different from ninety degrees here."

Her brows lifted delicately. "Ninety degrees isn't all that hot."

He chuckled and again wondered briefly at her ability to amuse him. It wasn't anything overt, just the subtle differences in her outlook and the way she phrased it. "That's the difference, one of attitude. Though, of course, it gets hotter than that occasionally, to a New Yorker ninety degrees is *hot*. To you, it's a nice day."

"Not exactly. Ninety degrees is hot to us, too. It's just that, compared to a hundred degrees, it isn't bad."

"Like I said, attitude." He sipped his wine. "I like New York for what it is. I like it down here for the same reason. In New York there's an air of excitement and energy, the opera and ballet and museums. Here, you have clean air, no overcrowding, no traffic jams. No one seems to hurry. People smile at strangers." His eyes lingered on her face, and when he continued his voice was a little deeper. "Though I admit I've been disappointed that I haven't heard you say 'y'all' at all. In fact, I've heard it very few times since I've been here."

She hid her smile. "Why would I say it to you? Y'all is plural. You're singular."

"Is it? That minor detail had escaped me."

"That you're singular?" She paused, aware that she was trespassing into his private life and that he might well shut down as he had that afternoon. "Have you ever been married?"

He sipped his wine again, and his eyes glittered at her over the rim of the glass. "No," he replied easily. "I was engaged once, when I was in college, but we both realized in time that getting married—particularly to each other— would have been a stupid thing to do."

"How old are you?"

"Thirty-six. To satisfy any other pertinent questions you may have, my sexual interest is exclusively in women. I've never done drugs and I don't have any communicable diseases. My parents are dead, but I have a sister, Madelyn, who lives in Montana with her husband and two sons. There are a few distant cousins, but we don't keep in touch."

She regarded him calmly. He was totally relaxed, telling her that he didn't regard those details of his life as being particularly revealing. They were simply facts. She listened, though, because such minutiae made up the skeleton of his life. "Becky and I have relatives scattered all over the state," she said. "One of my uncles has a huge farm down around Montgomery, and every June we get together there for a family reunion. We aren't a close family, but we're friendly, and it's a way to stay in touch. If it wasn't for the reunion, Jason and Paige would never know Becky's side of the family, only their father's, so we make an effort to go every year."

"Your parents are dead?" He knew they were, for that had been in the supplementary report he had received.

"Yes." The golden glow in her eyes dimmed. "Becky is the only immediate family I have. When Mom died, I lived with Becky and Paul until Matt and I married." Her voice faltered, just a little, at the end.

"What about afterward?" he asked gently.

"Then I lived with Matt's parents." The words were soft, almost soundless. "Where I live now. It was their house. The marina was theirs, too. Matt was their only child, and when they died, they left everything to me."

Robert was pierced by another arrow of jealousy. She was still living in the house where Matt had grown up; there was no way she could walk into that house without being reminded of him at every turn. "Have you ever thought of moving? Of buying a more modern house?"

She shook her head. "Home is important to me. I lost my home when Mom died, and though Becky and Paul made me welcome, I was always aware that it was their home and not mine. Matt and I were going to live in a trailer, at first, but after he died I couldn't…. Anyway, his parents asked me to live with them, and they needed me as much as I needed company. Maybe because they needed me, I felt comfortable there, more like it really was my own home. And now," she said simply, "it is."

He regarded her thoughtfully. He had never felt that sort of attachment for a place, never felt the tug of roots. There had been a large country estate in Connecticut, when he was growing up, but it had simply been the place where he lived. Now his penthouse served the same emotionless function. Evie wouldn't like it, though it was spacious and impeccably decorated. Still, he was comfortable there, and the security was excellent.

The restaurant featured a live band, and they were really very good. In keeping with the image of the place, they played old standards, meant for real dancing rather than solitary gyrations. He held out his hand to Evie. "Would you like to dance?"

A glowing smile touched her face as she placed her hand in his, but then she hesitated, and a look of uncertainty replaced the pleasure. "It's been so long," she said honestly, "that I don't know if I can."

"Trust me," he said, soothing her worries. "I won't let you come to grief. It's like riding a bicycle."

She went into his arms. She was stiff at first, but after several turns she relaxed and let the pleasure of the music and the movement sweep through her. Robert was an expert dancer, but then, she hadn't expected anything else. He held her closely enough that she felt secure, but not so close as to touch intimately. More of those exquisite manners, she thought.

As the music continued, she realized that he didn't have to be blatant. Dancing was its own seduction. There was the tender way he clasped her hand, the warm firmness of his other hand on her back. His breath brushed her hair; the clean scent of his skin teased her nostrils. This close, she could see the closely shaven stubble of his beard, dark against his olive skin. Occasionally her breasts brushed against his chest or arm, or their thighs slid together. It was stylized, unconsummated lovemaking, and she wasn't immune to it.

They left at midnight. During the forty-minute drive back to Guntersville, Evie sat silently beside him as he competently handled the black Renegade. They didn't speak until he pulled into her driveway and turned off the ignition, flooding the sudden darkness with silence. As their eyes adjusted, they could see the river stretching, soundless and glistening, behind her house.

"Tomorrow night?" he asked, turning toward her and draping one arm over the steering wheel.

She shook her head. "I can't. I haven't arranged for Craig to take over my shift, so he'll open the marina in the morning as usual. I wouldn't, anyway. That isn't the deal we made."

He sighed. "All right, we'll compromise. How about swapping shifts with him once a week? Would that be acceptable to your strange scruples? He works for you, rather than the other way around, you know."

"He's also a friend, and he does a lot of favors for me. I won't take advantage of him." The coolness in her voice told him that he had offended her.

He got out and walked around to open the door for her. As he lifted her to the ground, he said with a touch of whimsy, "Will you try to make a little time for me, anyway?"

"I'll talk to Craig about it," she replied noncommittally.

"Please."

She extracted her house key from her purse, and Robert deftly lifted it out of her fingers. He unlocked the door, reached inside to turn on a light, then stepped back. "Thank you," she said.

He delayed her with his hand on her arm as she started to go inside. "Good night, sweetheart," he murmured, and placed his mouth over hers.

The kiss was slow and warm and relatively undemanding. He didn't touch her, except for his hand on her arm and his lips moving over hers. Unconsciously she sighed with pleasure, opening her mouth to the warmth of his breath and the leisurely penetration of his tongue.

When he lifted his head, her breasts were tingling, her body was warm and she was breathing faster than normal. It gratified her to notice that his breath, too, was a little rough. "I'll see you tomorrow," he said. Then he kissed her again and walked back to the Jeep.

She closed the door, locked it and leaned against it until she heard the sound of the Jeep fade in the distance. Her chest felt tight, her heart swollen and tender. She wanted to weep, and she wanted to sing.

Instead, she kicked off her shoes and walked into the kitchen to get a drink of water. Her left foot landed solidly in something wet and cold, and she jumped in alarm. Quickly she turned on the kitchen light and stared in dismay at the puddle around the bottom of the refrigerator. Even more ominously, there was no faint humming sound coming from the appliance. She jerked the door open, but no little light came on. The interior remained dark.

"Oh, no, not now," she moaned. What a time for the refrigerator to die! She simply couldn't afford to get it repaired now. She supposed she could buy a new one on credit, but she hated to add another payment to the monthly load. The refrigerator had been elderly, but why couldn't it have lasted another year? By then she would have paid off a couple of debts and had more ready cash. Another six months would have made a difference.

There was nothing, however, that she could do about the refrigerator at nearly one in the morning. She was drooping with fatigue, but she mopped up the water and put down towels to catch any additional leaks.

When she finally got into bed, she couldn't sleep. That part-time job she had thought about during the afternoon now looked like a necessity, rather than an option. Her lower abdomen was dully aching. The evening with Robert, about which she had been so nervous, had turned out to be the best part of the day.

AT SEVEN O'CLOCK she was on the phone to Becky. While Becky was calling around to her friends, Evie began systematically calling in response to every Refrigerator For Sale ad in the paper. As she had suspected, even at that early hour there were a number of calls that weren't answered. One, which had seemed the most promising, had sold the refrigerator as soon as the ad appeared.

By nine o'clock, she and Becky had located a good refrigerator for sale. At a hundred dollars, it was more than she could readily afford, but considerably less than a new one would cost. Becky came to get her, and they drove out together to look at it.

"It's ten years old, so it probably has another five to seven years," the woman said cheerfully as she showed them into the kitchen. "There isn't anything wrong with it, but we're building a new house, and I wanted a big side-by-side refrigerator. We were getting one, anyway, but last week I found just what I wanted, on sale at that, so I didn't wait. As soon as I get this one sold, I can have the new one delivered."

"It's sold," Evie said.

"How are you going to get it home?" asked Becky practically. "Until your truck is fixed, you don't have any way to haul it." Having stated the problem, she set about trying to solve it, running down the list of everyone she knew who owned a pickup truck and might be available.

Evie's own list was formidable. After all, she knew a lot of fishermen. Half an hour later, Sonny, a friend who worked second shift and had his mornings free, was on his way.

Time was running short for Evie by the time they got the refrigerator to her house. She called Craig to let him know what was going on and that she might be a few minutes late. "No sweat," was his easygoing reply.

Sonny hooked up the ice maker while Evie and Becky hurriedly transferred what food had survived from the old refrigerator into the new one. The frozen stuff was okay, and since she hadn't opened the door, most of the food in the other compartment was still cool and salvageable. She threw away the eggs and milk, just to be on the safe side.

"Do you want me to haul off the old one?" Sonny asked.

"No, you need to go to work. Let's just push it out onto the deck, and I'll take care of getting rid of it when I get my truck back. Thanks, Sonny. I don't know what I'd have done without you today."

"Anytime," he said genially, and bent his muscles to the job of getting the old refrigerator outside.

After that was accomplished and Sonny had left, Becky grinned at her sister. "I know you're in a hurry to get to the marina, so I'll call you tonight. I can't wait to hear all the juicy details about your evening with Robert."

Evie blew a wisp of hair out of her face. "It was fine," she said, smiling because she knew the answer would disappoint Becky. "I was worried for nothing. He was a perfect gentleman all night long."

"Well, damn," muttered her once-protective big sister.

WITH MURPHY'S LAW in full effect, when Evie arrived at
the marina she found that the afternoon before had indeed
brought Burt several repair jobs on boats that had to be
done before he could get to her truck. Because the people
who used the marina were her livelihood, she didn't protest the delay. Financially, it would be better for her if even
more repair jobs came in. Enough of them would pay for
fixing her truck.

Craig met her at the dock, took one look at her and said,
with his tongue firmly planted in his cheek, "Boss, you
need to stop all this carousing and get a good night's sleep."

"That bad, huh?"

"Not really. Dark circles are in this month."

"If one more thing tears up," she said direly, "I'm going
to shoot it."

He put his brawny young arm around her shoulders.
"Aw, everything will be okay. Chin up, boss. You're just
tired. If you want to take a nap, I'll hang around for another couple of hours. I've got a date tonight, but I'm free
this afternoon."

She smiled at him, touched by his offer. "No, I'm fine.
You go on home, and I'll see about getting a morning job
to help pay for all this stuff that's going kablooey."

"What stuff?" asked a deep voice behind them. She and
Craig turned. A boat had been idling outside, and the noise
had masked the sound of Robert's arrival. Unlike her, he
looked well rested. His expression didn't give anything
away, but she sensed that he didn't like Craig putting his
arm around her.

"My refrigerator died last night," she replied. "I spent
the morning locating a good used one and getting it home."

That seemed to give him pause, for some reason. Then
he gave her a considering look and said, "You didn't get
much sleep, did you?"

"A few hours. I'll sleep like a log tonight, though."

Craig said, "If you're sure you don't want me to stay for a while...?"

"I'm sure. I'll see you tomorrow."

"Okay." He took off, whistling. Robert turned to watch him go, a tall, well-built boy who gave the promise of being an outstanding man.

"You don't have any reason to be jealous of Craig," Evie said coolly as she brushed by him, heading toward the office and the promise of air-conditioning.

Robert's eyebrows climbed as he followed her. When they were inside, he murmured, "I don't recall saying anything."

"You didn't, but it was plain what what you were thinking."

He was taken aback. God, her perception was expanding into mind reading. He didn't like the feeling of transparency.

"I've known Craig since he was a child. There's absolutely nothing sexual in our relationship."

"Maybe not from your perspective," he said calmly, "but I was a teenage boy once myself."

"I don't want to hear about raging hormones. If all you can do is criticize, then leave. I'm too tired to deal with it right now."

"So you are." He took her in his arms and tucked her head into the hollow of his shoulder. With one hand he stroked her sun-warmed hair, which was restricted into its usual braid. The night before, she had worn it in an elegant twist. One day soon—or rather, one night—he was going to see it down and spread across his pillow.

Gently he swayed, rocking her. The support of his hard, warm body was so delicious that Evie felt her eyes drifting shut. When she realized that she actually was dozing off, she forced herself to lift her head and step away. "Enough of that or I'll be asleep in your arms."

"You'll sleep there eventually," he said. "But in different surroundings."

Her heart gave a great thump. What he so effortlessly did to her simply wasn't fair. Unbidden, she thought of the one night she had slept in Matt's arms, the sweetness that had so shortly been overlaid with bitterness and regret when his life had ended the next day. Sleeping with Robert wouldn't be anything like that long-ago night....

He saw the sadness darken her eyes again, and he felt like swearing savagely. Every time he thought he was making progress, he slammed into Matt Shaw's ghost, standing like an ethereal wall between Evie and any other man. As unlikely—as damned *ridiculous*—as it seemed, he couldn't doubt that she'd been entirely chaste during her widowhood. Her connection with Landon Mercer, whatever else it was, certainly wasn't physical.

Her relationship with *him,* on the other hand, certainly would be.

"Did you come by for any particular reason?" she asked.

"Just to see you for a moment. Would you like to get a quick bite to eat tonight before you go home?"

"I don't think so. I'm so tired I just want to go home and get some sleep."

"All right." Gently he touched her cheek. "I'll see you tomorrow, then. Take care going across the lake tonight."

"I will. The days are so long, I'll be home before it gets dark."

"Take care, anyway." He leaned over and kissed her, then left.

As soon as he was out of her sight, his black brows pulled together in a frown. Last night's ploy hadn't worked all that well because of something he simply hadn't consid-

ered, and he was impatient with himself. He'd been born
into money and had made even more, so the option of buying a second-hand refrigerator hadn't occurred to him. He
had no idea what she'd paid for it, but he assumed that it
was considerably less than a new one, even the cheapest
model, would have cost. Though a little more financial
pressure had been brought to bear on her, it hadn't been
as much as he'd planned.

Mercer was beginning to find the financial waters a
little choppy these days, too. It wasn't anything for him to
worry about…yet. Soon he would find himself in a pinch
with a growing need for ready cash. The next time he
made a move, Robert would be ready for him. The net
was slowly closing.

He estimated another two weeks, three at the most. He
could make things move faster, but he was oddly reluctant to bring everything to a close just yet. If Mercer tried
to make another sale, of course he would have to act, but
until then, he intended to use the time to complete Evie's
seduction.

That was, if he could keep her mind off her dead husband. Robert's jealous fury was banked, but glowing hotly
under the restraint. It was ironic that he, of all people,
should be jealous. It wasn't an emotion that he'd ever felt
before, and he'd been coolly contemptuous of those who
allowed someone to become that important to them. But
he had never wanted a woman so violently, nor found himself up against such a formidable rival. That, too, was a
new experience for him. If a woman had been interested
in another man, he had simply moved on, on the theory
that battling for her affections was too much trouble and
complicated what was, for him, a fairly simple issue.

But then he'd met Evangeline. Her name whispered
through his mind, as musical and elegant as the wind sigh-

ing in the trees. Evangeline. A poetic name, associated with undying love.

He couldn't accept that she was Matt Shaw's forever, that he might never have her.

Damn it, what was this appeal that teenage boys had for her? He had wanted to punch Craig in the jaw for daring to touch her, but his own sense of fair play had restrained him. Craig looked to be as strong as a young ox, but Robert knew his own capabilities. He could easily have killed the boy without meaning to.

Because Matt had died so young, was Evie's taste forever frozen at that age? The idea was distasteful. He was disgusted with himself for even thinking it. He had no basis for the ugly speculation; he knew very well that there was nothing sexual between Evie and Craig. It was his own jealousy that had spurred the thought.

He had to have her. Soon.

CHAPTER ELEVEN

EVIE SLEPT SOUNDLY for ten hours that night, from nine until seven the following morning. She woke feeling much better, though she was groggy from sleeping so hard. She stumbled through the house toward the kitchen, keeping her fingers crossed that nothing else had gone on the fritz during the night, especially the coffeemaker. Everything seemed to be in working order, though, so she put on a pot of coffee and headed back toward the bathroom while it was brewing.

Fifteen minutes later, semidressed and with hair and teeth brushed, she was contentedly curled in a chair on the deck, sipping her first cup of coffee. She closed her eyes as the morning sun bathed her with soothing heat. It was a perfect morning, clear and still and fragrant. The birds were singing madly, and the temperature was still comfortable, probably in the high seventies.

She heard tires singing on the road, the particular note that meant four-wheel drive, and a few seconds later Robert pulled into her driveway. Though she couldn't see either the driveway or the road from the deck, and though she knew any number of people who had four-wheel-drive vehicles, she had no doubt of her visitor's identity. Her blood had started moving faster, her skin tingled and a subtle heat that had nothing to do with either the sun or the coffee had begun spreading through her body.

How many women had loved him? Instinct told her

that she was far from the first. Poor creatures. They, like her, had been unable to resist that gentle, ruthless charm. She knew just as certainly that he had never loved any of them in return.

Through the open patio door she heard the knock at the front. "Robert?" she called. "I'm on the deck."

His footsteps in the grass were silent as he walked around, but in fifteen seconds he was coming up the three shallow steps onto the deck. He stopped, his eyes kindling as he stared at her.

Surprised, she curled a little tighter in the chair. "What have I done now?"

His expression relaxed as he moved to take the chair beside her. "You mistake the matter. That was lust, not anger."

"Ah." She used the cup to hide her face as she took another sip. "That should tell you something."

"Should it?"

"That I see anger from you more often than I do lust." Her heart was pounding even harder. My God, she was *flirting*. She was stunned by the realization. She had never in her life engaged in suggestive banter with a man, especially not to discuss his lust for her. She didn't think she had ever even flirted with Matt; somehow things had always seemed settled between them, and they hadn't gone through that dizzying, intense stage of courtship before commitment. They had grown up committed to each other.

"Again you mistake the matter," Robert said idly.

"In what way?"

"The lust is always there, Evangeline."

The quiet, almost casual, statement left her breathless. This time she took refuge in good manners, unwinding her legs to stand up as she said, "Would you like a cup of coffee?"

"I'll get it," he said, stopping her with a hand on her shoulder. His touch lingered, his fingertips lightly caressing the curve of the joint. "You look as contented as a cat. Just tell me where the cups are."

"In the cabinet directly over the coffeemaker. I don't have any cream, only skim milk—"

"It doesn't matter. I drink it black, like you. While I'm in there, would you like a refill?"

Silently she handed him her cup, and he disappeared into the house.

As Robert got a cup from the cabinet, he noticed that his hand was shaking slightly. He was both amused and amazed at the force of his reaction to her, though he had gotten used to being at least semi-aroused whenever he was in her company. But when he had first seen her this morning...well, he had wanted to see her with her hair down, and now he had gotten his wish.

He just hadn't expected the potency of his response, hadn't expected that thick, tawny-gold, streaky mantle flowing halfway down her back, the sunlight glinting along the strands like precious metal. Only the ends curled, frothing in delight at having been released from the confines of her habitual braid. One lock hung over her shoulder and breast, the curl wrapping around her nipple as perfectly as if it had been created to do just that. It had taken only a glance for him to tell that she wasn't wearing a bra under the pale peach camisole top with the tiny tucks down the front that she probably thought disguised her braless state.

He should have become accustomed by now to the luminosity of her skin. He hadn't. Every time he saw her anew, he was struck by the way she seemed to glow. This morning the effect had been particularly acute. She had been curled in the chair like a cat, sleepy and slightly tousled, her shapely legs and delicate feet bare, the bright sunlight somehow lighting her from within.

He wanted to pick her up and carry her back into the dim coolness of her bedroom, strip her naked and sate himself on the golden pearl of her flesh. But he remembered, with an unpleasant jolt, that this was the house where Matt had grown up. He didn't want to take her here, where the memories of the boy abounded.

"Robert?" Her tone was questioning at his long delay.

"I'm just reading your coffee cups," he called back, and heard her chuckle in reply.

He chose the cup that said, "I'm forty-nine percent sweet. It's the other fifty-one percent you have to worry about," and poured coffee into it, then refilled her cup. He carried both of them out onto the deck and carefully gave hers to her, not wanting even a drop of the hot liquid to spill on her bare legs.

"That's quite a collection of cups."

"Isn't it? Jason and Paige are the culprits. Every birthday, every Christmas, they give me a cup as a gag gift. It's become tradition. They put so much time and effort into picking the cup that it's gotten to where unwrapping it is the highlight of the occasion. They don't let Becky or Paul see it beforehand, so it's always a surprise to them, too."

"Some of them are rather suggestive."

She grinned. "Paige's doing. She's an expert at finding them."

He raised his eyebrows. "That delicate, innocent child?"

"That precocious, inventive child. Don't let the shyness fool you."

"She didn't seem shy to me. She started talking to me right away when I first met her."

"Blame your own charm. She isn't that open with most people. But considering the way Sherry's baby took to you," she said judiciously, "it seems that little girls have an affinity for you."

"That's all well and good," he replied, watching her calmly over the rim of his cup, "but what about the grown-up ones?"

"I'll bring you a big stick tomorrow so you can keep them beat off." Very calmly he leaned over to place his cup on the deck, then took her cup from her hand and put it beside his. She eyed him warily. "What are you doing?"

"This." With one swift, deft movement, he scooped her out of her chair, and settled down in his again with her on his lap. She sat stunned, stiffly erect, her eyes big with surprise. He retrieved her cup and placed it in her hands, then shifted her so she was off balance and had to relax against his chest.

"Robert," she said in a weak protest.

"Evangeline." His voice lingered over the long *i*.

She couldn't think of anything else to say. She sat there wrapped by his strength, his warmth, his scent. She could feel the steady thumping of his heart. She had known that he was tall, but even now, with her sitting on his lap, her head wasn't as high as his. She felt physically overwhelmed and remarkably safe. Not from him, but from the rest of the world.

His thighs were hard under her, and something else was, too.

"Finish your coffee," he said, and unthinkingly she raised the cup to her lips.

They sat there in peaceful silence as the heat grew and the traffic on the river increased. When their cups were empty, he set them aside, then caught her face in his hand and turned it up for his slow, deep kiss.

Like a flower turning toward the sun, she shifted toward him, fitting herself more firmly against him. The taste of coffee was in his mouth and hers. His tongue gently explored, and she trembled, her arms lifting to encircle his neck. How long he drank from her mouth she didn't know; time was measured only by the heavy pulse of her blood, throbbing through every inch of her body.

His hand brushed across her breast, pushing her hair aside, then returned to firmly cup the soft mound. Evie stiffened slightly, but he soothed her with a deep murmur, not really a word, only a calming sound. He had had his hands and his mouth on her breasts before, but he could sense that she was still uncertain about allowing the caress. He petted her, gently circling her nipples with one fingertip until they stood temptingly erect, stroking the lush curves with tender care. He wanted her to relax, but instead the tension in her changed, became more finely charged, and he knew that he was arousing her instead.

Deliberately he unbuttoned the first three buttons of the camisole and slid his hand inside. With a sharply indrawn breath, she turned her face into his neck, but she didn't say the one word that would stop him. Her satiny flesh was cool to his touch, the small nipples puckered and tight. He played with them, rubbing them between his fingers, lightly pinching as he watched her with acute attention to learn exactly what she liked. Slowly her breasts grew warm from his touch, the paleness taking on a pinkish glow.

Evie held herself very still, barely breathing, her eyes closed as she tried to deal with the delicate, exquisite pleasure sweeping through her. She knew she was playing with fire, but she couldn't seem to make herself stop. What if he carried her inside? She would have to call a halt then, because she was still having her period, and she was neither sophisticated nor experienced enough to either let him proceed or tell him, without embarrassment, why he couldn't.

"Shall I stop?" he asked, the sound very low.

She swallowed. "I think you should." But she didn't lift her face, and that wasn't the agreed signal. He shifted her, lifted her, and the shocking heat of his mouth closed over the distended nipple of her exposed breast. She cried out, her nipple prickling at the sensation, and fire shot straight through to her loins.

Then, incredibly, his mouth left her body and he was sitting her up on his lap. "We have to stop," he was saying with gentle regret. "I don't think you're ready to give me the go-ahead, and I don't want to push my self-control much further."

Evie bent her head, struggling with a mixture of relief and chagrin as she fumbled with her buttons, restoring her clothing to order. He was right, of course. She didn't want their intimacy to go any further than it already had, though she intended to be prepared if it did.

She managed to smile at him as she scrambled out of his lap and bent down to get the coffee cups. "Thank you," she said, and carried the cups inside.

Robert rubbed his hand over his eyes. God, that had been closer than he'd let on, at least for him. Would she have let him make love to her, after all? Somehow he didn't think so; he could still sense reluctance in her. In a few more minutes she would have said no, and the way he felt now, the strain might well have killed him. Even if she had said yes, he didn't want to make love to her in this house, so it was just as well he'd had the sense to stop.

They spent the morning together without a repeat of the scene on the deck. He'd already had enough frustration for one day, he decided. When it was time for her to cross the lake to work, he kissed her goodbye and left.

The wind blowing in her face helped clear Evie's mind as she sped across the water. What did he do for most of the day? she wondered. He'd said that he was on vacation, but a person, especially a man like Robert, could take only so much relaxation.

To her relief, Burt had made real progress on the marina jobs and thought he would be able to get started on her truck that afternoon. The prospect of having a vehicle to drive home the next day made her cheerful. Perhaps the run of bad luck was over.

She called the local fast-food restaurants to ask about a part-time job in the mornings, but with school out for the summer, none of them needed any help, all of the part-time jobs being filled by teenagers. Call again after school starts, she was told.

"Well, that was a dead end," she muttered to herself as she hung up from the last call. It looked as if the pendulum of luck hadn't swung back her way, after all.

On the other hand, she had the knack of existing on practically nothing when she had to. Over the next few days Evie cut operating expenses where she could and her personal expenses to the bone. She ate oatmeal or cold cereal for breakfast, and allowed herself one sandwich for lunch and one for supper. There were no snacks, no soft drinks, nothing extra. She turned off the air-conditioning at home, making do with the ceiling fans and drinking a lot of ice water. She was pragmatic enough that she didn't feel particularly deprived by these cost-cutting measures. It was simply something that had to be done, so she did it and didn't think much about it one way or the other.

For one thing, Robert occupied a great deal of her thoughts. If he didn't drop by the house in the morning, he came by the marina in the afternoon. He often kissed her, whenever they were alone, but he didn't pressure her for sex. The more he refrained, the more confused she became about whether she wanted to make love with him or not. She had never bemoaned her lack of practical experience before, but now she did; she needed every bit of help she could muster in handling her feelings for him. With every passing day she wanted him more physically, but caution kept warning her away from letting him become more important to her than he already was. She loved him, but somehow, if she didn't make love with him, some small part of her heart remained hers. If he claimed her body, he would claim all of her, and she would have no reserve to fall back on when the end came.

Still, she was acutely aware of how gradually and skill-fully he was undermining her resolve. Every day she be-came more accustomed to his kisses, to the touch of those lean hands, until he had only to look at her and her breasts would tighten in anticipation. Frightened of the conse-quences if her willpower faltered, she began taking the birth-control pills on schedule, and as she did so, she won-dered if she wasn't actually weakening her own position, for knowing that she was protected might make her less inclined to say no. She was well and truly caught on the horns of that particular dilemma, afraid not to take the pills and afraid of what would happen if she did. In the end, the deciding factor had been that she would rather gamble with her own well-being than that of a helpless baby.

When the next weekend came, Robert once again asked her to swap shifts with Craig so they could have an evening out. Remembering with pleasure the first time she'd had dinner with him, and the dancing afterward, she quickly agreed.

When he picked her up the next night, a slow fire lit the green of his eyes as he looked her up and down. Evie felt a very female gratification at his response. She knew she was looking particularly good, her hair and makeup just as she had wanted, and her dress was very flattering. It was the only cocktail dress she owned, purchased three years before, when the chamber of commerce had organized a party for the local businessmen and women to meet some manufacturing representatives who were thinking about locating in Guntersville.

The deal had fallen through, but the cocktail dress was still smashing. It was teal green, a shade that did wonders for her complexion. There was a full, flirty skirt that swirled just above her knees, a sweetheart bodice supported by thin straps, and it was very low-cut in the back. She had pinned up her hair in a loose twist, with several tendrils left around her ears. Simple gold hoop earrings and her wedding band were the only jewelry she wore, but she had never liked a lot of jewelry weighing her down, so she was satisfied.

Robert was wearing an impeccable black suit with a snowy white silk shirt, but with the heat so oppressive, she wondered how he could stand it. Not that he looked hot; on the contrary, he was as cool and imperturbable as ever, except for the expression in his eyes.

"You're lovely," he said, touching her cheek and watching her bloom at the compliment.

"Thank you." She accepted his verbal appreciation with serene dignity as he drew her outside and locked the door behind them.

He helped her into the Jeep, and as he got in on the other side he said, "I think you'll like the club we're going go. It's quiet, has good food and a wonderful patio for dancing."

"Is it in Huntsville?"

"No, it's here. It's a private club."

She didn't ask how, if it were private, he had managed to get reservations for them. Robert didn't make a show of being wealthy and influential, but he obviously was, given the quality of his clothing, the things he'd bought. Any local bigwig worth his salt would be more than willing to extend an invitation for Robert to join his club.

There was no place in Guntersville that couldn't be gotten to rather quickly. Robert turned the Jeep off of the highway onto a small private road that wound toward the river and soon was parking in a paved lot. The club was a sprawling one-story cedar-and-rock affair, with manicured grounds and a soothing atmosphere. She had seen it before only from the water which glistened just beyond the club. It was only seven-thirty, still daylight, but already the parking lot was crowded.

Robert's hand was firm and very warm on Evie's bare back as he ushered her inside, where they were met by a smiling, very correct maître d'. They were seated in a small horseshoe booth, upholstered in buttery soft leather.

They ordered their meals, and Robert requested champagne. Evie didn't know anything about wines, period, but his choice brought a spark to the waiter's eyes.

The only time she had tasted champagne had been at her wedding, and that had been an inexpensive brand. The pale gold wine that Robert poured into her glass had nothing in common with that long-ago liquid except its wetness. The taste was dry and delicious, the bubbles dancing in her mouth and exploding with flavor. She was careful to only sip it, not knowing what effect it would have on her.

As before, the evening was wonderful, so wonderful that it was half-over before Evie realized that Robert was herding her toward some swiftly nearing conclusion as implacably as a stallion herded the mare he had chosen to breed, keeping after her, blocking all retreat, until she was cornered. Robert was unfailingly gentle and courteous, but nevertheless relentless. She could see it in those pale eyes, in which a fire smoldered. He intended to have her before the evening was finished.

It was evident in the way he touched her almost constantly, small touches that looked casual but were not. They were seductive touches, light caresses that both gentled her and accustomed her to his hand on her body, while at the same time patiently beginning the process of arousing her.

When they danced, his fingertips moved over her bare back, leaving a trail of heat behind and making her shiver in response. His body moved against hers in rhythm with the music, with her heartbeat, until it seemed as if the music flowed through her. And when they returned to their booth, he was close beside her. Several times she shifted uncomfortably, putting more distance between them, but he was inexorable; he would move closer, so that she could feel the heat of his body, smell the faint, spicy scent of his cologne and the muskiness of his skin. He would lightly stroke her arm, or trace the line of her jaw with one long finger, or rub his thumb over the curve of her collarbone. His leg would slide along hers, and then she would feel the hard curve of his arm behind her back, the firm clasp of his hand at her waist. With every move he made her more aware of him and at the same time broadcast his possession of her to any male in the vicinity who might be thinking of poaching.

Evie was both alarmed and excited, and therefore couldn't get her thoughts in order. She managed to retain an outward calm, but inside she was quietly panicking. Robert had always presented the image of an urbane, eminently civilized man, but from the beginning she had seen beneath the cosmopolitan surface to a far more primitive man, a man of swift and ruthless passion. Now she saw that she had underestimated that volatile streak. He meant to take her to bed with him that very night, and she didn't know if she could stop him.

She didn't even know if she *wanted* to stop him. Was it

the champagne, or the fever of desire he had been expertly feeding, not just tonight, but from the moment he'd first kissed her? Her usually clear thought processes kept getting tangled by the slowly increasing heat and hunger of her own body. She tried to think why she should say no, why he was so dangerous for her, but all she could bring to mind was his mouth on her breasts, the way it felt when he touched her.

Physically...oh, God, physically he had destroyed all the years of control, of peaceful solitude. She had wanted no man since Matt—until Robert—and she had never wanted Matt this much. Matt had died on the verge of manhood and was forever frozen in her memory as a laughing, wonderful boy. Robert was a man, in the purest sense of the word. He knew the power of the flesh. He knew that, in the taking of her body, he would also be forging a claim, a possession as old as time. His experience far exceeded hers, and he wanted all of her. She would never be able to hold herself, her inner self, inviolate against his taking. A small voice in her cried out in abject fear, and she struggled toward control.

But he seemed to sense whenever that clear inner voice would gather itself, whenever she would panic as she realized anew what he was doing, and with a warm, lingering touch and the brush of his hard body against her soft curves, he would fan the flames of physical desire to overcome the voice of sanity. He was too good at seduction; even though she recognized it, she couldn't stop it. She had the bitter realization that he could have had her any time he'd wanted, that her will was proving no match for his expertise. He had held back only for some reason of his own, and now he had decided that he wasn't waiting any longer.

He asked her to dance again, and helplessly she went

into his arms. She felt too warm, her skin too sensitive. She could feel the fabric of her dress sliding over her body, rasping her nipples, caressing her belly and thighs. Whenever he touched her, her entire body seemed to clench. They moved across the dance floor on the patio, and he held her close while his powerful legs slid against hers, sometimes thrusting his thigh between hers, and she began to throb with a hollow ache between her legs. In the distance, heat flashes lit the sky over the mountains with flickers of purple and gold. There was a sullen rumble of thunder, and the air was humid and still, waiting.

She felt weak, physically weak. She hadn't known that desire robbed the muscles of power. She melted against him, flowed against him, until she felt as if only his arm around her was holding her up.

He brushed his hard mouth over the fragile skin at her temple, his warm breath stirring her hair, touching her ear. "Shall we go home?"

A last, small vestige of caution cried, "No!" but she was so caught in his sensual web that she could only nod her head, and the cry remained unvoiced. She leaned against him as he walked her out to the Jeep.

Not even on the way home did he ease the relentless pressure. After he had shifted gears, he put his right hand on her thigh, sliding it up under her skirt, and the heat of his palm on her naked flesh almost made her moan aloud. She didn't even realize where he was taking her until he parked in front of his house, rather than hers.

"This isn't—" she blurted.

"No," he said quietly. "It isn't. Come inside, Evie."

She could say no. Even now, she could say no. She could insist that he take her home. But even if she did, she suspected, the outcome would be the same. All she would be changing was the location.

He held out his hand. The intent behind it was ruthless. She could feel the heavy arousal and hunger that tightened his lean, powerful frame. He was going to take her.

She put her hand in his.

Even though she sensed his savage satisfaction at her tacit surrender, he remained gentle. If he had not, perhaps her common sense would have won after all. But he was too experienced to make that mistake, and she found herself standing in his moonlit bedroom with his big bed looming behind her. She looked out the French doors to the lake, a black mirror reflecting the cool, pale moon. Another low rumble of thunder reached her ears, and she knew that the heat flashes were continuing, bright bursts of light that teased with their promise of rain but never delivered.

Robert put his hands on her waist and turned her to him. Her heart thudded painfully against her ribs as he bent his head and his mouth claimed hers. His kisses were slow, so slow, and devastatingly thorough. His tongue probed, and his mouth drank deeply from hers as his hands leisurely moved over her body, unzipping, loosening, removing. The bodice of her dress fell to her waist, and beyond. He paused a moment to caress her smooth back, the inward curve of her waist; then he gently removed the dress and tossed it aside.

She stood before him wearing only high heels and panties. He caught her to him for more kisses, his tongue stroking deeply within. His hands moved over her breasts, molding them under his lean fingers. Desperately Evie clung to his broad, muscled shoulders, trying to steady her spinning senses. His silk shirt slid across her tightly budded nipples, making her whimper. He murmured soothingly as he unbuttoned his shirt and shrugged out of it, dropping it, too, to the floor. Then her naked breasts were pressed full against his bare chest, nestled into the curly black hair, and she heard herself make a low, hungry sound.

"Easy, darling," he whispered. He kicked out of his shoes and unfastened his pants, letting them drop. His thick sex extended the front of his short, snug boxers. She arched against him, blindly thrusting her pelvis forward to nestle that rigid length. His breath hissed inward, and his control cracked. Fiercely he crushed her to him, his arms tightening until pain made her cry out, the sound stifled against his shoulder.

He lowered her to the bed, the sheets cool against her heated flesh. In a swift movement he divested himself of his shorts. Evie's eyes flared as she saw him totally naked, aroused, the muscles in his body taut with desire and the strain of control. His leanness was dangerously deceptive, for it was all steely muscle, the graceful strength of a panther rather than the bulk of a lion. He lowered himself beside her, one arm cradling her head, while his other hand efficiently removed her shoes and panties. Her total nudity was suddenly startling; she made a brief movement to cover herself, a movement that he halted by catching her wrists and pinning them on each side of her head. Then, very deliberately, he mounted her.

Evie couldn't catch her breath. He was heavier, much heavier, than she had imagined. The sensations were alarming, jarring through her consciousness, coming too swiftly on waves of pleasure that both panicked and beguiled. She was violently aware of his muscled thighs pushing between hers, holding them apart, of his furry, ridged abdomen rubbing against her much softer belly, of the hard press of his chest on her breasts. Between her legs, on her bare loins, she could feel the insistent push of his naked sex against her. Her own sex felt swollen and hot, throbbing in rhythm to her own heartbeat.

He loomed over her in the darkness, much bigger, much stronger. The moonlight was sufficient for her to see the pale glitter of his eyes, the hard planes of his face. His expression was stamped with savage male triumph.

Then he released her wrists and cupped her jaw in one hard, hot hand, turning her face up to him. He held her for the deep thrust of his tongue, the blatant domination of his mouth. Helplessly she responded, caught in the heated madness.

He suckled her breasts, lingering over them and making her writhe with pleasure, and all the while she could feel that hard length impatiently nudging her softest flesh.

The moment came too soon, and not fast enough. He braced himself over her on one arm and reached between their bodies with the other. She felt his lean fingers on her sex, gently parting the folds, finding and stroking her soft, wet entrance. Her hips strained instinctively upward. Her entire body was throbbing. "Robert," she whispered. The single word was taut with strain.

He guided his rigid shaft to her, leaning over and into her as he tightened his buttocks and increased the pressure against the tender opening, forcing it to widen and admit him.

Evie stiffened, her breath quickening. The pressure swiftly became burning pain, real pain. He rocked against her, forcing himself fractionally deeper with every controlled thrust. Her fists knotted the sheet beneath her. She turned her head away, closing her eyes against the hot tears that seeped out beneath her lashes.

He froze as realization hit him.

He turned her head so that she faced him. Her eyes flew open, brilliant with tears in the silver moonlight, and then she couldn't look away. His chest was heaving with the force of his breathing, the sound loud in the quiet, still bedroom. There was nothing of the urbane sophisticate in the man who leaned over her, his face hard with desire. For a split second she saw straight into his soul, into the frighteningly intense, primitive core of him. He held her, forced her to look at him, and with a guttural, explosive sound of control breaking, thrust hard into the depths of her silky body, forcing his way past the barrier of her virginity. She cried out, her body arching under the deep lash of pain. Beyond the pain was the stunning shock of invasion, worse than she had imagined, her delicate inner tissues shivering as they tried to adjust to and accommodate the hard bulk of the intruder.

A rough, deep growl sounded in his throat as he gripped her hips, pulling her more tightly into his possession.

He rode her hard, thrusting heavily, his hips hammering and recoiling as he imprinted his physical brand on her flesh. He had never before been less than gentle with a woman, but with Evie he was ferocious in his need. He couldn't be gentle, not with his head and heart reeling, his entire body exploding with savage pleasure. She was hot and tight, silky, wet…and his. No one else's. Ever. *His*.

He shuddered, gasping, convulsing, and she felt the hot wash of his seed deep inside her. Then he slowly collapsed, shaking in every muscle, blindly groping for support. His heavy weight settled over her, pressing her into the mattress.

Dazed, Evie lay beneath him. She felt shattered, unable to form a coherent thought.

And then she found that it wasn't over.

CHAPTER TWELVE

SLOWLY ROBERT SURFACED from the depths of pure physical sensation, his mind sluggishly beginning to function once more. The power of what he had experienced left him shaken, with a sense of being outside himself, not quite connected. He was intensely aware of his own body in a way he never had been before. He could feel the warmth of his blood pumping through his veins with the heavy, slowly calming beats of his heart. He could feel the harsh bellowing of his lungs decreasing to a more normal pace, feel the intense sexual satisfaction relaxing his muscles, feel the hot, delicious clasp of Evie's body as he remained firmly inside her, satisfied but not yet sated. She was naked beneath him, just the way he had wanted.

Then, with an abrupt shift, the sluggishness was gone from his brain and reality settled in with ruthless clarity. Robert tensed, appalled at himself. He had lost control, something that had never happened before. Gentleness on his part had never been more needed, and instead he had taken her like a marauder, intent only on his own pleasure, on the conquest and possession of her silky flesh.

She lay motionless beneath him, holding herself in a sort of desperate stillness, as if to avoid attracting his attention again. His heart squeezed painfully. Robert shoved aside the matter of her virginity—he would know the answer to that puzzle later—and concentrated instead on the task of reassuring her. His mind was racing. If he let her escape him now, he would have a hell of a time getting anywhere near her again, and he couldn't blame her for being wary. Wary, hell. She would probably be downright scared, and with good reason.

He had shown her the relentless drive of passion but none of the pleasure. She had known nothing but pain, and the scale was dangerously tilted; unless he could balance the pain with pleasure, he was afraid he would lose her. It was the first time Robert had felt that sort of fear, but a sensation of panic seized him and mixed with his determination. A part of his brain remained blindingly clear. He knew exactly how to bring a woman to climax in a variety of ways: fast or slow, using his mouth or hands or body. He could gently take her to ecstasy with his mouth, and that way would perhaps be the kindest, but his instinct rejected it. He had to do it fast, before she recovered enough to begin fighting—God, he couldn't bear that—and he had to do it the same way that had caused her the pain to begin with. He wanted her to find pleasure in his body rather than dread the thrust that brought their flesh together.

He was still hard, and once more he began moving, slowly, within her. She tensed, and her hands flattened against his chest as if she would try to shove him off. "No," he said harshly, forestalling her resistance. "I won't stop. I know I'm hurting you now, but before I'm finished I'm going to make you like having me inside you."

She stared up at him, her eyes darkened with distress. But she didn't say anything, and he gathered her close, adjusting their positions so she would have the maximum sensation. He could feel her thighs quivering alongside his hips.

He took a deep breath and gentled his voice, wanting to reassure her. "I can make it good for you," he promised, brushing her soft mouth with kisses and feeling it tremble beneath his. "Will you trust me, Evangeline? Will you?"

Still she didn't say anything, hadn't spoken a word since whispering his name at the beginning. Robert hesitated for half a heartbeat, then lifted her hands and put them around his neck. After a moment her fingers shifted slightly to press against him, and relief shuddered through him at that small gesture of permission.

Evie closed her eyes again, gathering herself to once more endure this painful use of her body. At the moment, that was the limit of her capability; she couldn't act, couldn't think, could only endure. She wanted to curl herself into a protective ball and weep in shock and pain and disappointment, but she couldn't do that, either. She was helpless, her body penetrated; she was dependent on his mercy, and he seemed to have none.

At first there was only more pain. But then, abruptly, the twisting thrust of his hips made her arch off the bed with something that wasn't pain, but was just as sharp. There was no warning, no gradual lessening of pain and buildup of pleasure, only that jolt of sensation that made her cry out. He did it again, and with a strangled moan she discovered that her body was even less under her control than she had thought.

She had been cold, but now she was suffused with heat, great waves of it, rolling up from her toes until she felt as if her entire body glowed. It concentrated between her legs, increasing with each inward thrust. Her hands slid from his neck to his shoulders, clinging now, her nails biting into the hard layer of muscle. He was gripping her buttocks, lifting her up to meet him, moving her, rocking her subtly back and forth, and each tiny movement set off new explosions of pleasure within her. She had the sensation of being relentlessly driven up an internal mountain toward some point she couldn't see, but now she was straining to reach it. He pushed her further with each hard recoil of his hips until she was panting and desperate, sobbing as she arched tightly into him. And then he forced her over the edge, and Evie screamed as her senses shattered.

She shuddered and bucked, trying to meld into his flesh, as devastated by the paroxysms of pleasure as she had been by the pain that went before. Robert held himself still and deep, gritting his teeth, but the frantic milking of her internal muscles was more than he could stand, and with a groan he gave himself over, pulsing with release. Somehow he forced himself not to thrust, to let her take her pleasure and not intrude with his, and that only intensified the sensation. From a distance he heard himself groan again as he dissolved, collapsing heavily in her arms.

If Evie had been dazed before, she was even more so now. She lay limply beneath him, drifting in and out of a haze. The demands he'd made on her body, the roller-coaster succession of pain and shock and ecstasy, had left her with neither mind nor body functioning. Perhaps she dozed; she knew she dreamed, flickering images that faded too swiftly to grasp as she surfaced into foggy consciousness once more. She felt him separate himself from her, knew he was trying to be careful, but couldn't prevent a moan at the pain of his withdrawal. She didn't open her eyes as he paused, then murmured softly, a soothing sound that also held a note of apology, and completed the motion. She felt instantly bereft, cold in the air-conditioned darkness. She would have curled protectively on her side, but her limbs were too heavy. The next moment the dark fog closed about her again.

A light snapped on, blindingly bright against her eyelids. She flinched away from it, but he stilled her with a touch. The mattress shifted as he sat down beside her and firmly parted her thighs. Evie made a faint sound of protest and tried to struggle upward, but again the effort was too much.

"Shh," he whispered, a mere rustle of reassurance. "Let me make you more comfortable, sweetheart. You'll sleep better."

A cool wet cloth touched her between her legs. Deftly, tenderly, he cleaned away the evidence of their lovemaking, then dried her with a soft towel. Evie gave a soft sigh of pleasure. He returned the washcloth and towel to the bathroom, and when he came back to turn out the lamp and slide into bed beside her, she was asleep. She didn't rouse even when he turned her into his arms, cradling her protectively against him.

EVIE WOKE IN the still, dark silence before dawn. The moon had long since set, and even the stars seemed to have given up their twinkling efforts. The darkness that pressed against the patio doors was more complete than at any other time of night, in the last moments before being dispelled by the first graying that heralded the approach of the sun. She was still sleepy, exhausted by the tumultuous night in Robert's arms. It was as if her body was no longer hers, the way he called forth and controlled her responses. He had seduced her past caring about fear, about pain, so that her body arched eagerly into his possessive thrusts.

Robert lay beside her, his breathing slow and deep. One arm was curled under her head, the other lay heavily across her waist. His heat enveloped her, welcome in the cool night. The strangeness of his presence beside her made her breath catch.

She didn't want to think about the night that had just passed, or the things that had happened between them. She was too tired, too off balance, to handle the riot of impressions and thoughts that whirled in her brain, but she was also too tired to fend them off. She gave up the effort and instead tried to make sense of what she was feeling.

She had never thought that giving herself to the man she loved would prove so traumatic, but it had. The physical pain, oddly, was the least of it, the most understandable. She had known that, under his urbane manner, Robert had the soul of a conqueror. She had also known that he had been sexually frustrated from the time they'd met. It would have made her very uneasy if, under those circumstances, his control *hadn't* wavered. She hadn't expected such a complete collapse, but then, to be perfectly fair, he hadn't expected everything that had happened, either.

She should have told him that she was a virgin, she knew, but the telling would have required an explanation that she simply hadn't been able to give. Talking about Matt, reliving those brief hours of their marriage, was too painful. Her throat tightened with dread, knowing that Robert would demand that explanation soon. She had hoped—foolishly—that he wouldn't be able to tell, that her first time would provide no more than a momentary discomfort that she could easily disguise or ignore. She felt like weeping and laughing at the same time. Had she told him, that might well have been the extent of her pain. As it was, she had paid dearly for keeping her secret, only to have it known, anyway.

The two most difficult things for her to deal with, however, were mingled grief and terror. She had known that sleeping with Robert would destroy her defenses, but she hadn't known how panicked she would feel, or that giving herself to him would call up such poignant memories of Matt. She couldn't distance herself from the grief; loving Matt, and losing him the way she had, had shaped her life and her soul. He had, in effect, made her into the woman she was now.

For twelve years she had been faithful to him, and his memory had wrapped around her like an invisible shield, protecting her. But now she had given herself irrevocably to another man, in both heart and body, and there was no going back. She loved Robert with an intensity that swelled in her chest and made her breath catch. For better or worse, *he* filled her life now. She would have to let Matt go, surrender his memory so that it became only a small, indelible part of her, rather than a bulwark between her and the world. It was like losing him twice.

"Goodbye, Matt," she whispered in her mind to the image of the laughing, dark-haired boy she carried there. "I loved you…but I'm his now, and I love him, too, so much." The image stilled, then nodded gravely, and she saw a smile, a blessing, move across the young face as it faded away.

She couldn't bear it. With a low, keening sound of grief she surged out of bed, awakening Robert. He shot out a hand to catch her, but she evaded it and stood in the middle of the floor, looking wildly around the dark bedroom, her fist pressed to her mouth to stop the sobs that pressed for release.

"What's wrong?" he asked softly, every muscle in his body tense and alert. "Come back to bed, sweetheart."

"I—I have to go home." She didn't want to turn on a light, feeling unable to bear his too-discerning gaze, not now, with her emotions stripped bare. But she needed to find her clothes, get dressed…. There was a dark heap on the carpet, and she snatched it up, touch telling her that it was her dress. Oh, God, her muscles protested every move she made, his lovemaking during the night echoing now in her flesh. A deep internal ache marked where he had been.

"Why?" His voice remained soft, compelling. "It's early yet. We have time."

Time for what? she wanted to ask, but she knew, anyway. If she got back into that bed, he would make love to her again. And again. Shaking with grief, caught in the transition between the old love and the new, she thought she would break into pieces if he touched her. She was irrevocably passing from one phase of her life into another, traumatic enough under any circumstances, but she had the sensation of leaving a secure fortress and plunging headlong into unknown danger. She needed to be alone to deal with what she was feeling, to get herself back.

"I have to go," she repeated in a ghostly voice, tight with suppressed tears.

He got out of bed, his naked body pale in the shadowy darkness. "All right," he said gently. "I'll take you home." She watched in bewilderment as he stripped the top sheet from the bed. His next movement was a blur, so swift that she couldn't tell what he was doing until it was too late. With two quick steps he was beside her. He swathed the sheet tightly around her, then lifted her in his arms. "Later," he added as he opened the patio doors and stepped outside with her.

The early morning was silent, as if all God's creatures were holding their breath, waiting for first light. Not even a cricket chirped. The water lapped at the bank with only a slight rustling sound, like silk petticoats. Robert sat down in one of the deck chairs and held her cradled on his lap, the sheet protecting her from the cool, damp air.

Evie tried to hold herself tight, all emotion contained. She managed for a few minutes. Robert simply held her, not saying anything, looking out over the dark water as if he, too, were waiting for the dawn. It was his silence that defeated her; if he had talked, she could have concentrated on her replies. Faced with nothing but her own thoughts, she lost the battle.

She turned her face into his neck as hot tears ran down her cheeks and her body shook with sobs.

He didn't try to hush her, didn't try to talk to her, simply held her more closely to him and gave her the comfort of his body. It was, despite her chaotic emotions, a considerable comfort. The bonds of the flesh that he had forged during the night were fresh and strong, her senses so attuned to him that it was as if his breath were hers, her jerky inhalations gradually slowing and taking on the steady rhythm of his.

When she had calmed, he used a corner of the sheet to dry her face. He didn't bother to wipe her tears from his neck.

Exhausted, empty of emotion, her eyes burning and grainy feeling, she stared out at the lake. In a tree close by, a bird gave a tentative chirp, and as if that were a signal, in the next moment hundreds of birds began singing madly, delirious with joy at the new day. In the time while she had wept, the morning had grown perceptibly lighter, the darkness fading to a dim gray that gave new mystery to details that had been hidden before. That dark hump out in the water—was that a stump, a rock or a magical sea creature that would vanish with the light?

Robert was very warm, the heat of his powerful, naked body seeping through the sheet in animal comfort. She felt the steely columns of his thighs beneath her, the solid support of his chest, the secure grasp of his arms. She rested her head against that wide, smoothly muscled shoulder and felt as if she had come home.

"I love you," she said quietly.

Foolish of her to admit it; how many other women had told him the same thing, especially after a night in his arms? It must be nothing new to him. But what would she gain by holding it back? It would allow a pretense, when he left, that he had been nothing more than a summer affair, but she couldn't fool herself with a sop to her pride. Probably she couldn't even fool him, though he would be gentleman enough to allow her the pretense.

All the same, she was glad of his self-possession. He didn't parrot the words back to her; she would have known he was lying, and she would have hated that. Nor did he act uncomfortable or nervous. He merely gave her a searching look and asked in a level tone, "Then why the tears?"

Evie sighed and returned to staring at the water. He was due some explanation, would probably insist on one, but even though she loved him, she simply couldn't strip her soul bare and blurt out everything. She had a deeply private core, and even if she remained Robert's lover for years, there would be some things she wouldn't be able to tell him, memories that brought up too much pain.

"Evie." It wasn't a prompt but a gentle, implacable demand.

Sadness haunted her eyes and trembled around her mouth. She was very familiar with it, had walked with it for twelve years, gone to bed with it at night, awakened with it on countless mornings. Sadness and a deep lonelines that neither friends nor family had been able to dispel had been her constant, invisible companions. But Robert wanted an answer. A man who had held a woman through such a bout of bitter weeping should at least know the reason for her tears.

"I realized," she finally said in a low, shaking voice, "that Matt is truly gone now."

Cradled against him as she was, she felt the way his muscled body tightened. His words, however, were still controlled. "He's been gone for a long time."

"Yes, he has." Only she knew exactly how long those twelve years had been. "But until last night, I was still his wife."

"No," he said flatly. "You weren't." He put one finger under her chin and tilted it up, forcing her to look at him. It was light enough now for her to see those pale eyes glittering. "You were never his wife. You never slept with him. I hope you aren't going to try to pretend you weren't a virgin, because I'm not a fool, and the stain on the sheet isn't because you're having your period."

Evie flinched. "No," she whispered. God, it was eerie how he had gone straight to the secret she had kept for so long.

"You married him," he continued relentlessly. "How is it that I'm the only man who's ever had you?"

Sadness still darkened her eyes, but she said, "I had a June wedding," and a wealth of grief and irony lay in those brief words.

He didn't understand, but he lifted his dark brows, inviting her to continue.

"It's impossible to book a church for a wedding in June unless you do it about a year in advance," she explained. "Matt and I picked the day when we were still juniors in high school. But there's no way to do any personal planning that far ahead of time." Evie turned her head away from him once more, toward her private solace, the water. "It was a beautiful wedding. The weather was perfect, the decorations were perfect, the cake was perfect. Everything went off without a hitch. And my period started that morning."

Robert was silent, still waiting. Evie swallowed, aching inside as she looked back at the innocent girl she had been. "I was so embarrassed that night, when I had to tell Matt that we couldn't make love. We were both miserable."

"Why didn't you—" he began, but then stopped as he realized that two teenagers wouldn't have the ease and experience of two adults.

"Exactly," Evie said, as if he had put his thoughts into words. "We had never made love, obviously. Matt didn't have any more experience than I did. What experience we had, we'd gotten together, but we'd both wanted to wait until after we were married. So there we were, two eighteen-year-olds on our wedding night, and all we could do was neck and hold hands. Matt was so miserable that we didn't even do much of that.

"But he was basically such a cheerful person that nothing depressed him for long. He was making jokes about it the next morning, making me laugh, but we both agreed that it was something we'd *never* tell our kids when we got old." Her voice wavered and faded until it was almost soundless. "He died that day."

Gently Robert pushed a strand of hair away from her face. So she had never made love with her young husband, but for over a decade had kept herself untouched for him. With an acuteness of insight that often made people uncomfortable, he saw exactly how it had been. Traumatized by Matt's death, she had doubly mourned the fact that they had never been able to make love and had sealed herself off from other men. If her first time couldn't be with Matt, it would be with no one. She had existed ever since as an animated Sleeping Beauty whose body had kept on functioning while her emotions had been suspended.

Robert felt a deep, savage satisfaction. Despite that enormous barrier, he had succeeded where others hadn't even been able to begin. Her first time had been *his*. She was *his*.

He had always despised promiscuity but hadn't prized virginity. It had seemed to him the height of hypocrisy to demand something from a woman that he himself lacked. All of his sophisticated affairs, however, had nothing in common with the powerful, primitive sense of jealous possessiveness that had swept over him the moment he had realized that he was the only man ever to make love to Evie.

Her association with Landon Mercer, whatever it was, was certainly not romantic in any sense. Sitting there in the early dawn, with Evie cradled on his lap, Robert made a swift decision. He wouldn't stop the investigation, wouldn't warn her in any way, because the espionage had to be halted before it did irreparable harm to both the space station and national security. But when the net was tightened and all the traitorous little fish caught, he would step in and use his influence to shield Evie from prosecution. She wouldn't escape punishment, but the punishment would be his, and his alone, to mete out. The simple truth was that he couldn't bear for her to go to prison. He was astonished at himself, but there it was.

He didn't know why she was involved in something so vile. He was a very good judge of people, and he would have sworn that honor was a cornerstone of her character. Therefore, she had to be doing it for what she considered a good reason, though he couldn't imagine what that could be. It was possible she didn't realize exactly what was going on; that explanation fit better than any other, and made him all the more determined to protect her. As he had told her once, he was good at taking care of his own, and last night Evie had become his in the most basic of ways.

He was fiercely glad that nature's rhythm had interfered with her wedding night all those years ago. Poor Matt. A lot of his jealousy for the boy faded away, and a rather poignant pity took its place. Matt Shaw had died without ever tasting the perfection of his young wife's body.

Robert remembered the moment the night before when

he had removed her last garment and seen her totally naked, nothing left to his imagination any longer. To his numb surprise, his imagination had fallen short. He had seen her breasts before, but each time he had marveled at how firm and round they were, delightfully upright, the nipples small and a delectable shade of dark pink. Her body curved in to a lithe waist, then flared again to very womanly hips. Her skin, in the silver moonlight, had glowed like alabaster. Instead of being model thin, like the women he had been accustomed to, her curves had been lush and sensual. He hadn't been able to wait but had mounted her immediately.

A gentleman would have been far more considerate of her than he had been, but he had always been wryly aware that, despite what all his acquaintances thought, he was definitely *not* a gentleman. He was controlled and intelligent and not a cruel man, but that wasn't the same thing as being gentlemanly. Where Evie was concerned, though, his control went right out the window. His mouth took on a grim line as he remembered the wild rush of passion, the primitive instinct to make her his, that had blotted out all reason. Not only had he hurt her, he hadn't used a condom. He, who had never before neglected to make certain some form of protection was used, hadn't even given a thought to birth control.

She might be pregnant. He allowed the possibility to seep into his mind just as the golden light began to seep over the ridge of mountains. To his surprise, he didn't feel any panic or disgust at his stupidity. Rather, he felt pleased—and intrigued.

He put his hand inside the sheet, resting it on her cool, flat belly. "We may be parents. I didn't wear a condom."

"It's all right." She gave him a composed look. The tears and grief were now well under control. "I went to my doctor in Huntsville and got a prescription for birth-control pills."

He felt a not altogether pleasant jolt. He should have been relieved, but instead he was strangely disappointed. Common sense prevailed however. "When?"

"Not long after meeting you," she said wryly.

Robert almost snorted at the amount of work he'd had his people doing, trying to find out what she had been doing, whom she had seen, that day in Huntsville. He would pull them off that particular job now, but he would be damned if he'd tell them what she *had* been doing.

He lifted his eyebrows at her, a sardonic look on his face. "I distinctly remember you saying that you didn't intend to sleep with me."

"I didn't. But that doesn't mean I'd leave something that important to chance, because you were determined, and I wasn't entirely sure of my willpower."

"Your willpower would have been fine," he said, "if you hadn't wanted me, too."

"I know," she admitted softly.

Dawn was well and truly upon them now, golden light spilling across the water. The roar of outboard motors broke the serene hush of the morning, and soon the river would be crowded with fishermen and pleasure boaters. Though Evie's position on his lap would keep anyone from seeing he was naked, Robert thought it best not to chance shocking the locals. After all, she ran a business here, and she might be recognized. He stood up easily, still cradling her securely in his arms, and carried her back through the open patio doors.

He had never been more content than he was at this moment. Evie probably didn't know what was really going on with Mercer and was involved only peripherally; he would be able to protect her without much problem. He had taken her to bed, and now he knew what had lain beneath her mysterious sadness. He doubted that Evie would ever completely stop thinking about Matt, but that was okay now, because Matt Shaw's ghost had been banished and she had emerged from her emotional deep freeze. She had said that she loved him, and he knew instinctively that she hadn't been mouthing the words merely to rationalize their lovemaking. If she hadn't already loved him, he would never have been able to seduce her.

Some of the women who had come before had also told him that they loved him—most of them, in fact. The declarations had never elicited more from him than a rather tender pity for their vulnerability. Though he had liked and enjoyed all his lovers, none of them had ever managed to pierce his shell; he doubted any of them had even known the shell existed.

Evie's simple statement, though, had filled him with a satisfaction so fierce that his blood had thrummed through his veins. She hadn't expected him to respond. Now that he thought about it, she expected less from him than anyone else ever had. It was a startling realization to a man accustomed to having people come to him with their problems, expecting him to make decisions that would affect thousands of workers and millions of dollars. Evie expected nothing. How was it, then, that she gave so much?

He carried her into the bathroom and stood her on her feet, then unwrapped her from the sheet. The sight of her creamy golden flesh aroused him again, drew his hands to cup her breasts and feel the cool, silky weight of them. His thumbs rubbed across her nipples, making them tighten. Evie's eyes were wide with alarm as she stared at him.

His mouth quirked into a crooked smile. "Don't look so worried," he said as he bent down to press his lips to her forehead. "I'll restrain myself until you've had time to heal. Get in the tub, sweetheart, while I put on the coffee. A bath will relieve some of the soreness."

"Good idea," she said with absolute sincerity.

He chuckled as he left her there. The feeling of contentment was even deeper. She was *his*.

CHAPTER THIRTEEN

How could experiencing such a night not leave an imprint on her face? Evie wondered as she got ready for work. After her leisurely soak in the soothing hot water and an equally leisurely breakfast, which Robert had cooked with the same easy competence with which he handled everything else, he had driven her home and reluctantly kissed her goodbye for the day, saying that he had some business to attend to in Huntsville but would try to get back before she closed the marina. If not, he would come to her house.

She had forced herself to do the normal things, but she felt as if her entire life had been turned upside down, as if nothing were the same. *She* wasn't the same. Robert had turned her into a woman who actively longed for his possession, despite the discomfort of her newly initiated body. She hadn't known, hadn't even suspected, that passion could be so savage and all-encompassing, that the pain would be as nothing before the need to link her body with his.

She wanted him even more now than before. He had brought up the long-buried sensuality of her nature and made it his, so that she responded to the lightest touch of his hand. When she thought of him, her body throbbed with the need to wrap her legs around him and take him inside her, to cradle his heavy weight, accept and tame the driving need of his masculinity. The scent of his skin, warm and musky, aroused her. Her memory was filled now with details that she hadn't known before, like the guttural growl of his words and the way his neck corded when he threw his head back in the arching frenzy of satisfaction.

She stared at her face in the mirror as she swiftly braided her hair. Her eyes had shadows under them, but she didn't look tired. She simply looked...like herself. If there was any change at all, it was in the expression in her eyes, as if there was a spark that had been missing before.

But if her face was the same, her body bore the signs of his lovemaking. Her breasts were pink and slightly raw from contact with his beard stubble, her nipples so sensitive from his mouth that the soft fabric of her bra rasped them. There were several small bruises on her hips, where he had gripped her during his climax, and her thighs ached. She was sore enough that every step reminded her of his possession and awakened echoes of sensation that made her acutely aware of her body.

It was much earlier than usual when she drove to the marina, but she needed the distraction to take her mind off Robert. If she was lucky, Sherry would bring Virgil by to spend the day with her.

Craig was gassing up a boat when she arrived. When he had finished, he came in and rang up the sale, putting the money in the cash drawer. "How come you're in so early? Have a nice time last night?"

Her nerves jumped, but she managed a composed smile. "Yes, we did. We went to a private club for dinner and dancing. And I came in early...just because."

"That's a good enough reason for me." He brushed his dark hair out of his eyes and gave her an urchin's grin. "I'm glad you're going out with him. You deserve some fun, after the way you've worked to build up this place."

"Thanks for swapping shifts with me."

"You bet."

Another customer idled up to the docks, and Craig went out again. Evie picked up the morning mail and began sorting through it. The junk mail and sales papers went into the trash. The bills went to one side, to be juggled later. One letter was from a New York bank she'd never heard of, probably wanting her to apply for a credit card. She started to toss it without opening it, but on second thought decided to see what it was about. She picked up the penknife she used as a letter opener and slit the envelope.

Thirty seconds later, her brows knit in puzzlement, she let the single sheet of paper drop to the desk. Somehow this bank had gotten her confused with someone else, though she couldn't think how they had gotten her name on one of their files when she had never done business with them. The letter stated, in brisk terms, that due to a poor payment record they would be forced to foreclose on her loan unless it was paid in full within thirty days.

She would have ignored it except that the amount noted was the same as what she owed her bank for the loan against the marina. She knew that figure well, had struggled to get it down to that amount. Each payment brought it even lower. She didn't know how, but obviously her file had gotten into this other bank's computers, and they wanted her to pay fifteen thousand, two hundred and sixty-two dollars within thirty days.

Well, it was obviously something she would have to clear up before it got even more tangled. Evie called her bank, gave her name and asked for her loan officer, Tommy Fowler, who was also an old school friend.

The line clicked, and Tommy's voice said, "Hi, Evie. How're you doing?"

"Just fine. How are you and Karen doing, and the kids?"

"We're doing okay, though Karen says the kids are driving her crazy, and if school doesn't start soon she's going to get herself arrested, so she can have some peace and quiet."

Evie chuckled. The Fowler kids were known for their frenetic energy.

"What can I help you with today?" Tommy asked.

"There's been a really strange mix-up, and I need to know how to straighten it out. I got a letter today from a bank in New York, asking for payment in full on a loan, and it's the same amount as the one I took out from you, on the marina."

"Is that so? Wonder what's going on. Do you have your account number handy?"

"Not with me, no. I'm at work, and all my bookkeeping is at home."

"That's okay, I'll pull it up under your name. Just a minute."

She could hear the tapping of computer keys as he hummed softly to himself. Then he stopped humming and silence reigned, stretching out for so long that Evie wondered if he'd left the room. Finally a few more keys were tapped, then more silence.

He fumbled with the receiver. "Evie, I—" Reluctance was heavy in his voice.

"What's wrong? What's happened?"

"There's a problem, all right, hon. A big one. Your loan was bought by that bank."

Evie's mind went blank. "What do you mean, bought?"

"I mean we sold off some of our loans. It's a common practice. Banks do it to reduce their debt load. Other financial institutions buy them to diversify their own debt load. According to the records, this transaction took place ten days ago."

"Ten days! Just ten days, and already they're demanding payment in full? Tommy, can they do that?"

"Not if you've fulfilled the terms of the loan. Have you…ah…were you late with the payment?"

She knew he must have her payment record there in front of him, showing that she had been late several times, though she had never fallen a full month behind and had always gotten back on schedule. "It's late now," she said numbly. "I had an unexpected expense, and it'll be next week before I can."

She heard him exhale heavily. "Then they're legally within their rights, though the normal procedure would be to make an effort at collecting the payment, rather than the full amount."

"What do I do?"

"Call them. It should be fairly easy to straighten out. After all, you're a good risk. But be sure to follow up by letter, so you'll have a record in writing."

"Okay. Thanks for the advice, Tommy."

"You're welcome. I'm sorry about this, hon. It never would have happened if we'd still held the loan."

"I know. I'll see what I can do."

"Call me if there's anything I can do to help."

"Thanks," she said again and hung up.

Her heart was pounding as she dialed the number on the letterhead. An impersonal voice answered and nasally requested her business. Evie gave the name of the man who had signed the letter, and the connection was made before she could even say please.

The call was brief. Mr. Borowitz was as brisk as his letter had been and as impersonal as the operator. There was nothing he could do, nor did he sound interested in trying. The outstanding amount was due in full by the time limit set forth in the letter, or the loan would be foreclosed and the property forfeit.

Slowly she hung up and sat there staring out the win-

dow at the blindingly bright day. The lake was crowded
with boaters, people laughing, having fun. The marina was
busy, with owners cleaning their craft, others using her
ramps to launch their boats, still others idling in for gas.
If she didn't somehow come up with over fifteen thousand
dollars within the next thirty days, she would lose it all.

She loved the marina. Because she and Matt had been
playmates before they had become sweethearts, she had
spent a lot of time here even as a child. She had spent hours
playing on the docks, had grown up with the smell of the
water in her nostrils. The rhythms of the marina were as
much a part of her as her own heartbeat. She had helped
Matt work here, and later, after his death, had taken over
the lion's share of the work from his parents. When they had
left the marina to her, she had channeled all her energy and
efforts into making it prosperous, but it had been a labor
of love. The marina, as much as her family, had given her
a reason for going on when she had been doubtful that she
wanted to even try.

This was her kingdom, her home, as much or more than
the house in which she lived. She couldn't bear to lose it.
Some way, any way, she would find the money to pay off
the loan.

The most obvious solution was to borrow against the
house. The amount of the debt would be the same, but it
would be stretched out over a longer period of time, and
that would actually lower the payments. She felt giddy for
a moment as the shock and horror lifted from her shoulders. She would be in even better shape than before, with
more free cash every month.

She called Tommy again and got the ball rolling. He
agreed that a mortgage was the perfect solution. He would
have to get an okay on the loan, but he didn't foresee any

problems and promised to call her as soon as permission came through.

When she hung up, Evie sat with her head in her hands for a long moment. She felt as if she had just survived combat. She was shaky, but elated at her victory. If she had lost the marina... She couldn't let herself imagine it.

When she finally lifted her head and looked out the window, driven by a need to see her domain still safe and secure, still hers, her face broke into a smile. Business was good today. So good, in fact, that Craig desperately needed a hand and was probably wondering why she wasn't out there helping him. Evie bounded to her feet, energy restored, and rushed out to help him with the sudden glut of customers.

ROBERT ARRIVED AT the marina just after seven that evening. It had been busy all day, and she was on the dock selling gas and oil to yet another happy, sun-roasted boater. Alerted by a sensitivity to her lover's presence, Evie looked around and saw him standing just outside the door, watching her. She lifted her hand. "I'll be there in a few minutes."

He nodded and stepped inside, and she turned her attention back to her customer.

Robert watched her through the big window as he stepped behind the counter. He had been notified that she had received the letter and called the bank that he had arranged to buy her loan, and that, as instructed, they had been totally unwilling to cooperate on the matter. Glancing down, he saw the letter lying on top of the stack of mail, the single sheet of paper neatly folded and stuffed back into the envelope.

She had to be uspet. He regretted the need for it, but he had decided to see the plan through. Though he was almost certain she didn't know exactly what Mercer was doing, that she was more of an unwitting accomplice than anything else, there was still the small chance that she was involved up to her pretty neck. Because of that, he couldn't relent in his financial pressure. If she *was* involved, she would be forced into another sale just to raise the money to pay the loan. If she wasn't involved, he would take care of her money problems just as soon as he had Mercer in jail. There were others, and he would get them, too. But Evie was his, one way or the other.

Since he had left her that morning, he had several times been struck with amazement that he wouldn't see her sent to jail, even if she was guilty. This was his country's security at stake, something he took very seriously indeed. He had risked his life more than once for the same principle. He had relished the adventure, but the underlying reason for taking those risks had been a simple, rock-solid love of country. If Evie had betrayed it, she deserved prison. But acknowledging that in no way changed his decision. He would protect her from prosecution.

The sunburned customer and his trio of friends, all young men in their early twenties, were obviously in no hurry to stop chatting with Evie. Robert scowled out the window, but he couldn't blame them. Only a dead man wouldn't respond to her curvy, glowing femininity.

He slipped the letter out of the envelope and unfolded it. There was no reason for doing so, except a meticulous attention to detail. He wanted to know exactly what it said. Swiftly he scanned the contents, satisfied with the way it had been handled. Then he read Evie's notes, hastily scribbled in the margin.

She had written down the name "Tommy Fowler," with a phone number beside it. Underneath she had written "mortgage house" and circled that.

A smile tugged at his mouth. She was certainly a resourceful, common-sense woman. Relief welled up in him. If she was truly involved in stealing the NASA computer programs, she wouldn't be trying to mortgage her house to pay the loan; she would simply arrange another buy. In his experience, criminals didn't think of things like honest work to pay off debts; they were leeches, living off the effort of others, and would simply steal again.

Robert returned the letter to the envelope. More than ever, he regretted the need to play out what he had begun, but he never left anything to chance, certainly not in a matter this serious. He would have to squash any attempt to mortgage the house, of course. Evie would be worried sick, but he would make it up to her afterward.

He sat down on the high stool and watched her as she finally got rid of the four admiring young men. She was dressed much as she had been the first time he'd seen her, in jeans and a T-shirt with her tawny blond hair in a thick, loose braid. His reaction, too, was almost the same: he was poleaxed with lust. The only difference was that it was more intense now, and he hadn't thought that possible. But now he knew exactly how she looked naked, knew all the delectable textures and curves of her body, and the hot, tight clasp of being sheathed deep inside her. He shivered with desire, his burning gaze locked on her as she walked up the dock. He knew the sounds she made at the peak of pleasure, knew how she clung to him, the way her legs locked convulsively around him, and how her nipples hardened to tight little raspberries. He knew the taste of her, the scent, and wanted to have it again.

She came inside, glanced at him and froze in place. He saw the shudder of awareness that rippled over her as she sensed his arousal. God, was she even more attuned to him than she had been before? The thought was unsettling.

"Come here," he said softly, and she blindly walked into his arms.

He didn't rise from the stool but pulled her between his thighs. Her arms circled his shoulders as he bent his mouth to hers. He kissed her for a long time, so hungry for her that he couldn't be gentle. Evie moved against him, her hips rolling in a languorous, wanton manner that made his heart almost stop in his chest. Kissing her when her response was reluctant had been intoxicating enough; now that she was willing, her mouth clung to his in a way that made him forget about Mercer and the stolen computer programs, about the mess she was embroiled in, even where he was, everything but the hot joy of holding her.

But she would be too sore for any more lovemaking today, and reluctantly he eased away from her mouth, trailing kisses across her temple and the curve of her jaw. He would have to restrain himself for a while yet.

"How did your day go?" he murmured, opening the door for her to tell him about the problem with the bank loan.

"It was as busy today as I've ever seen it," she replied, leaning back in the circle of his arms. Her eyes were soft and sleepy. "How about yours?"

"Tedious. I had some boring details to handle." That was a lie. No detail was boring to him.

"I wish you had been here today, I'd have put you to work. I think everyone who owns a boat was on the water today." She glanced over his shoulder. "There's another one," she said as she slipped out his arms.

This group didn't need any gas but trooped inside in search of some snacks and cold drinks. They had the ruddiness of people who had been out in the sun and wind all day, and brought with them the coconut scent of sunscreen lotion. Once inside, they seemed reluctant to leave the air-conditioning and milled around looking at the fishing tackle. Evie didn't try to hurry them, instead chatting pleasantly. They were two couples about her age, out for a day of relaxation on the lake. One of the women mentioned how nice it was to have a day away from the kids, and for a while the conversation centered on the antics of their children. When the group finally left, it was with friendly goodbyes.

"Alone at last," Robert said, glancing at his watch. "It's closing time, anyway."

"Thank goodness." Evie stretched and yawned, catching herself in midstretch with a wince that she quickly covered, but not quickly enough. He saw that slight hesitation. He would indeed have to exercise self-control.

He helped her to close up, then sent her home while he stopped for takeout. They ate dinner together, then sat out on the deck in the cooling night, talking softly about routine things. But Evie soon became sleepy, a direct result of not sleeping much the night before. On her third yawn, Robert stood up and held out his hand. "That's it, sleepyhead. Bedtime."

She put her hand in his and let him pull her to her feet. He led her to the bedroom and gently began undressing her.

"Robert, wait," she said uneasily, trying to draw away from him. "I can't—"

"I know," he said, and kissed her forehead. "I told you I'd give you time to heal. I didn't say anything about not sleeping together, but *sleep* is the operative word."

She relaxed into his arms again, and he finished the task of undressing both of them. It was too warm in the house for him to be comfortable, but when they were both naked and lying on the bed, the ceiling fan wafted a cooling breeze over them, and he began to get drowsy, anyway. They lay nestled spoon fashion, his hard thighs under her round bottom, one hand possessively covering a breast.

He lay quietly. She was already asleep, her breathing slow and even. All his objections to staying in this house had faded when he had found that Evie had never truly been Matt's wife. He would still have preferred being in his own house; the bed was much bigger, for one thing. But Evie would be more comfortable in her own home, and that was the most important thing. He had notified his people where he would be, just as he had notified them that Evie would be staying with him the night before.

He had given her every opportunity to tell him about the bank loan, but she hadn't said a word about it. Just as she had with the blown motor in her truck, she kept her trouble to herself rather than running to him for help or even emotional support. For someone who was so open and friendly, Evie was a very solitary person, accustomed to handling everything on her own. Though he would have had to turn her down if she'd asked for help, he wanted her to confide in him, to let him far enough into her life that he knew about the problems as well as the pleasures. When they were married, he would make damn certain he knew every time she stubbed her toe.

Until that moment, he hadn't let his plans for the future progress that far, but suddenly it seemed the thing to do. He had never wanted any other woman the way he wanted Evie, and he sincerely doubted that he ever would. After this mess was settled, he intended to keep her close by, which would mean taking her to New York with him. And he knew Evie. Though she had given herself to him, she was essentially a conventional soul. She would want the security of marriage; therefore, he would marry her. Other women had wanted marriage from him, but this was the first time in his life he'd been willing to give it. He couldn't imagine ever becoming bored with Evie, which had always happened with other lovers. Even more, he couldn't imagine letting any other man have the chance to marry her.

He didn't regret the impending loss of freedom. He thought of dressing her in silk gowns and expensive jewelry, of settling her in the lap of luxury—his—so that she wouldn't have to work seven days a week or worry about paying bills. She wouldn't have to make do with a second-hand refrigerator or drive around in a beat-up old truck. She wouldn't be so tired that dark smudges lay under her eyes. He would take her with him on his business trips, show her Paris and London and Rome, and they would take vacations on the ranch in Montana. Madelyn, he suspected, would gloat because he had finally been caught, but she would like Evie. Evie, despite that glowing sensuality, wasn't the type of woman that other women disliked on sight. She was friendly and courteous and unselfconscious about her looks. He had seen a lot of women who were far more vain than Evie, and with a lot less reason.

Within a month, perhaps even sooner, all of this would be behind them and they would be in New York. He fell asleep, thinking with pleasure of having her all to himself.

As usual, Evie woke at dawn. Robert lay close beside her, his body heat bathing her in warmth, despite the fact that the sheet had been kicked completely off the bed. He had done that, she supposed, because he wasn't accustomed to doing without air-conditioning. His arm was draped heavily across her hips, and his breath stirred the hair at the back of her neck.

She had slept with him for two nights in a row now and wondered how she would be able to bear the desolation when he was no longer there.

She turned within the circle of that enveloping arm and rose up on one elbow. He woke immediately. "Is anything wrong?" he asked, and just for a moment there was something feral and frightening in his eyes, and an instant tension in his muscles, as if he were poised to attack.

Quickly she shook her head to reassure him. "No. I just wanted to see you."

He relaxed at her words, lying back on the pillows. His olive-toned skin was dark against the whiteness. His thick black hair was tousled, and his jaw darkened by a heavy stubble. She was entranced by his sheer, uncomplicated masculinity, not yet smoothed over with grooming and clothes that somewhat obscured his true nature. Lying there with his iron-hard body naked and relaxed, he looked like what he was, a warrior honed down and redefined by years of battle.

She put her hand on his chest, and he lay quietly, watching her from beneath lowered lids but content to let her do as she wished. She didn't whisper her love to him; she had already told him how she felt and didn't intend to badger him about it. She concentrated, instead, on learning as much as she could about him. She had spent the first eighteen years of her life gathering memories about Matt, but she would have a much shorter time with Robert, and she didn't want to waste a minute.

She bent over him, her long hair trailing across his chest and shoulder as she planted a line of gentle kisses down his body. He smelled delicious in the morning, she thought, all warm and sleepy. The crispy curls of black hair on his chest invited her to rub her cheek against them, catlike. His nipples, tiny and brown, were almost hidden in the hair. She sought them out, tickled by the minute points that stood out when she rubbed her fingertip across them. Robert flexed restlessly on the sheet as desire tightened his muscles, then forced himself to relax again to better enjoy her attentions.

"I wonder if that's the same expression a pasha would have, lying back and letting his favorite concubine pleasure him," she murmured.

"Probably." He put his hands on her head, fingers sliding beneath the heavy fall of hair to massage her scalp. "You do pleasure me, Evangeline."

She continued her dreamy exploration, down the furry ridged abdomen toward his hips and thighs, detouring around his early morning erection. Something high on the inside of his left thigh caught her eye, and she bent closer to examine the mark. The morning sunlight clearly revealed a stylized outline of an eagle, or perhaps a phoenix, with upswept wings. The tattoo was small, not even an inch in length, but so finely made that she could see the fierceness of the raptor.

She was startled by the tattoo—not the design, but its very presence. Lightly she traced her finger over it, wondering why he had it. After all, Robert hardly seemed the type of man who would have a tattoo; he was too polished and sophisticated. But for all that sophistication, he wasn't quite civilized, and the tattoo matched that part of him. This was perhaps the only overt signal he permitted himself that he was more than what he seemed.

"How long have you had it?" she asked, looking up at him.

He was watching her with piercingly intent eyes. "Quite a while."

It was a very inexact answer, but she sensed that it was all she would get from him, at least for now. Slowly she leaned down and licked the tattoo, her tongue gently caressing the sign in his flesh that signaled the presence of the inner man.

A low, rough sound vibrated in his throat, and his entire body tightened.

"Do you want me?" she whispered, licking him again. She felt very warm, and slightly drunk with her feminine power. Desire was unfurling inside her, opening like a flower. Her breasts throbbed, and she rubbed them against his leg.

He gave a strangled laugh, almost undone by her natural sensuality. "Look a few inches to your right and tell me what you think."

She did, turning her head with slow deliberation to survey the straining, pulsing length of his sex. "I believe you do."

"The sixty-four-thousand-dollar question is, how do *you* feel?"

Evie gave him a slow, luminous smile of desire that promised him more than he thought he could survive. "I feel…willing," she purred, crawling up the length of his body to lie on him as she wound her arms around his neck.

His face was strained as he rolled, placing her beneath him. "I'll be careful," he promised in a rough whisper.

She reached up to touch his beard-roughened cheek and opened her thighs to clasp them around him. Her heart was in her eyes as he began slowly, with almost agonizing care, to enter her. "I trust you," she said, giving him her body as surely as she had given him her heart.

CHAPTER FOURTEEN

LANDON MERCER CAUGHT himself wearing a habitually worried expression whenever he glanced into a mirror. Nothing was going right, for no particular reason that he could tell. One day he had been feeling pretty damn good about himself and the way everything was going, and the next it all began to go to hell. It was just little things at first, like that bastard Cannon showing up and nearly giving him a heart attack, though it turned out that Cannon had been the least of his worries. The big boss's reputation had been vastly overstated; he was nothing more than another lazy playboy, born into money, without any real idea of what it was like to get out and hustle for what he had.

Sometimes, though, Cannon had a cold look in his eyes that was downright spooky, as if he could see right through flesh. Mercer wouldn't soon forget the panic he'd felt when Cannon had caught him in Shaw's Marina. For one terror-stricken minute, Mercer had thought he was caught, that they'd somehow managed to find out what he was doing. But all Cannon had seemed interested in was that he'd taken off from work for the afternoon, something he'd been careful not to do again. Of all the damn luck! There were plenty of marinas in Guntersville; why had Cannon picked Shaw's? It wasn't the biggest, or the best run. In fact, for him, its major attraction was that it was small, a bit out of the way and basically a one-horse outfit. Evie

Shaw didn't have time to pay attention to everything going on around her.

Of course, once Cannon had seen Evie, it was understandable why he kept hanging around. Mercer had been trying for months to get her to go out with him, but she was as standoffish as she was stacked. He just didn't have enough money, he supposed; she had latched on to Cannon fast enough.

Of course, if things had worked out, he *would* have had enough money to interest her. He wasn't stupid. He hadn't blown the payoffs; he'd invested them. The ventures he'd picked had all seemed sound. He'd stayed away from the high-interest but volatile money markets and opted for slower but more secure returns. In a few years, he'd figured, he would have enough money invested to be on easy street.

But stocks that had looked good one day went sour the next, prices going on a steady slide as other investors dumped their shares. In one terrible week the tidy little nest egg he'd built up had decreased in value to less than half of what it had been before. He had sold out, taking a loss, and in a desperate move to recoup his money had invested it all in the money markets. The money market had promptly plummeted, almost wiping him out. He felt like King Midas in reverse; everything he touched turned to dross.

When he was contacted about another sale, he was so relieved that he almost thanked them for calling. If his bank account didn't get a cash transfusion soon, he wouldn't be able to make his car payment, or the payments on all his credit cards. Mercer was horrified at the thought of losing his beloved Mercedes. There were more expensive cars, and he intended to have them eventually, but the Mercedes was the first car he'd had that said he was *somebody,* a man on the way up. He couldn't bear to go back to being nothing.

EVIE FELT AS IF she had been split into two separate beings. Half of her was deliriously happy, overwhelmed by the intoxication of having Robert for a lover. She had never dreamed she could be so happy again, or feel so whole, but the great emptiness that had lurked in her heart for so long had been filled. Robert was both passionate and considerate, paying her so much attention that she felt as if she were the center of his universe. He never ignored her, never took anything about her for granted, always made her feel as if she were the most desirable woman he'd ever seen. Whenever they went out, his attention never wandered to other women, though she was well aware of other women looking at him.

She saw him every day, slept with him almost every night. As she became more at ease with her own body and the passion he aroused, their lovemaking became more leisurely, and even more intense, until sometimes she screamed with the force of it. He was a sophisticated lover, leading her into new positions, new variations, new sensations, and he was so skilled that he didn't make her feel awkward or ignorant. He made love to her almost every night. Only once, but that once was long and complete, leaving her sated and sleepy. Then, in the morning when they woke, they would make love again, silently, drifting in that half-awake state when dreams still shadow consciousness.

His mastery of her body was so complete that thoughts of him were always with her, lurking just under the surface, ready to come to the fore and bringing desire with them. She didn't know which she enjoyed most, the intense sessions at night or the dreamy ones of early morning. It was amazing how quickly her body had learned to crave sexual pleasure with him, so that, as the afternoon hours advanced, she would become jittery with anticipation and need. He knew it, surely. She could see him watching her, as if gauging her readiness. Sometimes she had a violent desire to pin him to the floor and have her way with him, but she always restrained herself, because the buildup of desire, though maddening, was equally delicious.

She had become accustomed to containing her thoughts and emotions, guarding them behind a wall of reserve, but Robert drew her out. They had long, involved discussions about a wide variety of subjects. Sitting out on the deck at night, staring up at the stars, they would discuss astronomy and various theories, from the big bang to black holes, dark matter and the relativity of time. His intelligence and the scope of his interests were almost frightening. Without giving any indication of restlessness, his mind was always working, looking for new facts to absorb or arranging those he already had. They would trade sections of the newspaper, and debate politics and national events. They swapped childhood stories, she telling him about growing up with an older sister as bossy as Becky, he making her laugh with stories of his indomitable younger sister, Madelyn. He told her about the ranch in Montana, which he owned in partnership with Reese Duncan, Madelyn's husband, and about their two rowdy little boys.

The sense of closeness with Robert was at once seductive and terrifying. There was a powerful lure that drew her to him, creating an intimacy as much of the mind as of the body, so that she was no longer a solitary creature but half of a *couple,* her entire sense of being altering to include him. Sometimes, in the back of her mind, she wondered how she would survive if he were to leave—she had to think of it as *if* now, rather than *when*—and the thought of losing him made her almost sick with terror.

She couldn't let herself worry about that. Loving him

now, in the present, demanded all her attention. She couldn't hold anything back; she was helpless to even try.

At the same time, the other part of her, the part that wasn't preoccupied with Robert, worried incessantly about the bank loan and the mortgage on the house. Tommy hadn't called her back. She had called the bank twice; the first time he said that permission simply hadn't come through yet, but he didn't think there was any problem and that she should just be patient. The second time she called, he was out of town.

She couldn't wait much longer. It had already been eleven days, leaving just nineteen until the loan had to be paid. If her bank couldn't give her a loan, she would have to find a bank that would, and if all banks moved so slowly, she could find herself running out of time. Just thinking of the possibility was enough to make her break out in a cold sweat.

She tried to think of other options, of some way to quickly raise the money in case the loan didn't go through fast enough. She could put her boat up for sale, but it wasn't worth even half the amount that she needed and might not sell in time, anyway. Asking Becky and Paul for a loan was out of the question; they had their own financial responsibilities, and supporting two teenagers was expensive.

She could sell the rental boats, which would raise enough money but deprive her of a surprisingly tidy bit of income. Of course, with the loan paid, and if she didn't have to take out another one, she would have much more available cash and would soon be able to acquire more boats for rent. The only problem with that was time— again. In her experience, people took their time buying boats. Boats, even in a town like Guntersville that was geared toward the river, weren't a necessity of life. People looked at them, thought about it, discussed it over the dinner table, checked and double-checked their finances. It was possible, but unlikely, that she would be able to sell enough of them to raise the money she needed in the time she had.

Of the limited options available to her, however, that was the best one. She put a sign that read Used Boats For Sale in front of the marina and posted other notices in the area tackle stores. Even if she sold only one, that would lower the amount of money she would need to borrow.

Robert noticed the sign immediately. He walked in late that afternoon, removed his sunglasses and pinned her with a pale, oddly intense look. "That sign out front—which boats are for sale?"

"The rental boats," she calmly replied and returned her attention to waiting on a customer. Once she had made the decision to sell the boats, she hadn't allowed herself any regrets.

He moved behind the counter and stood in front of the window with his hands in his pockets, looking out at the marina. As she had known he would, he waited until the customer had left before turning to ask, "Why are you selling them?"

She hesitated for a moment. She hadn't told him anything about her financial worries and didn't intend to do so now, for a variety of reasons. One was simply that she was reticent about personal problems, disinclined to broadcast her woes to the world. Another was that she was fiercely possessive about the marina, and she didn't want word to get around that it was on shaky financial ground. Yet another was that she didn't want Robert to think she was obliquely asking for a loan, and she would be distressed if he offered one. He was obviously wealthy, but she didn't want the issue of money to become a part of their relationship. If it did, would he ever be certain, in his own mind, that her attraction to him wasn't based on his wealth? Still another reason was that she didn't want anyone else to have a share, and thus a say-so, in the marina. Banks were one thing, individuals another. The marina was *hers,* the base on which she had rebuilt the ruins of her life. She simply couldn't give up any part of it.

So when she answered, she merely said, "They're getting old, less reliable. I need to buy newer ones."

Robert regarded her silently. He didn't know whether to hug her or shake her, and in fact he could do neither. It was obvious that she was trying to raise money by any means available, and he wanted to put his arms around her and tell her it would be all right. But his instinct to protect his own had to be stifled, at least for now. Despite his decision that she was largely innocent in Mercer's espionage dealings, the small chance that he was wrong about her wouldn't let him relent. Soon he would know for certain, one way or the other. But if she sold the rental boats, what means would Mercer use to deliver the goods? Every one of those rental boats was now equipped with tiny electronic bugs that would allow them to be tracked; if Mercer was forced to use some other boat, or even change his method of delivery entirely, Robert would lose his control of the situation.

On the plus side, he was certain Mercer would act soon. They had intercepted a very suspicious phone call, putting them on the alert. It didn't matter if Evie managed to sell a couple of boats, or even most of them, so long as she had one remaining when Mercer made his move. He would simply have to monitor the situation and step in to prevent a sale if it looked as if she would manage to unload all of them.

Aloud he asked, "Have you had any offers yet?"

She shook her head, a wry smile curving her mouth. "I just put the sign up this morning."

"Have you put an ad in any of the newspapers?"

"Not yet, but I will."

That might bring in more customers than he could block, he thought with a sigh. The easiest way would be to stop the ads from being printed; there weren't that many area newspapers. The phones both here and at her house were being monitored, so he would know which papers she called. Somehow he hadn't expected to have so much trouble keeping abreast of her maneuvers. Evie was a surprisingly resourceful woman.

FIVE DAYS LATER, Evie rushed in from overseeing a delivery of gas to answer the phone. She pushed a wisp of hair out of her face as she lifted the receiver. "Shaw's Marina."

"Evie? This is Tommy Fowler."

As soon as she heard his voice, she knew. Slowly she sank down onto the stool, her legs so weak that she needed the support. "What's the verdict?" she asked, though she knew the answer.

He sighed. "I'm sorry, hon. The board of directors says we already have too many real-estate loans. They won't okay the mortgage."

Her lips felt numb. "It isn't your fault," she said. "Thanks, anyway."

"It isn't a lost cause. Just because we aren't making that type of loan right now doesn't mean other banks aren't."

"I know, but I have a deadline, and it's down to fourteen days. It's taken you longer than that to tell me no. How long would it take to process a loan at any other bank?"

"Well, we took longer than usual. I'm sorry as hell about it, Evie, but I had no idea the okay wouldn't go through. Go to another bank. Today, if possible. An appraiser will have to make an estimate of the house's value, but it's waterfront property and in good shape, so it's worth a lot more than the amount you want to mortgage. Getting an appraiser out there is what will take so much time, so get started as soon as you can."

"I will," she said. "Thanks, Tommy."

"Don't thank me," he said glumly. "I couldn't do anything. Bye, hon."

She sat there on the stool for a long time after she hung up the phone, trying to deal with her disappointment and sense of impending disaster. Though she had been worried, the worry had been manageable, because even though she had been making contingency plans, she had been certain the mortgage would go through.

She hadn't sold a single boat.

Time was of the essence, and she didn't have a lot of faith in getting a loan through any other bank. It was as if an evil genie was suddenly in control of things, inflicting her with malfunctioning machinery and uncooperative banks.

Still, she had to try. She couldn't give up and perhaps lose the marina from lack of effort. She *wouldn't* lose the marina. No matter what, she simply refused to let it go. If she couldn't get a mortgage, if she couldn't sell the boats, she had one other option. It was strictly last-resort, but it was there.

She picked out a bank with a good reputation and called to make an appointment with a loan officer for the next morning.

THE HEAT WAS already intense the next day when she was getting ready. Despite the ceiling fans, her skin was damp with perspiration, making her clothes cling to her. Robert hadn't asked why her house was so hot, but the past three nights he had insisted on taking her to his home and bringing her back after breakfast. This morning she had showered at his house as she usually did, then asked him to bring her home earlier than usual because she had a business appointment at nine. He hadn't asked any questions about that, either.

She retrieved her copy of the deed from the fireproof security box under the bed and braced herself like a soldier going to war. If this bank wouldn't give her a loan, she wasn't going to waste any more time going to another one. Time was too short. She would rather be too hasty than take the chance of losing the marina.

She rolled the truck window down, and the wind blowing in her face cooled her as she drove to the bank. The heat was building every day, and soon it would be unbearable in the house if she didn't turn on the air-conditioning. She smiled grimly. She might as well turn it on; one way or the other, she would have the money to pay the power bill.

Her appointment was with a Mr. Waldrop, who turned out to be a stocky, sandy-haired man in his late forties. He gave her a strangely curious look as he led her into his small office. Evie took one of the two comfortable chairs arranged in front of the desk, and he settled into the big chair behind it.

"Now then, Mrs. Shaw, what can we do for you today?"

Concisely, Evie told him what she needed, then pulled the copy of the deed from her purse and placed it on his desk. He unfolded it and looked it over, pursing his lips as he read.

"It looks straightforward enough." He opened his desk and extracted a sheet of paper. "Fill out this financial statement, and we'll see what we can do."

Evie took the sheet of paper and went out to one of the small seating areas off the lobby. While she was answering the multitude of questions, her pen scratching across the paper, someone else came in to see Mr. Waldrop. She glanced up automatically, then realized she knew the newcomer, not an unusual occurrence in a small town like Guntersville. He was Kyle Brewster, a slightly shady businessman who owned a small discount store, dealing in seconds and salvage material. He was also known as a gambler and had been arrested once, several years back, when the back room of a pool hall had been raided on the information that an illegal game was being conducted there. Evie supposed that Kyle was fairly successful in his gambling; his style of living was considerably higher than the income from the discount store could provide.

The door to Mr. Waldrop's office was left open. She couldn't hear what Kyle was saying, only the indistinct drawl of his voice, but Mr. Waldrop's voice was more carrying. "I have the check right here," he was saying cheerfully. "Do you want to cash it, or deposit it into your account?"

Evie returned her attention to the form, feeling slightly heartened. If the bank would lend money to Kyle Brewster, she saw no reason why it wouldn't lend money to her. Her business was more profitable, and her character was certainly better.

Kyle left a few minutes later. When Evie completed the form, someone else had come in and was with Mr. Waldrop. She sat patiently, watching the hour hand on the clock inch to ten o'clock, then beyond. At ten-thirty, the other customer left and she carried the form in to Mr. Waldrop.

"Have a seat," he invited as he looked over the information she had provided. "I'll be back in a few minutes." He carried the form out with him.

Evie crossed her fingers, hoping the loan would be okayed that morning, pending an appraisal of the property. She would get the bank's appraiser out to the house if she had to call him ten times a day and hound him until he appeared.

More time ticked by. She shifted restlessly in the chair, wondering what was taking so long. But the bank seemed busy this morning, so perhaps the person Mr. Waldrop had taken the form to was also tied up, and Mr. Waldrop was having to wait.

Forty-five minutes later Mr. Waldrop returned to his office. He settled into his chair and tapped his fingertips together. "I'm sorry, Mrs. Shaw," he said with real regret. "We simply aren't making this type of loan right now. With the economy the way it is…"

Evie sat up straight. She could feel the blood draining from her face, leaving the skin tight. Enough was enough. "The economy is fine," she interrupted sharply. "The recession didn't hit down here the way it did in other parts of the country. And your bank is one of the strongest in the country. There was an article in one of the Birmingham papers just last week about this bank buying another one in Florida. What I want to know is why you would lend money to someone like Kyle Brewster, a known gambler with a police record, but you won't make a loan on a property worth five or six times that amount."

Mr. Waldrop flushed guiltily. A distressed look came into his eyes. "I can't discuss Mr. Brewster's business, Mrs. Shaw. I'm sorry. I don't make the decisions on whether or not to okay a loan."

"I realize that, Mr. Waldrop." She also realized something else, something so farfetched she could hardly believe it, but it was the only thing that made any sense. "I didn't have a chance of getting the loan, did I? Having me fill out that form was just for show. Someone is stepping in to block the loan, someone with a lot of influence, and I want to know who it is."

His flush turned even darker. "I'm sorry," he mumbled. "There's nothing I can tell you."

She stood and retrieved the deed from his desk. "No, I don't suppose you can. It would mean your job, wouldn't it? Goodbye, Mr. Waldrop."

She was almost dizzy with fury as she went out to the truck. The heat slammed into her like a blow, but she ignored it, just as she ignored the scorching heat of the truck's upholstery. She sat in the parking lot, tapping her finger against the steering wheel as she stared unblinkingly at the traffic streaming by on U.S. 431.

Someone wanted the marina. No one had made an offer to buy it, so that meant whoever it was knew she wasn't likely to sell. This mysterious someone was powerful enough, well-connected enough with the local bankers, to block her attempts to get a loan. Not only that, the original transfer of the loan from her bank to the New York bank had probably been arranged by this person, though she couldn't think of anyone she knew with that kind of power.

She couldn't think why anyone would want her little marina enough to go to such an extreme. Granted, she had made a lot of improvements in it, and business was better every year. When she paid off the outstanding debt, the marina would turn a healthy profit, but it wouldn't be the kind of money that would warrant such actions from her unknown enemy.

Why didn't matter, she thought with the stark clarity that comes in moments of crisis. Neither did *who*. The only thing that mattered was that she kept the marina.

There was one move she could make that wouldn't be blocked, because she wouldn't be the one obtaining the loan. She wouldn't breathe a word about this to anyone, not even Becky, until it was a done deal.

Numbly she started the truck and pulled out into traffic, then almost immediately pulled off again when she spotted a pay phone outside a convenience store. Her heart was thudding with slow, sickening power against her ribs. If she let herself think about it, she might not have the nerve to do it. If she waited until she got back home, she might look around at the dear, familiar surroundings and not be able to make the call. She had to do it now. It was a simple choice. If she lost the marina, she stood to lose everything, but if she sacrificed the house now, she would be able to keep the marina.

She slid out of the truck and walked to the pay phone. Her legs seemed to be functioning without any direction from her brain. There was no phone book. She called Information and got the number she wanted, then fed in another quarter and punched the required numbers. Turning her back on the traffic, she put her finger in her other ear to block out noise as she listened to the ringing on the other end of the line.

"Walter, this is Evie. Do you and Helene still want to buy my place on the river?"

"She stopped at a convenience store immediately after leaving the bank and made a call from a pay phone," the deep voice reported to Robert.

"Could you tell what number she called?"

"No, sir. Her position blocked the numbers from view."

"Could you hear anything she was saying?"

"No, sir. I'm sorry. She kept her back turned, and the traffic was noisy."

Robert rubbed his jaw. "Have you checked to see if it was the marina she called?"

"First thing. No such luck. She didn't call Mercer, either."

"Okay. It worries me, but there isn't anything we can do about it. Where is she now?"

"She drove straight home from the convenience store."

"Let me know if she makes any more calls."

"Yes, sir."

Robert hung up and stared thoughtfully out at the lake as he tried to imagine who she had called, and why. He didn't like the angry little suspicion that was growing. Had she called the unknown third party to whom Mercer had been selling the stolen computer programs? Was she involved up to her pretty little neck after all? He had backed her up against a financial wall, just to find out for certain, but he had a sudden cold, furious feeling that he wasn't going to like the results worth a damn.

CHAPTER FIFTEEN

"WOULD YOU LIKE to go fishing this morning?" Robert asked lazily, his voice even deeper than usual. "We've never been out in a boat together."

It was six-thirty. The heat wave was continuing, each day seeing temperatures in the high nineties, and it was supposed to reach the hundred mark for the next few days, at least. Even at that early hour, Evie could feel the heat pressing against the windows.

It was difficult to think. Robert had just finished making love to her, and her mind was still sluggish with a surfeit of pleasure. He had awakened her before dawn and prolonged their loving even more than usual. Her entire body still throbbed from his touch, the echoes of pleasure still resounding in her flesh. The sensation of having him inside her lingered, though he had withdrawn and moved to lie beside her. Her head was cradled on one muscled arm, while his other arm lay heavily across her lower abdomen. She would have liked nothing better than to snuggle against him and doze for a while, then wake to even more lovemaking. It was only when she was sleeping, or when Robert was making love to her, that she was able to forget what she was doing.

But the throb of pleasure was lessening, and a dull ache resumed its normal place in her chest. "I can't," she said. "I have some errands to run." Errands such as finding a place to live. Walter and Helene Campbell had jumped at the chance to buy her house. They had wanted it for years and had decided to pay cash for it and worry about the financing later, afraid she would change her mind if she had a chance to think about it. Evie had promised she would be out within two weeks.

She couldn't bring herself to tell Robert, at least not yet. She was afraid he would feel pressured to ask her to live with him, when he seemed perfectly satisfied with things the way they were now. It was difficult to think of anyone pressuring Robert to do anything he didn't want to do, and he might not offer, but neither did she want him to think she was hinting that he should. It would be best to find an apartment or house for rent first, then tell him about it.

For that matter, she hadn't told Becky, either. She hadn't told anyone. She had made her decision, but hadn't managed to come to terms with it yet. Every time she thought about moving, tears burned in her eyes. She couldn't bear to go into the explanations and listen to the arguments.

She didn't let herself think about who was behind all these financial maneuverings. First she had to concentrate on saving the marina and finding a place to live. After that was settled, she would try to find out who had been doing this to her.

"What kind of errands?" Robert asked, nuzzling her ear. His hand stroked warmly over her stomach, then covered her left breast. Her nipple, still sensitized from the strong suckling he had subjected it to a short while ago, twinged with a sharp sensation and immediately puckered against his palm. Her breathing deepened. Rather than becoming less intense with familiarity, his sensual power over her body seemed to increase each time he took her.

"I have to pay a few bills and do some shopping," she lied, and wondered why he'd asked. He had no compunction about taking over every facet of her private life but seldom inquired about what she did when they weren't together.

"Why not put it off until tomorrow?" His nuzzling was growing a bit more purposeful, and she closed her eyes as pleasure began to warm throughout her body again.

"I can't," she repeated regretfully. He rolled her nipple between this thumb and forefinger, making it even harder. She caught her breath at the tug of desire, as if the nerves of her nipples were directly connected to those in her loins.

"Are you certain?" he murmured, pressing his open mouth against the rapid pulse at the base of her throat.

Going fishing didn't tempt her, at least not in this heat. Lying in bed with him all morning, though, was so tempting it took all of her willpower to resist. "I'm certain," she forced herself to say. "It has to be done today."

Another man might have turned surly at having his advances refused, but Robert only sighed as he rested his head once again on the pillow. "I suppose we should get up, then."

"I suppose." She turned into him, pressing her face against his chest. "Hold me, just for a minute."

His arms tightened around her, satisfyingly tight. "What's wrong?"

"Nothing," she whispered. "I just like for you to hold me."

She felt his muscles tense. Abruptly he rolled on top of her, his hair-roughened thighs pushing hers apart. Startled, she looked up into slitted green eyes, glittering beneath those heavy black lashes. She couldn't read his expression but sensed his tightly contained violence.

"What—" she began to ask.

He thrust heavily into her, the power of his penetration making her body arch and shudder. He had had her only a little while before, but he was as hard as if that had never happened, so hard that she felt bruised by the impact of his flesh against hers. She gasped and clutched his shoulders for support. Not since the first time he'd taken her had he moved so powerfully. A primal feminine fear beat upward on tiny wings and mingled with an equally primitive sense of excitement. He wasn't hurting her, but the threat was there, and the challenge was whether she could handle him in this dangerous mood, all raw, demanding masculinity.

Desire flooded through her. She dug her nails into his muscular buttocks, pulling him deeper, arching her hips higher to take all of him. He grunted, his teeth clenched against the sound. Evie locked him to her, as fiercely female as he was dominatingly male, not only accepting his thrusts but demanding them. The sensation spiraled rapidly inside her, burning out of control, and she bit his shoulder. He cursed, the word low and hoarse, then slid his arms under her bottom to lift her even more tightly against him. All of his heavy weight bore her into the mattress as they strained together.

The sensation peaked, and Evie cried out as she shuddered wildly in the throes of pleasure. His hips hammered three more times; then he stiffened and began to shake as satisfaction took him, too. He ground his body against hers, as if he could meld their flesh.

The room slowly stopped spinning about her. She heard the twin rhythms of their panting breaths begin to calm. His heartbeat seemed to be thudding through her body, until it was in sync with her own. Their bodies were sealed together with sweat, heat rolling off them in waves.

Their first lovemaking of the morning had lasted an hour. This time, it hadn't taken even five minutes. The fury and speed of it, the raw power, left her even more exhausted than she'd been before.

What had aroused him so violently? After their first

night Robert had been a slow, considerate lover, but he had just taken her like a marauder.

He was very heavy on top of her, making breathing difficult. She gasped, and he shifted his weight to the side. Pale green eyes opened, the expression still shuttered. His mouth had a ruthless line to it. "Stay with me today," he demanded.

Regret pierced her, sharp and poignant. "I can't," she said. "Not today."

For a split second something frightening flickered in his eyes, then was gone. "I tried," he said with rueful ease, rolling off her and sitting up. He stretched, rolling his shoulders and lifting his muscled arms over his head. Evie eyed his long, powerful back with pleasure and approval. The layered muscles were tight and hard, the deep hollow of his spine inviting kisses, or clutching hands. He was wide at the shoulders, his body tapering in a lean vee to his hips. She reached out and ran a lingering hand over the round curve of his buttocks, loving the cool resilience of his flesh.

He looked at her over his shoulder, and she saw a smile come into those green eyes. He leaned over to kiss her, his mouth lingering warmly for a moment; then with a yawn he was off the bed and heading toward the shower. She watched him until he closed the bathroom door behind him, drinking in his tall, naked body. She felt like smacking her lips, like a child drooling after a tasty treat. He was a fine figure of a man, all right. Sometimes, when she saw him sprawled naked and sleepy beside her, it was all she could do to keep from attacking him. She lay in bed for a while, listening to the shower run and entertaining a wicked, delicious fantasy in which he was tied to the bed and totally at her mercy.

But a glance at the clock told her that time was still ticking away. Sighing, she got out of bed and slipped into his shirt, then went to the kitchen to make coffee.

When she returned, he was just coming out of the bathroom, a towel draped around his neck but otherwise still completely naked. His skin was glowing from the shower, his black hair wet and slicked back.

"I put on the coffee," she said as she went to take her turn in the shower.

"I'll start breakfast. What do you want this morning?"

The thought of what she had to do that day killed her appetite. "I'm not hungry. I'll just have coffee."

But when she had showered and dressed, she went into the kitchen to find that he had his own ideas about what she was having for breakfast. A bowl of cereal, as well as a glass of orange juice and the requested coffee, was sitting at her customary place at the table. "I'm really not hungry," she repeated, lifting the coffee cup and inhaling the fragrant steam before sipping.

"Just a few bites," he cajoled, taking his own place beside her. "You need to keep up your strength for tonight."

She gave him a heated, slumberous look, remembering her fantasy. "Why? Are you planning something special?"

"I suppose I am," he said consideringly. "It's special every time we make love."

Her heart swelled in her chest, making it impossible for her to speak. She simply looked at him, her golden brown eyes glowing.

He picked up the spoon and put it into her hand. "Eat. I've noticed you haven't been eating much while it's been so hot, and you're losing weight."

"Most people would consider that a good thing," she pointed out.

His black eyebrows lifted. "I happen to like your butt as

round as it is now, and your breasts perfectly fit my hands. I don't want to sleep with a stick. Eat."

She laughed, amused by his description of her rear end, and dipped the spoon into the cereal. It was her favorite brand, of course; once he had seen the box in her cabinets, a box of the same cereal had taken up residence in his.

She managed to choke down a few bites, more than she wanted and not enough to satisfy him, which was a reasonable compromise. The cereal felt like a lump in her stomach.

Less than an hour later he kissed her goodbye at her door. "I'll see you tonight, sweetheart. Take care."

As she entered the house, she thought it a little odd for him to have added that last admonition. What on earth did he think she would be doing?

Sadly she dressed for work, so she wouldn't have to come back to the house before going to the marina. She wouldn't be braiding her hair in front of this mirror very many more times, she thought. After this afternoon, the house would no longer belong to her. Walter and Helene were getting a real estate agent, a friend of theirs, to handle the transaction immediately. They were supposed to bring all the paperwork to the marina this afternoon, along with a cashier's check in the specified amount. Evie was taking the deed to the property, the surveyor's report that she had had done when she inherited the house, as well as the certification of the title search that had also been done at that time. It was a measure of their trust in her that they were willing to forgo another title search, probably against their agent friend's advice.

She addressed an envelope to the bank in New York, stamped it and added it to her stack of papers. She would take the cashier's check immediately to her bank, desposit it and have another cashier's check made out in the amount of the outstanding loan against the marina. Then she would express-mail that check to New York, to Mr. Borowitz's attention. All her financial troubles would be over.

She wouldn't have her home any longer, but she could live anywhere, she told herself. The marina was more important, the means of her support. With it, she could some-day buy another house. It wouldn't hold the memories this one did, but she would make it into a home.

She took a last look in the mirror. "Standing here won't get anything done," she said softly to herself and turned away.

She spent the morning driving around Guntersville. She had checked a few of the rental ads in the newspaper but didn't want to call them yet, preferring to see the houses and the neighborhoods before calling. She knew she was just stalling, despite the urgency of the situation, but some-how actually making contact was beyond her at the moment. She gave herself a stern talking-to, but it didn't help much. She didn't like any of the houses she saw.

It was almost noon when she came to a decision. She made an abrupt turn, causing a car behind her to squeal its tires and the irate driver to lean on the horn. Muttering an apology, she cut through a shopping-center parking lot and back onto the highway, but in the opposite direction.

The apartment complex she had chosen was new, less than two years old, incongruously known as the Chalet Apartments. She stopped the truck outside the office and went inside. Twenty minutes later she was the new resident of apartment 17, which consisted of a living room and combination dining room/kitchen downstairs, along with a tiny laundry area just big enough to hold a washer and dryer, and two bedrooms upstairs. There were no one-bed-room apartments available. She paid a deposit, collected two sets of keys and went back out to the truck.

It was done. She doubted she would be happy there, but at least she would have a roof over her head while she took her time looking for a house.

THE CELLULAR PHONE BEEPED, and Robert answered it as he threaded his way through the traffic on Gunter Avenue, the one-way street that bisected Guntersville's downtown area and also ran through a neighborhood of grand old houses that looked turn-of-the-century.

"I think she spotted me."

"What happened?" he asked in a clipped tone.

"First she just drove around, all over town. I had to hang back so I wouldn't be as easy to spot. She slowed down several times but didn't stop anywhere. Maybe she was looking for something. Then she got on the highway, going south toward Albertville. She was on the inside lane, I was on the outside. All of a sudden, without a turn signal, she whipped the truck into a parking lot and nearly got hit doing it. I was in the wrong lane and couldn't follow her. By the time I got turned around, she'd vanished."

"Damn." Robert felt both tired and angry. Just when he'd been convinced of Evie's innocence, she was suddenly doing some very suspicious things. She was obviously worried about the marina, but there was something else on her mind, something she was trying to keep hidden. This mornng, in bed, he had been seized by the urgent need to keep her with him all day, thereby preventing her from doing anything foolish. He wasn't used to women refusing any request he made, but Evie didn't appear to have any trouble doing it. She had said no with insulting ease.

Furious, he had even tried to seduce her into staying with him, only to lose his control, something he'd sworn wouldn't happen again. And afterward she'd still said no.

"I'll pick her up again when she comes to the marina," the man said in his ear. "I'm sorry, sir."

"It wasn't your fault. No tail's perfect."

"No, sir, but I should have been more careful about letting her see me."

"Have two cars next time, so you can swap."

"Yes, sir."

Robert ended the call and replaced the receiver. It took all his self-control to keep from driving to the marina to wait for her so he could shake some sense into her as soon as he saw her. But he had to play this through to the end.

As mundane as it was, he had his own errand to run that day: grocery shopping. It wasn't something he normally did for himself, but it wasn't an onerous duty. Despite its strangeness, or perhaps because of it, he didn't mind doing it. Southerners imbued grocery shopping with the same casualness that characterized almost everything else they did. Shoppers ambled down the aisles, stopping to talk with chance-met acquaintances or to strike up conversations with strangers. The first time he had gone into the big grocery store, he had been amused by the thought that a New Yorker relaxed in the park with more energy than Southerners shopped. But when in Rome... He had learned to slow his own pace, to keep from smashing into old ladies who had stopped to pass the time of day.

Today, though, he wasn't in the mood to be amused. It went against his protective, controlling nature to leave Evie to hang herself with all the evidential rope he was feeding to both her and Mercer. He wanted to snatch her away from here, kidnap her if necessary. But if she *were* involved with Mercer, that would scare off the others and they might never be caught. Not knowing for certain, one way or the other, was driving him crazy with frustration.

Two more days. From the telephone calls they had intercepted, they knew that Mercer would transfer more stolen data the day after tomorrow. Evie hadn't been able to sell any of the rental boats, so that was one less problem for Robert. It didn't matter which boat Mercer took, since they were all wired. As a precaution, he had also had Evie's boat wired. In two days it would all be over except for the cleanup. In three days, if all went on schedule, he would be back in New York, and Evie would be with him.

He wouldn't need many groceries, just enough for three days, but he was completely out of coffee and almost out of food, and he didn't want to eat in restaurants for three days. He strode through the aisles of the grocery store, his expression remote as he planned the damage-control measures he would use. Operating with his usual efficiency, he was in and out of the store within fifteen minutes. As he walked out the automatic doors with a grocery bag in his arms, though, the woman just entering through the other set of doors stopped and stared at him.

"Robert."

He paused, immediately recognizing Evie's sister, Becky. Another shopper was exiting behind him, and he stepped out of the way. "Hello, Becky. How are you?" He smiled faintly. "And how's Jason? I haven't seem him at the marina again."

"Didn't Evie tell you? He can't come back to the marina for the rest of the summer. That's a real punishment to him," Becky said dryly. "The marina's one of his favorite places." She too, stepped away from the doors. "There's no sense standing here blocking traffic. I'll walk you to your car."

They strolled across the hot, sticky pavement. The heat was smothering, and sweat began to gather almost immediately on his skin. Wryly he waited, seeing Becky's determination plain on her face. The protective older sister wanted to have a heart-to-heart talk with him, to make certain he didn't hurt Evie.

They reached the Jeep, and he stored the groceries inside, leaving the door open so some of the heat inside could dissipate. He leaned against the vehicle and calmly eyed her. "You worried about Evie?" he prompted.

She flashed him a rueful look. "Am I that easy to read?"

"She mentioned that you're a bit protective," he murmured.

Becky laughed and pushed her hair out of her face. Her hair was darker than Evie's, but in that moment Robert saw a flash of resemblance, a similarity in expression and in the husky tone of their voices. "The big-sister syndrome," she said. "I didn't use to be this bad, only since—"

She stopped, and Robert felt his curiosity stir. "Since when?"

Becky didn't answer immediately, instead turning her gaze to the traffic on the highway. It was a delaying tactic, to give her time to think and organize her answer. He waited patiently.

"Are you serious about her?" she asked abruptly.

He wasn't accustomed to being interrogated about his intentions, serious or otherwise, but he quelled his surge of irritation. Becky was asking only out of concern for Evie, an emotion he shared. In a very level tone he said, "I intend to marry her."

Becky closed her eyes on a sigh of relief. "Thank God," she said.

"I didn't realize the state of our relationship was so critical," he said, still in that cool, dead-level tone.

Becky's eyes opened, and she gave him a considering look. "You can be very intimidating, can't you?"

He almost smiled. If he could, it obviously wasn't working on her. He'd never managed to intimidate Evie, either.

Becky sighed and looked again at the traffic. "I was worried. I didn't know how important Evie is to you, and... well, the success of your relationship *is* critical to her."

His curiosity became intense. "In what way?"

Becky didn't answer that directly, either. Instead she asked, "Has she told you about Matt?"

Robert's eyes glittered suddenly. "Probably more than even you know," he said, his voice deepening as he remembered the first time he'd made love to Evie.

"About how he died?"

Sweat trickled down his back, but suddenly nothing could have moved him from the scorching asphalt parking lot. "He died in a car accident, didn't he?" He couldn't remember if Evie had told him that, or if it had been in the report he'd requested on Matt Shaw.

"Yes, the day after they married." She paused, organizing her thoughts, and again she made what appeared to be a shift in topic. "Our father died when Evie was fifteen. I was twenty, already married, already about to be a mother. A year later our mother died. Can you understand the difference in the way losing our parents affected us?" she asked, her voice strained. "I loved them both dearly, but I had built my home with Paul. I had him, I had my son, I had an entire life away from my parents. But losing Daddy shook Evie's foundations, and then when Mother died... Evie didn't just lose Mother, she lost her home, too. She came to live with Paul and me, and we loved having her, but it wasn't the same for her. She was still just a kid, and she had lost the basis of her life."

Robert stood silently, all his attention on this insight into Evie's past life. She didn't talk about her childhood much, he realized. They had talked about a lot of things, sitting on the deck at night with all the lights off and the starry sky spread like a quilt overhead, but it was as if Evie had closed a mental door on her life before Matt's death.

"But she had Matt," Becky said softly. "He was a great kid. We'd known him all his life, and I can't remember when they hadn't been inseparable, first as buddies, then as sweethearts. They were the same age, but even as young as he was, when Daddy died, Matt was right there beside Evie. He was there with her when Mother died. I think he was her one constant, the only person other than me who had been there for as long as she could remember. But I had my own family, and Evie had Matt. He put a smile back in her eyes, and because she had him, she weathered the loss of our parents. I remember what she was like back then, a giggling teenager as rowdy as Jason is now, and full of mischief."

"I can't picture Evie as rowdy," he commented, because Becky's voice had become strained, and he wanted to give her a moment to compose herself. "There's something so solemn about her."

"Yes, there is," Becky agreed. "Now."

The jealousy he thought he had banished swelled to life again. "Because of Matt's death."

Becky nodded. "She was in the car with him." Tears welled in her eyes. "For the rest of my life, I'll carry two pictures of Evie in my mind. One is of her on her wedding day. She was so young and beautiful—so *glowing*—that it hurt to look at her. Matt couldn't take his eyes off her. The next time I saw her, she was in a hospital bed, lying there like a broken doll, her eyes so empty that—" She stopped, shuddering.

"They had spent the night in Montgomery and were going on to Panama City the next morning. It was raining. It was Sunday, and they were in a rural area. There wasn't much traffic. A dog ran out into the highway, and they hit it, and Matt lost control of the car. The car left the road and rolled at least twice, then came to a stop, on its right side, in a stand of trees. Evie was pinned on the bottom. Matt was hanging in his seat belt above her. She couldn't get out, couldn't get to him, and he b-bled to death in front of her, his blood dripping down on her. He was conscious, she said." Furiously Becky dashed the tears from her cheeks. "No one saw the car for a long time, what with the rain and the trees blocking the view. He knew he was dying. He told her he loved her. He told her goodbye. He'd been dead for over an hour before anyone saw the car and came to help."

Robert turned to stone, his eyes burning as he pictured, far too clearly, what a young girl had gone through that rainy Sunday. Then he reached out automatically and took Becky in his arms, holding her head against his shoulder while she wept.

"I'm sorry," she finally managed, lifting her head and wiping her eyes yet again. "It's just that, when I let myself think about it, it tears my heart out all over again."

"Yes," he said. Still holding her with one arm, he fished his handkerchief out of his pocket and gently wiped her face.

"She's never let herself love anyone else," she said fiercely. "Do you understand? She hasn't risked letting anyone else get close to her. She's stuck with the people she already loved, before the accident—Paul and me, Jason and Paige, and a few, very few, special friends, but no one else. If you hadn't pulled her and Jason out of the river, she would have drowned rather than let him go, because she couldn't have stood to lose anyone else she loves. She's been so...so *solitary,* keeping everyone a safe distance from her heart."

"Until me," he said.

Becky nodded and managed a wavery little smile. "Until you. I didn't know whether to be glad or terrified, so I've been both. I want her to have what I've got, a husband I love, kids I love, a family that will give her a reason to go on living when someone else dies." She saw the sudden flare in Robert's eyes and said quickly, "No, she never said anything about suicide, not even right after Matt died. That isn't what I meant. She recovered from her injuries—both legs were broken, some ribs, and she had a concussion—and did exactly what the doctors told her, but you could see that she wasn't interested. For *years,* life for her was just going through the motions, and every day was an effort. It took a long time, but finally she found a sort of peace. Evie's incredibly strong. In her place, I don't know if I could have managed it."

Robert kissed Becky's forehead, touched and pleased by this fiercely competent woman's concern for her sister. He would, he realized, like having her for a sister-in-law. "You can put down your shield and sword, and rest," he said gently. "I'll take care of her now."

"You'd better," Becky said, her fierceness not one bit abated. "Because she's already paid too much for loving people. God only knows where she found the courage to love you. I've been terrified that you didn't care about her, because if you waltzed out of here at the end of the summer, it might well destroy her."

Robert's eyes glittered. "When I waltz out of here," he said, "I'm taking her with me."

CHAPTER SIXTEEN

WALTER AND HELENE CAMPBELL were in their mid-sixties, retired, comfortable but not wealthy. Evie's house was just what they wanted, well-built and maintained, but old enough and small enough that her asking price was much less than what they would have paid for a new house on the lakefront. They were both thrilled to the point of giddiness at their unexpected good fortune, for though they had asked several times if she would sell, they had long since given up hope that she would.

They arrived at the marina over half an hour early, their estate agent in tow and bearing a huge sheaf of papers. Having never bought or sold a house before, Evie was struck by the amount of paperwork it evidently required and amazed that the agent had managed to get it all prepared in less than a day.

There weren't sufficient chairs for everyone to sit down, so they stood grouped around the counter. The agent explained the purpose of each document as he presented it first for her signature, then the Campbells'. After an hour of dedicated document-signing, it was finished. Evie had sold her house, and the check was in her hand.

She managed a smile to send the joyous Campbells on their way, but as soon as the door had closed behind them, her smile collapsed. She closed her eyes and shuddered in an effort to control the grief that had been growing since she had made the phone call the day before. No matter that she had told herself it was just a house and she could live anywhere, it was her *home,* and she had just lost part of herself. No, not lost it—sold it.

But the marina was a more important part of her foundation, and the green cashier's check in her hand had just saved it.

She wiped the betraying moisture from her eyes and braced her shoulders. She called Burt and told him she had to go to the bank and would be back in about half an hour. "Okay," he said, as laconic as ever, when she asked him to watch for customers.

The transaction at the bank took very little time. The Campbells' cashier's check was deposited and a new cashier's check cut in the amount she owed on the loan. Tommy Fowler saw her standing at the counter and came out to speak to her, his eyes anxious.

"How're you doing, Evie?"

She heard the worry in his tone and managed a version of the same smile she had given the Campbells. "I'm okay. I have the money to pay the loan."

Relief flooded his face. "Great! That didn't take long. So another bank gave you the mortgage?"

"No, I sold my house."

The relief faded, and he stared at her, aghast. "Sold your house? But, Evie… God, why?"

She wasn't about to tell him, with the teller and other customers listening, that she suspected someone of blocking the mortgage. "It was something I'd been thinking about," she lied. "Now my bank account is healthy, the marina is out of debt and will turn a pure profit, and I can take my time looking for another house."

Varying expressions were flickering across Tommy's face like slides. The final one, a rather uneasy relief, was testament to his belief in her pragmatic lie. "I guess it's worked out, then," he said.

She kept her smile intact with an effort. "Yeah, I guess it has."

The teller handed the check over the counter to her, and she slipped it into the envelope. "I'm getting this mailed today," she said to Tommy. "Thanks for all you did."

"I didn't manage to do anything," he replied.

"Well, no, but you tried."

She left the bank and drove straight to the post office, where the precious envelope was dispatched by express mail. She felt a sense of finality. It was done; she had gotten past this. It hadn't been easy, but now she could move on.

Robert was waiting at the marina when she got back. "Where have you been?" he demanded, striding up as she slid out of the truck.

She blinked at the unguarded fierceness of his tone. Robert was seldom overt in his reactions, except in bed. "The bank and the post office. Why?"

He didn't answer but caught her shoulders in a hard grasp and pulled her to him. His mouth was heavy and hungry, demanding rather than seducing a response from her. Evie made a muffled sound of surprise, her hands lifting to rest against his chest, but she gave him what he wanted, her mouth opening to admit the thrust of his tongue, her lips shaping to the pressure of his.

Passion rose sharply between them, strong and heady. She hadn't recovered her balance after the difficult events of the day and she melted against him, drawn irresistibly to the whipcord strength of his body. Although a whirlwind was tossing the rest of her life about, he wasn't swayed but remained solidly on his feet and in control. Though she had bitterly resisted—and feared—coming to depend on him, his very presence now made her feel better. She was both aroused and comforted by the familiarity of his body, his warm animal scent, all the subtle details by which she knew her mate.

He drew back, hampered by the public nature of the parking lot. Inside wouldn't be much better, with people coming and going. He threaded his hands through her hair, tilting her face back so he could read every nuance of her expression. He must have been pleased by the drowning look of desire he saw there, for his fingers tightened on her scalp. "Not here, damn it. But as soon as I get you home…" He didn't have to finish the sentence. Raw lust was on his face and in his voice, violent and intense.

Recalled to where she was, Evie cast a half-embarrassed look around and touched his hand as she slipped from his grasp. How many hours until they could go home? She didn't know if she could wait that long. Her body was throbbing.

THE LONG AFTERNOON was an exercise in self-control, and she wished the summer days weren't quite so long. She needed Robert, needed his driving presence within her, taking her into oblivion so she could forget everything but the almost narcotic pleasure of making love with him. She felt raw, her emotions sharp and too near the surface.

It was difficult, when she was finally able to close the marina that night, to hold to the schedule they had established. Robert wanted to take her straight to his house, but she resisted. "I don't want to leave my truck here overnight," she said. "You'd either have to bring me to pick it up in the morning or waste your morning hanging around so you could drive me to work."

"It wouldn't be a waste," he growled, his lean face taut, and she knew what she envisioned them doing to pass the time.

Temptation weakened her, but she shook her head again.

"It would be so blatant, if my truck was still here and you brought me to work. Craig—"

"You're worried about Craig knowing that we sleep together?" he asked, amusement lighting his eyes. "He's seventeen, sweetheart, not seven."

"I know, but…this isn't New York. We're more conventional down here."

He was still smiling, but he gave in with good grace. "All right, protect his tender sensibilities, though I have to tell you that most teenage boys have the sensibility of a rhino in heat."

She laughed, and it felt good, her heart lightening. "Then let's just say that *I* wouldn't feel comfortable."

He kissed her forehead. "Then go home, sweetheart. I bought some fillets this afternoon, and I'll get them ready to grill before I pick you up."

"I have a better idea," she said. "You start grilling, and I'll drive over. That will save even more time."

He smiled again as he rubbed his thumb over her lower lip in a gentle caress. "You make me feel like a teenage rhino myself," he murmured, and she blushed.

Anticipation heated her blood as she drove home, preoccupying her so much that she showered and dressed without more than a twinge of sadness. Her heartbeat pounded in the rhythm of his name.

It was still hot, so hot that she couldn't bear the idea of encasing her legs in clothing, but she didn't want to wear shorts. She opted instead for a gauzy blue skirt and a sleeveless, scoop-necked chemise, with her breasts unconfined beneath. The floaty skirt was virtually transparent, clearly showing her legs, but allowed air to filter through the flimsy fabric and cool her skin. She would never have worn it out in public, but to Robert's house…yes, definitely.

He came to the door when he heard the truck in his

driveway. His face tightened as he watched her walk toward him. "God," he muttered. As soon as she was inside, he slammed the door and caught her arm, pulling her rapidly down the hall to the bedroom.

"What about the steaks?" she cried, startled by his haste despite the pleasant frustration of the afternoon.

"Screw the steaks," he said bluntly, wrapping his arms around her and falling across the bed. His heavy weight crushed her into the mattress. With a quick motion he flipped the skirt to her waist and caught the waistband of her panties, tugging them down her legs. When her feet were free, he tossed her underwear aside and pulled her thighs apart, kneeling between them.

Evie laughed, the sound low and provocative. He hadn't even kissed her, and her entire body was throbbing. He was tearing at his belt buckle with impatient fingers, and she added her hands to the confusion, trying to find the tab of his zipper and pull it down. She could feel the hard, swollen ridge of his sex, pushing at his clothing. He grunted as his length sprang free and lowered himself between her legs.

No matter how many times he took her, she always felt a small sense of surprise at his size and heat, and a flutter of uncertainty at the stretching sensation that followed the initial pressure as he sank deep within. She gasped, her entire body lifting to the impact. She was tender from the unbridled lovemaking of the morning, his thrusting sex rasping against inner tissues that were sensitive to the least touch. Intense pleasure rippled through her, tossing her unprepared into paroxysms of satisfaction. She cried out, her hands digging into his back as the shivery delight went on and on, past bearing, until she thought she would die if he didn't let the pleasure ebb. He was muttering hotly in her ear, sex words, the sound indistinct but the meaning clear.

And then he shuddered, too, holding himself deep as the spasms took him. Afterward, he lay heavily on her, both of them breathing deeply in the exhausted aftermath. Drowsily she let her eyes drift shut, only to open them again as he suddenly chuckled, the small movement shaking them both. "Definitely like a teenager," he murmured, nuzzling the lobe of her ear before taking it between his teeth and gently biting it. "No matter how often I have you, I want you again almost as soon as I move off you. The only time I'm satisfied is when we're like this." He thrust lazily, their bodies still linked.

"Then let's stay like this." She ran her hands down his muscular back, feeling the heat of him through the fabric of his shirt. "Someone will find us in a couple of weeks."

He laughed and kissed her. "They'd probably think, wow, what a way to go, but I'd prefer both of us being warm and pliable. If I want to keep you that way, I suppose I'd better feed you, hadn't I?" He kissed her again and rolled away to sit up.

She stretched, replete, the afternoon's aching frustration relieved. Even the hollowness in her chest had faded, though by no means vanished. She had never had this before, she thought dimly, this bone-deep sense of connection. And she wouldn't have it now if Robert had been less ruthlessly determined to have his way.

They spent the next couple of hours grilling the steaks, then sitting out on the deck after they had eaten and cleaned the kitchen. The night was thick and warm, the temperature still in the high eighties. Robert stretched out on a chaise longue and pulled Evie down on top of him. There were no lights on in the house, and the concealing darkness was like a blanket. They lay there in the heavy, peaceful silence, with his hand slowly moving over her back. Slowly his caresses grew more purposeful, and Evie melted against him. Her chemise top was lifted off over her head and dropped to the deck. She hadn't put her underwear back on, so when his hand moved under the gauzy skirt, he touched only the bare flesh of her thighs and buttocks. He cupped the twin mounds in his hands and held her hard against him, nestling his arousal in the soft junction of her thighs.

"You have on too many clothes," she murmured, kissing the underside of his jaw.

"You, on the other hand, hardly have on any."

"Whose fault is that?" Her wandering mouth nibbled down his neck. "I was completely dressed when I arrived here."

"I wouldn't say that, sweetheart. Even if your nipples hadn't been sticking out like little berries, the delicious jiggle of your breasts when you walked made it obvious you weren't wearing anything under your top. And this thing," he continued lazily, grasping a handful of material, "doesn't qualify as a skirt." Tiring of her mouth being on his throat rather than his own mouth, he pulled her up for a long kiss, during which his own clothing was opened and removed. Sighing with pleasure, she lifted the skirt out of the way and settled over him, gasping a little as he slid inside her.

Then they lay quietly again, bodies linked, content with the sensation as it was. The lights of a night fisherman drifted by on the lake, but they were shielded by the darkness. Sometime later it became difficult to lie still. Hidden impulses twinged deep inside, inviting undulating movement. She resisted, but knew he was feeling the same compulsion. He was growing even harder, reaching deeper into her, and a fine tension invaded his muscles as he lay motionless beneath her.

She pressed her forehead hard against his jaw, fighting not to move. He throbbed inside her, and she moaned softly. Her inner muscles clenched in helpless delight on his invading length, then did so again, and her soft cries floated in the night air as the moment took her. In an effort to control his own reaction, Robert gripped her bottom hard, his teeth clenched against the almost overwhelming need to give in. He won, but sweat beaded on his forehead from the struggle.

When she stilled, he lifted her from him and bent her over the end of the chaise. He knelt behind her, his thighs cupping hers, and thrust heavily into her moist, relaxed sheath. She clung to the chaise, unable to stifle her moans of pleasure as his rhythmic motion increased in speed and power. He convulsed, flooding her with warmth, and lay heavily over her for a long time, while his breathing slowed and his heartbeat returned to normal.

Recovered, he gathered their scattered clothing and pushed it into her arms, then lifted her and carried her inside, to the big bed that awaited them.

THEY SLEPT LATE the next morning, until after nine o'clock. She yawned and stretched like a sleepy cat, and Robert held her close, stroking her tangled hair away from her face. As usual, he had awakened her at dawn with silent, drowsy lovemaking; then they had both gone back to sleep.

With a quick kiss and a lingering pat on her bare bottom, he left the bed and headed toward his shower. Evie yawned again and got up herself. She slipped into his shirt as she went to the kitchen to make coffee. "Robert, you need an automatic timer on your coffeemaker," she muttered to herself as she scooped the coffee into the round filter. Not that they would ever remember to prepare the coffee and set the timer before they went to bed.

Standing there in the sun-drenched kitchen, listening to

the coffeemaker pop and hiss, she became aware that she felt strangely light, almost carefree. She hugged herself in an effort to contain the elusive feeling. She was happy, she thought with some surprise. Despite selling the house, she was happy. She had saved the marina, and she had Robert. Most of all, she had Robert.

Her love for him quietly grew each time she was with him. He was such a complicated, controlled, private man; no matter how often he made love to her, he still kept that inner core of himself inviolate, not allowing her or anyone else inside. Knowing that had no effect on the way she felt about him. He hadn't opened his heart to her, but that in no way made him less worthy of love. He might never love her, she realized. But if this was all he could give a woman, then she would take it.

A ringing interrupted the quiet. It sounded like a telephone, but the phone there in the kitchen definitely wasn't ringing, and this sound was muffled, as if it were in a different room. The line in Robert's office must be a different number, she realized. He was in the shower and wouldn't be able to hear it. It rang only once, though, and she realized that the answering machine there must have picked up the call.

She walked down the hall to the office and opened the door. The whirring sound of the fax machine greeted her. So it hadn't been a call, after all, but a fax.

The machine stopped whirring and lapsed into silence after having spat out only one sheet of paper. As she turned to go, her eye was caught by a name on the page, and curiously she turned back.

It was her name that had caught her attention.

The message was brief. "Mr. Borowitz just reported that a cashier's check from E. Shaw, in full payment of the outstanding amount, was delivered by express mail and re-

ceived by him. His hands are tied. Further instructions?"
The scrawled signature looked like "F. Koury."

Evie picked up the page and read it again. At first she
was merely puzzled. Why would this F. Koury be telling
Robert that she had paid the loan? And why would Mr.
Borowitz be reporting it at all? Robert didn't even know
about the loan, much less the threat of foreclosure.

Her mind stopped, along with her breathing. She hung
there, paralyzed by a sickening realization. Robert knew
all about it because he was the one who had been blocking
her efforts to mortgage the house. He was also the reason
why her loan had been bought, and why Mr. Borowitz had
been so intractable in demanding full payment. He had
been instructed to give her no cooperation at all, instructed
by Robert Cannon. Her lover was her enemy.

Her chest was hurting. She gasped and resumed breathing, but the pain remained, a cold, heavy lump in her chest.
The sense of betrayal was suffocating.

Obviously Robert was far wealthier and more powerful than she had imagined, to have this much influence,
she thought with detached calm. She didn't know why he
wanted her marina, but he obviously did. There were a
lot of why's she couldn't comprehend, particularly right
now. Maybe later, when she could think better, some of
this would make sense.

Right now, all she could think was that Robert had tried
to take over her marina and had cost her her home.

That distance she had sensed in him had been all too
real. He hadn't committed his heart because, for him, it
had all been business. Had he seduced her simply so he
could stay close and keep tabs on what she was doing?
Given what else he had done, that seemed to her like a
reasonable assumption.

Her lips felt numb, and her legs moved like an automaton's as she left the office, carefully closing the door behind her. The damning fax was still in her hand as she returned to the kitchen.

The hopeless enormity of the situation overwhelmed her. How ironic that she had fallen in love with the man who was coolly trying to destroy her! Oh, she doubted he looked at it in such melodramatic terms, but then, he probably saw the whole thing as a successful business takeover, rather than a love affair.

She heard the shower cut off. With slow, achingly precise movements, she folded the fax and dropped it into the trash, then poured a cup of coffee. She desperately needed the caffeine, or anything, to bolster her. Her hands were shaking slightly as she lifted the cup to her lips.

She was standing in front of the window when Robert came into the kitchen a few moments later, wearing only a pair of jeans and still rubbing a towel across his chest. He stopped, his entire body clenching at the sight of her. God, she was breathtaking, with her mane of tawny gold hair loose and tousled. She was wearing only his shirt, and it was unbuttoned. There had never been another garment invented, he thought with a surge of desire, that looked better on a woman than a man's shirt. She was sipping coffee and looking out the window, lost in thought, her expression as calm and remote as a statue's.

He dropped the towel and went to her, sliding one arm around her as he took the cup and lifted it to his own lips. He imagined he could taste her on the rim, but then, his senses were so attuned to her that he could pick her out of a crowd blindfolded.

No woman had ever responded to him the way Evie did. She was pure fire in his arms, reveling in every thrust, tempting more from him. If he was gentle, she melted. If he was rough in his passion, she clung to him, clawed at him, her soaring desire feeding his own until they were both frenzied with need. He wanted her incessantly.

He smoothed his hand over the curve of her bottom, delighting in the silky texture of her flesh. "The shower's all yours, sweetheart."

"All right," she said automatically, but he had the impression she didn't really hear him. She was still looking out the window.

He tipped his head to see if he could tell what had her so interested. He saw only a wide expanse of lake, dotted with a few boats. "What are you looking at?"

"Nothing. Just the lake." She turned away from his embrace and left the kitchen.

Robert's brows briefly knit in puzzlement, but he was hungry, and breakfast took precedence at the moment. He had scarcely gotten the bacon started when Evie reappeared in the kitchen, fully dressed, and with her keys in her hand.

"A fax came in while you were in the shower," she said quietly.

He turned, going still at what he saw in her face—or rather, what he didn't see. She was pale and expressionless, her eyes empty. With a chill, he remembered how Becky had described the look in Evie's eyes after the accident and he knew it must have been something like this. She looked so terribly remote, as if she had somehow already left.

"Who was it from?" he asked, keeping his voice gentle while his mind raced, sorting through the possibilities, all of them damning. The worst-case scenario was if she was indeed working with Mercer and had found out that the trap was closing tight about them.

"An F. Koury."

"Ah." He nodded, concealing a sense of relief. "My secretary." Probably it had nothing to do with Mercer, then, but why was Evie looking so frozen?

"It's there in the trash, if you want to read it, but I can tell you what it said."

He leaned against the cabinet and crossed his arms, eyeing her carefully. "All right. Tell me."

"Mr. Borowitz notified your secretary that he'd received a cashier's check from E. Shaw for payment in full of the loan, and that his hands were tied. She asked for further instructions."

Robert's expression didn't change, but inwardly he was swearing viciously. Of all the things for Evie to stumble onto! It was less damaging, from a security standpoint, than anything connected with Mercer would have been, but a hell of a thing to try to explain to a lover. He'd never intended her to know about it. The pressure had been real, but he would never have let it go to foreclosure. He didn't rush into explanations but waited for her reaction so he could better gauge what to say to her. And how in hell had she managed to get the money to pay the loan?

"You're the reason I couldn't get a mortgage on my house," she said, her voice so strained it was almost soundless.

She'd put it together quickly, he thought. But then, from the beginning, she'd proven herself to be uncomfortably astute. "Yes," he said, disdaining to lie.

"You're behind the loan being sold to another bank in the first place."

He inclined his head and waited.

She was gripping the keys so tightly that her fingers were white. He noted that small giveaway of emotion held in check. She took several shallow breaths, then managed to speak again. "I want your boat gone from my marina by the end of the day. I'll refund the balance of the rent."

"No," he said gently, implacably. "I'm holding you to the agreement."

She didn't waste her breath on an argument she couldn't win. She had hoped he would have the decency to do as she asked, but given his ruthless streak, she hadn't really expected it.

"Then leave it there," she said, her voice as empty as her eyes. "But don't call me again, because I don't want to talk to you. Don't come by, because I don't want to see you."

Sharply he searched her expression, looking for a way to penetrate the wall she had thrown up between them. "You won't get rid of me that easily. I know you're angry, but—"

She laughed, but it was raw and hollow, not a sound of amusement. Robert winced. "Is that how you've decided to 'handle' me? I can see you watching me, trying to decide which angle to take to calm me down," she said. "You never just react, do you? You watch and weigh other people's reactions so you can manipulate them." She heard the strain in her voice and paused to regain control of it. "No, I'm not angry. Maybe in fifty years or so, it'll just be anger." She turned on her heel and started for the door.

"Evie!" His voice cracked like a whiplash, and despite herself, she stopped, shivering at the force of will he commanded. This wasn't the cool strategist speaking but the ruthless conqueror.

"How did you pay off the loan?" The words were still sharp.

Slowly she looked at him over her shoulder, her eyes dark and unguarded for a moment, stark with pain. "I sold my house," she said, and walked out.

CHAPTER SEVENTEEN

ROBERT STARTED TO go after her, then stopped. Instead he swore and hit the countertop with his fist. He couldn't explain anything to her, not yet. Every instinct in his body screamed for him to stop her, but he forced himself to let her go. He stood rigidly, listening as the truck door slammed and the motor started. She didn't spin the wheels or anything like that; she simply backed out of the driveway and drove away without histrionics.

God! *She had sold her house.* The desperation of the action staggered him, and with sudden, blinding clarity he knew, beyond the faintest doubt, that she wasn't involved with Mercer in any way. A woman who could make money by espionage would never have sold her home to pay a debt. She had appeared to be leaving the marina and meeting with Mercer on the lake, but it must have been nothing more than damnable coincidence. Evie was totally innocent, and his machinations had cost her her home.

She wouldn't listen to anything he said right now, but after he had the espionage ring broken up and Mercer safely behind bars, he would force her to understand why he had threatened foreclosure on her loan. That he had suspected her of espionage was another rocky shoal he would have to navigate with care. He didn't imagine it would be easy to get back into her good graces, but in the end he would have her, because he didn't take no for an answer when he really wanted something. And he wanted Evie as he had never wanted anything or anyone else in his life.

He would have to make amends, of course, far beyond apologies and explanations. Evie was the least mercenary person he'd ever met, but she had a strong sense of justice, and an offer of reparation would strike a chord with her. He could buy her house from the new owners—they probably wouldn't be willing to sell at first, but he cynically suspected that doubling the price would change their minds—and present her with the deed, but he far preferred that she have a newer, bigger house. The simplest thing would be to deed over his own house to her. It meant nothing to him, he could buy a house anywhere he wanted, but Evie needed a base that was hers and hers alone. It would be a vacation home, a getaway when they needed a break from the hubbub of New York, a place for her to stay when she wanted to visit Becky.

He fished the damning fax out of the trash and read it. Three concise sentences, Felice at her most efficient. There was nothing more he could do about the loan; realizing that, she had de-prioritized it and sent the information by fax so he could have it immediately but respond at his leisure, rather than calling and wasting both his time and hers. Felice was a genius at whittling precious seconds here and there so she would have more time to devote to the truly important matters. In this instance, however, her knack for superefficiency had worked against him and perhaps cost him Evie.

No. No matter what, he wouldn't let Evie go.

EVIE DROVE AUTOMATICALLY, holding herself together with desperate control. She tried to empty her mind, but it wasn't possible. How could she be so numb but hurt so much at the same time? She literally ached, as if she had been beaten, yet felt somehow divorced from her body. She had never felt as remote as she did now, or as cold and hollow. The heat of the sun washed over her, but it didn't touch her. Even her bones felt cold and empty.

Why? She hadn't asked him that and couldn't think of a reason that would matter. The why of it wasn't important. The hard fact was that he had sought her out for a reason that had nothing to do with love or even attraction, used the intimacy he had deliberately sought as a means to gather information that he wanted, and then turned that knowledge against her. How had he known about the loan in the first place? She supposed it was possible a credit report would have given him the information, but a far more likely explanation was that he had simply taken a look through the papers in her desk at home. There had been ample opportunity for him to do so; the very first time he had been in her house, she remembered, was when he had brought her home to change clothes after Jason had fallen in the water, and she had left him alone while she showered and changed.

She didn't know why he had targeted her marina, and she didn't care. She marked it down to simple avarice, the greedy impulse to take what belonged to others.

She hadn't known him at all.

She was still calm and dry-eyed when she reached her house. No—not her house any longer, but the Campbells'. Dazed, she unlocked the door and walked inside, looked at the familiar form and content of her home, and bolted for the bathroom. She hung over the toilet and vomited up the little coffee she had swallowed, but the dry, painful heaves continued long after her stomach was emptied.

When the spasms finally stopped, she slumped breathless to the floor. She had no idea how long she lay there, in a stupor of exhaustion and pain, but after a while she began to cry. She curled into a ball, tucking her legs up in an effort to make herself as small as possible, and shuddered with the violent, rasping sobs that tore through her. She cried until she made herself sick and vomited again.

It was a long time before she climbed shakily to her feet. Her eyelids were swollen and sore, but she was calm, so calm and remote that she wondered if she would ever be able to feel anything again. God, she hoped not!

She stripped, dropping her clothes to the floor. She would throw them out later; she never wanted to see that skirt again, or any other garment she had worn that night. She was shivering as she climbed into the shower, where she stood for a long time, letting the hot water beat down on her, but the heat sluiced off her skin just like the water, none of it soaking in to thaw the bone-deep cold that shook her.

She would have stood there all day, paralyzed by the mind-numbing pain, but at last the hot water began to go and the chill forced her out. She wanted nothing more than to crawl into bed, close her eyes and forget, but that wasn't an option. She wouldn't forget. She would never forget. She could stay in the shower forever, but it wouldn't wash his touch off her flesh or his image out of her mind.

He had never wanted her at all. He had wanted the marina.

The marina. Her mind fastened on it with desperate gratitude. She still had the marina, had salvaged something from the ruin Robert Cannon had made of her life. No matter how much damage he had done, he hadn't won.

The habits of years took over as she moved slowly about, getting ready to go to work. After towel-drying her hair, she stood in front of the bathroom mirror to brush out the tangles and braid it. Her own face looked back at her, white and blank, her eyes dark, empty pools. Losing

Matt had been devastating, but she had carried the knowledge of his love deep inside. This time she had nothing. The care Robert had shown her had been an illusion, carefully fostered to deceive her. The passion between them, at least on his part, had been nothing more than a combination of mere sex and his own labyrinthine plotting. The man could give lessons to Machiavelli.

He had destroyed the protective shield that had encased her for so many years. She had thought she couldn't bear any more pain, but now she was learning that her capacity for pain went far beyond imagination. She wouldn't die from it, after all; she would simply rebuild the shield, stronger than before, so that it could never be penetrated again. It would take time, but she had time; she had the rest of her life to remember Robert Cannon and how he had used her.

She hid her sore, swollen eyes behind a pair of sunglasses and carefully drove to the marina, not wanting to have an accident because she wasn't paying attention. She refused to die in a car accident and give Cannon the satisfaction of winning.

When she drove up to the marina, everything looked strangely normal. She sat in the truck, staring at it for a few seconds, bewildered by the sameness of it. So much had happened in such a short time that it seemed as if she had been gone for weeks, rather than overnight.

No matter what, she still had this.

ROBERT PROWLED THE HOUSE like a caged panther, enraged by the need to wait. Waiting was alien to him; his instinct was to make a cold, incisive decision and act on it. The knowledge of the pain Evie must be feeling, and what she must be thinking, ate at him like acid. He could make it up to her for the house, but could he heal the hurt? Every hour he was away from her, every hour that passed with her thinking he had betrayed her, would deepen the wound. Only the certainty that she would refuse to listen to him now kept him from going after her. When Mercer was in jail, when he had the proof of what he'd been doing and could tell her the why, then she would listen to him. She might slap his face, but she would listen.

It was almost three o'clock when the phone rang. "Mercer's moving early," his operative barked. "He panicked and called them from the office. No dead drop this time. He told them that he needed the money immediately. It's a live handoff, sir. We can catch the bastards red-handed!"

"Where is he now?"

"About halfway to Guntersville, the way he was driving. We have a tail on him. I'm on the way, but it'll take me another twenty-five minutes to get there."

"All right. Use the tracking device and get there as fast as you can. I'll go to the marina now and get ahead of him. He's never seen my boat, so he won't spot me."

"Be careful, sir. You'll be outnumbered until we can get there."

Robert smiled grimly as he hung up the phone. Everything he needed was in the boat: weapons, camera, binoculars and tape recorder. Mercer's ass was in a sling now.

He drove to the marina, ignoring the speed laws. He only hoped Evie wouldn't come out when she saw him and do something foolish like cause a scene. He didn't have time for it, and he sure as hell didn't want to attract any attention. He tried to imagine Evie causing a scene, but the idea was incongruous. No, she wouldn't do that; it wasn't her style at all. She would simply look through him as if he didn't exist. But when he reached the marina, he didn't take any chances. He went straight to the dock where his boat was moored, not even glancing at the office.

EVIE HEARD HIM drive up. She knew the sound of that Jeep as intimately as she knew her own heartbeat. She froze, trying to brace herself for the unbearable, but the seconds ticked past and the door didn't open. When she forced herself to turn and look out the window, she caught a glimpse of his tall, lean figure striding purposefully down the dock toward his boat. A minute later she heard the deep cough of the powerful motor, and the sleek black boat eased out of its slip. As soon as he was out of the Idle Speed Only zone, he shoved the throttle forward, and the nose of the boat rose like a rearing stallion as the craft shot over the water, gaining speed with every second.

She couldn't believe how much it hurt just to see him.

Landon Mercer walked in ten minutes later. Loathing rose in her throat, choking her, and it was all she could do to keep from screaming at him. Today, though, there was none of the slimy come-on attitude he thought was so irresistible; he was pale, his face strained. He was wearing slacks and a white dress shirt, the collar unbuttoned. Sweat beaded on his forehead and upper lip. He carried the same tackle box, but no rod and reel.

"Got a boat for me, Evie?" he asked, trying to smile, but it was little more than a grimace.

She chose a key and gave it to him. "Use the one on the end."

"Thanks. I'll pay you when I get back, okay?" He was already going out the door when he spoke.

Something in her snapped. It was a quiet snap, but suddenly she had had enough. Mercer was definitely up to no good, and today he hadn't even made the pretense of going fishing. The marina was all she had left, and if that bastard was dealing drugs and dragged her into it by using her boats, she might lose the marina after all.

Over her dead body.

It was too much, all the events of the day piling on top of her. She wasn't thinking when she strode out to the truck and retrieved her pistol from under the seat, then hurried to her own boat. If she had been thinking, she would have called the police or the water patrol, but none of that came to mind. Still reeling from shock, she could focus on only one thing—stopping Mercer.

ROBERT HAD POSITIONED his boat where he could see Mercer leave the marina and fall in behind him without attracting his notice. The tracking device was working perfectly, the beeping increasing in speed as Mercer approached his position, then decreasing as the rental boat sped past. Not wanting to get too close and scare off the people Mercer was meeting, he started the motor and began idling forward, letting Mercer put more distance between them.

Another boat was coming up fast on the left, intersecting his path at a right angle. There was enough space that Robert didn't have to back off his speed, and he kept his eye on the diminishing dot on Mercer's boat. Then the other boat flashed across his line of vision, and he saw a long blond braid bouncing as the boat took the waves.

Evie! His heart leapt into his throat, almost choking him. Her appearance stunned him; then, suddenly, he knew. *She was following Mercer!* That was what she'd been doing all along. With that unsettling intuition of hers, she had known that Mercer was up to no good and had taken it upon herself to try to find out what it was. He even knew her reasoning: by using one of her boats, Mercer was involving her marina. Robert knew better than most to what lengths she would go to protect that place. She would give up her home, and she would risk her life.

Swearing savagely, he picked up the secure phone and punched in the number even as he pushed the throttle forward. "Evie is following Mercer," he snarled when the call was answered on half a ring. "She's on our side. Pass the word and make damn sure no one fires on her by mistake!"

His blood ran cold at the thought. None of his people would shoot at her, but what about the others?

Mercer was heading toward the islands again, as she had known he would. She kept about five hundred yards between them, enough distance that her presence wouldn't worry him, at least not yet. She would close the gap in a hurry when he reached the islands and slowed down.

The pistol lay in her lap. It was a long-barreled .45 caliber, very accurate, and she not only had a license to carry it, she knew how to use it. Whatever Mercer was doing, it was going to stop today.

There was another boat anchored between two of the smaller islands, two men inside it. Mercer didn't take his usual circuitous route around and through the islands, but headed straight toward the other boat. Grimly Evie increased her speed and followed.

Mercer pulled up alongside the other boat and immediately passed the tackle box over. Evie saw one of the men point to her as she neared, and Mercer turned to look. She wasn't wearing a hat or sunglasses, and though her hair was braided, she knew she was easily recognizable as a woman. But she didn't care if Mercer recognized her, because the time for stealth was past.

The fact that she was a woman, and alone, made them less cautious than they should have been. Mercer was standing, his feet braced against the gentle rocking of the boat. Confident that they hadn't been caught doing anything suspicious, he said something in a low tone to the two other men, then raised his voice to call to her. "Evie, is something wrong?"

She waved to allay any suspicions. She was still twenty

yards away. She eased the throttle into neutral, knowing that the boat would continue nosing forward for several yards even without power. Then, very calmly, she lifted the pistol and pointed it at the man holding the tackle box.

"Don't make me nervous," she said. "Put the tackle box down."

The man hesitated, darting a petrified look at his partner, who was still behind the wheel of the boat. Mercer was frozen, staring at her and the huge pistol in her hand.

"Evie," he said, his voice shaking a little. "Listen, we'll cut you in. There's a hell of a lot of money—"

She ignored him. "I told you to put the box down," she said to the man who was holding it. Her mind still wasn't functioning clearly. All she could think was that if he dropped the tackle box into the river, the evidence would sink and there wouldn't be any way of proving what he was doing. She had no idea how she would manage to get three men and three different boats to the authorities, but there was a lot of boat traffic on the river this afternoon, and eventually someone would come over this way.

Another boat was coming up behind her already, way too fast. Mercer's attention switched to it, and a sick look spread over his face, but Evie didn't let her attention waver from the man holding the tackle box. A sleek black boat appeared in her peripheral vision, nosing up to the side of the boat holding the two men. Robert rose from the seat, holding the steering wheel steady with his knee as he leveled a pistol on the three men, his two-fisted grip holding the weapon dead level despite the rocking of the boat.

"Don't even twitch a muscle," he said, and the tone of his voice made Evie risk a quick glance at him. The facade of urbanity had fallen completely away, and he made no attempt now to disguise his true nature. The lethal pistol in his hand looked like a natural extension of his arm, as if he had handled weapons so often it was automatic to him now. His face was hard and set, and his eyes held the cold ferocity of a hunting panther.

The waves made by Robert's boat were washing the others closer together, inexorably sweeping Evie's boat forward to collide with them. "Look out," she warned sharply, dropping one hand to the throttle to put her motor into reverse, to counteract the force of the waves. The two other boats bumped together with staggering force, sending Mercer plunging into the river. The man holding the tackle box cursed and flailed his arms, fighting for balance, and dropped the box. It fell into the bottom of the boat. Robert's attention was splintered, and in that instant the driver of the boat reached beneath the console and pulled out his own weapon, firing as soon as he had it clear. Evie screamed, her heart stopping as she tried to bring her pistol around. Robert ducked to the side, and the bullet tore a long gouge out of the fiberglass hull. Going down on one knee, he fired once, and the driver fell back, screaming in pain.

The second man dived sideways into the rental boat. Mercer was clinging to the side, screaming in panic as the man hunched low in the boat and turned the ignition key. The motor coughed into life, and the boat leapt forward. Knowing she couldn't get a good shot at a moving target, especially with her own boat still rocking, Evie dropped the pistol and shoved the throttle back into forward gear. The two boats collided with a grinding force that splintered the fiberglass of both craft, her more powerful motor shoving her boat on top of the other. The impact tossed her out of the seat, and she hit the water with a force that knocked her senseless.

She recovered consciousness almost immediately but was dazed by the shock. She was underwater, the surface only a lighter shade of murky green. There was a great roaring in her ears, and a vibration that seemed to go straight through her. Boats, she thought dimly, and terror shot through her as she realized how much danger she was in. If the drivers couldn't see her, they might drive right over her, and the propeller would cut her to pieces.

She clawed desperately for the surface, kicking for all she was worth. Her head cleared the water, and she gulped in air, but there was a boat almost on top of her, and she threw herself to the side. Someone in the boat yelled, and she heard Robert's deep voice roaring, but she couldn't understand his words. Her ears were full of water, and dizziness made everything dim. If she passed out, she thought, she would drown. She blinked the water out of her eyes and saw the wreckage of the two boats, not five yards away. She struggled toward it and shakily hooked her arm over the side of the rental boat. It was very low in the water and would probably sink within half an hour, but for now it was afloat, and that was all that mattered.

The boat that had almost hit her was idling closer. Two men were in it, dressed in jeans and T-shirts. The driver brought the boat around sideways to her, and the other man leaned out, his arm outstretched to her. The sunlight glinted off a badge pinned to the waistband of his jeans. Evie released the rental boat and swam the few feet to the other craft. The man caught her arms, and she was hauled out of the water and into the boat.

She sank down onto the floor. The man knelt beside her. His voice was anxious. "Are you all right, Mrs. Shaw?"

She was panting from exertion, gulping air in huge quantities, so she merely nodded. She wasn't hurt, just dazed from the impact, so dazed that it was a minute before she could wonder how he knew her name.

"She's okay!" she heard him yell.

Gradually her confusion faded, and things began to sort themselves out. She remained quietly in the bottom of the boat, propped against one of the seats, and watched as the two men in the water were hauled out and roughly hand-cuffed, and the man Robert had shot was given medical aid. Though pale and hunched over, he was still upright and conscious, so Evie assumed he would live.

Four more boats had arrived, each of them carrying a team of two men, and all of those men wore badges, ei-ther pinned to their jeans or hung around their necks. She heard one of them briskly identify himself to Mercer as FBI and assumed that they all were.

Other boats who had seen the commotion on the water were approaching but stopped at a short distance when they noticed the badges. "Y'all need any help with those boats?" one fisherman called. "We can keep 'em afloat and haul 'em to a marina, if you want."

She saw one agent glance at Robert, as if for permis-sion, then say, "Thanks, we'd appreciate your help." Sev-eral of the fishermen idled foward and added their boats to the snarl.

Evie resisted the urge to look at Robert, though she could feel his hard, glittering gaze on her several times. For the rest of her life she would remember the cold ter-ror she'd felt when that man had shot at him and she had thought she would have to watch another man she loved die in front of her. The devastation she'd been feeling all day, bad as it was, paled in comparison to that horror. Rob-ert didn't want her, had used her, but at least he was alive. Reaction was setting in, and fine tremors were starting to ripple through her body.

The mopping-up seemed to take forever, so long that her sopping clothes began to dry, as stiff as cardboard from the river water. The wounded man was placed in another boat and taken for further medical attention, with two agents in attendance. Mercer and the other man were taken away next, both of them handcuffed. There was a lot of maneuvering around the two wrecked boats as the salvaging continued. Gathering her strength, she took control of the boat she was in, while the driver added his efforts to the job. Finally, though, it all seemed to be winding down. Robert brought his boat alongside the one Evie was handling.

"Are you all right?" he asked sharply.

She didn't look at him. "I'm fine."

He raised his voice. "Lee, get this boat. I'm taking Evie back to the marina."

Immediately the agent clambered back into the boat, and Evie relinquished her place behind the wheel. She didn't want to go anywhere with Robert, however, and looked around for anyone else she knew.

"Get in the boat," he said, his voice steely, and rather than make a fool of herself, she did. There was no way to avoid him, if he was determined to force the issue. If he wanted to discuss private matters, then she would prefer that they were private when he did.

Nothing was said on the ride back to the marina. The black boat moved like oiled silk over the choppy waves, but still every small bump jolted her head. She closed her eyes, trying to contain the nausea rising in her throat.

As Robert throttled down to enter the marina, he glanced over at her and swore as he took in her closed eyes and pale, strained face. "Damn it, you *are* hurt!"

Immediately she opened her eyes and stared resolutely ahead. "It's just reaction."

Coming down off an adrenaline high could leave a person feeling weak and sick, so he accepted the explanation for now but made a mental note to keep an eye on her for a while.

He idled the boat into his slip, and Evie climbed onto the dock before he could get out and assist her. True daughter of the river that she was, she automatically tied the lines to the hooks set in the wood, the habits of a lifetime taking precedence over her emotions. The boat secured, she turned without a word and headed toward the office.

Burt was behind the counter when she entered, and a look of intense relief crossed his lined face, followed by surprise and then concern when he saw her condition. It went against his grain to ask personal questions, so the words came reluctantly out of his throat, as if he were forcing them. "Did the boat flip? Are you all right?"

Two questions in a row from Burt? She needed to mark this date on her calendar. "I'm all right, just a little shaken up," she said, wondering how many more times that day she would have to say those words. "The boat's wrecked, though. Some guys are bringing it in."

Robert opened the door behind her, and Burt's expression went full cycle, back to relief. "I'll get back to the shop, then. How long do you reckon it'll take 'em to get the boat here?"

"About an hour," Robert answered for her. "They'll have to idle in." He went to the soft-drink machine and fed in quarters, then pushed the button. With a clatter, the bottle rolled down into the slot, and he deftly popped off the top.

"Well, don't make no difference. I reckon I'll stay until they get here." Burt left the unnatural surroundings of the office and headed back to where he felt most comfortable, leaving the oily smell of grease behind.

Evie walked behind the counter and sat down, wanting to put something between herself and Robert. It didn't work, of course; he knew all the moves, all the stratagems. He came behind the counter, too, and propped himself against it with his long legs outstretched and crossed at the ankle.

He held out the Coke. "Drink this. You're a little shocky and need the sugar."

He was probably right. She shrugged and took the bottle, remembering another time when she'd been fished out of the water, and how he had insisted she drink very sweet coffee. The last thing she wanted to do was faint at his feet, so she tilted the bottle and drank.

He watched until he was satisfied that she was going to follow his orders, then said, "Mercer was manager of my computer programming firm in Huntsville. We've been working on programs for the space station, as well as other things, and the programs are classified. They began turning up where they shouldn't. We figured out that Mercer was the one who was stealing them, but we hadn't managed to catch him at it, so we didn't have any proof."

"So that's what was in the tackle box," she said, startled. "Not dope. Computer disks."

His dark eyebrows rose. "You thought he was a drug dealer?"

"That seemed as plausible as anything. You can't sneak up on anyone in the middle of the river. He must have been weighting the package and dropping it in a shallow spot between the islands, and the others were picking it up later."

"Exactly. But if you thought he was a drug dealer," he said, his voice going dangerously smooth, "why in hell did you follow him today?"

"The federal seizure law," she replied simply. "He was in my boat. I could have lost everything. At the very least, he could have given the marina a bad reputation and driven away business."

And she would do anything to protect the marina, he thought furiously, including sell her house. Of course she hadn't balked at following a man she suspected of being a drug dealer! She had been armed, but his blood ran cold at the thought of what could have happened. She had been outnumbered three to one. In all honesty, however, she had had the situation under control until the waves from his boat had washed them all together.

"You could have killed yourself, deliberately ramming the boat like that."

"There wasn't much speed involved," she said. "And my boat was bigger. I was more afraid of the gas tanks exploding, but they're in the rear, so I figured they'd be okay."

She hadn't had time to consider all that, he thought; her reaction had been instantaneous and had nearly given him a heart attack. But a lifetime spent around boats had given her the knowledge needed to make such a judgment call. She hadn't known that reinforcements were almost there, she had simply seen that one of them was about to escape, and she had stopped him. Robert didn't know if she was courageous or foolhardy or both.

She still hadn't so much as glanced at him, and he knew he had his work cut out for him. Carefully choosing his words, he said, "I've been working with the FBI and some of my own surveillance people to set a trap for Mercer. I soured some deals he had made, put some financial pressure on him, to force him to make a move."

It didn't take more explanation than that. Watching her face, he saw her sort through the implications and the nuances of what he had just said, and he knew the exact moment when she realized he had also suspected her. A blank shield descended over her features. "Just like you did with me," she murmured. "You thought I was working with him, because he was using my boats, and because I'd been following him, trying to find out what he was doing."

"It didn't take me long to decide that if you were involved at all, you probably didn't realize what was going on. But you kept doing suspicious things, just enough that I didn't dare relax my pressure on you."

"What sort of suspicious things?" she asked, a note of disbelief entering her flat tone.

"Leaving the marina in the middle of the day to follow him. The day before yesterday, when you left the bank, you immediately stopped at a pay phone and made a call that we couldn't monitor. Yesterday you led the guy following you all over Guntersville, then ditched him by making an abrupt turn across traffic, and we weren't able to find you again until you came to work."

Evie laughed, but the sound was bitter and disbelieving. "All that! It's amazing how a suspicious mind can see suspicious actions everywhere. When the mortgage was turned down a second time, I realized there had to be someone behind it, someone who was blocking the loans. I couldn't lose the marina. The only thing left to do was sell the house, and I knew if I didn't make the call right then, I'd lose my nerve. So I stopped at the first pay phone I came to and called some people who have tried several times to buy the house, to see if they were still interested. They were so interested that they decided to pay me immediately rather than take a chance that I'd change my mind.

"Yesterday," she said softly, "I was looking for a place to live. But I knew I was just dithering, and that the longer I put it off, the worse it would be. So I made a quick turn, drove to an apartment complex and rented an apartment."

Yes, he thought, watching her colorless face. A quick, sharp pain was better than endless agony. Innocent actions based on desperate decisions.

She shrugged. "I thought you wanted the marina. I couldn't figure out why. It means a lot to me, but if you were looking for a business investment, there are bigger, more profitable ones around. Instead, you thought I was a traitor, and what better way to keep tabs on me than to start a bogus relationship and push it until we were practically living together?"

This was the tricky part, he thought. "It wasn't bogus."

"The moon isn't round, either," she replied, and turned to look out the windows at her kingdom, saved at such cost to herself.

"I wasn't going to go through with the foreclosure," he said. "It was just a means of pressure. Even if you'd been guilty, I'd already decided to prevent them from prosecuting you."

"How kind of you," she murmured.

He uncrossed his ankles and left the support of the counter, moving until he was directly in front of her. He put his hands on her shoulders, warmly squeezing. "I know you're hurt and angry, but until Mercer was caught, I didn't dare ease up on the pressure."

"I understand."

"Do you? Thank God," he said, closing his eyes in relief.

She shrugged, her shoulders moving under his hands. "National security is more important than hurt feelings. You couldn't have done anything else."

The flat note was still in her voice. He opened his eyes and saw that he hadn't cleared all the hurdles. The issue of the house was still between them.

"I'm sorry about your house," he said gently. "I would never have let you sell it if I'd known that was what you were planning." He cupped her cheek with one hand, feeling the warm silkiness of her skin under his fingers. "I can't get your house back, but I can give you mine. I'm having the deed made over in your name."

She stiffened and jerked her face away from his hand.

"No, thank you," she said coldly, standing up and turning to stare out the window, her back to him.

Of course she had jumped to the wrong conclusion, he thought, annoyed with himself that he had brought up the house before settling the other issue. "It isn't charity," he said in a soothing tone, putting his hand on the nape of her neck and gently rubbing the tense muscles he found there. "It isn't even much of a gesture, come to that, since it will be staying in the family. Evie, sweetheart, will you marry me? I know you love it here, but we can compromise. I won't take you completely away from your family. We can use the house for vacations. We'll come down every summer for a long vacation, and of course we'll visit several times during the year."

She pulled away from him and turned to face him. If she had been white before, she was deathly pale now. Her golden brown eyes were flat and lusterless, and with a chill he remembered how Becky had said she'd looked after Matt had died. What he saw in Evie's eyes was an emotional wasteland, and it froze him to the bone.

"Just like everything else, your *compromises* are heavily in your favor," she said, a rawness in her voice that made him flinch. "I have a better one than that. Why don't you stay in New York, and I'll stay here, and that way we'll both be a lot happier."

"Evie…" He paused, forced himself to take a deep breath and reached for control. She was wildly off balance, of course, with everything that had happened today. She loved him, and he had hurt her. Somehow he had to convince her to trust him again.

"No!" she said violently. "Don't try to decide how you're going to manipulate me into doing what you want. You're too intelligent for your own good, and too damn subtle. Nothing really reaches you, does it?" She spread her hands far apart and gestured. "You're over here, and everyone else is way over here, and never the twain shall meet. Nobody and nothing gets close to you. You're willing to marry me, but nothing would change. You'd still keep yourself closed off, watching from the distance and pulling strings to make all the puppets do what you want. What I had with Matt was *real,* a relationship with a person instead of a facade! What makes you think I'd settle for what you're offering?" She stopped, shuddering, and it was a moment before she could speak again. "Go away, Robert."

CHAPTER EIGHTEEN

EVIE'S ABSENCE LEFT a great, gaping hole in his life. Robert had never before in his life missed a woman or let one assume enough importance to him that he was lonely without her, but that was the predicament he found himself in now. After her flat rejection of his marriage proposal, he'd returned to New York the next day and immediately taken up the threads of his business concerns, but the social whirl he had enjoyed before seemed simultaneously too frantic and too boring. He didn't want to attend the opera or the endless parade of dinner parties; he wanted to sit out on the deck in the warm, fragrant night, listening to the murmur of the river and enjoying the array of stars scattered across the black sky. He wanted to lie naked on the chaise with Evie, motionless, their bodies linked, until their very stillness was unbearably erotic and they both shattered with pleasure.

Sex had always been a controlled but extremely important part of his life, but now he found himself unresponsive to the lures cast his way. His sex drive hadn't abated; it was driving him crazy. But he didn't want the controlled pleasure he'd known before, his mind staying remote from his body. He hadn't been remote when he'd made love with Evie, and several times he hadn't been controlled, either. Having her naked under him, thrusting into her tight, unbelievably hot sheath, and feeling her turn into pure flame in his arms…

The carnal image brought him to full arousal, and he lunged to his feet to prowl restlessly around the apartment, swearing between his teeth with every step. Nothing else made him hard these days, but just the thought of Evie could do it. He wanted her, and her absence was like acid, eating away at his soul.

He still couldn't decide what had gone wrong. He sensed the answer, but it was an ethereal thing, always floating just beyond his comprehension. His inability to understand the problem was as frustrating, in its own way, as his hunger for Evie. He had always been able to grasp nuances, see clearly to the crux of any problem, with a speed that left others in the dust. Now it was as if his brain had failed him, and the thought infuriated him.

It wasn't the house. As much as that had hurt her, she had understood his explanation; he had seen that in her eyes. Balanced against national security, her house was nothing, and she had believed him when he'd told her that he'd never intended to go through with the foreclosure. It was a dreadful miscalculation on his part, and though it chafed that he had made such a mistake, Evie had made a move that no one could have anticipated. Mortgage the house, yes, but not *sell* it. He was still stunned by the solution she had chosen.

But she had forgiven him for that, had even forgiven him for suspecting that she might be a traitor.

Why in hell, then, had she refused to marry him? The expression in her eyes still haunted him, and he lay awake nights aching with the need to put the glow back into her face. His golden, radiant Evie had looked like...ashes.

She loved him. He knew that as surely as he knew his heart beat in his chest. And still she had turned him down. "Go away, Robert," she'd said, and the finality in her voice had stunned him. So he had gone away, and he felt as if, every day away from her, he died a little more.

Madelyn had called several times, and she was becoming insistent that he come to Montana for a visit. Knowing his sister as he did, he was ruefully aware that he had maybe two more days to get out there before she turned up on his doorstep, holding one toddler by the hand and the other balanced on her hip, a ruthless expression in those lazy gray eyes. She knew him well enough to sense that something was wrong, and she wouldn't rest until she knew what it was. Her determination had been a fearsome thing when she'd been a child, and it had gotten worse as she'd grown older.

Robert swore in frustration, then made a swift decision. Other than Evie, Madelyn was the most astute woman he knew. Maybe, as a woman, she could put her finger on the reason that was eluding him. He called Madelyn to let her know he was coming.

With the time difference, it was still early the next morning when his plane landed in Billings. The ranch was another hundred and twenty miles, and had its own airstrip, so he had long since developed the habit of renting a small plane and flying the rest of the way, rather than making the long drive. As he banked to align the Cessna with the runway, he saw Madelyn's four-wheel drive Explorer below; she was leaning against the hood, her long hair lifting in the breeze. The color of her hair was lighter and cooler than Evie's tawny-blond mane, but still his heart squeezed at the similarity.

He landed the plane and taxied it close to the vehicle. As he cut the engine, he could see the two lively little boys bouncing in the cargo area, and a rueful smile touched his eyes. He had missed the little hooligans. He wanted some of his own.

As he crossed the pavement, Madelyn came to meet him, her lazy stroll fluid and provocative. "Thank God you're here," she said. "The imps of Satan have been driving me crazy since I told them you were coming. Did you know that when a one-year-old says Uncle Robert, it sounds remarkably like Ali Baba? I've heard it fifteen thousand times in the past hour, so I'm an expert."

"Dear God," he murmured, looking past her to where the two imps of Satan were shrieking what was undoubtedly their version of his name.

She went up on tiptoe to kiss his cheek and he hugged her to him. Something guarded inside him always relaxed when he set foot on the ranch. The sense of nature was much closer here, just as it had been in Alabama.

Madelyn waited until after lunch before broaching the subject he knew had been eating her alive with curiosity. The boys had been put down for their afternoon naps, and he and Reese were sitting at the table, relaxing over coffee. Madelyn came back into the dining room, sat down and said, "All right, what's wrong?"

He gave her a wry smile. "I knew you couldn't wait much longer. You've always been as curious as a cat."

"Agreed. Talk."

So he did. It felt strange. He couldn't remember ever needing help before in deciding what to do. He concisely outlined the situation with Mercer, explaining Evie's suspected involvement and the method he had used to force them into action. He described Evie, unaware of the aching hunger in his eyes as he did so. He told them everything—how Evie had sold her house to stop the foreclosure on the marina, how she had discovered that he was behind it all, and how Mercer had been caught. And how she had turned down his marriage proposal.

He was aware that Madelyn had stiffened during his

recital of events, but she was looking down at the table, and he couldn't read her expression. When he finished, however, she lifted her head, and he was startled to see the molten fury in her eyes.

"Are you that dense?" she shouted, jumping to her feet with a force that overturned her chair. "I don't blame her for not marrying you! I wouldn't have, either!" Infuriated, she stomped out of the dining room.

Bemused, Robert turned to stare after her. "I didn't know she could move that fast," he murmured.

Reese gave a startled shout of laughter. "I know. It took me by surprise the first time I made her lose her temper, too."

Robert turned back to his brother-in-law, a big, tough rancher as tall as himself, with dark hair and hazel-green eyes, coloring that he had passed on to his two sons.

"What set her off?"

"Probably the same thing that set her off when I was being that dense, too," Reese explained, amusement in his eyes.

"Would someone please explain it to me?" Robert asked with strained politeness. On the surface he was still in complete control, but inside he was dying by inches. He didn't know what to do, and that had never happened to him before. He was at a complete loss.

Reese leaned back in his chair, toying with the handle of his cup. "I almost lost Madelyn once," he said abruptly, looking down. "She probably never told you, but she left me. She didn't go far, just into town, but it might as well have been a million miles, the way I felt."

"When was this?" Robert asked, his eyes narrowing. He didn't like knowing that Madelyn had had problems and hadn't told him about them.

"When she was pregnant with Ty. I tried everything I

could think of to convince her to come back, but I was too stupid to give her the one reason that mattered."

Reese was going somewhere with this, Robert realized. He was a private man and not normally this talkative. "Which reason was that?"

Reese lifted his gaze to meet Robert's, and hazel-green eyes met ice-green ones, both stark with emotion.

"It isn't easy to give someone else that kind of power over you," Reese said abruptly. "Hell, it wasn't easy to even admit it to myself, and you're twice as bad as I ever was. You're a tough son of a bitch, more dangerous than you want people to know, so you keep it all under control. You're used to controlling everything around you, but you can't control this, can you? You probably don't even know what it is. I practically had to be hit in the head before I saw the light. You love her, don't you?"

Robert froze, and his eyes went blank with shock. Love? He'd never even thought the word. He wanted Evie, wanted to marry her, wanted to have children with her. God, he wanted all of that with a fierce passion that threatened to destory him if he didn't get it. But everything in him rebelled at the thought of being in *love.* It would mean a terrible helplessness; he wouldn't be able to hold himself apart from her, to keep uncompromised the basic invulnerability that was at the core of him. He was well aware of his true nature, knew the savage inside. He didn't want to unleash that kind of raw passion, didn't want anyone to even know it existed.

But Evie knew, anyway, he realized, and felt another shock. She had seen through him right from the beginning. With that maddening intuition of hers, she sometimes went straight into his thoughts. He could shut everyone else out, but he had never been able to shut out Evie, and he had spent the entire time they were together trying to regain control over himself, over the situation, over her. She knew him for what he was, and she loved him, anyway.

He swore, running a shaking hand over his face, blinding truth staring him in the eye. Evie wouldn't have loved him if that savage intensity hadn't been there. She had known real love with Matt, and lost it; only something incredibly powerful could take her beyond that. Loving Evangeline couldn't be a civilized, controlled affair; she would want him heart and soul, nothing held back.

The house hadn't been the issue. Neither had suspecting her of a crime. He could offer her a hundred houses, all the power his wealth could bring, and none of that would tempt her. What she wanted was the one thing he hadn't offered: his love.

"It was that simple," Reese said softly. "I told Maddie that I love her. More importantly, I admitted it to myself."

Robert was still stunned, still turned inward. "How do you know?" he murmured.

Reese made a low, harsh sound. "Do you feel as if you can never get enough of her? Do you want to make love to her so much that the ache never quite leaves your gut? Do you want to protect her, carry her around on a satin cushion, give her everything in the world? Are you content just being with her, listening to her, smelling her, touching her hand? Do you feel as if someone's torn your guts out, you miss her so much? When Maddie left me, it hurt so damn bad I could barely function. There was a big empty hole in me, and it ached so much I couldn't sleep, couldn't eat. The only thing that could make it better was seeing her. Is that the way it feels?"

Robert's green eyes were stark. "Like I'm bleeding to death inside."

"Yep, that's love," Reese said, shaking his head in sympathy.

Robert got to his feet, his lean face setting in lines of determination. "Kiss Madelyn goodbye for me. Tell her I'll call her."

"You can't wait for morning?"

"No," Robert said as he took the stairs two at a time. He couldn't wait another minute. He was on his way to Alabama.

EVIE DIDN'T LIKE her new home. She felt hemmed in, though she had a corner apartment and neighbors on only one side. When she looked out the window, she saw another apartment building, rather than the river sweeping endlessly past. She could hear her neighbors through the thin walls, hear them arguing, hear their two small children whining and crying. They were out until all hours, children in tow, and came dragging the poor little tykes in at one or two in the morning. The commotion inevitably woke her, and she would lie in bed staring at the dark ceiling for hours.

She could look for another place, she knew, but she couldn't muster enough energy or interest to do it. She forced herself to go to the marina every day, and that was the limit of what she could do. She was going through the motions, but each day it took more and more effort, and soon she would collapse under the strain.

She felt cold, and she couldn't get warm. It was an internal cold, spreading out from the vast emptiness inside, and no amount of heat could get past it. Just thinking his name was like having a knife jabbed into her, shards of pain splintering in all directions, but she couldn't get him out of her mind. A glimpse of black hair brought her head snapping around; a certain deep tone of voice made her heart stop for an instant—a precious instant—as uncontrollable joy shot through her and she thought, *He's back!*

But he never was, and the joy would turn to ashes, leaving her more desolate than before.

The sun burned down, the heat wave continuing, but she couldn't feel its heat or see its bright light. The world was colored in tones of cold gray.

I got through this before, she would think on those mornings when there didn't seem to be any reason to get out of bed. *I can do it again.* But the fact was, doing it before had nearly killed her, and the depression that sucked all the spirit out of her was getting deeper every day. She didn't know if she had the strength to fight it.

Becky had gone ballistic when she found out Robert had left town. "He told me he was going to ask you to marry him," she'd roared, so enraged her hair had practicallly been standing on end.

"He did," Evie had said listlessly. "I said no." And she had refused to answer any more questions; she hadn't even told Becky why she'd sold the house.

Summer was coming to an end, burning itself out. It was almost time for school to start. The calendar said that fall was a month away, but the scent of it was in the air, crisp and fresh, without the redolent perfumes of summer. She was burning herself out, too, Evie thought, and didn't much care.

She went to bed as soon as it was dark, hoping to get a few hours' sleep before her noisy neighbors came home. It was usually a useless effort. Whenever she stopped, she couldn't keep the memories at bay; they swarmed at her from all the corners of her mind. Lying in bed, she would remember Robert's warm presence beside her, feel his weight compressing the mattress, and the memory was so real that it was almost as if she could reach out and touch him. Her body throbbed, needing his touch, the exquisite relief of having him inside her. She would relive every

time he had made love to her, and her breasts would grow
heavy with desire.

He was gone, but she wasn't free of him.

That night was no different; if anything, it was worse.
She tossed about, trying to ignore the fever in her flesh
and the misery in her heart. The T-shirt she wore rasped
her aching nipples, tempting her to remove it, but she knew
better. When she had tried to sleep nude, her skin had become even more sensitive.

Someone banged on the door, startling her so much
that she bolted upright in bed. She glanced at the clock.
It was after ten.

She got up and slipped on a robe. The banging came
again, as thunderous as if someone was trying to beat
down her door. She paused to turn on a lamp in the living
room. "Who is it?"

"Robert. Open the door, Evie."

She froze, her hand on the knob, all the blood draining
from her face. For a moment she thought she would faint.
"What do you want?" she managed, the words so low that
she wasn't sure he could hear them, but he did.

"I want to talk to you. Open the door."

The deep, rich voice was the same, the tone as controlled as ever. She leaned her head against the door facing, wondering if she had the strength to send him away
again. What remained to be said? Was he going to try to
make her accept the house? She couldn't live there; the
memories of him were too strong.

"Evangeline, *open the door*."

She fumbled with the lock and opened the door. He
stepped in immediately, tall and overwhelming. She was
swamped by her reactions as she fell back a pace. The scent
of him was the same, the leashed vitality of his tall, lean
body slamming against her like a blow. He closed the door

and locked it, and when he turned back to her she saw that his black hair was tousled, and a dark shadow of beard covered his cheeks. His eyes were glittering like green fire as they fastened on her. He didn't give the apartment a glance.

"I'm only going to ask you once more," he said abruptly. "Will you marry me?"

Evie shuddered with the strain, but slowly shook her head. She could have married him before, when she'd thought he cared for her at least a little, but when she had realized he'd only been using her... No, she couldn't do it.

A muscle clenched in his jaw. She could feel the tension in him, like some great beast coiled to jump, and she took another step back. When he spoke, however, his voice was almost mild. "Why not?"

The contrast of his voice to the energy she could feel pulsing in him was maddening. All the misery of the past weeks congealed inside her, and she felt herself splintering inside. "Why not?" she cried incredulously, her voice shaking. "My God, look at yourself! Nothing touches you, does it? You'd take everything I have to give, but you'd never let me inside where you really live, where I could reach the real man. You keep yourself behind a cold wall, and I'm tired of bruising myself against it!"

His nostrils flared. "Do you love me?"

"Is that what you came for?" Tears welled in her eyes, rolled slowly down her cheeks. "A sop to your ego? Yes, I love you. Now *get out!*"

She saw his powerful muscles tense, saw his eyes flare with something savage. Her heart leapt, and too late she saw the danger. She turned to run, but Robert grabbed her, whirling her to face him. Confused, Evie thought at first it was one of his carefully gauged actions, designed to impress upon her how serious he was, but then she saw his eyes. The pupils were contracted to tiny black points, the irises huge and glittering like pale fire. His face was tight and pale, except for two spots of color high on the blades of his cheekbones. Not even Robert, she thought dazedly, could control those physical reactions.

His hands tightened on her waist until his fingers dug painfully into her soft flesh, a grip that she knew would leave bruises. "You're right," he said almost soundlessly. "I've never wanted anyone to get close to me. I've never wanted to care this much for anyone, to let you or anyone else have this kind of power over me." His lips drew back over his teeth, and he was breathing hard. "Shut you out? My God, I've tried to, but I can't. You want the real man, sweetheart? All right, I'm yours. I love you so much it's tearing me apart. But there's a flip side to it," he continued harshly. "I'll give you more than I've ever given any other human being, but by God, I'll take more, too. You don't get to pick and choose which qualities you like the best. It's a package deal. You get all the bad with the good, and I warn you now, I'm not a gentleman."

"No," she whispered, "you're not." She hung in his grip, her eyes fastened on his face, seeing the sheen of sweat on his forehead and the ferocity of his expression. Her heart thundered at what he had just said, her mind reeling with joy. He loved her? She almost couldn't take it in, couldn't believe he'd actually said it. She stared up into those fiery eyes, too dazed to say anything else.

"I'm jealous," he muttered, still in that tone of stifled violence. "I don't want you even looking at another man, and if any fool tries to come on to you, he'll be lucky if I only break his arm." He shook her with enough force to make her teeth snap together. "I want you all the time, and now, damn it, I'll take you. I'll be on you so often, four and five times a day, that you'll forget what it's like not to have me inside you. No more being a gentleman and restricting myself to twice a day."

Her golden brown eyes widened. "No," she said faintly. "I wouldn't want you to restrict yourself." There were no controls on him now; she could feel the passion surging through him, a wild and savage force that caught her up in its tide and swept her along with him.

"I'll want you at my beck and call. I can't ignore the business, so I'll expect you to fit your schedule around mine, to be available whenever I'm home." As he talked, he moved her backward and roughly pushed her against the wall. His hands tugged at her panties, stripping them down her legs. He leaned against her, his heavy weight pinning her to the wall as he tore his pants open. She gave a brief, incoherent prayer of thanks that her neighbors were gone, then clung to his shoulders as he hooked one arm under her bottom and lifted her. Her heart pounding, her blood rushing through her veins on a giddy tide of joy, she parted her thighs, and he shoved himself between them. His penetration was fast and rough. She bit back a cry and buried her face against his neck. She could feel his own heartbeat thudding against her breast.

They were both motionless, overwhelmed by the stunning relief and pleasure of their bodies being joined once more, she trying to adjust to the hard fullness of him, he groaning at the tightness of her inner clasp on his sex. Then, still caught in the savage exaltation of emotional freedom, he drove mercilessly into her.

"I don't want to wear a condom," he said fiercely, his breath hot against her ear. "I don't want you to take birth-control pills. I don't want you to act like my semen is some hostile marauder that you have to protect yourself against. I want to give it to you. I want you to want it. I want you to have my babies. I want a house full of kids."

With each word he thrust, pushing himself deeper and deeper into her.

She moaned, shuddering around him with the force of her pleasure. "Yes." She had unleashed a monster of passion, a total dictator, but she could meet his power with her own. This was the real man, the one who made her feel alive again, who sent heat throbbing through every cell of her body. She wasn't cold any longer, but radiant with vibrant life.

"I want marriage." His teeth were ground together, and a drop of sweat ran down his temple. "I want you tied to me—legally, financially, every way I can devise. I want you to take my name, Evangeline, do you understand?"

"Yes," she said, and splintered with joy. "Robert, *yes!*"

He bucked violently against her with his climax, flooding her with moisture and heat. Evie locked her legs around him and took him deep within, her senses whirling and fading, all consciousness gone except for the primal awareness of him inside her.

Some endless time later, she realized that she was on the bed and he was stretched out naked beside her. She hadn't fainted, but neither had she been aware of anything else but him. He hadn't released her during the entire time he had stripped both her and himself, struggling out of clothing while still keeping her in his grasp. She turned to snuggle closer, and the lure of his body, after the long deprivation, was too great. She found herself on top of him, wriggling to find the right contact and nestle his sex against the soft heat between her legs. He caught his breath, and she felt him begin to harden again.

"You might get started on that house full of kids sooner than you thought," she murmured, moving against him again in voluptuous delight. "I stopped taking the birth-control pills the day you left."

"Good." He caressed her bottom and hip, urging her closer to him. "I don't want to hurt you," he said even as he slipped inside her.

She heard the worry in his voice and knew that he was uneasy with releasing all the force he'd kept contained for so long. She kissed him and bit his lip as his subtle movements made her nerve endings riot with pleasure. "You can't hurt me by loving me," she said.

His eyes glittered in the faint light coming from the lamp in the living room. "That's good," he murmured. "Because God knows I do."

EPILOGUE

EVIE HEARD THE elevator arrive and crouched down beside the tiny, adorable creature who was clinging unsteadily to the chair in the entrance hall. "There's Daddy," she whispered, and watched her daughter's big eyes go round with delight. She barely restrained herself from gathering the baby into her arms; sometimes the surge of love was so strong that she thought she would burst from the force of it.

The elevator doors slid open, and Robert stepped out, an indescribable light flaring in his pale green eyes as he saw them waiting for him. With a joyous gurgle, the baby let go of the chair and hurled herself toward him, every toddling step teetering on the edge of disaster. Robert turned absolutely white, dropped his briefcase with a thud and went down on one knee to swoop her into his arms. "My God," he said, shocked. "She's walking!"

"For a couple of hours now," Evie said, smiling as Angel caught her father's silk tie in one tiny, chubby hand and began babbling at him. "It makes my heart stop every time she lurches across the floor."

"She's too young to walk. She's only seven months old." Aghast, he stared down at the small head, covered with downy dark hair, that butted against his chest. He had been just as aghast when she had started crawling at five months. If he could, Robert would have kept his darling offspring as a babe in arms for the first five years of her life. She, however, was blissfully oblivious of his panic at her daring.

Still holding the baby, he hugged Evie close for a long kiss, one that quickly grew heated despite his squirming burden, who tried to poke her fingers between their mouths. They had named her Jennifer Angelina, intending to call her Jenna, but instead she had been Angel from the day she'd been born. She was angelic only when she was asleep, however; during waking hours, she had the fearless spirit of a daredevil.

Evie clung to his mouth for a long time, her hand clenching his hair to hold him in place. She had been waiting all day for him to come home, feeling shivery and excited and a little frightened.

"You were right," she murmured.

He lifted his head, and the green eyes gleamed. "I was, huh?"

She laughed and pinched him. "You knew you were." They had decided to have another baby as soon as possible. Both pregnancy and delivery had been easy for her, and though they had decided that two children would fill the house they were building just fine, they had both wanted to have them close together.

Three weeks ago, they had spent the night locked together, lost in the passion that hadn't faded during the sixteen months of their marriage. When they had awakened at dawn, for their ritual of morning love, Robert had looked down at her with his sleepy green eyes barely open and said, "We made a baby last night."

She had thought so, too, her instincts certain even before the early pregnancy test she'd taken just that morning had confirmed it. Already it was as if she could feel that hot, tiny weight in her womb, pulsing with life.

She leaned her head against his broad shoulder, remembering the sheer terror she'd felt when she had realized that she was pregnant the first time. Taking a chance on loving Robert had required all her courage, but now there was to be someone else to love, someone who was part of her, part of Robert. She would have no defense against this new little person, and she had thought she would shatter from the fear. But Robert had known how she was feeling, had seen the raw fear in her eyes and hadn't left her side all day. He had called Felice and announced that he wouldn't be in, cancel everything, and had spent the day holding Evie on his lap or making love to her. His solution, she thought wryly, had been to overwhelm her with what had gotten her in that condition to begin with; the tactic had been amazingly successful.

Angel was trying to throw herself bodily out of his arms. Sighing, he released Evie to bend down and set the baby on her chubby feet. As soon as he released her, she was off like a wobbly rocket. Evie went back into his arms, but they both kept a weather eye on their precocious daughter as she began investigating a fascinating crack in the hardwood floor.

Evie rested her head on his chest, reassured by the strong, steady thump of his heart beneath her ear. Far from losing himself in his work and demanding that she structure her time around him, as he'd said he would, Robert had instead ruthlessly reorganized his office schedule so he could spend every available moment with her and Angel. She had known that he was a man of alarming intensity, but instead of being frightened when he focused it on her, she had bloomed. Robert wasn't a man who loved lightly; when he loved, it was with every fiber of his being.

His hand moved to Evie's belly and pressed in gentle reassurance. "Are you all right?" he asked softly.

She lifted her head and gave him a luminous smile. His

love had renewed her strength, banished the shadows. "I've never been better."

Robert kissed her, savoring her sweet taste and the familiar, delicious tension of desire that quivered in their bodies. "I love you, Evangeline," he said, gathering her close to him. Loving her was the most joyous, satisfying thing he'd ever done. She demanded everything from him and gave him all of herself, and sometimes he was staggered by the richness of the bond between them. He'd been right; loving Evangeline took everything he had, heart and soul.

* * * * *

Welcome to Honey Ridge, Tennessee, where
New York Times bestselling author

LINDA GOODNIGHT

invites you to a house rich with secrets and
brimming with sweet possibilities.

NEW YORK TIMES BESTSELLING AUTHOR

LINDA GOODNIGHT

THE MEMORY HOUSE

A HONEY RIDGE NOVEL

"Linda Goodnight is a genuine treasure.
The Memory House is a beautiful, rich, unforgettable
story filled with tenderness and heart."
—NEW YORK TIMES BESTSELLING AUTHOR
RAEANNE THAYNE

Memories of motherhood and marriage are still fresh for Julia Presley—though tragedy took away both years ago. Finding comfort running the Peach Orchard Inn, she lets the historic place fill the voids of love and family. Life is calm…until a stranger with a young boy shows up and disrupts the loneliness of her world. Julia suspects there's more to Eli Donovan than his motherless son, Alex. Offering the guarded man work, she glimpses someone who—like her—has a heart in need of restoration. But with the chance discovery of a stack of dusty love letters found in the lining of an old trunk, a Civil War romance envelops Julia and Eli, challenging them to risk facing yesterday's ghosts for a future bright with hope and healing.

Pick up your copy today!

"Linda Goodnight is a genuine treasure. *The Memory House* is a
beautiful, rich, unforgettable story filled with tenderness and heart."
—*New York Times* bestselling author RaeAnne Thayne

Be sure to connect with us at:

Harlequin.com/Newsletters
Facebook.com/HarlequinBooks
Twitter.com/HQNBooks

HQN™

www.HQNBooks.com

PHLG912

LINDA HOWARD

77840 ESCAPE   ___ $7.99 U.S. ___ $8.99 CAN.

(limited quantities available)

TOTAL AMOUNT	$ _____
POSTAGE & HANDLING	$ _____
($1.00 FOR 1 BOOK, 50¢ for each additional)	
APPLICABLE TAXES*	$ _____
TOTAL PAYABLE	$ _____

(check or money order—please do not send cash)

To order, complete this form and send it, along with a check or money order for the total above, payable to HQN Books, to: **In the U.S.:** 3010 Walden Avenue, P.O. Box 9077, Buffalo, NY 14269-9077; **In Canada:** P.O. Box 636, Fort Erie, Ontario, L2A 5X3.

Name: _____
Address: _____ City: _____
State/Prov.: _____ Zip/Postal Code: _____
Account Number (if applicable): _____

075 CSAS

      *New York residents remit applicable sales taxes.
    *Canadian residents remit applicable GST and provincial taxes.

HQN™

www.HQNBooks.com

PHLH0216BL